Over the Fence

MELANIE MORELAND

This is for all of you who think you aren't "enough."

I have something to tell you—YOU ARE.

You are *you*—which is perfect.

Never let anyone tell you different.

We are all enough.

For my online readers who asked—this is for you.

And finally, to my Matthew—my reason for everything.

I love you.

Chapter One

STEPPED INSIDE THE HOUSE, forcing the door shut behind me with a resounding slam. It echoed off the walls of the almost empty rooms, the floor under my feet shaking from the impact.

That felt good.

When I bought the place, the woman presenting the house had pointed out all the "little features" of the space. Her demeanor was enthusiastic as she showed me drawers that shut on their own, cupboards that closed without a sound, and explained about the extra soundproofing in the walls. The best feature, she insisted, was all the entry doors were the same—no matter how hard you pushed them, they closed with the smoothest whisper. "It's great"—she had beamed—"you'll never disturb your neighbor with the sound of a slamming door!"

I removed one of the gadgets as soon as I moved in, and left all the others, but off came the "silencer" on the door leading from the garage. I used that door the most.

Some days, you had to be able to slam a door. Today was one of them.

I moved through the house, dropping keys and my wallet, shedding my clothes. I hit the shower, letting the hot water pour over my back and loosen the tight muscles. They were a direct result of spending all day hunched over a keyboard.

It was bad enough having to service people who knew nothing about computers all the time. The days were worse when a moron turned off the antivirus software on purpose, so they could watch porn movies at their desk. Because of one person's inane action, the entire system was infected and had to be fixed. The worst part—he didn't even look ashamed at being caught doing it.

I groaned as my head hit the wall; spare me from these fucking idiots.

Toweling off my hair, I grabbed a beer from the refrigerator and stepped into the small backyard. Despite the sun, the early summer air was cool. I slumped into my chair, cracked the top and took a deep swallow of the cold liquid. I threw my towel on the table and looked around at the bleak space. My small patio led to an even smaller patch of grass consisting mostly of weeds and dirt. Surrounding the entire yard was a fence; an eight-foot tall, solid fence. I had paid extra to have it taller than normal. Thick, cedar planks and a wide top rail, which added another six inches to the height, completed the structure, offering complete privacy from the world around me.

I had only one neighbor to worry about—the townhouse complex was situated on a small cul-de-sac, the houses grouped in varying sizes. This small section had only two houses and backed onto the dense woods behind us, which was why I chose this particular house. Between the fence and the property layout, it was a small oasis. Bleak—but private.

I polished off the beer and went inside to grab some dinner, cursing when I studied the contents of the refrigerator. Aside from the remaining beer and condiments, it was basically empty. The freezer held nothing except a bottle of vodka and an empty ice cube tray. I had meant to go grocery shopping, but after the day I experienced, it had slipped my mind. Grabbing the last of some lunch meat and slightly stale bread, I threw together a sandwich. I took it, and another beer, out back and sat down to eat. After swallowing, I sniffed at the meat before taking another bite. It had a distinctly strange flavor to it. With a shrug, I continued to munch away; figuring if I consumed enough beer, it would cancel out any danger contained within the sandwich. I'd go to the grocery store tomorrow, but for tonight I'd have to make do with what I had on hand.

I heard movement next door and shifted in my seat, remembering I had a new neighbor. The last one was a business man who was scarcely home, and had moved out a few weeks ago. We exchanged the occasional greeting if we ran into each other while I was washing my car or grabbing the paper. I had seen the moving truck on the weekend, and heard a woman's voice at one point, but otherwise I didn't pay much attention. I hadn't known my other neighbor well at all, and didn't expect the new one to be any different.

As I listened, I heard someone moving around, the unmistakable sound of boxes being broken down and papers folded. A pleasant voice humming softly made me aware it was a woman in the other yard. Another sound caught my ear and I wasn't sure what it was until the scent hit me a few moments later.

She was cooking something on a barbeque.

I inhaled the scent, my mouth instantly watering. The strange tasting sandwich I was holding no longer appealed to me in any way.

My head fell back and a groan escaped my lips, because it smelled fucking amazing.

"I beg your pardon?" A shocked, sweet-sounding voice came from behind the fence.

Oh shit.

Did I say that out loud?

I chuckled. "Sorry." I cleared my throat. "Your, ah, dinner smells awesome. It's making my sandwich look pretty pathetic."

"Oh. Sorry?"

I noticed how quiet her voice was, yet I had the feeling she was speaking louder than normal for my benefit.

"Not your fault."

Only silence greeted me.

"So, welcome to the neighborhood."

"Thank you."

"It's a nice area."

"Yes, it's lovely."

"I'm sure you and your, ah, husband will like it."

"There's no husband."

"Oh. Well then, your partner, girlfriend, significant other, son, daughter, cat, dog . . . whew, have I missed anyone?"

She laughed—a husky, rich sound; very different from her faint-speaking voice. "No, I think you covered it all. It's only me, though."

"Same as me, then."

There was no reply, but I could hear the sound of food being turned and the smell was driving me crazy. My mouth was watering at the delicious aroma wafting over the fence. I looked down at my partially eaten sandwich with sudden distaste.

I couldn't help but ask. "What are you cooking?"

"Chicken and vegetables."

"Hmm. Sounds good. It smells amazing."

"Don't you cook?" Her hesitant voice asked.

I snorted. "No, I burn, I char, I destroy. I never quite got the hang of cooking."

Now the sweet voice sounded horrified. "What do you eat?"

"Take-out, mostly. But I mix it up with frozen entrees, cereal, and I make a mean sandwich." I looked down at the one currently in my hand and set it on the table in front of me with a grimace. It was no longer tempting at all. "Well, usually," I added quietly.

"Oh, that's sad."

I took another pull from my bottle and snickered. "If you think that's sad, you don't want to know about the expired meat

I'm trying to choke down because I forgot to go to the store and pick up supplies. At least I usually have something half-edible on hand to eat."

I heard footsteps move away and the sound of a sliding screen door. Obviously, I had bored her enough with my sob story. Leaning back, I finished the last of my beer. Maybe I would order a pizza. I sighed. I was sick of pizza. I was sick of take-out. Shaking my head, I admitted I was sick of this lonely, solitary life. All the time I spent alone was starting to get to me. I realized how much I had enjoyed the few minutes of conversation with my new neighbor. Although, it would seem I had effectively scared her away with my choice of subject.

Standing up, I went inside and grabbed another beer and threw out the sandwich. I opened the cupboard and found a box of cereal with a little still left in the bottom. I was out of milk, but at least it was something. Back outside, I opened up the box and munched away; it was a little stale, but still edible. I needed to make a list of things to pick up tomorrow.

Beside me, I heard movement again, but I refrained from trying to start up another conversation. I could hear her talking to herself, the sound of an item being dragged, and I caught a muffled grunt and the words *"height"* and *"stupid idea,"* then the sound of more rustling. All of this was followed by a solid thump, a brief silence, and a little gasp. I looked at the fence in amusement wondering what the hell was happening on the other side of it.

Then I heard a nervous sounding, "Hello?"

"Are you all right?" I asked, unsure what was going on.

"Oh. Good. You're there."

I grimaced. I didn't have anywhere else to go. "Yeah, I'm here."

"I, um, I put something on the fence for you."

I sat up. "What?"

I heard the sound of retreating footsteps and the door opening again. "I can't let a neighbor starve. Goodnight."

I stood up and looked at the fence.

Holy shit.

Was that really a plate sitting on the top?

Dragging my chair to the fence, I stepped up, stretching as far as I could. I was able to snag the unexpected treasure and bring it down. Stepping off the chair, I immediately tore off the foil and basked in the incredible aroma that hit me.

The plate was filled with chicken, grilled vegetables and salad. It was a real meal—complete with a plastic fork and knife.

A huge grin broke out on my face—it was mine—all mine.

I dragged my chair back to the table and began to devour the best meal I'd eaten in ages. The logical part of my brain reminded me I had no idea who the person was giving me the food. She could have spat in it, or even poisoned it for all I knew. Cautiously, I picked up the plate and inhaled. It smelled far too good to be poisoned. Why would she poison me anyway? I hadn't done anything to piss her off—at least not yet. I hadn't heard any spitting either, so I was certain it was safe.

Nothing could keep me from this feast.

The first bite was heaven—the second tasted even better.

I knew she was inside and probably wouldn't hear me—but, I did it anyway.

"Thank you!" I bellowed. "This tastes as fucking awesome as it smelled!"

The sound was low and distant, but I heard it.

A giggle, lilting and strangely delightful, came drifting over the fence from somewhere inside her house—an odd sound in my world, yet I liked it.

I smiled around my mouthful.

This new neighbor thing was okay—so far.

Chapter Two

THE NEXT DAY, I MADE good on my promise of getting some food in the house. When I had gone inside for the night, I discovered I was also almost out of other necessities, including laundry soap, so I knew I'd put it off long enough. There was something indelibly sad about shopping alone all the time. I knew when I arrived back home I'd unpack it all, stow it away and still be alone.

I grimaced at my strange melancholy—I needed to snap out of it.

The grocery store was fairly empty at this time of night. Most people were at home eating dinner, not shopping. I filled the cart with my usual list; supplies purchased so often I could do it blindfolded. The same frozen dinners and canned items—even the usual cold meats at the deli. I changed up the eggs, buying brown ones instead of white, chuckling at my own idiocy. They all tasted the same to me when I was done with them—usually runny, sometimes overcooked, but edible and at least the toast was okay. I threw in toilet paper, laundry soap, and fabric softener, since I hated static cling, and liked my sheets to smell nice. To finish off, I grabbed milk and some pop to fill up the cart; planning another stop at the liquor store for some beer. I stopped and looked longingly at the fresh meat counter, but walked away without adding anything. No matter how hard I tried, everything I cooked became inedible, aside from my feeble egg attempts. I did stop at the hot food section and pick up a rotisserie chicken and a few sides for dinner. The leftovers would make good lunches.

Once I was home and unpacked, I tore into the chicken and pasta salad, standing at the counter and wolfing it down. I didn't even bother with a plate, using my hands to tear the chicken apart and a plastic fork to scoop out the pasta. When I was done, I stowed the rest into my reasonably full refrigerator and grabbed a beer.

I sat at the table outside, slumping down in the chair, and opened the newspaper. When I heard a noise next door, I sat up, looking expectantly toward the fence.

"Hey, neighbor!" I called out, wondering why I was so eager to talk to her again.

"Um, hello."

"Dinner was great last night, absolutely delicious. Thank you." I hoped she heard my sincerity.

"I'm glad."

I chuckled. "It was very generous of you—you have no idea. I think I licked the plate clean."

I heard her giggle—the light, heartwarming giggle that made me smile last night. It had the same effect on me today.

"Not usually the best idea with a paper plate," she observed. "Paper fibers really . . . suck. And they stick to the roof of your mouth. Ewww."

I laughed. "Ewww, indeed. I'll keep that in mind."

"Did you, um, char something tonight?"

"Nah, I got a pre-cooked chicken at the supermarket."

"Ah, I'm glad you ate something good."

"I always thought so before, but now I'm not as convinced."

"Sorry, before?"

"Before I ate *your* chicken. I always thought the one I bought at the store was a treat; something fresh and tasty, instead of my frozen dinners. Now it tastes like cardboard, frankly."

"Oh . . . thank you."

"Did you eat?" I wondered what she had cooked tonight.

"Yeah, I had some leftovers."

I took a swig of beer. For some reason I didn't want this conversation to end. I relaxed back in my chair, trying to think of something to say to keep her talking.

"Settling in okay?"

"Well, it's coming along."

"Finished unpacking?"

"No. Not yet. I'm trying to do a few boxes every day. In fact, I should go and unpack some now."

I felt an unusual flash of disappointment flicker because she was leaving. "Okay, then. Goodnight . . . and thanks again."

"Um, can you come closer to the fence?" Her voice seemed even more hesitant than last night. Being curious, I approached the fence, where I estimated she was standing. The boards were so thick and close together that I couldn't even see a shadow through them.

"I'm here."

"Okay. Heads up, neighbor." A small package came over the top of the fence, and I easily stretched my arm out and caught it. I looked at it for a minute, grinning.

In my hand was a tightly wrapped, thick slice of Rice Krispies square.

No fucking way.

Another giggle alerted me to the fact I had, once again, spoken aloud.

I heard muted footsteps retreating, and the door starting to close. "Goodnight."

"Wait!"

There was no answer.

"Chefgirl!" I blurted out.

"Um, yes?"

"Thank you. This is my favorite thing. I swear."

Her voice was quiet, almost endearing in its gentle quality. "You're welcome."

"What if I'd told you I hadn't eaten?" I teased, not wanting her to leave quite yet. "Would you have had a plate for me?"

"I guess you'll never know, now will you?" She teased back.

I snickered as I unwrapped the sweet treat, groaning when I bit into the gooey texture.

The door shut with a dull click before I could thank her again. I frowned as I took another bite, realizing I didn't even know her name. I needed to change that sad fact.

I grinned as I walked into the house. One thing at a time, I supposed.

Last night dinner, tonight dessert, tomorrow her name.

Or maybe, if I was lucky, tomorrow night, I would get all three.

THE NEXT DAY WAS ONE disaster after another. The building we serviced was mostly comprised of various businesses that rented office space and time on our servers. This morning, another idiot had downloaded a nasty virus, although this time no porn was involved, so we all spent the day with patches, going from office to office because of his error. I shook my head in frustration as I finished off the last client. It wasn't the first time, and it certainly wouldn't be the last. My boss had been on a tear about overtime and expenditures, and I'd had to listen to a lecture on cutbacks and reducing extra hours. When I questioned how that was possible when we couldn't control the tenants, I was told to figure it out. Then I was chewed out for rolling my eyes at that inspiring solution.

I went home as early as possible—looking forward to some down time. Grabbing a beer, I headed out back to the deck, sat down, closed my eyes, and enjoyed the silence. The next thing I knew, I woke up with a start. I whipped my head around in panic, then realized I was sitting in my backyard, alone and safe. Dropping my head in my hands, I took some deep breaths to calm my pounding heart. I must've had another nightmare; the dull memory of terror still lingering. Reaching for my beer, only to find it warm and flat, I scowled and set down the bottle with the loud thump.

"Are you all right?"

I started at hearing her caring voice come over the fence. Looking down at my watch, I was surprised to see how long I'd been asleep.

I glanced toward the sound of her voice, scrubbing my face hard.

"Yeah, I'm good. Thanks."

"You shouted out in your sleep."

"How do you know I was sleeping?"

"Um, you snore."

"I do not."

"Okay then, I have x-ray vision and could see you through the fence." She huffed. "You still shouted."

I grinned at the huffing. But I frowned at her next statement.

"You sounded frightened." I was surprised to hear a twinge of worry in her voice. I needed to nip that in the bud right now.

"I had a nightmare. I dreamed I was out of beer," I said flatly.

"Oh," was her dubious response.

"Hate when that happens." I laughed without humor, because I really did.

I inhaled deeply and immediately began salivating.

"What are you cooking?"

"Dinner." Now her tone was flat.

Ah. She didn't like my flippant answers. I went inside and got a fresh beer. Going back outside, I cracked the top and took a swallow.

"Obviously, it *was* only a dream," she observed dryly. "You still have beer."

Snickering, I took another swallow. "Yep."

I could hear her moving around; the sound of boxes being refolded. I approached the fence.

"Still unpacking?"

"Uh-huh."

"Almost done?"

"Almost."

I ran a hand through my hair in vexation. I wasn't going to tell her what I'd been dreaming about. Yet, I didn't like the one-word answers either. I searched for something to say.

"The dessert slice was delicious last night. Thank you. It's always been a favorite of mine. It tasted different than usual. Better."

"I add toffee."

"Well, that explains it. It was incredible."

I heard the barbeque lid open and smelled the appetizing aroma as she moved the food around on the grill. The scent almost had me on my knees.

"I'm glad you liked it." Her soft voice was warmer now.

"I did. Very much. It was kind of you to share."

"That's what neighbors are for, right?"

I smirked. I had nothing to share with her. I glanced down at the bottle in my hand.

"You want a beer?"

She laughed, the sound sweet. "No thanks, not big on beer."

"What do you like?"

"Red wine sometimes, but usually water—and coffee."

I nodded in agreement, even though she couldn't see me. "I'm addicted to the stuff."

"Beer? Or coffee?" She teased.

I grinned. "A little of both."

"Well, somehow I didn't think it was the water."

I chuckled at her wit.

"Do you use a lawnmower or only a weed whacker to cut your grass?"

I snickered at the randomness of the question. "Pardon me?"

"I was trying to decide if I should buy a small lawn mower or if I would even need it. Once I add some flower boxes, there won't be much of a lawn to cut. Maybe a weed whacker, you know?"

I looked around at my bedraggled excuse for a lawn. Flower boxes?

"Or maybe one of those small, manual push ones? What do you think?" she mused, moving around. I assumed she was inspecting her yard—checking out its landscaping potential. I grimaced, wondering what she would think of my barren space.

"I don't really have much grass," I admitted.

"Oh, you have a garden?"

"Um, no." I drew in a deep breath. "I have weeds. And dirt."

"Oh."

Why the fuck did that one word sound so sad?

"I keep it simple," I offered lamely. I moved away to sit back down, suddenly feeling too tired to stand anymore.

"Of course."

I rested my head back on the chair, listening to her movements. Papers rustled, boxes were folded, food was checked, but she said nothing. I did hear her low humming again. A distinct thump had me turn my head toward the fence, but I saw nothing. I shrugged, drained my bottle, standing up to head inside and finish off the cold chicken. Now I smelled her dinner, I was starving.

"I'm going in now. Good night. Your dinner is . . . up there."

I turned, looking back in the direction of her voice and I saw it. A plate was perched on the top of the wide top rail of our fence, waiting for me.

"Hey, wait!" I yelled, picking up my chair, and heading to the fence. Reaching up, I grabbed the covered plate, wondering how she managed to get it up there.

"Enjoy your dinner, neighbor." I knew from the distant sound of her voice, she was already at her door.

"Nathan!" I blurted out.

"I'm sorry?"

"My name is Nathan."

"Nice to meet you, Nathan. Enjoy your dinner and have a nice evening."

"No, wait! You can't go in and not tell me your name!" I pleaded.

There was a tiny sigh. "Kourtney. My name is Kourtney—spelled with a K."

A grin tugged at my lips. Even her name was soft.

"Well, nice to meet you, Kourtney, spelled with a K. Whatever this meal is, I know it'll be great."

Only the click of the door greeted me.

Shaking my head, I took my plate and headed to the table. My eyes almost rolled backward when I lifted the cover and saw the steak and vegetables—and *holy shit*, I was sure those were *real* mashed potatoes; not the kind that came frozen with a Hungry-Man dinner. She even added an actual knife and fork. I didn't hesitate to begin devouring the meal, moaning as the first bite exploded on my taste buds.

I thought about our conversation as I ate. She was obviously intelligent, caring, and also had a droll sense of humor. I liked that—and man, could she cook.

I thought about my goals for the night: dinner, dessert and her name.

Smirking, I swallowed the last of the feast she had left me.

Two out of three ain't bad.

Chapter Three

ON MY WAY HOME THE next day, I impulsively stopped at the local garden center. Wandering around until I found what I was looking for, and with the help of one of the women working there, I picked up two pots of lilies. I remembered how much my mom loved lilies, and her saying they needed plenty of sunshine. My yard got a lot of sun, especially in the afternoon, and I was sure Kourtney's was the same. She seemed determined to make her yard look nice, and considering how kind she'd been to me, a couple pots of flowers seemed the least I could do to be neighborly.

When I got home, I carried them out to the back and set them on the table. I hesitated as I looked over toward the fence, suddenly nervous. Would she like the gesture, or would it be too forward? Then I chuckled. She had fed dinner to a complete stranger—one she'd never even seen or met—twice. Somehow giving her a small start on her flower pots didn't seem quite as generous.

I glanced at the fence, then behind me toward the front door. Should I go and put them on her doorstep? She'd certainly find them. Picking up the pots, I hesitated; I always entered the house via the side door from the garage. If she did the same thing, she might not see them. The fence exchange was already a little routine for us, so I decided to continue with it. I dragged my chair over, returned to the table, and retrieved the pots. It was a little trickier putting the plants on the ledge than it was to snag a flat plate off it, and again I questioned how she did it. I wondered if she was tall. I was 6'3" and I had a little trouble reaching that high, even with my long arms. I doubted she was taller than me. I chuckled a little at the mental image I had of living next door to a giant. When I had both pots on the ledge, I pushed them safely to the center of the wide rail on top.

I went in, grabbed a beer, sat down and waited. The last couple nights, she'd been home around five. Glancing at my watch, I nodded—she should be there soon. I rolled my eyes.

I already knew her schedule? Really?

I grabbed my iPad and started watching some lame movie to pass the time. I had almost watched every new release from *Netflix* already, and my choices were getting slim.

Eventually, she arrived. Through her open windows I could hear her moving around inside; soon afterward came the slide of the screen door when she stepped outside.

Staying silent, I listened to the noises coming through the fence. She seemed to be moving back and forth. I could discern the sounds of something being dragged and various items being set down onto different places in her yard. Lastly, I heard the sound I was waiting for: the barbeque lid being lifted and the grill lit.

I spoke up. "What's for dinner, Kourtney with a K?"

A small gasp greeted me.

"Oh, hi, Nathan. I . . . *oh!*"

I knew she had seen the lilies I left on the top of the fence.

"I wanted to say thanks for feeding me. I thought you could add those to your flower pots?"

Utter silence.

"Kourtney?"

Nothing.

Fuck. It *was* too forward. She didn't want flowers from me.

I got up and walked toward the fence when I heard the strange thumping noise and a few seconds later one of the lilies disappeared. All I caught was the fastest glimpse of pale fingers before the pot was gone.

"Thank you." Her voice quavered. "Lilies are . . . They are my favorite flower."

Shit. Was she crying?

She was crying over a couple of potted plants?

I ran my hand nervously through my hair. I heard her moving around and the thump sound again. This time I watched closely and saw a hand come over the ledge to grab the pot. It stretched but couldn't quite reach. She muttered a curse, then the hand reappeared and the pot disappeared.

"Are you on a ladder?" I asked. I now understood the thumps and ability to reach the top of the fence.

"Yes." Her voice was low and thick.

"So you're not a giant?"

"Not the way you think, no." She sighed.

I frowned. What did that mean?

"You didn't have to do this, Nathan. It was only a plate of food."

I snorted. "Two plates—and it wasn't only food. It was fucking beyond this world. It meant a lot you would share with me, and I wanted to say thank you."

Again, I was met with silence.

"Kourtney?"

"They're so pretty. Thank you so much."

She was definitely crying.

Fuck. Why was she crying?

"I was hoping to stay in your good books, Chefgirl," I teased, wanting her to stop crying. For some reason it made my chest hurt. "Ya know, hoping you'd be willing to share again some night."

"Oh, are you hungry?" she asked, sounding more the way I was used to.

I chuckled. "I'm *always* hungry."

"Do you have anything you can snack on?"

"Um, yeah?" I'd been to the store so I had cereal in the house.

"Okay, well, dinner won't be ready for a bit. It takes a little longer. If you can wait, I'm happy to share."

"What are you making?"

"Ribs."

Ribs?

I was pretty sure I whimpered. There was no way I was ruining my appetite with any kind of snack if ribs were on the menu.

"Yeah, I can wait. Not a problem."

"Okay!"

I heard the screen door open and shut, and I sat back perplexed. She sounded almost *excited* about feeding me, which seemed like a strange reaction. At least she had stopped crying, though.

I shook my head.

Women.

Never had understood them.

"SOON, KOURTNEY?"

"Yes, Nathan, very soon," she answered, although not as patiently as the last time.

I grinned listening to her move around. I'd been bugging her for the last half hour. The aroma from the grill was driving me crazy. I had managed to be patient for the first hour; constantly chatting with her while she worked on planting the flowers in the pots she'd brought home with her. She made me laugh with her wit and quick comebacks, and the time had passed quickly. Now, however, I was starving and about ready to scale the fence to get to the food she was cooking.

"Do I need to come over there and get it myself?"

"No!"

I was taken back at the panic I could feel in that one word.

"Relax. I don't own a ladder," I assured her, unsure why she panicked.

"I don't want you to hurt yourself, that's all. It's almost done."

Wow—she was a bad liar. I didn't believe that excuse for a second, especially with the nervous tremor in her voice when she spoke. Although I was puzzled over why seeing me would make her panic, I let it pass.

The aromatic smoke from the barbeque filled the air when I heard the lid being lifted. I got up and moved closer to the fence.

"You're killing me here, Kourt. Can I call you Kourt as long as I say it with a K? Or do you hate nicknames?"

Her laugh was even more endearing than her giggle. It was low, warm, husky and made me smile hearing it.

"Since you've already given me two of them, I better get used to it."

"I won't use them if you hate it."

She sounded shy. "No, I like them. They're nice ones. As long as they're nice, I'm okay with it."

My brow furrowed. She'd been called some not nice ones? Simply the thought of that made me angry, and I gripped my beer bottle a little tighter.

"Only nice ones, I promise. You can call me Nat if you want—my mom always did."

I swallowed the sudden lump in my throat when I realized I hadn't let anyone call me Nat in years. Yet, I was okay with letting her use it. I shook my head before the memories started back up.

"Gnat like a bug? A pesky ant who keeps trying to take your food on a picnic?" She giggled. "It suits you."

I barked out a laugh. She was funny and I enjoyed her fast comebacks. "Whatever, Chefgirl. Now, dinner? I'm dying here."

"You're a big boy, Nat. I'm sure you can wait five more

minutes."

I groaned, leaning my head on the fence. "I had no idea ribs took this much work. Are they all like this?"

She hummed. "These ones are worth it."

"Why?"

"You'll find out."

Ten minutes later, I was literally moaning as I tore into the food that appeared on the top of the fence. As soon as I heard the thump of the ladder being leaned on the wood, I dragged my chair over, snatching the plate before Kourtney had barely set it on the rail. Returning to the table, I groaned at the full plate, piled high with thick, sticky ribs and steaming, roasted corn—the aroma mouthwatering. I knew, without a doubt, there was enough food on my plate I would have leftovers. No cafeteria lunch for me tomorrow.

"Are you there?" I asked between mouthfuls.

"Yes."

"These are fucking incredible. How do you make them?"

"Planning on having a go, are you, Nat?"

I laughed. "Trust me, no. That wouldn't end well. But tell me." I wanted to hear her talk. I liked the sound of her voice and enjoyed listening to her. "I've never tasted sauce like this. It's delicious."

"I made it."

I smirked into my plate. "Of course you did. Do you stay up all night cooking?"

"No. I just like to cook. And having someone to cook for again is fun." Shyness crept back into her tone. "I guess I'm showing off a little."

"Showing off?"

"A bit."

"Feel free to show off anytime. If this is your A game, bring it on. I like it." I stopped eating, eyeing my huge plate with suspicion. "You didn't give me all the food, did you?"

"No, I didn't. I'm eating, too."

"Okay. Keep talking."

"As fascinated as I'm sure you are with cooking techniques, I think you've probably heard enough," she insisted sarcastically.

"Nah—your cooking terms are cool." I took another bite and swallowed. "God, I fucking love these ribs."

She giggled. "I'm going to leave you alone with your . . . *ribs* now."

I dropped another clean bone on my plate. "I don't imagine you know how to make souvlaki, do you?"

"Yeah, I do."

I groaned. "I think I'm seriously turned on right now, Kourt."

She laughed out loud. "Over souvlaki?"

"Over the ribs, your sauce and yes, the promise of souvlaki," I answered seriously. I never joked about food.

Her reply was laced with sarcasm. "Good thing God gave you hands then, Nathan. They should help alleviate your, ah, *problem*—when you're finished eating, of course." She was struggling not to laugh. again. "I hope, after you wash your hands, you and the Palmela sisters have a good night."

I gaped at the fence as I heard her door shut. I started laughing because, really, she was fucking brilliant. I laughed so hard, I almost missed the dessert plate sitting on top of the fence.

Almost.

Chapter Four

THE THURSDAY OF A LONG weekend was quiet in the building. Often in the summer the smaller offices shut down and stretched it into a four day break, as was the case today. I loved it, since it gave me a chance to catch up with the never-ending paperwork, and I could sneak away early on occasion.

My head was bent over a pile of forms I had to fill out when the clearing of a throat from my door made me look up. One of the building's tenants was leaning on the doorframe languidly. "Between your unruly hair and long beard, you're beginning to resemble a demented leprechaun, Nathan. Too busy to shave?"

Running a hand over my face, I grinned at her description. She was right; I needed to go to the barber, but kept putting it off. Sylvia only visited when she wanted something. That something being me. Both of us were single, unattached, and happy to remain that way—neither one of us were interested in a relationship. We got along well, but aside from the occasional evening together, we didn't seek each other out. It had been a while since she'd come to see me.

"I'm always busy. In this case, though, simply lazy. It's on my list."

She sashayed in, dropping gracefully into one of my visitor's chairs, crossing her long legs. One foot swung slightly as she leered at me, her short blonde hair gleaming in the light. "You always have a list. What about later—are you busy then?"

"I'd like to be."

"Dinner . . . or just fucking?"

I smirked, my body tightening at her blunt words; a reminder of how long it had been. Usually, I was enough of a gentleman, I bought her dinner first. I licked my lips as I studied the graceful lines of her body. "Both—as long as my 'demented leprechaun' look doesn't frighten you off."

She lifted one shoulder. "I can work with it."

"Okay."

"It'll have to be your place, my roommate is home sick."

"I'll change the sheets."

"How thoughtful."

I shrugged my shoulders. I knew she wouldn't care—it wasn't as if she ever spent the night. It wasn't that kind of relationship—if in fact it was any relationship at all. I ignored the fleeting thought that lately I wanted that kind of relationship—something deeper than a physical release. The truth was, I was getting tired of waking up to an empty bed, and being alone all the time.

I pushed aside my melancholy thoughts, turning my attention back to her. I knew she liked Thai food. "Lemon Grass?"

"Sounds good."

"I want to get a fresh shirt before we go—this one has ink on it from an uncooperative printer."

"The blue color is nice—it matches your eyes."

I rolled my eyes. "I'm a sure thing, Sylvia. No need to get all complimentary on me."

She laughed at my comment. "I'll leave my car here and come with you."

I nodded. Maybe we'd have dessert first.

SYLVIA WALKED AROUND MY LIVING room, her long nails tapping out a fast beat on the bottle of beer she held. "You've done so much with the place, Nathan."

I shrugged. "It's fine."

It was terrible. I knew it and chose to ignore it most of the time. I had a place to sit, somewhere to sleep and the fact it wasn't cozy and inviting rarely made any difference to me. Although lately, it seemed more desolate than usual. My only concessions to comfort were the huge chair in the corner I preferred to sit in, and the large flat screen TV that provided most of my entertainment.

A knock at the door made me frown. "I'll be right back. Grab a seat."

"Take your time."

Thinking it would be some random kid at the door, looking to sell me something I didn't want, I dug in my pocket for a five so I could quickly get rid of them. I was surprised to find Mrs. Webster on the other side of the door, smiling at me.

"Ah, Nathan. Good, I caught you home. Not a bad time, I hope?"

It was impossible to be rude to Mrs. Webster. She lived down the street, on the corner, and no matter how I tried to ignore her, she always came over to say hello if I was outside. Her grandson Kyle, who lived with her, cut my lawn and shoveled my driveway. Both were tasks I hated, and it gave the kid some spending money. He reminded me of myself at that age—tall, and lanky—not comfortable in his own skin yet.

I forced a smile on my face. "Not for you, Mrs. Webster. Do you need something?"

"Kyle's out and Ricky has himself stuck up a tree again. He's just out of reach and I knew with those long arms of yours, you could get him for me. If, of course, it wouldn't be too much trouble."

Damn cat was always getting stuck in a tree, which was

how I first met Mrs. Webster. I was washing my car when she appeared, hands wringing, asking me to help. I had followed her down the block and climbed the tree to rescue her precious Ricky, handing him to her quickly so he'd stop scratching and hissing at me. She'd been so grateful; she insisted I come inside for cookies. At the time I'd been happy to agree, since I loved cookies.

Mrs. Webster, however, as I discovered, was a terrible cook. I was barely able to choke down one, and the bag of them she sent home with me ended up being eaten by the birds.

I stifled a sigh and nodded. "Of course. I'll be right there."

I called to Sylvia, telling her I would return soon, then I followed Mrs. Webster down the block.

Swinging myself up onto the same tree, I reached for the little spitfire cat, handing him down to her. He swiped his angry paws at me, not happy at being disturbed. Mrs. Webster clucked her tongue at him calling him naughty, the whole time stroking his fuzzy head. I narrowed my eyes at him as he lapped up her attention. She was the one who made me pull him out of the tree and all I got were growls and attitude. I suspected Mrs. Webster could have gotten him down herself, using the small stool I'd seen her scramble up and down on in her kitchen, so I wasn't surprised when she asked me a nosy question. "Have you met your new neighbor yet? Kourtney?"

"With a K," I added without thinking.

"Oh, you have then! What a lovely girl she is!"

I shook my head. "We've chatted over the fence, that's all. She was kind enough to share her dinner one night."

She clucked. "I keep telling you to come let me cook for you. Kyle barely eats at home."

I managed to keep a straight face. Kyle had told me once if I thought his grandmother's cookies were bad, I needed to stay clear of her dinners. He ate at the restaurant where he washed dishes more often than not.

"I'm pretty picky, Mrs. Webster. Mostly, ah, vegetarian," I lied, figuring if I was forced into a meal with her, at least she'd make salad. The truth was I rarely ate vegetables. I liked meat—with a side of meat.

She frowned. "A strapping young man, such as you, needs to eat more than vegetables. How tall are you again, dear?"

"About six foot, three."

"My late husband was a short man." She sighed. "I always liked taller men."

I bit back my smile. She'd told me that fact many times.

"She's very shy."

I blinked at her. *Who was she talking about?*

"Kourtney. She's very shy. But so sweet."

I had rather figured that out myself, but I simply agreed, catching on to her plan. Meddlesome old woman—I wouldn't be getting to know my neighbor any better than I did now. She was far too nice for the likes of me. The kind of relationship I could handle was sitting on my sofa waiting for me. "I, ah, have someone waiting. I have to go."

"Of course. Thank you. Come for dinner soon!"

I nodded and turned, hurrying back to my place. Inside, I could hear voices and I followed the sound to the backyard. Sylvia was sitting at the table and chatting, it seemed, to the shy Kourtney. Her empty beer bottle was beside her on the table, and a second bottle was in her hand.

"Ah, Nathan. Finished your rescue attempt?"

I nodded, glancing toward the fence, wondering why I was uncomfortable with Sylvia talking to Kourtney.

"Your neighbor thought I was you. She offered to feed me and although it smells great, I declined on your behalf," Sylvia explained, arching her eyebrow at me. "I assured her, I'd make sure you ate."

Anxiety prickled down the back of my neck. I should never have brought Sylvia home with me.

"We should go."

Sylvia rose from her chair, smirking. "Anxious for the main event, Nathan?"

I grabbed her elbow, dragging her into the house. "I'm

starving actually. Let's go."

"Good night, Kourtney!" she called over her shoulder. "Enjoy your dinner!" She leered up at me. "I know I certainly will."

I glared at her for some reason, but all she did was shrug.

"I'm going to go powder my nose."

I stared after her, but didn't follow her inside. I couldn't walk away. Something held my feet to the deck. Instead, I approached the fence.

"Thanks for the offer, Chefgirl. It smells delicious."

"It's nothing. I'm glad you're going out. Have a pleasant evening," Kourtney replied, sounding . . . off.

"I doubt it's nothing. I don't think your cooking would ever be considered 'nothing.'"

"It's only dinner." She sighed, the sound making my shoulders tense. "You'll have a much better time out."

How did I explain the sudden feeling I had? That I would rather be sitting on my deck eating the dinner she cooked, talking to her for twenty short minutes, than going out with Sylvia?

How could I explain that to her, when I couldn't explain it to myself?

"Thank you anyway. Your offer was most generous."

"Good night, Nathan."

I had the feeling I'd been dismissed. I didn't like it.

Unsure what else to say or do, I turned and went inside.

MY FRACTURED MOOD LASTED ALL throughout dinner. The meal I ate wasn't anywhere near as appetizing as the one Kourtney had shared the other night. Sylvia's banter, which I always thought amusing, was suddenly banal and annoying. I found myself having to pretend to smile, and force myself to laugh at her jokes.

Finally, she laid down her chopsticks and stared at me.

"What seems to be the problem, Nat?"

"Nathan."

"Your neighbor called you Nat when she thought it was you in the backyard."

I bristled at her tone, but had no desire to share anything with her. Even more, I didn't want her talking about Kourtney. "I can't help what she calls me. I don't like to be referred to as Nat."

"Fine, *Nathan*. What the hell is up with you?"

"Nothing."

"You're acting like an ass."

I shifted in my chair. I *was* acting like an ass. "I have a headache."

She rolled her eyes, throwing her napkin on the table. "I think you have more than a headache, and I think I'm done with this."

"Where are you going?" I demanded as she stood up.

She shook her head, her hand resting on her hip. "I always enjoyed our time together. You were fun and easy—sex with you was great. But whatever or whoever has you all tied up in knots has changed something. I don't think you're any more interested in anything past dinner than I am now."

I met her gaze head-on. She was right—something was off for me and I didn't want to take her home.

"I'm sorry."

She shrugged. "It was great while it lasted."

I nodded, and started to stand up. "Let me take care of the bill and I'll drive you back to get your car."

She held up her hand. "Don't bother. I'll grab a cab. Figure it out, Nathan—before it's too late."

She turned and left, leaving me wondering what she meant.

THE NEIGHBORHOOD WAS QUIET WHEN I arrived home. I pulled into the driveway slowly, taking in Kourtney's house. It was dark, except for a porch light illuminating a bright-colored wreath that hung on the front door. There were two vivid, red flower pots flanking it, making the entryway homey. I glanced at mine. I had no decorations, no lights, and no flowers. There were a few shrubs that had been planted already when I moved in, but I had added nothing.

I parked the car and went inside, not bothering to turn on any lights. Grabbing a beer, I stepped out back, listening for sounds from next door, only to be greeted with complete silence. I sat down, feeling strange, wondering what had happened earlier and why it bothered me so much that Kourtney knew about Sylvia. I had only spoken to Kourtney a few times, and never officially met her. I had no idea what she looked like or anything about her life—even if she had a boyfriend who could start hanging around.

I certainly didn't understand why *that* idea made me want to punch something.

She was my neighbor, who was kind enough and had fed me a couple times. Neighbors did that. I got Ricky out of the tree for Mrs. Webster on occasion; Kourtney made me dinner.

It was simple. Neighbors helping neighbors.

I looked over at the empty house next door, wondering why I felt I should be doing something for her.

Why it felt like more than us being neighbors.

Why she felt like more.

Chapter Five

WELL, SHIT.

Grimacing, I watched the milk curdle in the cup of coffee I had made. I shook my head, groaning in frustration; that was what happened when you left the milk out on the counter overnight.

Kourtney had been conspicuously absent all day yesterday, even though it was a holiday. I didn't hear or see her at all. Her house remained dark, and there were no great aromas drifting over the fence to tempt me. Although, I wasn't sure even if she was there she'd share her food with me again. I had finally eaten some cereal later in the evening when I couldn't handle the hunger pangs anymore.

Dumping the offending cup, I grabbed the jar of instant and made another one, which I carried out to the deck with the newspaper.

It was still early. I sat down with a sigh and took a sip of the hot beverage, frowning at the bitter taste of the black coffee. Without the tempering edge of cream or milk, I wasn't very fond of it. A trip to the grocery store later was needed.

I scanned the headlines and sipped coffee, trying to decide what to do with the rest of weekend ahead. I had been invited to a barbeque, but I wasn't sure I was in the mood to be with other people. Of course, I wasn't sure I was in the mood to be alone, either.

Reaching over for my mug, I overshot and knocked it with my hand, sending the hot liquid spilling out all over the table. Jumping up, I swore in frustration.

"Not having a good morning, neighbor?"

Turning my head fast, I gazed at the fence with a wide grin. She was there—I hadn't even heard her moving around—but she was there!

I cleared my throat and tried to keep the excitement out of my voice. "Not so much."

"It's awful early for all that cussing and jumping around," she teased.

I relaxed at the tone. She wasn't upset with me.

"Some of us were home and asleep at a decent hour yesterday. Where were you? Out partying?"

Her adorable giggle made me smile. "I was working. We have a big seminar coming up and I had to put in some extra hours."

I sighed in relief at the knowledge she hadn't been out with someone. "Life's too short to work all the time."

"I'm not much for night life. I'll leave that to you."

I sucked in a fast breath, and moved a little nearer to the fence. "Yeah, Kourtney, about the other night. Sylvia may have given you the wrong impression."

"Oh?"

"We weren't on a date."

"You weren't going out to dinner?"

"Well, yes, we were, but it wasn't like a *date* . . . date."

"It's really none of my business."

"I think she gave you the impression we were, um, closer than we are." I exhaled a big breath, unsure why it was so important I made her understand. "I came home alone. It was only dinner, in fact only part of dinner, since she walked out."

"Maybe you should have sprung for a better restaurant."

I began to laugh, relieved at her teasing. "Pretty sure it wouldn't have made much difference."

"Maybe you would have gotten some action."

I laughed even harder. "I got plenty of action the other night. The Palmela sisters, as you called them, were highly cooperative."

"Ewww, Nathan. TMI."

She began to laugh, and everything felt right; the anxious feeling in my chest eased.

"I don't suppose you have some milk or cream I could borrow, do you? This coffee is bad enough, and without it, I'm having a tough time drinking it, but I really need a cup."

"I'm impressed, Nathan."

"Sorry?"

"You make coffee."

I snickered at her sarcasm. "It's instant. That's why it's extra bad without anything in it."

She sounded horrified. "That's not coffee—it's brown-colored water."

"It's all I've got."

Her chair creaked as she moved, and the sliding door opened. I'd gotten smart and left an extra chair by the fence. As I was waiting, I thought about adding a quick trip to Home Depot to the list today to get myself a ladder. Or, at least, a tall step stool.

A noise had me look up. I was surprised to see a large, steaming mug on the top of the fence. "Hey, why didn't I hear you move the ladder?"

"I gave up taking it down. I figured it was easier to leave it in place."

Chuckling, I reached up and retrieved the mug. It was a little trickier than a plate, and some of the liquid spilled over as I moved it.

Yeah, I definitely needed a ladder.

I stepped down and took a swallow, moaning in appreciation.

She made kick-ass coffee.

"Thanks. I'll add it to my list of attributes," she stated wryly.

I snickered at my lack of ability to keep my mouth shut where she was concerned. My thoughts seemed to find a way out without me realizing.

Ignoring the sodden mess in front of me, I returned to my chair and enjoyed the hot coffee for a few minutes.

"Thanks," I called out.

"You're welcome."

"So if you're leaving the ladder up, you plan on feeding me again, I assume?"

"Well, I figured I was the one to start the whole stray cat syndrome, so I suppose you're right."

I snorted. "Stray cat? Kourtney with a K, are you calling me a pussy? Seriously woman, you're insulting my manhood here."

She laughed loudly and I reveled in the sound. It was rich and full; filled with warmth. The sound was different than her delightful giggle and quiet voice. I liked hearing it. I wanted to be the one to make her laugh.

Grinning, I walked over and placed the mug back on the top of the fence. "But, I'd purr for you if there was another cup of your coffee," I begged, enjoying teasing her.

My mug disappeared. After a few minutes, it reappeared, this time with the addition of a plate on top. Eagerly, I grabbed at it, almost giddy to find a toasted bagel with cream cheese waiting for me.

"Yes," I hissed as I took a bite.

"Don't get so excited, I was merely saving the fire department a trip. I think I'm actually scared of what you might do to a toaster."

I took another bite, chewed, and made a semi-growling noise toward the fence.

"Excuse me?"

"I'm purring."

"Oh. Is that what that was? I thought you had gas."

The coffee burned as I struggled not to choke on it while I sniggered.

Gasping for air, I sat back; my bad morning suddenly became enjoyable. Kourtney was on a roll today.

"Are you okay, Nathan?" she asked, concerned.

"I'm good. Warn a guy before you're gonna make him laugh, okay?"

"Yeah, I'll get right on that."

"And call me Nat." I hesitated. "I like it when you call me Nat."

"Okay then . . . Nat."

Satisfied, I had another bite of the bagel.

It was quiet for a short while. As I ate and took my time with the second mug of coffee, I heard the rhythmic clicking of keys being hit. Kourtney must be working on a laptop. After a few minutes the clicking got louder and there was an occasional low-muffled curse. Next came the unmistakable sound of a laptop being shut in frustration.

"Problem, Chefgirl?"

"I was trying to find some information," she responded with a deep sigh.

"Oh?"

"My laptop is doing strange things and being all . . . wonky. It won't let me get to my list of stuff—you know, the document list thing—and there's a recipe I want. And my connection doodad is so slow and keeps dying. I need to take it somewhere and I was trying to find a computer repair shop."

I grinned at her distinctive description. Obviously, she didn't know much about computers.

"But?"

"Well, because it's acting so weird, it won't let me. I can't get to the internet to find a shop, so I guess I'll have to drive around and look for one. Unless you can recommend a place?"

"Why don't you use your phone to find one?"

"I don't have a phone book. I haven't picked one up yet."

"I mean your cell phone. You can get the internet on your phone."

"I don't have a cell phone."

I gaped at the fence. "What?"

"Yeah, I'm not much for technology."

"Hence the 'wonky' laptop?"

"I guess."

Standing up, I went over to the fence. "Hand it over."

"What?"

"You happen to live next door to the most brilliant IT man to ever walk the face of the Earth," I informed her. "Give me your laptop and I'll look at it."

"I can't ask you to do that, Nat."

"You didn't. I offered. Hand it over, Chefgirl. I promise I won't steal your recipes."

"Are you sure?"

"Kourtney," I began, now serious, "with all the generosity you've shown me since you moved in? The least I can do is look at your laptop."

She was silent.

"Besides," I teased, "sending you into a computer repair shop would be like throwing raw meat into a lion's den. They'd eat you alive. Let me look at it."

Her footsteps were slow as she approached the fence. Her laptop slid across the top.

"Thank you."

"I assume you have a password?" I asked as I reached for it.

"Oh, yeah, it's *emptiness,* and I used capital E and the number one for the 'i.' They always tell us to have a number and capital in our password at work."

Frowning, I paused. It wasn't the word I'd have expected from her. Opening up the laptop, I typed in the password, took a quick look at the hard drive, and groaned at the mess.

"When was the last time you defragged this?"

"I de—did what?"

I shook my head. "Your antivirus is expired. Do you know

that?"

"Oh, right. I meant to do something about getting a new one. But I found it all confusing and I couldn't tell what I should get."

Amused, I rolled up my sleeves. "I'm gonna need more coffee. This is gonna take me some time."

"Okay. I can do that. Anything else?"

"Probably lunch. Maybe even dinner. You have a real mess here."

"Are you sure you have time? I don't want to take you away from your plans."

I laughed without humor. "My huge plan today was going to get some cream for my brown-colored water, and having a nap, after I got my hair trimmed. I'm pretty sure I can still squeeze it all in at some point."

"I'll get you cream while I go get the stuff for dinner."

My ears perked up. "Dinner?"

"Yeah, a little birdie said something about souvlaki."

I groaned as my fingers flew over the keyboard, thinking about how amazing her dinner would be. She was getting this laptop back in perfect working order.

"Off with you, Chefgirl. I need to work for my dinner."

A thump made me turn. There was a thermos on top of the fence.

I grinned—what a great fucking weekend this was turning out to be.

Chapter Six

"IS THERE MORE?" I ASKED, wiping my mouth, looking toward the fence in expectation.

"Seriously?" Kourtney's voice was incredulous. "You already ate two burgers, Nat! Two *big* burgers. You have room for another one?" Then she sighed and laughed. "Wait, who am I talking to? Of course you have room for more, don't you?"

I chuckled as I approached the fence, grinning in anticipation of eating a third burger. "First, they're fucking awesome and I'm a growing boy; so yeah, lots of room. And second, it's not like the usual, where you pile on the vegetables and salad . . . no side dishes. All I got is the meat, so gimme another one, Chefgirl. Please?" I pushed my plate to the middle of the fence. "I've been working hard all morning. I even got my hair cut while I grabbed a couple things at the electronics store."

I heard her melodious giggle—the sound that made my chest feel lighter. I smiled wider as another fat burger appeared on the plate, only glimpsing the end of her fingers. I grabbed the plate and climbed down. "Are you short?" I asked. "As in stature wise?"

"Um, sort of."

"Maybe I need to cut a hole in the fence, to make it easier for you."

"No! It's fine, honestly."

I frowned at the sound of the panic I could hear radiating from her voice. "Relax—I was only teasing. I don't own a saw anyway. I don't want anything to hinder the feeding cycle."

"Well, I don't want you in trouble with the co-op. You know, for destroying the fence. That's all."

I threw a disbelieving glance toward the fence. Really, the girl was a lousy liar. But rather than challenging her, I grunted as I chewed on the delicious burger in front of me. "Thanks."

"Head's up."

I looked up in time to see an object come sailing over the fence. I caught it without a problem, and burst out laughing.

"Chips? A package of potato chips? From you?" I gasped, pretending to be horrified.

"You wanted a side dish. It's all I got. Maybe they'll help fill you up."

"You make me proud. This is the sort of side dish I take to potlucks. I'm famous for it. If I'm feeling extra creative, I buy the dip, too."

Kourtney began to laugh, and I couldn't stop my grin listening to it. Whereas her giggle was delightful and filled with mischief, her laugh was almost sultry; low, warm and filled with life. The sound was so much louder than the usual level I associated with her when she spoke. It was as if her amusement simply couldn't be contained and spilled out on its own accord. It made me happy.

"I like that," I mused.

"Like what?"

"Your laugh."

"*My laugh?*"

I nodded, even though she couldn't see me. "It's like unexpected sunshine on a dark cloudy day, Kourtney," I said, after swallowing a mouthful. "I love hearing it. Your giggles light me up, too."

The silence on the other side of the fence was deafening. Nothing moved, and there was no sound for what seemed an eternity. I cursed myself for once more speaking aloud, except this time I had wanted her to know what I was thinking.

Then Kourtney giggled.

"That was, without a doubt, the cheesiest thing you have ever said to me, Nat. Did you hear it in some bad chick flick you were forced to watch?"

I chuckled with her in relief. "I was hoping for another meal later," I teased half-heartedly, glad she wasn't upset. It was obvious she didn't like personal remarks, unless it was to compliment her cooking.

I wondered why that was. I thought women liked compliments—at least the ones I knew did.

"No worries, Tomcat. Dinner's on me. But stay away from the Romance channel, okay?"

"No problem. Your mess of a laptop should keep me away at least until the end of the day," I stated dryly.

"It's that bad?"

"I've seen worse. Not many, but a few. Not to worry. It'll be as good as new soon enough. Better even, when I'm done."

"I appreciate it."

I finished the burger and leaned back. "I know, Kourtney. I'm happy to help." I wanted her to know I truly meant it.

"I'm gonna go and make something right now. The door is open. If you need anything; you can holler, okay?"

"Yep."

I sat motionless after she went inside. I could hear her moving around and the sound of Celtic music filled the air—the lilting notes tranquil. I was perplexed thinking about her reaction to my statement. I did like her laugh, and her giggles, which I often found irritating in most women. However, hers, for some reason, made me smile. In fact, I liked everything about her.

I had never *listened* to voices before now—heard the

nuances or inflections that set them apart from one another, but with Kourtney I did. I could tell so much about her mood from the tone of her voice. I looked forward to talking with her, sharing my day. Listening to her soothed me and made me feel as though I was no longer alone. It was a new feeling for me; but one I was strangely okay with. Somehow, though, I knew I needed to keep those thoughts to myself.

Sighing, I went back to work, my lips quirking up as I caught sight of the bag of unopened chips beside me. My side dish.

Maybe I was rubbing off on her.

"OKAY, LISTEN UP, KOURTNEY WITH a K."

I pushed the laptop across the top of the fence. "I defragged it. I got rid of the *multitude* of viruses and spyware you had. I added a good antivirus software. I cleaned up your hard drive. I backed it up and saved your data. You do know what a backup is, right?"

"Yes."

"You need to do that on a regular basis."

"Um, my computer at work is automatically backed up nightly. I guess I never think about it."

I pushed another small device her way. "Here's an external hard drive. Plug it in every Sunday. It'll automatically back up everything you've done in the past week."

"Oh. Really? Just plug it in?"

I rolled my eyes at the worry I could hear. "Yes, all you have to do is connect it. It's programmed to do everything automatically. I also added some more memory to the laptop so it should be faster. Plus, I upgraded your operating system. And lastly, here is a USB key. It's a portable memory drive. You can take files back and forth to work." I paused and cleared my throat. "Do you have something against your screen, by the way? Do you poke it on a regular basis? It was covered in fingerprints. Dusty ones."

She giggled. "It's habit. The computers at the lab are all touch screen and sometimes I forget mine isn't. I try and scroll up when looking at a recipe and it doesn't work."

"Well, that explains the unusual amount of flour I found on the keyboard. I sucked it all out with my vacuum tool, but you should wipe your fingers."

"Okay."

Her chair moved as she sat down and I heard the slight squeak of the laptop lid being opened. "Wow. I didn't expect all this. Thank you. Please let me pay you for this little, um, backer upper? And the memory stuff?"

"Nope. Consider it a trade. You keep feeding me, Chefgirl, and I'll keep your laptop functional. Next, we'll work on a cell phone for you. Should I ask about your cable hook-up? Do you have cable?"

"Um, yes?"

"Why does that sound more like a question than an answer?" I replied, sitting back down at the table, packing up the various items I'd been using to fix her laptop.

"Well, I have it. I haven't quite figured out how to hook up everything."

I shook my head. Of course she hadn't. Seeing the shape her laptop was in, I wasn't surprised she hadn't attempted to wire up her TV and components.

"You want me to come over? I can do that for you?"

There was no mistaking the sound of a chair toppling over as she stood up quickly. "*No!*"

Now she *really* had my attention. *What the hell?*

"Why not, Kourtney?"

"I'll do it. I'll figure it out. I always do. Really, it's fine, Nathan. Thanks for doing this." Her movements sounded fast as she scurried to the door. "I have to go check on things. Thank you for fixing my laptop." Before I could react to the utter panic in her voice or actions, I heard not only the screen door, but the inside one, shut and lock.

She had, in fact, run away from me.

I gaped at the fence. Her reactions were so odd at times. I pondered the few things I knew about her. She was funny, smart, generous, witty, and could cook like a dream. She obviously had a caring nature, considering she'd started feeding a complete stranger, and had never asked for anything in return. She lived alone, was shy, but once she was fond of you, she was warm and giving—unless you got personal, then she was skittish as hell.

I looked back toward our shared fence.

Why would she have such a panicked reaction at the thought of me coming to her home? Had she been hurt? Was she hiding from something, or someone? Did some asshole hurt her so severely she somehow felt the need to lock herself away from the world?

Those thoughts bothered me. I didn't like to think of her hurt, or alone. She was too special.

I shook my head.

Where were all these thoughts coming from?

Chapter Seven

I WAITED A WHILE, BUT she never came back. I gave up and went inside to try and have that nap I had been looking forward to. Yet, somehow, I had trouble relaxing and falling asleep. I kept thinking about Kourtney and how skittish she became every time I suggested some sort of face-to-face meeting, however casual.

What could she possibly have to hide that would make her not want to meet me?

We were already friends; at least I thought we were. We talked almost every day. In fact, the highlight of my day had become talking to her over the fence at night, while we ate the dinner she had cooked, and afterward. She was droll and smart, and I enjoyed our conversations. I also enjoyed her food. Even the odd night she didn't feed me, it was listening to her talk and hearing her laugh that made the day a good one.

I wondered what kind of secrets she was hiding, then snorted. I was one to talk—she wasn't the only one hiding things, was she?

Eventually, I gave up and decided to go back outside. I stopped to grab a beer and was surprised when I saw how many I had left in the refrigerator. I thought back and realized I hadn't been drinking anywhere near as many since Kourtney came into my life. My time was filled with conversations and staying busy, rather than sitting around drinking alone. I hadn't even noticed.

I went outside, opened up my laptop and looked over a few things. I had copied Kourtney's email address and Yahoo chat info. I got busy and finished setting up the account I had started earlier, so I could send her messages. Somehow, the thought of being able to chat with her on occasion during the day, or the evenings when she wasn't outside, pleased me.

The whole time I had worked on her computer, I had struggled with my conscience. Time and again my fingers hovered over her directory wanting to see what information I could glean from her laptop, while I told myself not to snoop. It was fairly new with a bright red cover. Aside from the much abused screen I had teased her about, and the many smudges of flour on the keyboard, it was in good shape. I finally gave in and peeked at her documents.

I noticed a lot of medical stuff on her laptop and had bookmarked a few of the sites she seemed to look at a lot. She had a ton of documents saved, mostly recipes, but aside from that there had been very little personal stuff. There were no saved funny items, no personal pictures, or family information; nothing that gave me anymore insight into *her*. She had no Facebook, Twitter, no sort of social media on her laptop at all, aside from the one chat box. The only bookmarked sites she visited regularly, aside from the medical or cooking sort, were ones with pictures of baby animals. She had a lot of those. I knew I should feel bad for looking around her computer, but I wanted to know a little more about her. Her laptop had revealed nothing. Even her friends' list on chat was small, only six people. Well, seven now, I grinned, wondering if she would notice her new friend, *Gnat*, on the list.

Her door slid open. I remained quiet, listening to her move around. I heard her light the barbeque, and keeping my tone neutral, called over to her. "Hey, Chefgirl."

"Oh, hey, um, Nat."

I chuckled quietly at the way she still stumbled over my name. "Are you getting ready to feed the masses?"

"Well, I was only gonna feed you, but if you want me to share—"

I gasped in horror. "Don't even tease! That's not even remotely funny!"

Her giggle made me relax into my chair. "Sorry. I know how . . . *possessive* you are about your food. But really—you're a mass unto yourself."

I snorted. "You have no idea, on either count; especially when it comes to souvlaki. Is it chicken or pork?"

"Um, I did chicken and lamb."

I tilted my head back and groaned. "Get to it, woman."

"Keep your pants on Tomcat, it's coming."

"Tease."

Her laughter drifted back as she entered her house. I needed to keep it light. She was comfortable with that type of conversation.

I wanted her to be comfortable. Somehow, the way she felt had become important to me.

I LEANED BACK FROM MY small table, trying to slow myself down. "Fuck, this is incredible. Have you always liked cooking?"

"Pretty much."

"Was your mom a good cook?"

"She was a simple cook. I don't think she liked it. She used a lot of canned stuff."

"So you learned to cook in self-defense?"

She hesitated, and when she spoke her voice was strained. "I learned how to cook after she died. She was in a car accident when I was young. My dad had no idea how to cook, so I sort of took over."

"Shit, I'm sorry. I bet he appreciated it, though."

Her laugh was bitter. "You'd think, right?"

I glanced toward the fence, not liking the sudden tone the conversation had taken. I'd struck a nerve—obviously a painful one. I needed to make her smile.

Clearing my throat, I picked up my fork again. "Well, I fucking appreciate it. This is remarkable."

"I'm glad you like it."

We were both silent while we ate and enjoyed our meal. I wanted to keep her talking, though. I liked the cadence of her voice—I liked it more than I realized.

"Are you a doctor?"

"What?"

"Are you a doctor? I noticed you had a lot of medical stuff on your laptop. I wasn't snooping; I happened to see it as I was on cleaning up some files. There were a lot of big medical terms I didn't understand."

"Um, not the way you think. I don't treat people like a medical doctor. I have a PhD, but I do research."

"What kind?"

"I'm a cancer researcher."

I stopped chewing and glanced over to the fence. "That's impressive, Kourtney."

"It's intense and rewarding."

"I bet you're brilliant at it."

"Why would you say that?"

I shrugged, even though she couldn't see me. "I get the feeling you're brilliant at whatever you put your mind to."

There was silence.

I cursed myself internally but quickly added, "Unless it's computer-based of course. Hence the wonky laptop." I paused; curiosity making me ask, "How do you manage at work with computer-related medical programs?"

"Oh, I was trained on the software. It's very structured there. And, I took a basic course in Word and Excel. But that's all I know. I have no idea about all the other stuff. I find it very confusing," she explained, then sighed.

"Yeah, I figured that out from the state of your laptop." I snickered.

Truthfully, it was awful.

I relaxed when I heard her chuckle in return. "I guess it's a good thing I live next door to the most brilliant IT guy on the face of the planet—right, Tomcat?"

I leaned back in my chair and scowled at the fence. "Listen, Chefgirl. That's the third time you've called me Tomcat today. What did I say about referring to me as a pussy?"

Her giggle made me smirk.

"You had better be picturing some sleek, sexy, mean, hell-on-wheels kind of pussy when you refer to me that way." I growled menacingly. "Like the fucking King of the Alley Cats."

Huge, rich peals of laughter rang out over the fence and I was struggling to hold in my own. I loved hearing her happy sound. It made me feel as if I'd done something right.

"Stop laughing! I swear I'll do something drastic!"

"What are you going to do?" She gasped between peals of laughter. "Stop eating?"

"Well, now you're talking crazy, woman." I snorted in disgust. "I was thinking more like . . ." I grinned. "Cooking for you one night and making you eat it."

"Now, Nat, that's beyond drastic . . . it's cruel," she deadpanned.

I let go and began laughing with her. "Then behave. I'll do it, Kourtney with a K. And it won't be pretty."

She snorted, then tried covering it up, only to snort again. I laughed harder. How adorable.

Smiling, I tucked back into my dinner. She moved around, bumping into something, muttering a curse that made my smile wider. When dishes appeared on the top of the fence, I eagerly stood and went to retrieve them. "What's this?" I grabbed the two containers and walked back to the table.

"It's a thank you." She sounded nervous.

I opened the first lid and grinned. "Cookies? You made me cookies?"

"My laptop is . . . better than new. I wanted to say thanks. I don't bake very often, but I thought you'd enjoy those."

Grabbing a cookie, I bit down and moaned as the taste exploded in my mouth. Was there anything she made that wasn't awesome?

I picked up the second container and found it filled with more souvlaki and vegetables. There was enough I could take lunch for a few days. I fist pumped the air. No cafeteria for me!

"Kourtney, dinner was thanks enough. But this is incredible. Thank you."

"You're very welcome. Are you done with your plate?"

"Yeah, I'll wash it and return it tomorrow."

"No, it's fine; I'm loading the dishwasher. You can hand it over the fence."

I walked over, climbed the chair, and lifted the plate. I saw her hand come up, reaching for it. For the first time, I strained to catch a small glimpse of her, but because of the angle, only caught sight of fingers. On impulse, I pulled the plate back and instead reached out for Kourtney's hand with my own. I grasped her fingers in mine and I heard her small gasp. Her palm trembled, but I held on. I was afraid she would pull away, ready to let go if she did, but not wanting her to break our first connection. My large hand easily encompassed her much smaller one, and I squeezed her fingers.

"What are you doing?" she whispered.

"Saying hello. And thank you."

"Can I have my hand back?"

I squeezed her hand again. "Hello, Kourtney."

I waited patiently.

She sighed. "Hello, Nathan."

"Are you on the top step?"

"Um, no. I don't like heights much."

"Ah. Not a midget then?"

She giggled at my comment. "No. Shorter than most, but

not a midget."

I shook my head in wonder. "So you don't like heights, yet almost every day you climb up some steps and make sure I have dinner—Is that right? Even though it makes you uncomfortable?"

"I go only as high as I have to in order to reach the top of the fence. It's not too far."

I smiled at how she brushed off the question or any indication of her own feelings.

Pressing her fingers one more time, I noticed how right they felt clasped in mine. "Thank you, Kourtney. Thank you for being brave and climbing the ladder, for dinner, the treats, and your company. All of them were exceptional."

There was a few beats of silence before she spoke. "You're welcome, Nat."

I released her hand, feeling a small pang of regret in doing so. I wanted to get her to come up another couple steps and let me see her. From the angle I was standing, I wouldn't get much more than a glimpse of the top of her head probably, but still I wanted it. I wanted to tell her I'd hold her hand and she'd be safe doing so. I wanted to talk to her some more. However, I knew, it would only upset her if I asked, so I kept quiet.

"Goodnight, Kourtney."

"Goodnight."

Climbing down the chair, I picked up my containers and went inside. There was no sound behind me—I didn't hear Kourtney climb down or move toward her door.

It was then, I realized, it was the first time I had gone in before her. The feeling that I had left her out there alone made me uncomfortable. It made my heart ache.

I wasn't sure what to do with those strange and unfamiliar emotions.

Chapter Eight

I WAS UP AND GONE early the following Sunday morning. The sun wasn't even up when I left the driveway, but I had a long drive ahead of me.

I noticed lights were already on in Kourtney's windows, and it made me wonder how early she got up.

She had been busy at work the past week since I fixed her laptop. We had only shared a couple of evenings through the fence. I found myself unable to relax completely until I knew she was home. She never failed to come out back even if it was just for a few minutes on the nights she was later than usual. I realized those brief periods were the best parts of my day; I looked forward to them, no matter how short they were.

She had, however, been her typical, generous self and kept me fed. She made sure I had enough food for the nights she wasn't home until later. She still refused to take any money toward groceries, and I was still trying to figure out a way of getting around her refusal. I threatened not to eat the meals she made anymore, but she laughed, and I had to join in. I wasn't stupid enough to really mean it. But, the nights she was gone I found I missed her company as much as I missed her food. She always found a way to make me smile. She had sounded more tired than normal last night and, for some reason, it bothered me. I was extra outrageous, making her laugh at my comments, enjoying the sound of her amusement. She rewarded me with more leftovers.

The rest of the complex was still shrouded in darkness as I drove through the streets to the main intersection. I noticed a woman jogging to my right and I frowned. It was still so early, and the streets were deserted. Should she be out running on her own? As I drove past her, I looked in my rear view mirror; she was moving at a good pace, her bowed head under a hoodie, her face hidden from view. She was short and voluptuous-looking from what I could see, and I frowned again. Shouldn't her husband or boyfriend be with her? I saw her cut down the next street and shrugged. There was nothing I could do about it, but it gave me an unsettled feeling, and I hoped she was safe.

I stopped at the lights and waited for them to turn green. I needed to grab some coffee for the drive, then I would hit the highway. It was always a bittersweet day.

Both a reminder of my past—the lonely years I'd spent in prison because of mistakes I'd made, and the one unexpected friend I had found during that bleak part of my life.

⟲⟳

GRANT SLID INTO THE BOOTH across from me. "Nathan," he greeted me and smiled as we shook hands.

"Hey, Grant."

"How goes it?"

I shrugged. "Living large."

He waited for his mug to be filled, and we both ordered breakfast. He studied me over the rim of his mug.

"Knock it off."

"What?"

I shook my head at the man who had started out as a

mandatory counselor to me, and, over time, morphed into my friend. "I'm not your patient anymore. Stop looking for my 'tells.' I'm fine."

He sniggered. "Old habits die hard, Nathan."

I changed the subject. "How's Claire?"

"She's fine. Says hello and she wants you to come to the house next time. Stay for the weekend so she can cook for you. She always worries you're not eating enough."

"She can stop worrying now."

"Oh?" His eyebrow rose, his expression curious.

"I'm eating better."

"What, two sandwiches with every case of beer instead of one? Or you're actually adding lettuce to your BLT's?"

I smirked at him, since he had it about right—at least before Kourtney.

"I told you the place next to me was sold . . . I have a new neighbor."

"And?"

"She's great. We've become fence friends."

"Fence . . . what? What the hell is that?"

"She's shy, I think—extremely shy. I've never actually seen her face-to-face, but she feeds me. I sorta told her how great her dinner smelled one night and she fed me."

"How does it work if you can't see her?"

"You know how tall the fences are. She slid a plate on to the rail at the top and told me it was there."

He shook his head, frowning in disbelief. "And you ate it? Not knowing who was on the other side?"

I chuckled and winked at him. "Trust me, Grant. If you'd smelled this, you would have to."

"So now, what, she feeds you?"

"Basically. We're . . . friends. She feeds me, I fixed her laptop and we talk."

"You talk. What do you talk about?"

"Everything really—how our days have been, stuff in the neighborhood, the news, the weather—just conversation. She's incredibly smart—a cancer researcher. And she has a wicked sense of humor—she's constantly putting me in my place."

"And you do this through the fence."

I nodded, waiting as the waitress slid our plates in front of us, then walked away. "As I said, she's shy. She likes to keep things impersonal—she gets a little skittish otherwise."

"Impersonal. No wonder the two of you get along so well."

I ignored his jibe. "Well, it's nice to have her next door. The past year there was a tenant in the place who I never saw since he traveled all the time."

"Sounds as though you don't see her, either."

"One day I will, no doubt. It's inevitable since we live next door to each other. But I won't push her."

"You like her."

"What's not to like? She's funny, cooks like a dream, and I enjoy her company."

"Through the barrier of a fence."

I looked at Grant as I considered his words, then I nodded. "She's not ready for anything else yet. Neither am I. So for now . . . Yes."

He chuckled. "Fence friends. Now I've heard it all. I'll be interested to see where this goes next time I see you."

"It's not going anywhere. There's nothing more to it—we're just friends."

"Be careful, Nathan. Life has a way of springing surprises on you when you least expect it."

We were both quiet as I thought about Kourtney and kept eating my breakfast. There was no need for his warning. It would go nowhere. Kourtney and I were neighbors—that was it—all we could be.

Yet, the thought made me strangely sad.

Grant's voice broke in through my musings.

"Have you thought about reaching out again, Nathan?"

My fork paused midair and I narrowed my eyes at him. "That part of my life is over, Grant. You know it is."

"A lot of time has gone by. Things change, people change."

I shoved my plate away, my appetite now gone. "They made it crystal clear how they felt about me."

"Families are complicated."

"No. You were there the day I got out. You saw what happened." I shut my eyes as the memory of the car driving away, leaving me behind, hit me—the pain as tangible now as it was then. "I reached out—I tried. My letters were returned. They moved. It was obvious; they wanted me to stay as far away as possible."

"You moved yourself."

"I had to start over."

"I could help. I have lots of contacts with the police and private investigators . . ." His voice trailed off, when I shook my head.

"No, Grant. Leave it. They washed their hands of me when I went to jail. They have their life. I have mine."

He regarded me in silence, and sighed.

"I'm not sure what you're doing is called living, Nathan. You need to figure that out."

AS USUAL, WHEN I GOT back from seeing Grant, I was restless. Memories of the past were too close to the surface for comfort. It was mid-afternoon and the sun was out, so I grabbed a beer, went outside and paced for a while as I sipped. I stopped, listened, but heard nothing from Kourtney's side of the fence. I called her name, hoping to hear her quiet reply—only silence greeted me. I called louder in case she was inside, but there was no answer. I went inside, grabbed a handful of cookies and my laptop. After I opened it up, I logged onto Yahoo Messenger and was rewarded with the yellow light blinking by Kourtney's name.

Gnat: Hey Chefgirl. Where are you?

I waited, bouncing my knees, and finally saw what I was waiting for: WhyteElephant typing.

WhyteElephant: Nathan?

Gnat: Yeah, it's me. How many other people do you know called Gnat? Or call you Chefgirl?

WhyteElephant: Should I even ask how you did this?

Gnat: Nah, too technical for you.

WhyteElephant: I suppose I shouldn't be surprised you added yourself to my chat list. Kinda stalkerish, Tomcat. Just saying.

I smirked.

Gnat: Where are you?

WhyteElephant: At work.

Gnat: You're at work too much these days—and it's Sunday. Why?

WhyteElephant: I have a deadline. I needed to finish some things. Why?

I hesitated.

Gnat: I was looking for you.

WhyteElephant: OMG

Gnat: What?

WhyteElephant: Don't tell me you've eaten everything I gave you. Not even you could eat all that and still be hungry . . . could you?

Huh. I hadn't even thought about her food. I just wanted her.

Gnat: No, Chefgirl. I wasn't looking for food.

WhyteElephant: What do you need?

I paused.

Gnat: I was having a bad day . . . kinda wanted to talk.

WhyteElephant: I'm sorry, Nat . . . I have to do this. I'll be home in a couple hours?

Gnat: Yeah, you do your research—brilliant girl you are. I'll be here.

There was a long wait until she responded. I sat waiting patiently until she did.

WhyteElephant: Steak for supper?

I smiled. Avoid the personal comments.
But her grilled steak? Hell, yes.

Gnat: I'll go to the store and buy some. No arguments. You buy stuff all the time. Only fair.

WhyteElephant: OK, Nat. Not arguing. See you later.

Gnat: Hurry home, Chefgirl. I'll be waiting.

Her light clicked off.

A FEW BEERS HELPED RELAX me once I got home from the store. I wasn't sure what Kourtney was going to think of my purchases, but I'd find out soon enough. I might have gone a little overboard with the meat shopping. I knew she'd make everything taste delicious, though, and I gave up trying to decide what to buy and bought it all.

I'd heard her car a few moments ago, so I went inside, gathered up the bags and placed them on top of the fence. Then I sat down and sipped on my beer. My legs felt a little wobbly and I tried to remember just how many beers I had actually consumed, losing count after four. It must have only been four—maybe five—couldn't be six—could it?

A few minutes later, her screen door opened and I heard her footsteps outside.

"Nat?"

"Hey, Chefgirl."

Okay, that sounded a little slurry.

"Are you okay?"

I felt the oddest warming sensation at the concern in her voice. No one ever worried about me anymore. "Yeah, I'm good. Better now that you're home."

"Oh . . . I . . . um . . ."

I chuckled. "I'm hungry, and I'm trying not to dig into the leftovers you gave me. Those are to make co-workers jealous and promise me huuuuge favors for tastes. Big ones. Yep."

Okay, definite slur.

She giggled, and I beamed at the sound. She was home and we could spend some time together. She made me so happy.

"Is that what you do with them?"

"No. Unless there's something I really want. Then I may consider a trade . . . but to be honest, it hasn't happened yet. Nobody's had anything remotely equal to your fucking awesome leftovers." I smacked my hand on the table for emphasis. "Not even fucking remooootely . . . close."

"How many beers have you had?" She laughed, now sounding incredibly amused.

"A few."

"I think more than a few . . . Still having a bad day?"

I leaned my head back. "Nah, it's better now. You're home." I grinned in the direction of her voice. "I went shopping for us." I pointed to the top of the fence. "It's up there." Then I laughed, realizing she couldn't see me pointing. Maybe I should show her. I stood up on my slightly wobbly legs, climbed the chair and moved the bags around. "Here, Kourtney. It's here."

I heard her climb the ladder and I held tight to one of the rather large bags. She tugged one to her side and I watched it disappear, grinning while I waited for her to get the other. I felt the tug on the bag and held on. She tugged harder. "I think the other one is caught on something, Nat," she called patiently.

Smiling, I reached up and grabbed onto her hand. "Gotcha!"

Her unexpected shout of laughter surprised me and I started laughing with her, only to sway a little before losing the grip on her hand. I tipped myself off the chair and landed on my ass on the deck, with a loud thud. I continued to laugh as I sat there, my ass now throbbing in pain.

Kourtney stopped laughing. "Are you okay?"

I snorted. "Well, *fuck*, that's gonna leave a mark. My ass is gonna be black and blue tomorrow." I looked to the top of the fence. "You may have to perform CPR, Chefgirl."

Now she snorted. "On your ass? I don't think so."

I sniffed dramatically. "I'll have you know I've been told it's a nice ass. More than once."

She began giggling again. "Modesty becomes you."

I rubbed my aching butt. "Seriously, I may need medical attention here." I smirked. "You know doctor stuff; maybe you could . . . kiss it better?"

Once again, she snorted.

Seriously, she was snorting over kissing my ass? Some people would happily kiss it.

"Heads up!"

Startled, I looked up and snagged the item that was sailing over the fence. Confused, I regarded the package containing one of the thick steaks I had bought. "What's this for? It's not cooked yet!"

"Raw meat works to bring down the swelling on a bruised eye. Maybe you could sit on that and it would do something for your ass—and your overinflated ego."

Wordlessly, I looked at the steak, then glared at the fence. "You know, Kourtney with a K, my other girl doesn't give me lip the way you do; I could go back to her. She's always waiting."

"Other girl?"

"Yeah. She's pretty hot stuff. Warm, soothing, always there when I need her, with none of this back-talking shit. You've probably seen her at the grocery store."

"And does she have a name?"

I bit back a laugh. "Yeah, she does. Marie Callender."

There was silence for a minute.

I could tell she was trying not to laugh when she spoke.

"Nathan?"

"Yeah?"

"I don't know how to say this . . . but your *other* girl?"

"What?" I could feel my lips twitching.

"She's a total tramp. She's warm and soothing to a lot of guys. A few women, as well."

I gasped in mock horror. "Chefgirl, are you talking smack about Marie?"

Her voice dropped. "Only telling you what I've heard. The guys think she's easy, and she's pretty cheap most of the time. Rumor has it you can often get a 'twofer.' Maybe I give you some lip, deservedly so, I might add, but I'm a little more exclusive."

I threw my head back, hooting in laughter.

My girl was fucking hilarious. I loved it when she teased me.

On her side of the fence, Kourtney joined in my amusement. The second bag disappeared over the fence, then I heard a gasp as she discovered the contents inside the two huge bags. "Exactly how hungry are you? You don't expect me to cook all this at once, do you?" she asked, horrified.

I shook my head, still laughing. "No, Kourtney. I wanted to contribute. You've cooked so much for me. Throw it in your freezer and cook it when you want." I climbed gingerly back up on the chair. "The steaks are for tonight, though," I said, pushing the package over the top. "I am not putting that Grade-A beef on my ass. I want you to cook it for me. It'll work its way to my ass eventually."

"Oh, my God! You're so rude! Do you not have a filter at all?" Kourtney gasped, but then another fit of her warm laughter drifted over the fence. I loved making her laugh—even with my rude comments. She just got me. Nobody had ever gotten me the way she did.

"Nat?"

"Yeah?"

"Are you okay—seriously?" Her tone was warm and reflected her genuine worry.

"I am now. Thanks for the laugh."

"Sorry about your, um, ass."

I snickered. She was adorable. It sounded as if she was embarrassed simply saying the word. "I'll survive . . . unless you're offering that kiss . . ."

"Dream on, Nathan."

She walked away from the fence. "And stay off the chair after you've had a few beers . . . please."

I sighed, rubbing my sore ass.

Good advice.

Chapter Nine

THE SMELL DRIFTING OVER THE fence was driving me crazy. "Soon, Chefgirl?"

She sighed in frustration, but her voice was amused when she answered. "Get your fork ready, Nat. It's almost done."

"Not my fault you make it smell so fucking delicious I can't wait, you know."

Kourtney laughed. "I'm going as fast as I can, Tomcat. Your incessant 'are we there yet' queries won't cook it any faster, *you know*. I'm not a miracle worker."

"Pretty fucking close, if you ask me. You got me eating salad, and other . . . green things. If that's not a miracle, I'm not sure what is."

Her warm laughter filled the air, and grinning, I got up, went inside and grabbed the bottle of wine I had bought. It was one of my favorites when I was in the mood for wine and I thought Kourtney would enjoy a glass with her dinner. I had even bought a special glass; one of those flat-bottomed wine goblets so I could give it to her easily. I had my doubts a stemmed wine glass would make it intact being slid across the fence top. Those suckers were wobbly enough on a flat surface. I had mostly sobered up, but wasn't totally sure my coordination skills were up to pushing a tippy glass around. I approached the fence and carefully climbed on the chair, waving my hand frantically over the top. "Are we there yet?"

A subtle giggle close to me indicated Kourtney was up on the ladder. A plate appeared, and reaching out, I touched her hand, pleased when her fingers didn't immediately pull back.

"Hi, Kourt."

"Hi, Nat."

"I got you something."

"What?"

I grabbed the plate and carefully pushed the glass her way. "You mentioned once you liked red wine. I thought you'd enjoy a glass with your steak."

She seemed surprised. "You remembered that?"

I wanted to tell her I remembered everything she had ever said. However, I knew better than to be too forthcoming. "Yeah," was my simple reply.

For a minute there was silence. I heard her climb another step, allowing her to reach for the glass. I glimpsed the pale skin of her forearm and saw her hand wrap around the glass before disappearing back over the fence. I heard a relieved sigh and I knew she was off the ladder. "Safe now?" I teased as I reached for my plate. "Back on solid ground?"

"Yeah. Thanks, Nat. I appreciate the wine."

I surveyed my heaping plate in anticipation. Then I frowned. "Kourtney?"

"Hmm?"

"Why do I have two steaks? One of those was for you."

"It's only one and a half. They're huge—I'd never be able to eat more than half. Somehow I knew you would have no problem with the added portion."

"You don't eat enough."

She snorted. "I eat plenty, Tomcat. Not everyone is a bottomless pit like you."

I carried my plate to the table and dug in, closing my eyes as the first bite hit my taste buds. "It isn't possible to eat enough of this deliciousness."

"Enjoy your dinner."

"No doubt of that, thank you." I took another huge bite and ate steadily, enjoying every morsel. Damn it, my girl could cook. I wondered what Kourtney would think if she knew I now thought of her as my girl. I decided to keep that little bit of information to myself for the time being.

"How's the wine?"

"It's lovely. You chose well."

"It's my favorite," I stated, without thinking. "My mom used to drink it, too."

"Oh."

"Otherwise, to be honest, I don't know much about wine. I know one good red and one good white. She always said I should know that in order to impress a date."

"Sounds like a smart woman."

I sighed. "I thought so."

Kourtney was quiet for a moment. "Is your mom not . . . here . . . anymore?" she asked hesitantly.

I shut my eyes as the sudden pain seared in my chest. I had to swallow several times before I could answer her, and even then I could only tell her the partial truth.

"No. I have no family."

"Oh, Nathan, I'm sorry."

I looked toward the fence. She sounded sad. Almost as if she was crying again, like the day I bought her the lilies.

Wanting to lighten the moment, I chuckled. "She would have loved you. She was never able to get me to eat vegetables on a regular basis. Or even on an irregular basis."

"Why do you eat them for me?"

I looked down at my almost empty plate, mystified. I had no idea.

"Maybe because *you* made them, Chefgirl? Because you share your company and food with me every day—it seems rude not to." I thought for a second. "Besides, you make them taste *real* good. She always cooked the living shit out of them. Not sure there was much nutrition value left when she was done." I sighed as a small reminiscent smile crossed my face. "But man, could she cook a mean pot roast."

Kourtney laughed and I was pleased to hear the sound. I didn't want her sad. I finished my dinner in silence, savoring each mouthful.

"What about you, Kourtney? You said you cooked for your dad and brother after your mom died. Did they eat their vegetables like good boys?" I teased, in hopes of discovering something about her. "They must have loved having you cook for them. Lucky bastards."

Kourtney was quiet for a moment. "They ate what I cooked, but I don't think they saw it quite like that."

I snorted. "How could they not?"

"I never . . ."

"Never what?"

"I never did much right in their eyes. I wasn't the daughter or the sister they wanted. I never measured up. No matter how well I cooked."

The pain in her voice was so prevalent; I turned in the direction of her sad tone, my body itching to find a way over the top of that fence. The urge to comfort her was overwhelming. Even though I knew she wasn't ready for it, I wished I had bought a ladder so I could get to her.

"Kourtney . . ."

"Don't," she pleaded with me. "Don't say it."

I shook my head in frustration. She was shutting down.

"Nathan, do you miss your family?"

"Every day."

Her voice was low and angry. "I don't miss mine. Not one bit. In fact, every day I don't have to be subjected to them is a good day."

I was speechless.

"Do you have good memories?" she asked. "Laughter and

happy times? Fun-filled holidays?"

They were from a long time ago, but I did have good memories. "Yes."

"Hold onto them. The last happy memory I can think of, I was eight. After that, life was pretty wretched."

"Did you want to talk about it?"

I heard her stand up. "I don't even want to think about it. Are you done?"

Without another word, I picked up my plate and walked over to the fence. I could hear her climb the ladder and I pushed my plate over the top.

"Kourtney . . ." I beseeched her in a quiet voice.

"What?" The word sounded tired—exhausted even.

I tapped the top of the fence, holding out my hand. "Please."

She sighed and I felt her hand touch mine. I stretched my arm as far as I could and grasped her fingers tight. "I didn't mean to upset you. I'm really sorry."

"I know. I'm not upset with you, but I don't want to talk about it."

"Fair enough. But Kourtney, you're an amazing woman. An incredible cook. Whatever their problem is, it's obviously them, not you. Clearly they're assholes."

Kourtney laughed without mirth. "Clearly."

I squeezed her hand. "I mean it—I think you're wonderful." I hesitated, afraid of saying too much. "I'm glad you're in my life. That you moved in next door."

She didn't respond, but her hand squeezed mine back. Finally she spoke. "Thank you, Nathan. You're a good friend." She withdrew her hand from mine. "I'm going in now. Goodnight."

I stood, listening to her gather up her plate and walk inside. The too quiet click of the door shutting seemed to echo in the still of the evening. It sounded as defeated as she did.

I climbed off the chair and sat in it.

A good friend—she thought of me as a friend. I leaned my head back and stared at the sky as I thought about it. I realized, despite what I had said to Grant earlier, I wasn't happy with only being her friend. Somehow, in a ridiculously short period of time, she had grown to be more than that in my mind. I shook my head at the absurdity. We had never even seen each other, never sat face-to-face to talk, yet somehow I had developed feelings for the woman with the soft voice, sweet giggle and giving nature, who lived next door. Who was so skittish she would probably panic if I suggested we get together in a setting that didn't include the barrier of a fence. It was what I wanted, though—more than anything.

I wanted to get to know the woman behind the warm sound and thoughtful ways. I wanted her to know me. I groaned, thinking about what that meant. How would she feel about me if she knew about my past? I would have to tell her—it wasn't something I could hide from her forever.

I was surprised to discover I wanted to talk to her and tell her about my life. Be honest and up front. Grant constantly told me being honest was the best thing. He often said I still hadn't faced my past since I refused to talk about it with anyone, unless I was forced to, as with him. Maybe he was right: I needed to tell someone else.

Maybe I needed to tell Kourtney and see if she could accept me—past and all. Maybe if I shared with her, she would open up to me and we could both move on from our pasts.

Together.

My fingers drummed restlessly on my knee as I thought about it. Obviously, her past had left her with issues—the same way as mine. I felt my anger build at the faceless people who had done this to her.

From the little she had said, her family had left long-lasting scars. The kind people couldn't see—the same way my family's rejection had scarred me, causing me to refuse to get close to anyone.

Family should love and protect, not hurt one another. From what I gleaned she had been hurt—badly—maybe even worse than I had been. Bastards. They better hope we never meet. It sounded as if her hurt stemmed from many years, whereas mine had been abrupt, leaving me reeling at a time when I needed my family the most.

I sighed. I wasn't sure I was prepared for this, or if she was either. I needed to be patient and understanding; be a friend to her, until she was comfortable with being . . . more. I could do that. For her, I could be patient.

I glanced behind me at the tall barrier that made her feel safe, yet kept me from her. At the moment it was a necessary evil.

I planned on buying a ladder, though—soon.

Chapter Ten

TOSSED AND TURNED ALL NIGHT. The pain in Kourtney's voice when she spoke about her family tormented me. I knew, without a doubt, whatever had happened in her past was what made her so skittish when it came to her present life. She always deflected the conversation away from personal subjects. She didn't accept compliments well. It was almost as if she didn't believe them. Any time I even hinted at removing the barrier of the fence between us, she panicked. She was hiding something and I wasn't sure what it was, or exactly why. I only knew it had something to do with her past and the way she was treated by her father and brother.

I snorted, remembering the day she had moved in. I had been in the backyard wondering if anyone else in the complex was hiding a secret.

Guess I got my answer.

I gave up and got out of bed. I had a busy week ahead of me so getting into work early wasn't a bad idea. After showering, I went into the kitchen, not bothering to put on any lights. Looking out the back door, as I ate some dry cereal from the box, I was surprised to see light coming from Kourtney's backyard. I opened the door and went outside.

There were no sounds indicating she was there, but her outside light was on. I wondered if her lights worked the same as mine. If you turned on either the front or back door lights, both came on. It was touted as a safety feature with the house, like the built-in carbon monoxide and smoke detectors. I called her name but there was no response. She probably had left one of the lights on. I went inside, grabbed my phone and got in the car, entering via the garage as I always did. Pulling out of the driveway, I backed the car up a little and confirmed her front light was on. I also noticed diffused light from behind the living room curtains, and I frowned. She was up early, and I wished I was able to go knock on her door and make sure she was okay. I shook my head at that idea. As if a knock at the door at five in the morning wouldn't startle her.

I drove through the subdivision, the houses mostly dark and the streets deserted. As I was stopped at the corner, movement caught my eye and I saw the same girl from yesterday, jogging toward me. Again, I couldn't help but observe her pleasingly curvy figure and the flexing muscles in her legs as her sneaker-clad feet pounded on the pavement. Her hood was up and her head down as she ran past, her legs pumping out a steady rhythm, not even lifting her head to spare a glance at my idling car.

The first thought that entered my head as I watched her run by was: she shouldn't be out alone. I looked in the rear view mirror and saw her turn the corner—and my frown intensified. There were only two streets in that direction, one of them being the one I lived on. Both streets were cul-de-sacs and sat on the fringe of dense woods. Surely to God she wasn't going running in the woods? As yesterday, the same restless feeling overtook me when I thought about this unknown woman out alone this early. She seemed too vulnerable and diminutive to be on her own. I had no idea why the sight of a stranger running in the early dimness made me feel uneasy, but unable to stop myself, I turned the car around and drove back in the direction she had turned.

I drove slowly, stopping at the corner of the first street, scanning the road for her. I didn't see her so I went back to my corner and viewed the quiet street. It was still deserted and the only light on was Kourtney's. I turned the car and headed back out, relief flooding through me when I saw a light snap on in one of the houses on the first street. She must live there and had made it home safely. Obviously, I had missed her arriving home. I had no idea why this concerned me, so I drove on, unsure of my strange reaction. I didn't understand why I was worried. I never worried about anyone else other than myself, and now in the short space of time I was worried about two women?

I sighed as I merged onto the main road, my speed picking up as I left the subdivision behind. I had other problems to deal with besides an unknown woman who liked to run in the dark. No matter how appealing they were to me.

WHEN I WAS FINALLY ABLE to get back to my desk, I grabbed a coffee and sat down with a heavy sigh. Despite being swamped all morning, Kourtney had been on my mind. She kept creeping into my thoughts, no matter what task I was dealing with at the time. I needed to check on her, but I wasn't sure how I would be received today. Regardless of what she had said last night I had upset her, and it bothered me. I liked it when I could make her happy.

I turned my chair to the window and studied the sky outside. The heavy clouds filling the atmosphere matched my mood well. I grinned as an idea hit me. Turning back to my desk, I clicked on Yahoo chat and was pleased to see WhyteElephant's light on.

Gnat: Hey, Chefgirl—emergency—call 911.

WhyteElephant: What seems to the problem?

Gnat: It's gonna rain.

WhyteElephant: Emergency indeed. I'll alert the media for you.

I grinned at her wit.

WhyteElephant: Should I ask why rain constitutes as an emergency?

Gnat: If it's raining, you can't BBQ. If you can't BBQ, I can't eat. Hence emergency.

WhyteElephant: Oh, how silly of me. I never thought of your stomach when I saw it was raining.

Gnat: Hmmmph.

WhyteElephant: Nathan—do you EVER go in your kitchen?

Gnat: Of course. I'm not completely useless.

WhyteElephant: Have you ever noticed the large square silver item there?

Gnat: I know the name of the appliance you're referring to.

WhyteElephant: Oh, excellent. And surprised you know the word appliance.

Gnat: Being rather sassy again, Missy. It's called a refrigerator. It's my friend. My hero actually.

WhyteElephant: Your refrigerator is your HERO? Do tell.

By now I was grinning widely. I *could* make her smile today.

Gnat: It's magic. I put warm beer in it and a few hours later it comes out cold.

WhyteElephant: Oh. My.

Gnat: And even better, it protects some of my most prized things.

WhyteElephant: You keep imported beer in there, too?

I chuckled. I loved her sense of humor.

Gnat: No, smartass. The food you give me. It keeps it safe and fresh. My hero.

WhyteElephant: Wow. That is a little frightening, but I was referring to the other large square appliance—the one that is waist high.

Gnat: Sniffing at you haughtily—I know that, too. It's called the stove. I am aware.

WhyteElephant: Impressed again. But do you know what it does?

Gnat: Yes!!! It also is multi-functional. It acts as extra counter space to lay out the pizza and wings on Football Sunday, and hides the empty containers and paper plates until garbage day. Duh.

I sat back, smiling, waiting for her reply.

WhyteElephant: OMG—I somehow never thought to use it for that. How silly of me. I've only ever used it for cooking INDOORS when it's raining or snowing OUTSIDE. My bad.

Gnat: Happy to have taught you something new. You should always keep your mind open to new ideas, you know.

WhyteElephant: You are seriously deranged.

I threw back my head, laughing. I knew without a doubt, she was laughing, too. Mission accomplished.

WhyteElephant: Don't worry about dinner—I got it covered. I promise you won't go hungry. Still holding onto the leftovers for bribes?

Gnat: I brought some for lunch. I did a thorough inventory last night. I think I'm good until Thursday. No cafeteria crap for me. But, I will heat it up, then take it down and sit with my co-workers as I eat it and watch them weep when they smell the awesomeness my containers hold.

WhyteElephant: Please refer to the seriously deranged comment above.

Gnat: Chefgirl?

WhyteElephant: Yes, Tomcat?

Gnat: I think you're the best hero of them all.

WhyteElephant: You're a nut!

I hesitated then went for broke.

Gnat: Nuts for you, Chefgirl. ;)

WhyteElephant: I have to go. You shouldn't be drinking on the job, Nat. I doubt the computers you work on today will work tomorrow. Just saying.

I rolled my eyes. As usual, she deflected.

WhyteElephant: Meet you at the fence at 7. I'll have your dinner.

Gnat: Have a good day, Kourtney. You just made mine.

Her light went out.

I stared at the screen. There was so much I found myself wanting to say to her, but I knew she wasn't ready to hear it. Somehow, I knew I needed to let her move this . . . relationship—or whatever it was—at her own pace.

A knock startled me and I looked up. "Hey, Shannon," I greeted and smiled at one of my co-workers.

"Hey, Nathan. Heather told me you wanted one of the old cell phones reactivated under your name?"

I nodded, holding out my hand for the slightly outdated phone, smiling when I saw the color—red. Kourtney liked the color red, given her flowerboxes and laptop cover, and I knew she'd at least be happy with the color.

She frowned as she handed me the small phone. "I have newer ones, you know—ones with more features and capabilities? This one seems rather backward for you."

"No. I need one as simple to use as possible. You added a text plan to it?"

"Yes, and it's billed to you as per your instructions, but under our group plan. I am going to assume it's not for your use?"

I shook my head. "No, it's for my girlfriend."

It wasn't until her eyebrows shot up I realized what I had said.

"Oh. I didn't know . . ." She trailed off.

I waved my hand. "No. It's fine. We're pretty, ah, new." Internally, I snorted. So new I didn't even know it myself. "She isn't much for technology. I'm trying to bring her a little more up to date."

Shannon laughed. "That should be fun for you. A new project."

"She's rather leery of a lot of technical gadgets. She needs things simple and easy to use." I smirked as I thought about her laptop.

"Well, I guess it explains your recent good mood." Shannon winked with a knowing grin. "And all the homemade lunches you've been bringing in."

I paused, surprised anyone had noticed a change, or even the fact there had been one. Thinking about it, I knew she was right. I had been laughing more and bringing a decent lunch. I nodded happily. "She takes care of me. I'm trying to return the favor."

"I'm sure she'll appreciate it, Nathan. See you later." Shannon waved as she left the office.

I picked up the phone I got for Kourtney and set to work. After getting the information, I programmed her number into my phone and added a ringtone for her. Then, opening hers, I set up a few things and added my cell and work number into her contacts and made sure the text option worked. Smirking, I added *"Tomcat Prowl"* as the ringtones for the numbers, knowing it would make her laugh. I looked at her contact list snickering; there were only the two numbers: Gnat Cell and Gnat Work. As far as I was concerned, they were all she needed, but tonight I would explain to her how to add others, plus use the phone and text option. Patiently.

I drew in a deep breath, letting it out slow.

I needed to be patient on a lot of levels, because as soon as the word left my lips I knew that was what I wanted. I repeated the word out loud. *Girlfriend*. I snorted and shook my head—I hadn't had a girlfriend since I was sixteen—I wasn't even sure if I knew how to be a grown-up version. I'd avoided all close relationships since I got out of prison. Ones like I had with Sylvia suited me fine—scratched the proverbial itch, but I steered clear of emotional attachments.

Until Kourtney—my shy but friendly, mysterious neighbor.

I wanted Kourtney to be my girlfriend. I wanted to learn how to be the guy for her. It was an odd sensation, one I didn't think I'd ever want in my life. For the first time in many years I wanted to be close to someone else. I wanted to get to know her, and her to know me. I wanted to take care of her. Everything in me told me it was what she needed; the same way I needed her to take care of me. She was alone as I was. I wanted to remove the fence permanently—then we could take care of each other.

For now though, I wanted her to have this phone. I would feel better knowing she had a cell phone and knew how to use it. I knew, without a doubt, if she decided to get one, she would be talked into some long-term plan with a high-tech cell phone she would never figure out how to use. This one was basic, wouldn't overwhelm her, and when she was ready, I would help her upgrade to a newer one if she wanted. Until then, I wanted to be able to get hold of her, and should the occasion arise, I wanted her to be able to contact me if she needed to, and especially if she wanted to.

I needed her to want to talk to me.

And I wanted her to need me.

Chapter Eleven

TAPPED THE TOP OF the fence, ignoring the container sitting there, beckoning me with its contents. "Chefgirl. You know the rules."

"Nat, it's raining."

"I saw the umbrella. Give it up." I tapped again.

"I'm not sure why this new ritual is so important to you," she grumbled.

"It just is." I shrugged, even though I knew she couldn't see me. "Hand, please."

I heard her overdramatic sigh and smirked. It grew wider as I saw the umbrella come into view and her hand appear. I stretched and clasped the tips of her fingers. "My chair is slippery, so I need you to come closer. Only one more step—please?" I implored. Her hand withdrew as she used it for leverage and reappeared. This time I was able to grasp it almost entirely.

"Hi, Kourtney."

"Hello, Nathan."

"I can feel you rolling your eyes at me, you know," I teased.

"Oh, now you have magical powers? Like your fridge?"

"I always have. How do you think you got here?"

"Um, in a car?"

"Only because I let you think that. I wished for my own personal chef and abracadabra—here you are."

"Wow. I think I need to add delusional to my earlier deranged comment." she stated dryly, then let out a string of her sun-filled giggles.

I chuckled with her, loving the sounds she made when happy. Her voice soothed all the rough edges, leaving me relaxed.

"Go eat your dinner."

I clutched her hand, feeling nervous. "Wait. I need something."

"What now?"

"I need you to come back after you're done. I have something for you."

"Something for me?"

"Yeah. But not until after dinner. Meet me back here . . . unless I come over?"

The question hung heavy in the air; the silence was deafening, but telling.

"I'll meet you back here in half an hour."

I sighed, not surprised by her answer, but knew not to push. Releasing her hand, I tugged at the container. "Holy shit, this is heavy. What's in here?"

"Something I thought you might like. I hope you enjoy it."

As soon as I was on firm ground, I opened the lid and groaned. "I'm gonna need forty-five minutes for this!"

Her laughter drifted across the fence. "See you then."

CAREFULLY, I HAULED MYSELF BACK up on the chair, glad it had stopped raining. I wanted to be able to talk Kourtney through how to use the phone without worrying she was getting soaked while doing so. If she didn't have an umbrella in her hand she couldn't smack me with it for giving her the phone, either. It was a win-win situation for me.

The door opened and her footsteps approach the fence. "You there?"

I grinned. "Yep. But you're lucky I can walk after that feast."

"I'm sure it wasn't as good as your mom's, but I thought you'd enjoy it."

"It wasn't as good, Kourtney. It was better. I almost licked the container."

Her tone was shocked. "You didn't eat all of it, did you?"

"I wanted to, but no. I saved some. It was the best pot roast I've ever tasted. Did you make it because I mentioned my mom's?"

"It was in your bag of beef yesterday. And you talked about it, so I thought it was a good indication you wanted one. I've had it cooking since last night."

"Thank you. It was amazing. I'm quite sure I'll have people weeping tomorrow as I eat the leftovers at lunch," I added with glee.

"Hmm, not sure I should be encouraging your continued torture of your co-workers."

"They deserve it. It's all good."

"Okay, then . . ."

There was my cue. Reaching in my pocket, I pulled out the small phone. "Hand, please."

She sighed. "We already did this, Tomcat."

I laughed. "Humor me."

I heard her small huff, but her hand came into view, palm side up which was perfect. Stretching over, I placed the phone in her palm with a gentle squeeze as her fingers curled around it. Her hand disappeared and for a minute there was silence.

"What's this?"

"It's called a *cellphone*, Kourtney. Say it with me. Celllllphonnnne."

"I know *what* it is, Nathan, but why are you giving it to

me?"

"It's for you."

"Why?"

"Because I want you to have it."

"But—"

"No buts, Kourtney. Please. You should have one. What if your car broke down or you needed something?"

"I could walk to a phone booth. I've managed to get along without one until now."

"Well, now you don't have to."

Her voice dropped. "It seems such a waste for me to have one."

I was confused. "A waste? Why would you say that?"

"I don't, um, have anyone to call." By the time she finished speaking, her voice was almost inaudible.

My throat felt tight. "You can call me—anytime; day or night, I mean it."

"I don't know how, and I don't know your number."

"You do now."

"What?"

"Pay attention, Kourtney. You're about to get cellphone lesson number one."

I GRINNED DOWN AT THE screen at Kourtney's text. "Well, aside from the horrendous spelling errors, you did it. You have now called and texted me."

She huffed—the air rising in white wisps above the fence. "It's cold and my fingers are shaking, Nathan. Even my socks are damp."

I realized she was right, the air was very cold. I hadn't even noticed, and as much as I didn't want her to leave, I also didn't want her chilled. "You wear socks in the summer?"

"My feet get cold a lot. I prefer fuzzy ones most of the time."

I stored that piece of information away for later.

"Are they red?"

"Yes. How did you know?"

I snickered. "Magic."

"Whatever."

"Okay, go inside. Send me some more texts."

"Yeah?"

I liked her quiet enthusiasm. She had understood everything I had shown her, and I thought she was quite excited about her little phone. "Yeah."

"Okay. But, wait. You have to pay for this, right? Will I get a bill or something?"

Right there was the part I was dreading; her refusal to accept this one small thing from me. "No, Chefgirl."

"Why? I know they aren't free."

"It's magic?" I offered hopeful she would leave it alone.

"Nathan. Tell me, or I am giving it back. I mean it."

I smirked at her stern tone.

"The phone cost nothing—it was a recycled phone from work. I added you to my work plan—my treat."

"You can't do that."

"Yeah, I can. It's cheap, I promise. With everything you do for me, I wanted to do something for you."

"Nathan—"

"Kourtney. The honest truth is: I'm doing it for myself."

"What do you mean?"

"I feel better knowing you have a means of on-the-go communication. I like knowing if you needed something, you can call me and ask. And the same for me—I can call you. Please, let me do this for you."

"You can call me?"

"Yeah, it's the latest craze, Kourtney. It sends *and* receives calls."

"Ass."

I hit speed dial, amused as *"Tomcat Prowl"* hummed over the fence, and I snickered as Kourtney's giggles filled the air.

"I don't know how to answer it!"

"Hit accept."

"Um . . . hi?"

"Hi," I murmured into the phone.

"Wow, it's like stereo. You're all around me."

I loved her choice of words. I wanted to be all around her. "Hit end. See? Easy." I stared at the fence. "So we're good? No more arguments?"

"I guess this could be very useful, even if I only use it for emergencies."

"Especially for those. Be sure to keep it charged and take it with you when you leave the house."

"Can it be bounced around?"

"What?"

"If it was in my pocket and I was running, would it get damaged?"

My breath caught and I had to clear my throat before I spoke. "You, ah, run?"

"Yeah."

"When?"

"In the morning, usually, before I go to work."

I swallowed, trying to keep my voice neutral. "*Early* in the morning?"

"Yes."

I leaned my head on the fence, my mind racing. "You should definitely have it with you. In fact, I want you to promise me you'll take it with you from now on. *Always* have it with you when you run. Okay?"

"Okay."

"You promise me?"

"Yes. I promise."

I sighed in relief. "All right, go get warm and practice your texting skills. I'll be waiting."

"What should I text you?"

"Whatever you want. Send me next week's menus or describe your socks every day, if you want. I'll read it. It's all good."

I lifted my head at the unexpected sound of tapping and I saw her hand stretched toward my side of the fence. Smiling, I reached up and clasped her cold fingers, pleased she had been the one to reach out this time.

"Thank you, Nathan."

I held her hand tight, not wanting to let go. "Night."

Reluctantly, I loosened my grip, noticing she took her time withdrawing from my grasp, before climbing down the ladder.

I heard the door close and stood there, lost in my thoughts.

Chefgirl and my voluptuous little runner—could they be the same person? The coincidence was too close for it not to be true. I thought about the strange pull I had experienced to the unknown runner. How it bothered me she was out alone. This morning, I had assumed she lived on the other street, when, in fact, she could have turned down this street and I hadn't realized it. Maybe the lights being on at Kourtney's house happened every morning, and this was only the first time I had been awake early enough to see it. The attraction I had felt to the runner now made sense. It had to be her.

I wanted them to be the same person. But how could I be sure?

My musings were interrupted when my phone alerted me to a new text.

My socks are red with yellow triangles on them.

Chuckling, I sent her a return message.

Are they fuzzy?

Yes.

Mine are white—at least they used to be. Now I think they'd be considered gray. They aren't fuzzy—more leaning toward threadbare.

Here's a tip—bleach. And get some new ones.

I walked into the house as I replied, enjoying her texts.

Here's a tip—I'm a guy. Don't much care.

Do I need to teach you about using a washing machine, Nathan?

I think I need you to teach me a lot of things.

Not sure I have the strength.

I think you do. Keep practicing—you're doing great.

Yeah, I'll keep you informed on my sock color.

I will wait with bated breath daily.

Dork. Night.

Night. Remember to take your phone when you run. Promise me, Kourtney.

I will. I promise.

I sighed. Was she my curvy runner?
There was only one way to find out.

I LEANED MY HEAD ONTO the dark window. It was five in the morning and I'd already been standing there for half an hour, waiting. I blinked wearily as I watched, wondering if I was wrong. Maybe Kourtney wasn't the runner; otherwise I would have seen her by now, wouldn't I? While those thoughts crossed my mind, light spilled over the front lawn.

I moved to the door, opening it fast, staying in the shadows, hoping I wouldn't be noticed. From next door, I heard the opening and closing of the front door and footsteps as they walked down the driveway. Kourtney appeared at the end of our shared driveway, shaking her arms and warming up prior to starting her run. The dimness of the early morning made it impossible to see her face, but I could make out a long ponytail. She reached up and slipped the hood over her head, confirming my Chefgirl was indeed the voluptuous little runner from the past couple days. My eyes drank in the sight of her curves as she stretched and broke into a jog, disappearing from my view.

Swiftly, I walked to the end of the driveway, watching her as she moved away from me. I scanned the street which was deserted, feeling both relieved at the quiet, but worried at the thought of her out on the empty streets alone.

Sighing, I went back into the house and waited. It was only when I saw her return, I was able to relax. She walked past at a slow pace, her hood still in place, her breath a misty fog around her head. She stopped, and turned toward the window where I was standing. Although I knew she couldn't see me with the deep tint on the window, I moved back, feeling somewhat guilty for watching her. She stood looking for a minute staring at my house, then disappeared from my sight. I didn't move for a while, wondering what she had been looking at and wishing I could have seen more of her in the early morning gloom. Had she somehow known I was watching her? Was she looking for me?

"I'm right here, Chefgirl. I'm waiting. Whenever you're ready, I'm here," I breathed.

Chapter Twelve

FOR THE NEXT WHILE, MY mind raced with my discovery. Kourtney and the little runner were one and the same. My Chefgirl. I didn't know what to do with the information but the thought of her out there, running in the dark every morning, alone, made me tense. It wasn't as if I could appear beside her while she warmed up and expect her to be happy I joined her. So, every morning I watched and waited for her to leave and return.

I knew I couldn't keep doing that, but for the moment, it was the only acceptable course of action I could come up with. She had been busy at work and had come home later than usual, even working on the weekend, and I had missed her company as well as her cooking. The few words we exchanged over the fence, when she would finally arrive, were no longer enough. I missed the soothing sound of her talking and the way her laughter made my chest feel lighter. I missed *her*.

Monday morning, returning to my desk after my usual morning workout, I was surprised to see a message waiting from WhyteElephant on my computer. It was the first time she had reached out and contacted me and I was curious why.

WhyteElephant: Nat—I'm sorry to bother you—are you there?

I shot her back a reply, grinning at how formal she sounded in her message.

Gnat: I am now, Chefgirl. Never a bother. What's up?

WhyteElephant: I have a problem.

Gnat: How can I help?

WhyteElephant: I have a document I need but it tells me the file is corrupted. What can I do? I really need it.

Gnat: Do you have it backed up somewhere?

WhyteElephant: At home. It's from my laptop. I put it on the stick thingy you gave me.

I couldn't resist teasing her.

Gnat: The stick thingy?

WhyteElephant: The UPS stick.

I threw back my head in laughter. Fuck, she was utterly endearing—and totally lost when it came to technology.

Gnat: USB memory key, Chefgirl. UPS does deliveries.

WhyteElephant: Oh. I knew it had a U in it.

Gnat: Good try.

WhyteElephant: Nat? I really need this, it's very important.

Gnat: OK, stay calm. Remember the small red thing I gave you the other night? The one you use to update me on your daily sock color?

WhyteElephant: Sigh. Yes, Nat. The cell phone. I know the name. I'm not completely useless.

I chuckled at her throwing my words back at me.

Gnat: I'm impressed. Use it.

WhyteElephant: For what?

Gnat: Call me. Pick up the phone, find my number and call me. The way I taught you.

I waited and my cellphone rang a moment later, the quiet strains of *"She"* filling the air. I smiled hearing it.

"Hey."

"Hi," she mumbled. "I'm sorry, Nat . . . I hate asking anyone here. They all make fun of me about computer stuff."

I could hear how upset she sounded and I felt a quiet pleasure knowing she would call me for help.

"It's okay, Kourtney. I'll try and help. You don't have another copy at work?"

"Not as recent as this one."

"Did you try to open it again?"

"Yes. It says file corrupted. I don't know what I did wrong. I thought I did everything you told me, correctly. The little light was green on the UP . . . the stick."

I smirked. I needed to teach her about Dropbox. *That* should be interesting.

"When did you create the document?"

"About three weeks ago. It's a chart and graph I had been working on to go with this presentation I'm writing."

I was surprised. "When are you giving a presentation?"

"I write it, I don't give it. And, I need to have it ready in an hour. I don't have time to go home. I'm screwed, aren't I?"

My gaze drifted to the memory key on my desk. Leaning forward, I plugged it into my laptop. "Was this on your computer when I fixed it?"

"Yes."

I sighed in relief. I could help. "Have you made any changes to it since then?"

"No."

"Good. What is the name of it?"

"Test Case Study Results 2011. Why?"

I was quiet as I scrolled through the folder called

"Kourtney's stuff." I found the file and took a deep breath. I wasn't sure how this was going to be received.

"I, um, I have a copy."

"What? How?"

"I was worried something would happen to your computer and I did another backup, which I kept."

There was silence for a moment. "I didn't look at anything, Kourtney. I was going to erase it after I made sure you were okay."

"Can you send it to me?"

"Give me your email."

I typed in her address as she dictated it to me and attached the file. "I sent it."

The line was quiet.

"Are you angry with me?"

"Why would I be angry, Nat? Because you thought ahead, knowing my lack of computer savvy? Because you're thoughtful enough to care that I might need a backup someday?" I heard her exhale a big breath. "Anger isn't the emotion I'm feeling right now."

"What is?"

"I'm grateful—so grateful—and thankful I live next door to the world's most brilliant IT guy."

I laughed, relieved. "That you do. Is it there yet? I want to make sure you can open it."

I heard the clicking of her keys. "Yes."

"You, ah, know how to open a file?"

Her relieved giggle made me smile. "*That* I *can* do. And it worked, Tomcat! Thank you!"

"Okay, Chefgirl . . . glad to have helped. Go finish your speech."

"I owe you. I'll make you something special."

"Pretty sure I owe you more. But if you insist—"

"I do. Thank you, Nat. You have no idea how much you helped me," she assured me.

"You can text me anytime, Kourtney. I always have my

phone with me. You don't have to use chat."

"I didn't want to bother you if you were busy."

"I'm *never* too busy for you. Call or text me—anytime."

"Oh," she breathed out, the surprise in her voice so obvious.

"See you at home, Chefgirl."

The line was silent for a moment. "At home. Yeah. See you at home."

I was still grinning when she hung up.

I WASN'T SMILING LATER. I was late getting home, only to discover Kourtney wasn't there, either. Her house was dark and there was no response when I called to her over the fence. By ten o'clock I was beyond worried. After no response to my texts and having my calls go straight to voicemail, I began to pace. I turned on the laptop but she wasn't signed into chat. Alternately, I paced, and stared at the silent screen, while running my hands through my hair in worry. Where could she be? She said she was coming home.

My stomach tightened as I thought of what could have happened. An accident: maybe something happened at work, or she became ill. Groaning, I realized nobody would know to contact me. She could be hurt and I wouldn't even know it. I started to look up the contact information for the local hospitals, but stopped. How could I even inquire if she had been admitted? I didn't even know her full name. I reached into my pocket for my memory key, knowing her name would be registered on her computer. Except, my pocket was empty; I had left it on my desk, after I sent her the file.

Cursing, I began pacing again. I didn't know anything about her aside from the few personal things I had gleaned from our conversations. I knew her voice. I knew her sweet laughter. I knew how her caring ways made me feel. But nothing about her—personally. Nothing I could use right now to find her.

Standing up, I walked into the kitchen, grabbing a beer. I took a deep swallow and tried to calm myself. Maybe she went for dinner with a friend and lost track of time. Maybe there was some big discovery at work and she was deeply entrenched in lab work. Both of those were valid possibilities—except somehow, I sensed, if either had happened, she would have sent me a text, or left me a message. She knew I expected her home tonight and I would worry.

I sat down on the sofa, exhausted. The early mornings, watching to make sure she was okay after her run, were catching up with me. I was tired, hungry, feeling stressed, and I could feel a headache coming on. I rested back against the cushion, closing my eyes, unsure what I should do next.

My eyes snapped open as the sound of Kourtney's ringtone drifted across the room from the desk where I had left my phone. I got up, stumbling as I lunged toward the edge of the desk, grabbing it, already speaking as I raised it to my ear. "Kourtney? Where are you? Are you okay?"

Her voice flowed over me like a calming wave. "I'm sorry if I woke you."

I glanced down at my watch, shocked to see it was after midnight. I must have fallen asleep.

"I don't care about that. Baby, where are you? Are you home now?"

Silence. I closed my eyes when I realized what I had called her.

"Kourtney?"

"No, I'm in Vancouver."

"What? What are you doing there?"

"Mark got sick."

I snorted. "Well, I'm fucking sorry about Mark, but what does it have to do with you being in Vancouver?"

Kourtney sighed. "He was to present the paper I wrote for this medical convention, Nat. He wasn't feeling very well this morning, and he was too ill to travel by lunch. They sent me in his place—there was no one else who could go." She was quiet for a minute. "I didn't want to go."

"Fuck, Kourtney, I was so worried. You weren't here—I

couldn't get hold of you."

"I know. I'm sorry. Do you know they make you turn off your cell phone before you get on a plane?"

I ran a hand through my hair. "Yes, I knew that, but you could have sent me a text, so I didn't worry as much."

"Didn't you get my note?"

I glanced around as if I expected to find something sitting on the desk. "What note?"

"The one I left with your care package."

"Kourtney, what are you talking about?"

"I left you some stuff on your doorstep."

I shut my eyes. "I haven't looked at my doorstep. I always use the door from the garage when I come home from work."

"Oh, well, it was windy and I was afraid to leave it on the fence. I figured you would see it on the doorstep. I never thought . . ." she rambled. "It happened so fast, Nat, and I wasn't really given a choice. I had to rush home, pack, and get to the airport—I barely made the plane. I've been traveling since mid-afternoon. I just got to the hotel."

I sighed as I sat down, feeling relief now that I knew she was all right.

"It's okay, Chefgirl. I'm glad you're safe. You must be tired, though."

"I'm . . . Yeah, I am."

I could hear more than exhaustion in her tone. She sounded tense. "Why do you sound so nervous?"

"I hate speaking in front of people. I'm not good at it. The deal is: I write it, someone else presents it."

"I bet you're better than you think."

She snorted. "I doubt it."

I frowned. "You are always too hard on yourself. You have a great voice, Kourtney. You're smart and witty. You wrote the words. No one would know them as well as you do. You'll be brilliant," I assured her.

"I wish I had your confidence," she mumbled.

"I believe in you. You can do this. I know you can."

"Thank you," she breathed.

"When are you coming home?" I asked, unsure how long she would be gone.

"Thursday."

"That's three more days. I'll miss you."

"I left you food, Tomcat," she stated wryly.

I liked her endearment. "It's not the food I'll miss, Kourtney. It's the cook."

"Have you been drinking?"

"No. Only speaking the truth."

"I'll . . . I'll miss you, too," she whispered, so low I almost didn't hear her. Her hushed confession made my heart soar.

"Nat?"

"Yeah?"

"Can I . . . can I call you again?"

"Anytime, Chefgirl. Day or night. Text me, too. I won't make it through the next few days if I don't know what color socks you're wearing," I teased.

"Okay, go back to bed. Don't forget to get your package."

"I'll go right now. What are you going to do?"

"Um . . . practice the presentation for a bit, then go to bed."

"You, ah, don't have to use PowerPoint or anything, do you?" I grimaced, thinking about how stressed out it would make her.

"No, Annie does that and she's got it covered."

"Good." I didn't want to let her go yet. "Call me if you want a captive audience to practice on."

"You'd listen, wouldn't you?" Her voice was filled with wonder.

"For as long as you wanted me to." I chuckled. "Or until I fell asleep. Whichever came first."

"I think the dialogue would put you to sleep. Unless you love big medical words and a lot of statistics, it's kind of dull."

"Doubt it. I know the person who wrote it. Nothing dull about her."

"Good night, Nat."

"Night."

I hung up, gazing around the room, feeling strangely lost. A thought occurred to me and I sent her a text.

What hotel are you staying at?

The Crowne Plaza.

Room number?

1416.

Last name, please.

Why?

Because I should know. Please.

Whyte.

Sock update?

Plain, boring, white.

I smiled.

Nothing plain or boring about you. Sleep well, Kourtney Whyte. I wish it was Thursday already.

Me, too. Night x

I stared at the small x for five minutes, wondering if she even realized she had added it. Then I got up and retrieved my package from the front step. I was amazed that despite the rush she was in and how nervous I knew she would have been, she had thought about me before leaving.

Inside the basket was a large casserole, some cookies and a note.

Nat—

I had to go out of town to the medical convention.

I don't want to go.

I had the casserole in the freezer it should keep you going until I get back. You have to bake it. I was saving the cookies for you but thought you would enjoy them while I was gone. A good substitute, right? Sweet and they won't give you any lip.

Please take care of yourself. I'll call you when I get to Vancouver.

I'm sorry for the short notice.

Chefgirl

I put the casserole in the refrigerator and grabbed a cookie, munching it as I walked down the hall to bed.

I sent one last text before I hit the mattress.

> The cookies are great, Chefgirl, but I would far rather be subjected to your lip. There isn't anything sweeter than that. Call me tomorrow.

I hesitated. Then I added it.

> Night x

Chapter Thirteen

9 a.m.

You awake, Chefgirl? I know you're 3 hours behind me.

Yes.

Are you going for a run?

Yes I am—why?

Be sure to take your phone.

I will.

Promise?

Nat, I run every morning. I'll be fine.

Running around this quiet, little subdivision is one thing—Vancouver is a big place—it's dangerous. Keep your phone on and don't have your music on too loud. Pay attention to your surroundings.

How did you know I listen to music?

Shit. I couldn't exactly tell her I noticed the earbuds in her ears the other morning while I was watching her run, so I decided to go with the most obvious thing I could think of.

Most people do while running—only stands to reason you do. Text me when you get back so I won't worry.

You don't have to worry about me.

Well, I do. Get used to it. Text me.

OK. Thank you.

Anytime.

12 p.m.

Chefgirl, my co-workers are indeed weeping over today's leftovers. One offered to cover the next virus cleanup to trade.

Sounds like a good deal.

Nope. Not happening. He had a (gasp) frozen mac and cheese. Can't let that shit pass my lips anymore. Do you make mac and cheese?

Yes.

Would you make it for me?

Yes.

I knew you would. x

I wasn't surprised when she didn't respond to that, so I forged ahead.

What time is your presentation?

In 2 hours.

You OK?

Nervous.

You'll be great. I know it. Then it's done.

Until tomorrow. I have to present to two different groups.

By then you will be a pro. You can do this. You're brilliant.

Thanks, Nat.

Anytime, Kourtney.

1:50 p.m.

Nathan?

Hey—you okay?

I can't do this.

Yes, you can.

I racked my brains, trying to figure out a way to help her. I dialed her number, frowning at the stress in her voice when she answered.

"I'm right there with you, Kourtney."

"What?"

"Keep the cell on; lay it on the podium beside you. I'll listen. Pretend you're talking to me over the fence the way you always do."

"Really? Doesn't it cost a lot?"

"Nah," I lied effortlessly. "My plan is an all-inclusive one."

"They're calling my name now," she blurted, panicked.

"Go. I'm right here," I assured her. I plugged in my headphone jack and continued to type away, listening to her begin to speak; her anxiety evident in the slight tremble of her voice.

She was right; I had no idea what she was talking about, but I found her voice captivating. For the first few minutes, there was a strange repetitive noise and it took me a moment to realize she was running her thumb over the cell phone. Gradually, the noise stopped as her speech lost its panicky edge and she became engrossed in the topic in which she was speaking. I worked away as I listened, my pride growing during the question and answer period at the end. She really was clever, answering all the questions without hesitation. She knew her subject matter. At the conclusion, she picked up her phone, asking if I was still there, sounding relieved when I answered.

"Of course I am, Kourtney. You were fucking amazing. How could you doubt yourself?"

"I kept looking down at the phone. I knew you were there, and it helped so much. Thank you, Nat. Nobody has ever—"she drew in a deep, stuttering breath—"nobody has ever cared that much," she whispered. "Ever."

It made me sad to hear her heartfelt confession, and my throat tightened. "Well, I do. Get used to it, because it's not gonna change."

"I have to go."

"I know. I'll call you later."

"Promise?"

"Promise, Chefgirl."

"Okay. Thank you, again."

ON THE WAY HOME I stopped at Home Depot and bought a ladder. The only way to move this relationship forward was to be able to breach the high fence between us, and that wasn't going to happen on a chair. I carried it into the backyard, leaning it up on the fence. Feeling somewhat guilty, I climbed the ladder, and for the first time, looked over into Kourtney's yard.

Curious, I glanced around, taking in the neat, trimmed grass and the bright pots of planted flowers she had scattered around, the lilies I had given her in full bloom; pink amidst the other plants in the containers. I looked over my shoulder, grimacing at the barren appearance of my own yard. I thought how similar the two were to the people who owned them; Kourtney's yard reflected the bright, lovely oasis she had become in my dark, lonely life.

I scanned the rest of her small yard. Leaning up on the fence, almost directly across from me, was her ladder, a much smaller version of mine. Beside it was her barbeque, and by her patio doors was a small table, where I knew she sat when we were outside.

My eyes kept straying to the table, something bothering me, until I realized what it was that had caught my attention. There was only one chair. I searched around the small yard, but I didn't see another one anywhere. I viewed my table and the four chairs around it. As solitary as my life was, there was still the need, the desire for company. Occasionally, all the chairs were occupied when I would have people from work over to watch a game and we would sit, laughing and drinking, sharing some time. My gaze traveled back to Kourtney's table and solitary chair; its singleness speaking volumes to me. She was alone and expected to remain alone. I stared at it for a moment before climbing back down the ladder and heading inside. I was probably thinking too much. Maybe the other chair broke or she used in her kitchen. But for some reason, the image of that one chair bothered me all evening.

6 p.m.

Chefgirl—this pan won't fit in my microwave—how can I bake it if it won't fit?

The pan is aluminum Nat—you CAN'T put it in the

microwave—it will spark.

You said to bake it.

You have to use the stove.

Use it as in turn it on?

Sigh. Yes. You have never used it?

For other than its intended purpose in this house, no.

Ah, yes. Counter space/garbage collector.

Yep. It performs well.

Is there garbage in it now?

Um, no Chefgirl. Football doesn't start for a few weeks. It's empty.

Oh, so sorry. Wasn't aware.

Gasp. You cannot be serious. I'm in shock you don't know this.

OK—you need to remain open to new ideas. I will teach you how to use the stove.

Great. Not sure how this will work, but I'll try.

If I can learn to use a cell phone, you can learn to turn on the oven.

Good point, but highly unusual for a cell phone to catch fire. Me and stoves . . .

Okay, first—do you know how to dial 911?

Yep. 9–1-1

Good, just checking. I don't want your dinner to be the reason you are homeless. Are you in front of the stove?

Would you really let me be homeless, Chefgirl?

No.

Knew it. x I am ready to be taught, wise one.

I am going to assume since the houses were built at the same time we have the same stove. Does it say LG on it?

Yep.

Good. See the button that says BAKE? Push it twice. It will beep.

Beeping has commenced.

It's going to heat up now. It automatically goes to 350 degrees. You can put the casserole in and once it beeps again, it should take about an hour and it'll be ready.

How will I know?

It will be bubbly and hot.

Bubbly and hot. Got it. Then?

Um, you take it out and let it cool for a few minutes and eat it. Be sure to turn off the oven! Then you can cut it and put it in containers and take it for lunch.

Turn off the oven — good point. And leftovers? Excellent. More weeping co-workers.

You get too much satisfaction in that.

You have no idea. What are you doing?

On a break from another presentation. Going back to the room in a bit.

Going out for dinner?

Annie and I are going to get something. Then I'll be back.

OK, let me know when you're back. I'll be lying on the sofa in a food-induced haze.

Laughing here.

The term is LOL, Chefgirl.

Right. Later?

Call me when you get back. I'll be right here.

11 p.m.

I SMILED WHEN I HEARD Kourtney's ringtone. "Hey, Chefgirl."

"Hi."

"How was dinner?"

There was a small giggle. "Good. Yours?"

"Fucking awesome casserole. I love stuff with noodles."

Another giggle. "I love how enthusiastic you always are over my cooking."

"What's not to be enthused about, Kourtney? As I said—fucking awesome."

"How many beers have you had?"

"A few."

"I had some wine."

"Yeah? How much?"

"Um . . . Annie and I shared a bottle." Her voice dropped. "I'm not much of a drinker. I can't feel my nose."

I laughed. "Uh-oh. Celebrating the day being done too much?"

"Glad it's over."

"One down, one to go, right?"

"Yeah. Then I can come home."

"I miss you."

She paused, her voice now timid. "Really?"

I rubbed my face. "Really, Kourtney."

"But I left you food."

"I told you it's not the food. It's you. Your company. I miss you giving me lip. And your laugh." I eased back into the sofa. "God, I love your laugh."

There was silence.

"Chefgirl?" I prompted her.

"Why?"

"Why what?"

"Why do you love my laugh?"

I thought about it. "I dunno. Maybe because when it happens, it's such an honest reaction and your laugh is so contagious. It makes me smile. It makes me happy. I miss hearing it. And I miss you."

"Nobody ever misses me, Tomcat."

"I'm not nobody."

"I know," she whispered, sounding wistful.

"And I do miss you, Kourtney. A lot, actually, and I want you home."

"I'll be there Thursday afternoon."

"Good."

I grinned when I heard her deep yawn. "Did you sleep at all last night?"

"Not much."

"Go to bed and get some rest. Are you running in the morning?"

"Yes."

"The rule?"

"I'll have my cell phone with me."

"And?"

"I'll let you know when I get back."

"Good. And if you need to call me before your talk tomorrow, I'll be there, okay?"

"Thank you. Night, Nat."

"Night, Chefgirl."

I hung up, not wanting to break the connection, but

knowing she needed some sleep. However, I felt her sadness when she hung up, too. I wanted to leave her smiling. Picking the phone back up, I texted her.

Kourtney, did you forget something today?

Um, no?

Sock color?

Oh.

?

Black and pink.

*Black and pink as in you forgot to do laundry so you wore one of each, or are you giving me more info than I asked for—which is fine, too. *wink wink**

wink wink?*

I thought maybe you were telling me your sock and underwear color. You know, as an added bonus for today.

Rude. My SOCKS are black with pink hearts on them, perv.

I chuckled at her reaction to my teasing. I loved hearing about her various socks. It was a simple thing, but it made me smile.

And who says I'm wearing underwear anyway?

I threw back my head in laughter. My Chefgirl was teasing *me* now. The wine must be making her brave.

Commando? I'm blushing here, Chefgirl.

You started it.

I did. I'll finish it as well. Gray.

Your socks are gray?

No, my underwear. I'm not wearing any socks.

Well, thank God it's not the other way around.

LOL

TMI, Nat. TMI.

Just wanted to give you something to think about, Chefgirl. My ass looks good in gray.

Thanks for the mental image. I need to go and find some brain bleach now. I don't want to think about your gray-covered ass.

That's the second time you have dissed my ass, you know. I'll have you know it's a fine-looking ass. Many have commented on this fact.

You have an unhealthy obsession with your own ass. You should talk to someone about it.

I am. I'm talking to you.

You're nuts. I think I may have mentioned this before.

And as I stated before . . . nuts about you, Chefgirl.

Go to bed, Nat.

Are you?

Going to bed?

No . . . Commando?

Sigh. You won't give this up will you?

No. Color, please.

Nathan . . .

Please.

Black.

Nice.

Go to bed, perv.

With that mental image, happily.

Eeewww.

Not in my mind, Kourtney. Sleep well, Chefgirl.

You, too.

xx

I waited. And waited. Finally, I sent her a prompt.

Waiting here, Chefgirl. I got one last night. Give it up.

Finally it came back.

x

I shook my head at how big I was smiling over a little x. But I couldn't help it.

One small x for me was one huge step for Chefgirl.

Laughing at my own corniness, I went to bed, taking the phone with me.

Just in case she wanted to drunk text me later.

I could only hope.

Chapter
Fourteen

Wednesday 10 a.m.

Hey Chefgirl—going for a run?

A short one. I'll go for another one later.

LOL—feeling the effects of your wine? Can you feel your nose again?

I told you that? What else did I say?

I smirked at my phone, then decided against telling her what she had said, and the fact she could check the text history and find out for herself.

Not much, Chefgirl, you were a little out of it. Cute though.

I have never been cute, Nat.

I huffed in frustration. The little I had seen of her, she was more than cute. Short and curvy—I liked that.

We never think that of ourselves. What time are you on today?

11 a.m. my time—2 p.m. for you.

So, 4 hours from now . . . You holding up?

I think so. Did you remember to turn off your stove?

For your info, Chefgirl, I did. There was a button that said END like my cellphone and I used it. I'm a smart man, you know. I figured it all out on my own.

Impressed. I bow down to your new kitchen expertise.

I can feel you rolling your eyes at me from here, Missy.

Nope. Not me. Only impressive feelings.

Use those feelings and wow them today, okay?

I will try.

Call me if you need me, Kourtney. I'm right here.

I know. And that . . . that is an amazing thing to me. Thank you.

That one line kept me smiling all morning.

12:05 p.m.

MY PHONE RANG AND I picked it up, wondering why she was calling so early. I had finished my work, and was about to head downstairs to have lunch and tease people while I ate it.

"Hey, Kourtney. You're early."

She was almost hyperventilating with her panic. "Annie is sick now. I have to do the PowerPoint thing myself, as well. Oh, my God, Nathan, I'm going to screw this up."

I shut my eyes at her fear. "Have you ever done it before?"

"Once—and it wasn't pretty. I *always* mess these things up. Annie assures me it's all set up. I only have to click to start it going. But . . ."

I took in a deep breath and interrupted her, breaking her panic. "Kourtney. Listen to me. You can do this. I know you can. I'll stay on the phone and talk you through it if you need me to."

"What if it doesn't work?"

"Can you do your presentation without it? If Annie had dropped her laptop and there was no PowerPoint to be had, could you still do this?"

"Um, yes."

"If it doesn't work, shut it down, make a joke about a technical glitch and keep talking. Okay?"

There was silence. Then I heard a deep sigh of relief.

"You're right. Thank you."

"You want me to stay on the line?"

"No. I'm okay."

"That's my brave girl."

"Can I . . . ?" She hesitated. "Would you mind . . . ?"

I interrupted her. "Yes—you don't even have to ask. Call me before you go on, or after, or both. I'm here for you, all right? I'll listen again, if you want me to. Whatever you need."

I was met with silence.

"Kourtney?"

"Yeah, I'm here. I . . . I don't know how to say thank you."

I could hear the emotion behind her words. Why was she so overwhelmed by a simple gesture of kindness? She handed them out to me daily without even thinking.

"None needed. I've got you, okay?"

"Okay," she breathed.

I hated hearing how vulnerable she sounded. "Kourtney?"

"Yeah?"

"I'm not nobody—remember that, please." I drew in a deep breath. "I'll be *whatever* you want me to be. You only have to tell me."

"Nathan . . ."

"We'll talk about it when you get home. Go do your

presentation. You'll be excellent again. And, I'm right here. *For you.* Understand me?"

Her voice was stronger. "Yes."

"Okay. Go wow them."

4 p.m.

I did it! Power Pointing and all!

I knew you would. So proud. What's the plan now?

Want to listen to one last presentation on gene structure. I'll go back to the hotel to change and go for a run. I'll get some room service in later.

No big wrap-up dinner?

There is. Not going.

I sighed in relief for some reason. I had the image in my mind of my Chefgirl, looped on red wine, sitting alone in the corner, giggling and unable to feel her nose. Then some rich, good-looking doctor swooping in, enticed by her brains and sexy curves, taking her away from me before I even got close enough to kiss her.

Okay. Not your scene?

No.

I sensed she didn't want to discuss that topic and I needed to change the subject.

You haven't given me my update.

?

Socks. Color please.

Not wearing socks.

What? Commando-style feet?

LOL—no I'm wearing a suit so no socks. Would look funny with dress shoes.

A suit—nice . . . what color?

Taupe . . . ish

Shirt?

Well, yes. Generally, they frown on nudity at these functions. At least during the daytime.

I chuckled at her quick wit and frowned at the second part. The good-looking doctor came to mind again. I didn't want him to see her topless.

Color, smartass.

Ivory. And it's called a blouse. But since you can't take care of your own socks, I suppose I shouldn't expect you to know that.

I smirked. I had listened to the women in my office talk about fashion daily. I knew enough to surprise her.

I will ignore your sarcasm, Chefgirl, and stun you with my fashion expertise. Taupe power suit and ivory blouse. Classy. Sexy. Nice.

Wow—impressed you know the words power suit. Second part—I don't think so.

Why did she always brush off compliments? I was sure she looked great.

I bet others say differently.

I doubt that.

I frowned at the phone. I knew she was curvy and had dark hair. I bet she looked beautiful in her outfit—and, without a doubt, sexy. Again, I was glad she wasn't attending the dinner that evening. There was no doubt more than one doctor interested already. I didn't want any of those bastards near her.

We'll agree to disagree. Take your phone on your run.

Yes, sir.

I grinned.

Sir. I like that.

Don't get used to it.

LOL. Never, Chefgirl. Let me know when you're back from your run. I assume you will have socks on then?

I will.

I shall remain in a guessing frenzy until later . . . black . . . white . . . pink . . . maybe yellow? And God knows what pattern you'll be sporting—the possibilities are endless.

Deranged.

Call me.

10 p.m.

I WAS PACING. SHE HADN'T called. She hadn't answered my calls. She should have been back from her run by now. Agitated, I tore at my hair, twisting the ends. She probably never made it to her run. That goddamned imaginary doctor was real and had cornered her before she even left the conference. She was sitting, at this very moment, having drinks with him while he planned on all the ways he would have her before the night was out. Her cell phone was buried in her purse, forgotten, and that fucking doctor . . .

That fucker was touching what should have been mine.

I sat on the sofa, finishing off another beer, frowning at my wild imagination. What was I thinking? This was Chefgirl. The woman so shy she wouldn't even meet me face-to-face. She must have gotten caught up in the presentation on genes . . . and their structure—whatever the fuck that meant. I bet it was fascinating stuff. She was late going for her run. That was all. Yeah.

Nope, she's late because that fucker cornered her, my mind whispered. *Charmed her.*

I growled in the silence of the room, my imagination out of control. Where was she? I went to the kitchen to grab another beer, almost falling over my feet when my phone rang and I lunged for it.

"Chefgirl, are you all right?"

"Um, I'm fine. Why do you sound as if you're upset?"

"I called you," I insisted petulantly. "You didn't answer. I was worried."

"I was running, Nathan. I had my iPod in my hand and my phone in my pocket. I can't carry both."

Her explanation made perfect sense, but I still didn't like it. I sat down, huffing. "We need to upgrade you. We'll get you an iPhone and you can run and listen to music, but when I call, you can pick up."

She chuckled. "That is not necessary. All you'd hear is me panting in your ear as I run. I doubt there is anything so urgent it can't wait until I'm done and can speak normally."

I had to laugh at her logic, and I couldn't resist the chance to tease her, as I leaned back in relief. "I'd love to hear that, Kourtney."

"Hear what?"

"You . . . panting in my ear."

"Stop it," she breathed out.

I smirked; I loved teasing her and her reactions. "Why were you running so late? I thought you were going right after the gene thing."

She laughed. "It's only seven here. The presentation was very interesting, I stayed behind to talk to the doctor who was speaking, and my run started late."

Once again tense, I sat up. I knew it.

That bastard.

"A doctor? You were talking to a doctor?"

"It's a medical convention. There are a lot of us medical types around here."

My stomach clenched. "Are you okay? Was he pushy? Did he make you uncomfortable?"

"What are you going on about?"

"The doctor, was he bothering you? Did he come onto you?"

Kourtney's laughter floated over the phone. "No one came on to me. *She* was great. She does research, the same as me, and we got a coffee and talked for a while. Have you been drinking?"

"No. I was worried."

"Why do you worry about me so much?"

I sighed. "Because I do. I think you need someone to worry about you."

"I can look after myself, Nathan. I've been doing it most of my life."

I wanted to tell her she didn't have to do that anymore—I wanted to look after her. But her tone told me the statement wouldn't be welcome and I was in dangerous territory.

"It's what fence friends do, Chefgirl," I quipped. "It's in the rule book. Number four."

There was a pause, then she giggled, her humor restored. "Oh. I guess I missed that one."

"Maybe you need to study up a little better."

This time she laughed. "I'll do that. I need to find my copy. Maybe you can loan me yours?"

"I'll email you a copy."

"You do that."

"So," I hedged, "no one bothered you today? No smarmy doctor got pushy or tried to get you drunk?"

"Nathan, the only drunk one here is you. What is it with you and hating doctors today?"

I shrugged to myself. "I bet there are a lot of them on the prowl, that's all."

"If they are, they aren't after me. Did you have dinner?"

"Um, no."

"Why? Are you sick? You never miss dinner."

I smiled, although I enjoyed hearing the worried tone. "I was distracted."

"Doing what?"

"I was waiting for your call."

"You need to learn to multitask."

I laughed. I heard the sound of a knock in the background. "Who's that?" I asked, my mind immediately seeing the lecherous doctor leaning on the other side of her door, waiting to pounce.

"The room service I ordered."

"Oh," I sighed in relief. "I guess I'll let you go and eat. Talk after?"

"Really? You want to?" She sounded nervous again.

"Yes. You should know that already," I scolded gently. "I'll go eat some more of your delicious casserole and you can call or text me after you're done with your meal, okay?"

"I'd like that."

I sat, eating her scrumptious casserole, and thinking. I missed her, and not only for her cooking. The fact she was going to be home tomorrow made me strangely happy, and it wasn't a feeling I was used to. The more I thought about it, the more I realized how much I had come to depend on her presence. How quick I had grown attached to her company. Unless I was mistaken, she had missed me as well.

She thought of us as friends. Fence friends. I frowned, realizing it wasn't enough. I wanted more. She made me want so much more and if I was being honest, I already felt so much more.

But would she allow it to change? Girlfriend rather than fence friend? Or was I simply the funny guy next door; the proverbial stray cat, the one she feels sorry for and feeds? Would she let me be more?

Part of me wanted to pick up the phone and ask her, but I knew I couldn't do it. I knew I had to take it slow, but I wanted to move things forward. I simply wasn't sure how. I didn't want to scare her away, and I had the feeling I could easily do so.

I sat staring at my phone, waiting for her to call. I already knew she would be wondering if she should call or text, or if she would be overstepping some invisible line she had in place, so I decided to take matters into my own hands. She was much braver on text, and I knew how to make her smile.

You know, I'm still waiting. It seems you forgot again, Chefgirl.

?

Socks?

Oh.

Give it up.

Pink yellow blue green orange.

Wow—did a color wheel roll by and throw up on you?

Ha-ha, polka dots, Nat.

Polka dots—sexy.

Yes, polka dot socks are sexy. NOT.

On you, I bet they are.

Stop it.

Nope. Part of my charm.

Is that what that is?

Yep. Get used to it; I'm only getting warmed up.

I've been warned I guess?

I'd say. You'll be here when I get home tomorrow?

Yes, my flight gets me there mid-afternoon.

I'll meet you at the fence.

OK.

I'll be waiting. My hand misses yours.

Nut.

We've covered this. Only for you.

Rolling my eyes. Did you eat?

Yes. Awesome. And still leftovers for torturing. Life is good.

Go to bed.

I will . . . You're not going out, are you?

I may go for a walk—it's nice out. But I'll take my phone and not go far, OK? Relax.

OK– but stay away from all the doctors—in fact, if anyone comes near you, kick them in the nuts and run like hell.

Laughing very hard here. I don't get your sudden dislike of the medical profession.

I'll explain one day.

I'll hold you to that. If I have to stay away from doctors, you stay away from that tramp, Marie.

I laughed as I typed her reply.

Done. Her charms are cold to me now. Get it?

You are on a roll tonight.

Text to let me know you're back safe.

It's a walk. I don't want to wake you.

Please.

Okay. Worrywart.

That's me. Night xx

Night.

Chefgirl . . . waiting.

For ?

You know what. Give it up.

x

Nice. I gave you 2 though.

xxxxxxxxxxxxxxxxxxxxxxxxxxxxxxxxxx

Well, now I'm feeling a little cheap. We've only been texting a few days . . . I don't put out that fast.

LOL. Refer to the deranged comments again. I take them all back but 2 okay?

Nope. They're all mine now. Keeping them.

I give up. You're worse than a child.

Kourtney?

Yes?

I'm glad you're coming home tomorrow.

Me, too.

Enjoy your walk.

I will.

I grinned as I flopped down on the mattress. Kourtney would be home tomorrow. We had missed each other. The last few days had proven we had a relationship of some sort. Now I wanted to figure out exactly what kind it was.

I had a ladder. Either I was going over the fence, or through it, but it was time to stop it from being the boundary that separated us. It was time to meet my neighbor.

Face-to-face.

Chapter Fifteen

THE DAY COULDN'T END FAST enough. Kourtney was coming home.

I arrived home in record time, anxious for the evening to begin. Tonight, I would hear her sweet voice and laughter as we ate dinner. Dinner, I knew, she would make for us. I had missed everything about her the past few days—talking with her, the way she teased me, her cooking, and especially the hesitant brush of her fingers with mine over the fence. I felt as empty as her house had been the past few days without her presence.

Tonight, after dinner, I was determined to ask her out. If she wasn't comfortable with my idea, I'd settle for coffee. It could be in her backyard; I didn't care, as long as it was together. No fence. If that failed, I was climbing the ladder and sitting on top of the fence until she was comfortable enough to let me get closer. I would be patient. I knew she liked me, and I *more* than liked her. I wanted to get to know her and the fence had to go— for good.

Pulling into the driveway, I frowned. A large, overly decked out truck was parked in Kourtney's driveway. I had never known her to have any visitors and I would certainly remember such a hideous truck. I snorted as I looked it over; someone wanted attention. You didn't drive that monstrosity unless you wanted people to notice you. Brilliant yellow flames across a bright orange paint job, sitting on top of too-large tires, all screamed *"look at me!"*

I parked in the garage and made my way to my room for a quick shower and change of clothes. As I ran a comb through my hair, I studied myself in the mirror, wondering if Kourtney would like what she saw. A true ginger, my hair was a force unto itself, which I had learned to ignore. Maybe the fact she liked red would work in my favor. I was tall and lean, almost gangly looking, unless I worked out and kept up the muscle mass. My face was all right, and women commented on my bright blue eyes a lot. I certainly wouldn't win any modeling contracts, but I hoped Kourtney would approve.

I stopped in the kitchen to pick up the wine and little bouquet of flowers I had bought on impulse for Kourtney at the store. The lilies in the middle had made me think of her and I thought she would be pleased at the welcome home gesture. I wanted her to know how *much* I had missed her. I hesitated, wondering about who was at her house, then decided to go outside and have a beer while I waited. When her company left, no doubt she'd come outside, and I would give her the flowers. She knew I was waiting for her.

Once outside, I climbed the ladder, placing the small bouquet on the top of the fence. She would see it when she came out and it would make her happy.

Sitting down, I cracked open the beer and had a long, appreciative swallow. I sat back, preparing to get comfortable, only to sit straight back up. I could hear raised voices next door. More specifically, I could hear the angry voice of a man, berating someone—and that someone had to be Kourtney. I hurried back over to the fence and stood still, listening. For a heartbeat, there was nothing, but then, I heard it again, louder. Whoever was next door was shouting at Kourtney, their menacing tone and curse words insulting, filling me with anger.

Without thinking, I climbed the ladder and swung myself up onto the top of the fence, hesitating for a moment. As soon as I heard her muffled voice carry through the air, its tone scared and pleading, the decision was made. Something was wrong and Kourtney was in trouble. Ignoring her ladder leaning on the fence, I dropped down to the deck, my sneakers absorbing the impact, and hurried to her door. I looked inside, my stomach clenching at the sight before me. This stranger had hold of her arms, pinning her to the wall while he screamed in her face. She was shaking, cowering and pleading; and fury tore through me was a hot flame. I had to stop him.

Right. The. Fuck. Now.

The sliding door creaked as I tore it open in my haste. The shouting was louder now; his abusive words ricocheting round the room. I charged; my shoulder slamming into his side, sending him flying away from her body. He hit the opposite wall hard, causing the pictures to shake and one to fall off, the glass shattering as it hit the floor. Kourtney's gasp of shock and his surprised curse were both followed by silence.

"The lady asked you to stop," I snarled at him, stepping in front of her in protection.

He gaped at me, stupefied. "Who the fuck are you? Where did you come from?"

I glared at him. "You don't get to ask any questions, asshole. Who the fuck are *you*, coming into her house, screaming at her? Hurting her?" I stepped forward, my stance threatening.

He scowled toward Kourtney, pointing an angry finger my way. "Kourtney, who the fuck is this?" Looking back at me, he yelled, "Get out of here—this is a private family matter. We don't need some snoopy neighbor sticking his nose in where it doesn't belong. Go back to wherever the fuck you came from."

I shifted over, blocking his view, as I glared at him, my voice low and furious. "You don't get to make that decision and you don't get to talk to her anymore, fucker. And I'm not going anywhere. You are."

I reached behind me, finding Kourtney's trembling hand. "Kourtney, call the police." I felt her hand clutch mine, and I squeezed it in reassurance, letting her know she was safe.

He let out a snide laugh. "Yeah, do that, *Kourtney*. We'll see who they deal with first—your family or a nosy neighbor who came in uninvited and assaulted me," he sneered.

I stared at him in horror. This was Kourtney's brother. Her words came back to me. *"Every day I'm not subjected to them is a good day."*

"Just go away, Andy. Please . . . leave me alone," she pleaded.

"We're not done here. Tell this asshole to—"

I lurched forward, catching him by surprise, cutting off his words. My arm bent at his throat and I leaned in, pushing into him as my other hand slammed into his stomach. His gasp of pain was rewarding and I stared at him in loathing. "She *asked* you to leave. You have two choices. Either do what she says or I send her to call the police. While she's gone you and I are gonna find out what happens when you try to pick on someone your own size." I lowered my voice even more. "I promise; it's not going to end well for you." I pressed forward again, further cutting off his airway. I watched without regret as his face began to turn red and his eyes bugged out of their sockets.

"Nathan, let him go." Kourtney spoke up from behind me. "He'll leave. Right, Andy?"

Andy made a small, grunting noise and I stepped back, watching as he struggled to get air into his lungs. He glared at Kourtney behind me. "We aren't done here. You owe us, you lazy, ungrateful bitch," he panted.

I was done with this asshole. I grabbed his arm, twisting it as I turned him away, this time smashing his face into the wall. His other arm shot out wildly, knocking another picture off the wall, plus the table beside it, both crashing to the floor. Behind me, I heard Kourtney's terrified whimper. I was desperate to turn around and check on her, to make sure she was okay, but I had to deal with the problem causing her fear. I clutched the back of his neck, forcing him toward the door, keeping his arm twisted up in what I knew was a painful angle. I got the front door open and pushed him outside. He fell to his knees, grunting with pain as I towered over him.

"Stay the fuck away from her. Do you understand me?"

He was slow to rise; hatred in his eyes. "This is none of your goddamned business."

I narrowed my eyes, curling my hands into fists. "That's where you're wrong, asshole. Everything about that woman is my business. Stay the fuck away from her. If you come anywhere near her again, you'll regret it. You have to get past me to get to her—which is *not* going to happen."

He narrowed his eyes at me. "I know people on the police force. I'll bring you up on assault charges."

I laughed without humor. "Go for it, shithead. I know people too—higher up than the local police force. I'll have Kourtney press charges and I'll file some myself," I threatened, my anger barely contained. "We'll start with breaking and entering, add in assault and go from there. Your life as you know it will be over. Done. You won't fucking know what hit you."

He faltered. I smirked—bullies never took threats very well. They preferred to be the one doing the threatening.

I stepped forward, sneering, as he moved back. "Are you listening to me? *Stay. The. Fuck. Away.* And, whatever you *think* she owes you? She doesn't. The slate is clean. She owes you *nothing*." I glared at him, not surprised when he broke eye contact first.

"I'm sick of your face already." I jerked my chin toward the truck. "Get your ass in that pathetic piece of shit you concocted to make up for whatever physical deficiencies you have and leave. You're not welcome here. Ever."

He hesitated, looking behind me. "Don't even think about looking at her." I stared him down. "Leave. Now."

I watched with narrowed eyes as he limped toward his truck. The loud rumbling of his engine made me roll my eyes. I disliked him for his stupid attention-seeking vehicle alone.

Adding in how I had witnessed him treating Kourtney, had brought the dislike up to loathing.

I waited until I could no longer hear his engine. Turning, I hurried back into the house, locking the door behind me. I walked down the hall, only to find Kourtney on her knees, her shaking hands trying to gather up the broken glass on the floor.

I crouched down beside her, my hand covering hers. "Stop, Kourtney," I whispered. "I'll do that. You'll cut yourself."

She ignored me, trying to pick up more glass. I could feel her entire body vibrating. I longed to pull her to me and cradle her in my arms. Squeezing her hand, I lifted it off the floor and out of the glass. "Please. Leave it."

"I'm sorry you witnessed that, Nathan." Her voice was thick and full of pain.

"That was your brother?"

She nodded, her hands covering her face, her shoulders hunched and shaking. I stood up, pulling her with me, and guided her to the sofa. She curled into the corner, trembling hard. I sat beside her and wrapped my arm around her shoulders, pulling her close. She was tense and stiff, fighting any comfort I was trying to give her.

"Kourtney," I began.

"You need to go. Please."

I looked down at her lowered head, wanting nothing more than to lift her chin and see her face.

"I'm not leaving you alone."

"Nathan . . . *please*. Give me a little time . . . I'll get your dinner in a while."

Was she serious?

"Chefgirl, I don't give a fuck about dinner." I felt her tense even further and I softened my voice. "I'm not leaving you alone after what happened."

"I can't . . . I can't . . ." she whispered.

I tightened my arm around her. "Can't what?"

"I can't . . . hold it in . . . I . . . don't . . . want . . . you to see . . ."

I could feel her shoulders start to shake. I shifted her as I turned, pulled her to my chest and cradled her head in my hand, my fingers stroking through the thick tresses of her hair in gentle passes. "I *want* to see, Kourtney. Let it out. I have you." I spoke low into her ear, tightening my arms as she tried to move away, her body taut with tension. "I'm here. You're not alone. I'm *not* leaving you alone."

A shudder ran through her as she melted into me, her arms wrapping around my neck as sobs began wracking her body. I drew her closer, running my hands up and down her back, my heart clenching at the sounds of her pain-filled cries. She felt supple in my arms, her lush curves fitting against me so well. I held her tight, listening as she let her emotions escape, finally accepting the comfort I wanted to give. Incoherent words poured out of her mouth and I didn't try to stop their muffled sounds. She needed to say them, even if they made no sense to me. The ones I caught made me frown.

Unworthy. Unloved. Useless.

I didn't understand. She was none of those. I knew it in my heart.

I dropped loving kisses on her head, resting my cheek on the softness of her hair, breathing in her scent. I hummed and rocked her, hating her pain, but grateful I was there to help her get through it. This was not the homecoming I had envisioned for us tonight.

Slowly, her sobs quietened. The shudders and tremors shaking her body eased. Leaning over, I grabbed the box of Kleenex from the side table. I felt her stiffen up, pulling back, and I released her from the circle of my arms with regret.

I pressed some tissues into her hand, gathering her heavy tresses with my fingers, smoothing them away from her face. I could see her pale skin, blotchy and wet from her tears, but her eyes remained downcast. I studied her features as she used the tissues to wipe her cheeks, her breath coming out in small, shuddering gasps as she collected herself. She was as lovely as I imagined her to be, if not more so.

"I'm—"

"Don't, Kourtney. You don't have to say it," I interrupted her. "You don't owe me an apology."

We were both quiet. "I'm going to go and make us a drink," I said, keeping my voice soft, my hands continuing to stroke her hair. "I think we both need it."

"I don't have much, but the liquor is in the kitchen cabinet by the table," she mumbled.

"Okay." But I didn't move. "Kourtney . . . look at me—please."

She stiffened further, anxiety pouring off her body at my quiet words. Reaching out, I cupped her chin and lifted her face. "Open your eyes, Kourtney. Let me see you."

Her hands clenched hard on my chest. Her eyelids opened, slow and hesitant.

And, for the first time I gazed into Kourtney's wide eyes, a surprised gasp escaping my lips.

Chapter Sixteen

I SIGHED AS I DUMPED the last of the broken glass in the garbage bin. After Kourtney had pushed away and flown down the hall to her bedroom, I needed to stay busy so I didn't follow her. I had righted the table, picked up the broken pictures, and ordered some pizza. I studied the limited supply in the liquor cabinet, grabbed the vodka, and mixed us some strong drinks. God knew I needed one, and I suspected Kourtney did, too.

Standing in the kitchen, taking a deep swallow of my drink, I studied the photos. Both were black and white pictures taken in a forest; lone trees set apart from the rest of the woods, bent and twisted out of shape, stark and hauntingly beautiful in their simplicity. I picked up one and studied it, smiling when I saw the small signature on the corner of the mat. *Kourtney.* I wasn't surprised to discover she had taken the photos. They screamed isolation and sadness. The same emotions I had seen pouring out of her eyes when she had looked at me.

My gaze drifted down the hall, my stomach a mass of undecided knots. I wasn't certain she still wanted me here, but I didn't want to leave. I couldn't leave her alone. Not given what had transpired with her brother or my ill-concealed reaction to her eyes.

I had gazed at her, waiting for her to open her eyes, eagerly absorbing the details of her face. She had rounded, full cheeks, with freckles scattered over the bridge of her nose and a deep pink set of plump lips that begged to be kissed. Under the corner of her left eye was a petite beauty mark that stood out next to the paleness of her skin, adding to her unique charm. Her hair was a long, thick mass of waves around her shoulders, and my fingers caressed the strands as I pleaded with her to look at me. She was as curvy and voluptuous as my glimpses had promised.

However, it was the vision of her eyes meeting mine that caused me to gasp out loud. With the deep color of her hair, I expected brown eyes, or perhaps blue like my own. What I hadn't expected under her long lashes, was one blue and one green eye; their uniqueness all the more apparent due to the vividness of the color of her unmatched irises. I had never seen anything as beautiful as the intensity of her stare. The sound that escaped my lips, when I saw the brilliance, shocked us both. She had immediately dropped her gaze and scrambled off my lap, running down the hall before I could stop her. Her door closed, and my head fell into my hands in regret, knowing my reaction had startled her.

Still thinking about my unexpected, but involuntary response, I put her broom away, and picked up my drink again. I heard the sound of her door opening, and her steps came closer. She hesitated in the doorway before entering the kitchen. I handed her a drink, a small grimace crossing her face after she sipped it.

"Too strong?" I murmured, afraid if I spoke too loud it would frighten her.

"I, ah, don't drink much," she admitted, her eyes glancing toward the photos. I removed the glass from her hand and poured some of it down the drain, adding more orange juice, handing it back to her. She sipped it again with no grimace, her fingers tracing the broken frames.

Now she was standing beside me, I could see how short she was, not even reaching my chest. It pleased me somehow, knowing she would fit perfectly under my chin when I held her. I found myself having to resist the urge to pull her close to me; the desire to feel her curves molded to my body so strong, I almost couldn't contain it.

"The photos aren't damaged," I pointed out. "We'll get some new frames for them tomorrow and I'll rehang them for you. You took the pictures, Kourtney?"

"Yes, I did."

"They're stunning. You're very talented."

She shrugged, not speaking, her finger continuing to trace the frames.

"I ordered a pizza for dinner."

"I'm fine, Nathan. You don't need to babysit me."

"Good. Because that's not what I'm doing."

Her beautiful eyes flew to mine, only to glance away again. I didn't like that. I wanted her eyes on me. I stepped in front of her, taking her glass and putting it on the counter.

"Hey. Look at me." I dipped down to her level, trying to encourage her to do so, reaching out my hand to touch hers.

Resigned, sad, extraordinary eyes slowly met mine. I drew in a breath, clasped her hand, and spoke the words I had been anxious to share with her. "Hello, Chefgirl. It's wonderful to finally meet you."

She blinked up at me. "Hello, Nathan." Her stunning eyes were filled with emotion: confusion, apprehension and sadness swirled in their depths.

"Kourtney," I breathed. Gradually, so I didn't startle her, I lifted my hand and caressed her warm cheek, my finger reaching up to tenderly stroke the edge of her eyes. "I'm sorry."

She shrugged; her expression sad. "It's okay, I know it's abnormal. People always react." Her voice dropped. "I don't like it, but I'm used to it."

I frowned, tightening my hand on her cheek. "No—you

don't understand."

Her brow furrowed in confusion.

I stared at her, holding her gaze. "Your eyes are not abnormal." I exhaled hard. "They are, without a doubt, the most gorgeous pair of eyes I have ever seen. I wasn't prepared for the sheer . . . *beauty* I saw. You took my breath away."

Her gaze was one of disbelief.

"Your eyes mesmerize me. I want to lose myself in them." I hesitated, but decided to forge on. "I want to lose myself in you."

"What?" she whispered in confusion.

To hell with slow. I knew what I wanted and she was right here in front of me. I knew it was fast, but, somehow, I also knew I wouldn't have another chance—she was far too skittish.

"I don't want to be the neighbor guy on the other side of the fence anymore. I want to be here, spend time with you and get to know you. Share our time face-to-face—not separated by a fence." I traced my finger under her eyes. "I want to see these exotic eyes sparkle when you smile. When you laugh. God, Kourtney, I love your laugh."

"Exotic? You think my eyes are exotic?"

I nodded. "Exotic, intriguing, dazzling—" I sighed in frustration. "But too sad. I don't want them sad." I stepped forward, wrapping one arm around her, pulling her to me. I could feel the tension in her body. "Give me a chance to make your eyes shine. Give me the pleasure of seeing that vision. Of knowing I can do that for you." Leaning forward, I kissed her forehead, nuzzling the warm skin of her brow. "Please."

A small whimper escaped her throat. Her arms wound around my neck as she buried her face in my chest, fitting to me just the way I knew she would. I could feel her body trembling as I gathered her close, loving how her rich, full curves felt against me. I buried my hand in her thick, silken hair as I held her, swaying us, and she clung to me. Somehow I sensed this was what she needed. To be held and comforted. I knew I needed it.

The ringing of the doorbell had her pulling back from me. "It's okay—it's the pizza. You get us some plates, okay?" I assured her. "I'll be right back."

"Okay."

I came back, boxes in hand, to find Kourtney standing at the counter. "I, um, prepared your usual surface for you," she offered with a shaky smile, indicating the top of the stove.

I deposited the boxes on the flat surface. Without thinking, I leaned over and kissed her cheek, lingering on the delicate skin. "Good thing I taught you the proper usage."

I winked. "And I'm glad to see you're open to new ideas." The subtle blush on her cheeks made me grin. I flipped open the lids. "My turn to feed you. Meat lovers or veggie?"

"Veggie, please."

"Somehow, I knew it."

WE WERE BOTH QUIET AS we ate. Kourtney picked at her pizza and I refrained from trying to get her to eat more, knowing she was still upset. Her eyes darted around the room, only resting on me occasionally. I could sense she was nervous about me being there with her, but I didn't quite understand why. I got up and made us both another drink; this time she didn't object to the amount of vodka I mixed in with the orange juice. I hoped the alcohol would help her relax.

After dinner, we moved to the sofa and she sat in the corner, drawing her legs up to her chest. I sat beside her, tentatively reached over, clasping her hand in mine. She regarded me for a minute, then dropped her gorgeous gaze down.

"So, do you want to talk about what happened?" I asked.

She sighed, the sound filled with pain. "That was my brother."

"Yeah." I snorted. "Loved his dumbass truck. What did he want?"

"My father is in a medical care facility and doesn't like it. He wants to come home, but he needs constant care now. He had a stroke, and never fully recovered."

"Okay?"

"He and Andy think I should move back there and look after him again."

"What about your job? Your life?"

She shrugged. "That's not important, Nathan. To them, anyway. Andy doesn't want to look after Dad, or give up his life to do so."

I frowned. "And they think you should?"

"Yes."

"That doesn't make any sense. Why?"

"They think I owe them."

"So the asshole said a couple of times. What exactly does he think you owe them for?"

Her eyes looked at me, wide and unblinking. "Because it was my fault."

"What was?"

"I was the reason my mother was in a car accident."

I stared, unsure what to say. She had told me her mother died when she was a child. How could it possibly be her fault? She jerked to her feet, wrapping her arms around herself.

"You should go home now, Nathan."

"Kourtney . . ."

She shook her head furiously. "I don't want to talk about it. You don't need to be worried about this. I'm fine, really. I'm sorry you had to witness that . . . *spectacle*. I'll make sure he doesn't bother you."

I got to my feet, feeling anger course through me. "He isn't fucking coming near me—or you."

"I thought they'd finally left me alone and let me live. He won't like the fact you interfered, but I'll talk to him."

"No, Kourtney." She stared up at me, her spectacular eyes troubled and damp.

"You don't need to talk to him. He had no right to come in here and threaten you."

She rubbed her arms as if trying to get warm. I laid my hands on top of hers. "He isn't coming back here. He won't get near you. I won't let him." Tenderly, I pressed her hands, still resting on her upper arms, frowning when she grimaced. Ignoring her startled gasp, I pushed her sweater off her shoulders and scowled when I saw the large bruises forming, where he'd been gripping her.

"He hurt you," I hissed.

"It's nothing, Nathan."

"Nothing? *This* is nothing?"

"It's not the first time." She began to pull away from me. "It won't be the last."

I didn't give her the chance to step away. I tugged her into my arms, refusing to let her go, despite how stiff she was holding herself. "Yes—it's the last fucking time."

She trembled against my chest; reflexively my arms tightened around her. "It is," I insisted fiercely.

"I can't ask you to get involved."

"I am involved." I stepped back, my hand cupping her chin, and gazed into her weary eyes. "Do you trust me?"

I felt a glimmer of intense satisfaction when she whispered, "Yes," without hesitating.

"Let me do this. Let me do what I need to do, okay?"

She hesitated, her gaze unsure. "Why?"

I frowned. "I want to do this for you. I *need* to do this. Please."

"Okay."

I pulled down her sleeves again, and using my phone, took pictures of the bruises.

"What are you going to do with those?"

"I have a friend who can tell us what you need to do. I'll show the pictures to him." I pulled her sleeve back into place. "If you'll let me?"

"You think he'll help?"

"I know he will."

"All right," she breathed out.

I dropped a kiss onto her head. "Thank you."

I got some ice and wrapped it in a tea towel, then handed it to her. "Keep this on for fifteen minutes; it'll help with the pain. I'd give you some Tylenol, but I already gave you alcohol, so it's not a good idea." I winked. "Although I'm sure you already knew that, Dr. Whyte."

Her smile was shaky, her wondrous eyes fatigued and swirling with emotion. I knew she must be exhausted given the traveling and stress she'd been under—speaking at the conference, then coming home to be attacked by her brother.

I tucked a strand of hair behind her ear. "You need to go to bed."

She nodded, looking weary. "Yeah, I'm tired."

"Okay. You get ready, and I'll be right back."

"What?"

"I need to go get a few things and lock up the house. I'll be right back."

I took in her stunned expression. "Do you really think I'm going to leave you alone tonight?"

"But . . ."

"No buts. I'll sleep on the sofa. You'll be safe."

"I can't ask you to do that, Nathan."

"You're not. And it's not up for discussion."

She glanced over my shoulder toward the patio doors. "How did you get here earlier?"

I grinned. "Over the fence." When I saw her confused face, I shrugged sheepishly. "I, ah, I bought a ladder."

Her eyes widened. "Oh."

"I wanted to be able to reach your hand easier, Chefgirl. I wasn't going to come over until you were ready—until you asked me. But when I heard what was happening, I had to."

Her hand cupped my cheek and I leaned into her touch. "Thank you."

I lowered down, and kissed her forehead. "I'm here for you. I'll be right back. You'll be okay?"

She nodded.

I went outside and climbed her ladder, swinging myself

over the top and climbing down my side.

I grabbed some stuff for the morning and my iPad. After locking the door behind me, and grabbing the bottle of wine I'd left on the table, I went back the way I came; over the fence. When I landed back on her side, I found the little bouquet I had bought her lying on the ground. I must have knocked it off in my haste to get to her earlier. I carried it inside and set it on the table, and put the wine on the counter.

In the living room, I found the sofa made up with blankets and a couple pillows and I smiled when I caught Kourtney's subtle scent on the pillowcase.

She appeared in the doorway, her hair up and dressed in a long baggy T-shirt and leggings. "I left you some towels and a toothbrush in the bathroom," she offered shyly.

I nodded in gratitude. "Thanks, I forgot that." Picking up the bouquet, I walked up to her slowly, not wanting to frighten her. "I got you these earlier, to, ah, welcome you home. They fell off the fence," I explained, handing her the rather wilted-looking flowers.

"Nathan, they're lovely," she whispered; her eyes luminous.

"They're kinda crushed on one side," I pointed out.

She buried her nose into the small nosegay, inhaling deep. "They're perfect."

Her words made my heart beat a little faster. I felt as if I had handed her dozens of roses rather than a simple, somewhat damaged, little bouquet. She filled a small vase with water and placed them into the glass with care, her fingers caressing the blooms. Her reaction filled me with a sense of warmth, and I got the idea getting flowers wasn't something that happened often, if ever, for her. I would have to change that.

Crossing over, I drew her to me, nuzzling her head. I couldn't stop myself from touching her. "Do you want to take those with you?"

She nodded, and I guided her down the hall into her room. I smiled as she placed the bouquet on her bedside table and touched the flowers again. I lifted the light blanket and indicated she should get in. She hesitated, then slid in, and I tucked the cover around her body. Leaning down, I stroked her thick hair. "I'm right down the hall, Kourtney, if you need *anything*. You're safe. Do you understand? I won't let anything happen to you."

"I know."

"Get some sleep. I'll be here in the morning."

She grabbed my hand, squeezing tight. "I don't know what might have happened if you hadn't—"

My stomach tightened at the thought of her being hurt. "Don't think about it. It's over and he isn't coming near you again."

"I want to believe that."

"Believe it."

I smiled, hoping to reassure her, dropping one more kiss on her head, turning out the light. I closed her door and waited in silence for a minute.

It took everything I had not to crawl into her bed and pull her into my arms. I wanted to offer her the safety of my embrace for the night, but I wasn't sure she was ready.

Pushing myself off the door, I sat on the sofa, grabbed my iPad and got to work. Half an hour later I got up, satisfied with what I had accomplished. I got ready to go to bed, using the toothbrush Kourtney had left me. As I was passing her doorway I paused, listening. I could hear something, and when I held my ear to the door, I realized it was the sound of muffled sobs. Sighing, I opened the door and stepped into the room. I could see her curled into a ball, her face buried in a pillow as she cried. My heart clenched at the sounds she was making; without a second thought, I gave into my instincts and slipped in beside her, pulling her into my arms. She stiffened, but I kept my arms around her, tucking her head into my chest as I spoke in a quiet, comforting voice. She began to relax, letting me gather her closer as her tears soaked my shirt.

"Let it out. I have you." I crooned into her hair. "I won't let him come near you again."

She gripped my shirt. "Not . . . me . . ."

I lifted her chin. "What?"

"I couldn't . . . take it . . . if he came after . . . you . . ." she stuttered out between her tears.

I pulled her back, holding tight. She was worried about *me*. "Ah, Chefgirl, not gonna happen," I promised her. "I've got this. You're safe. I'm safe. We're gonna take some precautions for a few days, all right?"

"Pre—precautions?" She hiccupped.

I combed my fingers through her hair in comforting passes. "You're not going anywhere alone. I'll go with you on your run in the morning and I'm driving you to work. I'll pick you up and stay here with you for the next few days."

"But—"

"He isn't coming near you again. Trust me on this."

Her face tilted up. "Why are you doing this?"

Gazing down at her, the dim light from the hall allowed me to make out the look of uncertainty on her face, I said, "I want . . . more, Kourtney."

"More?"

"Do you consider me a friend?"

"I consider you my best friend," she whispered in response.

Her words made me beam. "I think of you that way, too. But I want more than friendship with you. I told you I'd be whatever you wanted me to be, and if a friend is all you can do right now, then I'll be patient." I took in a deep breath. "But I was hoping you'd want the same thing I want."

"What do you want?"

"To belong to each other."

She sounded incredulous. "You want to belong—to me?"

"Yes."

"Even after this? Even after seeing me?"

I frowned. "I'm not sure what you mean, but yes. This isn't how I pictured myself telling you how I felt or how I had hoped the evening would happen, but it doesn't change what I want."

"You really want . . . *me*?"

"So much."

The room was silent. I gazed down on her; her incredible eyes were large as she stared back. "Nobody ever wants me."

"Then they're fucking idiots. Lucky for me."

Her brow furrowed. "I don't understand."

I rubbed small circles on her back. "It's too complex for right now. We're both exhausted. We'll talk about it tomorrow night." I wanted to make her think of something other than the events of the evening. I wanted her to smile before she fell asleep. "Think of me like a cell phone—you didn't know you wanted one, but once you got used to having it around, you wondered how you ever did without one."

She let out a combination giggle-sob and I grinned, continuing to rub her back. I could feel her relax; easing into my chest as her tears stopped and she calmed.

"Do you want me to go to the sofa?"

"No."

"Good. I like it right here."

She sighed, and we were silent for a few moments.

"Chefgirl?"

"Hmm."

"I didn't see them."

"See what?"

"Your socks. I was distracted and I forgot to look."

She giggled. "They're gray—no designs tonight."

"Excellent. They match my underwear. The pair that cover my fine ass."

I was granted another giggle.

Bending my head, I got close to her ear. "Play your cards right and I'll show you one day soon."

Her shoulders began to shake in laughter.

Grinning, I kept going.

"You know—I knew I was charming," I mused. "But even I have surpassed myself."

Her head tilted up, and her eyes met mine. "I'm almost afraid to ask, but why?"

"You're not even home a day and we're already sleeping

together," I teased.

She gasped, then started to laugh, the rich sound filling the room, and I joined in.

"I am goooood."

As her laughter quieted, I ghosted a kiss on her head. The feeling of her lips, brushing along my jaw, made me sigh; I knew I had made her feel a little better. She had smiled again. I loved making her smile.

"You're a nut," she whispered into my neck.

"Just about you, Chefgirl. Just about you."

I relaxed beside her, content, watching as she fell asleep; one hand curled into mine. A feeling of belonging filled me, and for the first time in years, I didn't feel alone. My arms tightened, keeping Kourtney close.

I was smiling as I fell asleep.

Chapter Seventeen

WAKING UP WITH KOURTNEY STILL curled into me felt like the most natural thing in the world. I grazed her cheek with my finger, smiling when she opened her eyes. She blinked and seemed a bit shocked, but her eyes were still stunning in the pale morning light.

Leaning forward, I kissed her cheek. "Hey, Chefgirl."

A small, shy grin appeared as she stretched, and it was then I realized how entangled we were under the covers. Lifting the blanket, I looked down at our entwined legs. "Guess I don't have to ask how you slept." I waggled my eyebrows. "I think last night was good for you. You can't stop yourself from touching me."

She stared at me for a second, then began laughing. I chuckled at her reaction, enjoying the sight before me. Her dark hair was a mass of tangles around her face, her cheeks a warm shade of pink from her amusement and her glorious eyes shone—the pools of color lit with mirth.

"You never stop, do you?" She gasped between guffaws.

Shaking my head, I rolled her under me, leaning on my elbows, and stared down at her. Her laughter stopped as she met my gaze. "I'll never stop if I can see this breathtaking vision when I'm being entertaining."

Her brow furrowed. "Vision?"

I traced my finger under her eye. "I knew you'd be beautiful when you laughed. But I didn't know how beautiful. Your soul shines in your eyes, Kourtney. They draw me in."

The color on her cheeks deepened. "Nobody has ever said anything like that to me before."

"I'm not nobody—remember?" I dropped a kiss on her full lips, wishing I could really kiss her, but knowing she wasn't ready.

"I don't know what to say," she confessed.

"You don't have to say anything. We'll talk tonight and this weekend." I paused, then asked, "If you want to?" I studied her face, noticing she still looked tired and her eyes were anxious. "Am I overwhelming you?" I swallowed hard; worried I had pushed too hard last night. "Is this too much for you right now?"

"It's just . . ."

"Tell me."

"It's unexpected."

"I was hoping for a cup of coffee with you last night. It's a little unexpected for me too, but I'm certainly not complaining about waking up with you."

Her answering smile was shaky.

"Tell me—what are you thinking behind those gorgeous eyes?"

"You seem so sure of this."

"I am." I frowned down at her. "You're not?"

"It's a little frightening for me."

I drew my knuckles down her cheek. "I won't hurt you, Kourtney. I promise."

"I don't know how to react to some of the things you say, Nathan. I've never had anyone say them before. Or treat me the way you do."

"Do you like it?"

She inhaled in a deep breath. "Yes."

"But you're still scared? Why?"

"Because I worry how I'll feel when it stops."

I frowned at the word "when."

"It's not going to stop. I meant what I said last night. I want us to be together, as long as you want it, too."

"I do."

"Good." I kissed her, my lips nuzzling hers, loving how right they felt on mine. "We'll figure it out, together, yes?"

"Yes."

I breathed out a sigh of relief. "Okay. Run time?"

"You don't have to go with me. I'll be fine."

I sat up, pulling her with me. "You aren't going anywhere alone. Understand? It's with me or a treadmill at the gym in my building. With me right beside you. Your choice."

"Guess I'm stuck with you?"

I kissed her again. "Yep. Cell phone, remember?"

"Okay then, Samsung. Let's get at it."

AN HOUR LATER I WAS grateful to see the houses come back into view. "Do you run this far every morning, Chefgirl?" I gasped, collapsing at the table with a glass of water.

"Usually. I didn't go as fast today as I normally do."

I paused in between sips. "You went at a pretty good pace."

"I can do faster." She got up, wrinkling her nose. "I'm going to go have a shower and get ready for work."

I frowned. "Okay."

"What?"

"I need to shower as well, but I don't want to leave you alone."

"Nathan." She sighed; her voice patient. "Andy hasn't seen this side of ten a.m. since we were teenagers. He would never think to show up here this early. He doesn't even go into work before eleven. It's perfectly safe for you to go home and have a shower."

"What does he do that allows him to go in so late?"

"He's a mechanic. He owns his own shop. I think he goes in late every day."

"Good business man. So responsible." I snorted. "Although, it explains how he can afford to deck his dumbass truck like that."

"You have a hate on for it, don't you?" She grimaced a little, wrinkling her nose. "It is rather hideous—and noisy. I never understood why he liked it so much."

I stood up and stretched. "He likes the attention, and it makes him feel better about his, ah, shortcomings."

Her brow furrowed. "Shortcomings?"

I nodded, keeping my expression serious. "Guys who drive souped-up vehicles like his are often trying to compensate for having, um," I hesitated.

"Having what?"

"Small dicks." I shrugged.

Kourtney stared at me wide-eyed. Peals of laughter bounced off the walls as she sat down, her hand clamping over her mouth to stifle the snorts as she shook with amusement.

I beamed; pleased I could make her laugh again.

"Only saying, Chefgirl. He needs to try and impress a woman with his truck, because once he gets her into bed, she ain't gonna be too impressed with what he's got going on under *his* hood."

"Stop it!" She gasped, between guffaws. "I don't like him, but he's still my brother and . . . ewww!"

"That's what they say once they get a load of what's waiting for them—or not waiting I should say. Ewww."

Her eyes were bright from the tears of her laughter, the sight of her amusement, making my chest warm.

Unable to resist, I crouched in front of her. "I drive a sleek, discreet, but rather sexy looking Acura." I grinned. "*Turbo*. I promise, Kourtney with a K, you won't be saying . . . ewww."

Her eyes grew large, her mouth forming a small O.

Snickering, I kissed her nose and stood back up. "I'm going next door to have a shower. I'll be at the end of the driveway in thirty minutes. Don't leave the house until I'm there. And keep your cell phone with you. Call me if anything makes you nervous. Anything. I'll be right over. Okay?"

"You're being over protective."

"I disagree. Lock up behind me."

I had gotten to the fence when I heard Kourtney's teasing voice behind me.

"Nat?"

I turned to look at her.

"What if you were in the shower when I called?" She grinned at me, her face lit with mischief.

I smirked over my shoulder as I continued to climb the ladder, loving her teasing. "I guess you'd be seeing my fine naked ass a lot sooner than I even hoped, Chefgirl." I winked before I dropped down to the other side, enjoying her giggles. "Feel free to test out the theory, though—I'm happy to oblige!" I called then I went inside.

She was still giggling as I shut the door behind me.

◦◦◦

WE PULLED UP IN FRONT of her building after checking in at the front gate. It pleased me to know there was an extra layer of security at the building.

I put the car in park and turned in my seat. "Kourtney," I began, pulling an envelope from above the visor.

"What?" She looked at the envelope, frowning. "What is that?"

"A picture of your brother."

"Where did you get it?"

"I used Facebook and found him. His settings are ridiculously low, and it was easy to snag one of his many selfies, send it to my printer and grab it this morning."

"Why?"

I drew in a deep breath. "I want you to let me give it to security and make sure they know he isn't allowed in the building."

She stared at me, then at the envelope. "He wouldn't show up."

"You didn't think he'd show up at your house, either," I argued. "Please let me do this—your safety is important."

She didn't say anything, but her fingers gripped and pulled on the edge of her coat.

"You can take it to them if you want. Or give me their email and I'll handle it." I wrapped my hand around hers to stop the nervous fidgeting. "For me, please."

"Okay," she agreed. "But, I don't want to call attention to myself."

"You want me to handle it?"

For a moment she didn't move, then nodded.

I breathed a sigh of relief she was letting me help. "Okay. I will. Jason Benson, right—he's the head of your security?"

"Should I ask how you know that?"

I gave her a soft smile, and ran my fingers down her cheek. "I'm smart, Chefgirl. I'll take care of this, okay?"

"Okay."

☙

LATER THAT MORNING, MY PHONE alerted me to a new text.

> *Nathan—Jason came to see me. He got your email and wanted to talk to me. The front gate now has the picture you attached.*

> *Good. I'm glad he took it seriously.*

> *I still think you're overreacting and being far too protective.*

> *I disagree. It would seem he feels the same way.*

> *He showed me the letter. It mentions a possible restraining order. Anything else I should know?*

146

I grimaced. I hadn't counted on him showing her the letter. I thought I could ease into the restraining order part over the weekend.

I think you should consider one. To keep him away from you. To keep you safe.

As I waited for her—no doubt—unhappy reply, I mulled over the email I had sent Grant last night, explaining the situation and asking his advice. He had replied, agreeing I should keep an eye on her. He also suggested she consider a restraining order; especially after viewing the pictures I attached of the bruises on her arms. He had other suggestions, but I decided to hold off discussing those with her quite yet. She wasn't ready to confide in me—I doubted me suggesting some sort of counseling would go over well.

I knew I was going overboard, but I had been reckless once in my life and it cost me everything I loved. I wasn't taking that chance again. I realized telling Mr. Benson about a possible restraining order might have been overstepping, but I didn't regret it.

Meanwhile, there was no reply from Kourtney, so I sent her another text.

I know you're angry with me. But I can't let him near you again. I have to do everything I can to keep him away from you—to keep you safe. I won't let him have the chance to hurt you again. I can't even stand the thought of that happening.

Silence. I tried calling her, but it went right to voicemail. I knew she must be furious I had invaded her privacy. I waited a few minutes, and I texted her again.

I get it—you're angry. Promise me you won't leave before I come get you. You don't have to talk to me. But don't make me worry all day that you'll leave without me. Stay where I know you're safe.

I waited, and finally got a reply.

I won't leave.

I sighed in relief.

Good. I won't apologize for trying to keep you safe. But you can yell at me tonight. I'll take it.

There was no response.

I DROVE UP IN FRONT of the lab and got out of the car just as Kourtney exited the building with two other people. A man and woman accompanied her, and I was surprised to see Kourtney was wearing sunglasses. She hadn't been wearing them this morning. I pushed off the car and held out my hand, unsure if she would take it, but was grateful when she allowed mine to grasp her shaking one. I pulled her close and wrapped my arm around her as the man stepped forward, his hand extended. "Mr. Fraser, I'm Jason Benson. You contacted me this morning."

I shook his hand. "Thanks for your prompt attention to my email."

He nodded. "Happy to help. Kourtney is an important member of the staff, as well as a friend of my fiancée." He indicated the woman who was standing to his side, staring between Kourtney and me in amazement.

Smiling, I offered her my hand. "Nathan Fraser."

"Annie Baker." She cocked her head to the side. "Kourtney hasn't mentioned you."

Inside I snorted, not surprised. Kourtney wouldn't have any reason to mention the guy she fed at night over the fence.

"We're pretty private people, and still new in our relationship." I smiled warmly, and fibbed a little. "She has spoken about you often." I turned back to Jason. "I know Kourtney isn't happy about the situation, Jason, but I wanted to take every precaution." I tucked Kourtney closer. "She is too important to me to take any chances."

Annie's eyebrows shot up and she stared at Kourtney, her facial expression saying everything.

Lucy, you got some 'splainin' to do!

Jason's face was far more impassive as he studied us. "Of course. We take care of the women in our life, yes?"

"Yes," I reaffirmed. "Thank you again. I hope you both have a pleasant weekend." I began to step back with Kourtney. I wanted to get her home so she could yell at me and I could start trying to get her un-angry with me. I hadn't expected to be in the doghouse this soon. I was sure I had a good week before she got mad with me.

Annie stepped forward and gave Kourtney a quick hug. "You'll be okay?"

"I'm fine—you're all making too much of this situation." Kourtney's tone was low and raspy sounding.

Shit, she was so mad she'd been crying. That explained the glasses.

All three of us sighed at her words. Jason shook his head. "Nathan is right, Kourtney. Better safe than sorry."

I opened the car door and let Kourtney slide in, closing it and walking around to the driver's side. I wondered if we would make it home before the yelling commenced. I was pretty sure I was going to hear the words "privacy" and "violation." As well as "get out" and "leave me alone." I slid in and started the car, pausing before I drove away. "Do you need anything on the way home?" I asked quietly.

"I do need to stop at the grocery store, if you don't mind?" Her reply was just as quiet.

I nodded. "Sure."

I followed her around the store, holding the basket. She didn't have a list, but she moved quickly through the aisles, picking up specific items. I was smiling as I noticed the makings for what I was sure was macaroni and cheese, and I knew she had remembered our texts, even if she was angry. Maybe she wouldn't kick me out after all. I admired the view as she walked ahead of me—her pretty skirt flowed over her hips and rounded backside, swirling about her shapely legs as she walked. I also noticed a few other guys checking her out and I glared at all of them.

Fuckers. She was mine.

I only had to convince her of that fact.

The drive home was silent and I parked in her driveway. "Do you want me to come in now so you can yell at me or should I go next door and change first?"

She turned toward me, but didn't say anything except to shake her head and open the door. I grabbed the bags and followed her, depositing them on the counter and leaning back beside it.

For a minute there was silence. Then she removed her glasses, tossing them on the counter behind me. Her vivid eyes blazed at me, awash with emotion, the redness telling me how much she had been crying.

"Why are you so worried?"

"I need to keep you safe."

"So you told me." She took in a deep breath and let it out slowly. "The question is *why*, Nat? You don't know me. Why would you care so much about my asshole of a brother and how he treats me?"

I gaped at her. "I don't *know* you?

"You live alone, and unless I'm mistaken, you're as alone as I am. You're a brilliant medical researcher, but you can't use a computer to save your life. You're very kind and loving. Despite your horrible, shitty upbringing, you give to people unconditionally and respond with your heart." I took hold of her hand, running my thumb over her knuckles. "I love our conversations. How you call me out when you disagree with me. How you respond to my teasing. How witty and smart and funny you are." I softened my voice. "I don't think you see yourself clearly because you've been hurt too much." I touched her cheek with my finger. "You're very shy—and also very sweet and brave. You cook like a dream, wear funny, fuzzy socks all the time, love the color red, and take care of me better than I deserve."

I yanked my hand through my hair in exasperation. "Maybe the past few weeks haven't been a conventional start for a relationship, but we have gotten to know each other, Kourtney. There's barely a day since you moved in where we haven't spent some sort of time with each other. I've talked to you more than any other person in my life in the past few years. And the last few days without you, have been some of the loneliest of my life. I missed everything about you."

I moved closer to her. "Maybe I don't know all about you *yet*, but what I do know, I like—very much. And no matter how mad you get with me, I'm not going to let someone hurt you when I can do something to stop it. I'm sorry I embarrassed you at work. I know you're a very private person and don't want the attention. It wasn't my goal." I shrugged, unsure how to explain it. "I . . . I needed to do whatever I could do to make you safe."

We stared at each other and Kourtney's eyes filled with tears that slid down her cheeks. I pulled her to me. She wrapped her arms tight around my waist, and buried her face into my chest as she began sobbing. I held her close, nuzzling her hair, shocked at her surprising reaction. I expected yelling and accusations, not tears. I stood, swaying us from side to side. She cried, the quietness of her tears somehow sounding even more painful than last night, but I knew she needed to get it out and I had to let her. I rubbed small circles of comfort over her back and rested my forehead on her hair. I whispered her name, crooning to her as she began to calm. Finally, she moved back, her eyes still swimming with tears as she tried to offer me a small, tremulous smile.

"Better now?"

"Sorry," she whispered.

"No, Kourtney. It's okay to be mad."

"I'm not," she insisted, interrupting me. "I'm not mad."

"You're not angry with me?"

"No. I'm not normally this way. I rarely ever cry. But I can't stop crying today and I didn't want everyone to see. It was an awful day, Jason came to see me and people kept asking questions, then—" Her gaze dropped.

My gut tightened. "Then what?"

"Andy called me."

"How did he get your number?"

"He has my contact information. He knows where I work. It's not as if I'm in the Witness Protection Program or something. I only moved to another town to get away from them. I hadn't given him my home address; although he must have looked it up. I thought with Dad in a care home he wouldn't bother me anymore."

"What did he say?" I asked.

"He was his usual . . . charming self."

"Kourtney, tell me."

She sighed in resignation. "He called me a bunch of unpleasant names and said to tell you to watch your back. He assured me you'd come to your senses soon and once you'd gotten over your fat fetish you'd be long gone and I'd come crawling back to them anyway. He says he'll be waiting." She looked up at me, her lip trembling. "He called me a 'lousy sister' and a 'horrible daughter'—all the usual things. He reminded me I was a loser, and 'once a loser always a loser.'"

I stared at her, shocked. I could feel my anger raging toward the asshole. My hands tightened into fists at my side; I wanted nothing more than to drive them into his face for his hateful words. I pushed my anger down and shook my head. "You are *not* a loser—and don't even get me started on the fat comments. That fucker needs a lesson in manners."

Kourtney shrugged. I hated seeing the look of utter resignation on her face. Her lips were still trembling as she looked at me. "I don't care what he says about me. I was so scared, Nathan, thinking he would hurt you. I didn't know if I should call you or what to do. All I could think about was how you didn't ask for any of this, and now because of me you could get hurt." Her voice shook. "I can't let that happen."

"It won't."

"He's violent at times," she explained. "He loses his temper."

I cupped her soft cheek. "That's why I have to keep him

away from you, Kourtney." I paused. "Did you think about the restraining order? At least talking to the police about it?"

"A little."

"And?"

"I don't know," she replied. "I just don't know."

I was grateful it wasn't a direct no. I'd discuss it with her tomorrow.

"I have to know you're safe too, Nathan. If you were hurt because of me . . . I'm not sure I could live with myself," she told me.

Embracing her, I sighed. "My brave girl," I crooned. "He won't get near me and he won't hurt me. I promise, but thank you." I wasn't going to argue with her; she had been overwhelmed all day and struggling with her emotions. I was relieved she wasn't angry with me.

She shuddered in my arms.

"How about a hot bath?" I remembered how my mom always enjoyed soaking in a warm bath after she had a rough day. "I'll look after dinner."

"Um—"

I held up my finger. "This is highly talented. I push a few buttons and soon food arrives at the door."

She grinned, her lips still trembling. "Magic again?"

I nodded. "Let me take care of you tonight, Kourtney. We'll have dinner and relax. Talk if you're up to it, or watch a movie. As long as we're in the same room, I don't care."

She stared at me, clearly unsure how to react to someone wanting to take care of *her*.

Finally, she nodded. "That sounds nice."

Leaning down, I kissed her nose. "Okay."

Chapter Eighteen

KNOCKED ON THE BATHROOM door. "You decent, Chefgirl?"

"Um, I'm in the tub, Nathan. I don't usually have clothes on."

I chuckled at the sarcastic remark from behind the door. "You got bubble action?"

"Yes?"

"Pile them up then, I'm coming in." Grinning, I opened the door, striding in with a glass of wine in my hand. "I come bearing gifts."

I stopped cold at the vision before me: Kourtney in the tub. Her eyes were wide with panic as she stared at me, her skin wet and glistening in the light, and frantically gathered up a large pile of bubbles, trying to hide herself. Her hair was piled up on top of her head, damp tendrils hanging around her face. She was utterly captivating. I swallowed the sudden lump in my throat.

"What are you doing?" She hissed. "I'm in the tub."

"I can see that." I smirked. "How hot do you have the water,

Kourtney? You're doing a great imitation of a cherry tomato right now." Leaning down, I dipped my finger in, only to find a pleasant warmth, not the boiling temperature I expected.

"Hmm. The temperature is fine. Why are you so red? Are you okay?"

"Nathan. I. Am. In. The. Tub. *Naked.*"

"You're all covered up."

"*Underneath* the bubbles I'm not."

"Ah. I. see. I have embarrassed you," I mused. "How ungentlemanly of me."

She glared at me. I offered her the glass of wine. She accepted with a frown, putting it down on the ledge of the tub.

"I'll even the playing field." Looking innocent, I smirked and dragged my shirt over my head, throwing it over my shoulder.

As I reached for the button on my jeans she sat upright, the bubbles beginning to dislodge around her body. Her voice was a few octaves higher and way louder than I was used to hearing. "*What* are you doing?"

"Getting naked. I thought it would make you feel better. We'd be equal." I winked as I started pushing off my jeans.

"Stop! Stop it right now!" She looked at me with shocked eyes.

"What?"

"I don't want you naked!"

"That's what your mouth is saying. But your eyes are saying something altogether different."

She snorted, backing up to the edge of the tub as she gathered more bubbles up against her in defense. Internally, I grinned. They really weren't doing much to hide anything, but if she felt better I would let her build her useless wall of suds. I was quite enjoying the view.

"And what are they saying?"

"You want me to join you in the tub."

"They are not!" she squeaked.

"No?"

She shook her head. "No."

I sighed. "Deny it all you want. You've wanted me all wrapped around you since we had to get out of bed this morning."

"I think you have that backward."

I stepped forward and leaned over, bracing myself on the edge of the tub. I stared down at her flushed cheeks, bringing my face close. "Truer words have never been spoken, Kourtney. I can't wait to crawl back into bed with you and feel you wrapped around me."

Her eyes widened at my words.

I lifted a hand, burrowing it into her thick hair and pulled her forward. I could feel her breath on my lips, small gasps of air that were warm and damp. I wanted those puffs of air in my mouth. I kissed her fast, but hard, before drawing back. Our gazes locked. I reached over and handed her the glass of wine I had brought in.

"Drink your wine and finish your bath. Stop trying to seduce me, woman. I have to get dinner ready."

"Get out, Nathan."

As I turned to walk out, I heard her mutter, "Incorrigible bastard."

Bending down, I grabbed my shirt off the floor and said with amusement, "Not true, Chefgirl. My parents had been legally married for almost two years before I came along."

"Out."

"Are you sure? I can leave the money on the doorstep for the food and join you. I'm already half-naked." I waggled my eyebrows.

"Get out!" She shrieked at me, but I didn't fail to see her fighting to hide her smile.

I shrugged. "Your loss. I would have scrubbed your back," I teased as I left the room, closing the door behind me.

I heard her giggle as I walked down the hall. I loved making her laugh. She never failed to respond to my outrageous behavior.

Next I needed to figure out how to make her respond to me, physically.

I grimaced a little as I adjusted myself. I was certainly responding to her.

☙

"DID YOU NOT EAT LUNCH?"

"What?" I asked, looking innocent, knowing full well to what she was referring.

"I'm not sure you ordered enough food."

I shrugged, chewing a mouthful of noodles. "Leftovers—then you don't have to make dinner tomorrow either." I tapped my forehead. "I'm smart like that. I was thinking of you, Kourtney."

"Ah."

Munching on an egg roll, with her feet tucked under her on the sofa, she looked relaxed and utterly adorable after her bath. The urge to lean over and brush the hair that curled around her ears was constant. I wanted so much to be free to touch her whenever I wanted. Her tongue peeked out as she licked plum sauce off her lips. All I could think of was how those lips had felt underneath mine earlier—how much I wanted her tongue in my mouth.

Kourtney looked up and caught me staring.

"What?"

"Nothing—I like looking."

She rolled her eyes at me, and I chuckled.

"Is the TV operational?" I inquired, looking askance at the components scattered haphazardly on top of an unopened box and the TV sitting on a small table beside it.

She nodded. "It works. I don't have it quite set up, ah, correctly."

I laughed at the understatement as I took in the vast amount of loose wires and remotes. "We'll make do tonight and tomorrow we'll get it set up properly. It's supposed to rain all day tomorrow, so it's a good project."

"Really?"

"Yeah, really."

"You don't have to do that for me."

"But I do, Kourtney. I plan on being here a lot and it would drive me crazy."

She blinked, looking shy. "You do?"

"Yep—you okay with that?"

Her cheeks bloomed into a pretty shade of pink. She looked at me from under her lashes, her eyes wary, but hopeful.

"Yeah, I am."

"Good."

DURING THE COURSE OF THE movie, I moved closer. Every time I reached for my drink or to grab a handful of the popcorn she'd made, I edged nearer to Kourtney, who was nestled in the corner of the sofa, with her legs drawn up to her chest. When I noticed her drink was almost gone, I paused the movie, and filled up her glass. When I returned, I plunked down next to her and lifted her legs over my lap; handing her the glass. I draped one arm along the back of the sofa, the other hand resting on her calf, while I pretended to be caught up in the movie. I felt her nervous glance, but I stared at the screen, rubbing my hand in small circles on her leg. I felt her relax, and I had to hide my smile.

She was such a contradiction to me. She seemed to enjoy my caresses, yet always reacted in shock when I offered them freely to her. It took her time to relax into my touch, which I didn't understand; it was as if she was guarding herself for a moment each time. I stole a peek, seeing her gaze locked on my hand. I gently caressed her leg. "Does this bother you, Kourtney?" I enquired, keeping my voice low.

Her marvelous eyes flew to mine and she shook her head. "Does it bother you?" she whispered.

"No. I like touching you."

"Oh." The small word was filled with confusion.

"Do you like me touching you?"

"It . . . it makes me nervous."

I turned to face her. "I'm not going to hurt you, I promise. You tense up every time—why?"

"I'm not used to people being so close."

I had a feeling there was a story behind her quiet statement, but decided it was best left for another time. "I like being close to you, but if it makes you nervous, I'll back off." I offered sadly, lifting my hand off the back of the sofa to stroke her warm cheek. I didn't want to stop touching her, but if it made her uncomfortable and was what she wanted, I would stop.

She leaned into my touch, her eyes fluttering shut. "No," she murmured so low, I almost didn't hear.

I shifted closer, lowering my face to hers. "Kourtney, open your eyes."

Brilliant, nervous eyes met mine.

"I want to kiss you. Really kiss you."

Her breath caught. "What?"

"Please, Chefgirl."

She was silent, but her hand covered mine on her cheek and I took it as her permission.

Her lips were so silky when they met mine. I could feel them trembling as I brushed along their warmth, slipping my hand up to cup the back of her head, holding her close. Sweetly, our lips moved together. I remained patient, letting her relax, before I parted mine, my tongue stroking her bottom lip. She hesitated, then her lips opened, and with a quiet sigh of pleasure, I tasted her for the first time. The rush of desire was almost overwhelming and I groaned low into her mouth.

I felt the slight stiffening of her posture, so I drew back, ghosting my lips up to her ear. "It's me, Chefgirl. Relax, pretty girl." She shivered as I brought her mouth to mine again, thrilled when she responded—her tongue tentative as it touched mine. The intense need to have her close was strong. I gathered her up, but continued to kiss her, moving us so she was straddling my lap. I felt her tense once more, but tightened my hold, until I felt her relax. She shuddered and became fluid and supple in my embrace, her arms winding around my neck, her grip firm.

I found the clip in her hair and released it, threading my hand into the thick waterfall of curls. My other arm remained wrapped around her as our lips moved, tongues swirling and touching as we explored and tasted. Further and further we melted into each other. Nothing else existed but the lush woman in my arms. Everything about her was heightened: her taste, the quiet whimpers that escaped her throat, the rich voluptuousness of her body melded into mine.

Her closeness banished the lingering loneliness I had been living with for so long, filling me with a sense of belonging. Yearning coursed through my body, spiking hot and rampant— my cock hard and throbbing between us, the desire building to a point of almost painful proportions. I knew I needed to slow down, before I ravaged her soundly on the sofa. Kourtney moved with me, and I fought a groan at the sensations she was causing, my erection aching with need for release.

It was with regret I moved away, dropping tender kisses on her parted, swollen lips. My thumb traced the warm flesh, my eyes taking her in flushed cheeks and rapidly heaving chest.

"Kourtney," I whispered, smiling as her eyes opened, still hooded in want. "Hi."

"You stopped."

"I had to."

Her brow furrowed in confusion, and I flexed my hips subtly, drawing her attention to the hardness trapped between us. Her gaze flew to mine and she attempted to scramble off my lap, but I held her tight. "No, Kourtney. Stay."

"I don't want you uncomfortable," she mumbled; her cheeks now a brilliant red.

I lifted her chin, forcing her to look at me. "It's fine. I know you're not ready. I'm not expecting anything but this. I only want you close."

Her eyes remained downcast. "Chefgirl . . ." I waited until

her eyes met mine. "I only want to kiss you. It's all I need right now. Just . . . ignore everything else." I glanced down toward my lap.

Her lips fought a smile. "Not sure I can ignore . . . *that*." She looked down, as well.

I grinned. "Good information to have for the future, but for now, try. I want your mouth back, Kourtney. Give it to me."

I crashed my mouth to hers, having already missed the feeling of her lips meshed with mine. She held herself stiff, trying to angle away from me, but I refused, holding her close. "Like this, Kourtney. You feel so good, just like this." I moaned into her mouth, sighing when she relaxed into me. "Kiss me . . ."

Time lost all meaning as our tongues swept together and our hands touched and explored. I paid attention to what seemed to make her uncomfortable and kept my touches to light caresses on her arms and shoulders, as I guided her lips with mine.

I gasped as I felt her undulate over me, pressing herself down on my aching erection. Her lips moved on my throat, nipping, licking, teasing up and down as she continued moving over me. I grasped her hips in silent warning, needing her to stop. Her breath was hot in my ear. "Let me, please."

I groaned and bucked up into her, my eyes rolling back in my head at the intense sensation.

"I won't . . . ugh . . . be able to stop." Another moan escaped my lips.

"I don't want you to. I want to do this for you, Nathan."

She rose up, our mouths meeting again, her hand stroking me over my sweats, moving upward before plunging under the waistband. She wrapped her fingers around my hardness, stroking firmly, and I groaned deep into her mouth. It had been a long time since I had been touched intimately by someone other than myself. The unexpected pleasure from her hand was so great, I erupted; straining upward, needing the feeling of her wrapped around me as I came; gasping and shaking. Her hand continued its gentle stroking until I was spent and loose, pulling her to me tight.

The room was silent, except for my heavy breaths. Kourtney's face was buried into my chest, one hand running through my hair, the other tucked between us. I wiped her hand on my shirt, grinning at her instant blush. I wrapped my arms back around her.

"Chefgirl?"

"Hmm?"

"That . . . that was phenomenal—and totally unexpected." She giggled.

"I kinda need to change now."

"Me, too."

I lifted her chin, meeting her gaze that had become shy and questioning. I grazed her sweet lips with mine. "We missed the end of the movie. You want to re-watch it?"

"No."

"You want to go to bed?"

She looked nervous, but then nodded her assent.

"I'll sleep on the sofa."

She bit her lip. "I don't . . . I don't want you to."

"Good. I don't want to either." I traced the shape of her lips with my finger. "Nothing is going to happen until you're ready—I'm happy only to hold you." I couldn't help my smile. "Especially right now."

I kissed her forehead. "You go get ready and I'll make sure the place is all locked up."

She stared at me. "You take such good care of me."

I kissed her again. "That's my job now, Kourtney."

She blushed.

"Meet you there?" I murmured.

Her smile was wide. "Meet you there."

Chapter Nineteen

THE SAFETY OF THE NIGHT was all around us. Kourtney was curled into my arms, and I stroked her back, keeping my touch light. Neither one of us had spoken much since I came to bed, automatically moving next to Kourtney, pulling her close. Her quiet sigh of happiness had made me smile when she had finally relaxed into my embrace.

"Chefgirl?"

"Hmm?"

"I was wondering . . ." I trailed off, unsure if I should ask her or not.

"What?"

"Could I, um, return the favor from earlier?"

I felt her stiffen.

"No. I'm fine. I wanted to do that for you."

Leaning down, I found her lips in the darkness, dropping a warm kiss on them. "I'd like to do it for you, too."

"I'm fine."

"*Fine*. I don't like that word." I huffed.

She sighed. "Leave it alone, Nathan. Please."

I leaned back, wanting to see her face. "No, I don't think I want to." A thought occurred to me. "Kourtney, are you . . . a virgin?"

"No."

"Okay." I felt both a sense of relief knowing what a huge responsibility that would be, and at the same time a pang of jealousy at the thought of someone else loving her.

"Do you, ah, not like sex?"

"I don't know, Nathan. I don't think I'm very good at it," she admitted, the pain in her voice evident.

"Why would you say that?"

She sat up, pulling her legs to her chest in a defensive action that I was beginning to recognize. I sat up, and reached over to stroke her arm in a comforting manner. "Talk to me, Kourtney."

She sighed, a sad sound in the room. "I didn't have a boyfriend until my second year of University. I met Ryan a couple months after summer break. He was like me—kind of shy and not experienced. We became friends, and started dating. Neither of us really knew what we were doing, you know? I had no experience at all and he hadn't had much more. We fumbled around a lot. It was awkward and not very, um, satisfying."

I chuckled, despite the twinge of jealousy I was feeling. "We all have to start somewhere."

"We had only slept together a few times when his father became ill and he had to go home." She shifted her feet a little. "His father died and he never came back. He stayed and took over the family business he said he never wanted."

"He didn't want a long distance relationship?"

She shook her head in the darkness. "We were pretty new. He told me it was too hard for him to think of a long-term relationship with everything else he had going on. He felt, well, he said, I wasn't important enough to him, yet, to make a decision like that. I understood what he meant."

I smiled ruefully. Of course she did. I had the feeling she was never important enough in anyone's life—until now.

"What about after?"

"I was shy and introverted. Plus, I was busy with school

and working. I tried, but I wasn't very good at the social thing."

I couldn't keep the surprise out of my tone. "You didn't date anyone else? Ever?"

"One." Her voice was tight.

I winced at the pain in the single word. "Sorry—I didn't mean to bring up something painful from your past."

She shrugged. "It turned out, he wasn't very nice. We didn't date long and we only slept together, ah, once. It was awful. He said he thought a fat girl would be grateful to get laid." She laughed—the sound bitter. "And, according to the stories he spread around, apparently I was far better with my hands than I was in bed." She turned her head in my direction. "You may have had the best of me, Nathan. Maybe you want to run while you can."

I didn't need to see her face to feel her hurt or the pain I knew I would see in her eyes. I lay down, pulling her to me. "First off, I'm not going anywhere. And second, he sounds like a selfish bastard, and a fucking lousy human being. He didn't deserve you." I hated the fact she had been hurt and embarrassed. "And you didn't deserve to be treated like that. How did you handle it?"

"I had no choice really. I buried myself in schoolwork and ignored the whispering and laughter. Eventually, they got tired of trying to get a reaction out of me, and I was left alone. I decided it wasn't worth trying to be something I wasn't, and I gave up on the social aspect and concentrated on my studies."

"You were young and inexperienced, Kourtney—and shy." I nuzzled her hair. "You still are. It's kind of endearing."

She snorted in obvious disbelief.

I lifted her chin, wishing I could turn on the light and see her eyes. They were so expressive and I was learning fast they often said more than her words did. "And since then, has there been anyone else?"

"No."

I sucked in a surprised breath.

"At all?"

"No."

"I don't understand how that's even possible."

Kourtney sighed. "Nathan—I'm not used to getting the sort of attention you give me. Growing up I was only ever ridiculed for how I look. I got used to the snide remarks about my height, my weight, my looks, especially my eyes. At University, things were different and yet they weren't. I wasn't shunned as much, but there were still more people willing to ignore me than there were to be a friend. Often, there were still nasty remarks and rude laughter when I left the room. I got used to being alone. I found it easier to hide than to be rejected all the time. I found if I stayed to myself I could almost be invisible. People ... *men* ... don't usually have the same reaction you do."

I hated the pain in her voice as she spoke of her past. "Is that why you didn't want to meet me?"

"I didn't want to see that look in your eyes. The disappointment of reality versus fantasy." She confessed. "I'd seen it so much in my life already."

"Did you see that look, Kourtney? From me?"

"No."

"And you never will. I like what I see when I look at you."

"I'm trying to get used to that, and how you think of me," she admitted.

"I'll keep reminding you."

We were both silent as I traced circles on her back while her fingers played on my arm.

Hesitating, I took in a deep breath, but I had to ask. I felt I already knew the answer; however, I needed to hear her say it. I trailed a finger down her cheek. "Kourtney, have you ever had an orgasm?"

The sudden heat under my finger told me what she couldn't. "Ever?" I breathed.

"Not with anyone. No. And when I, um, tried ... yeah, well, I ... um ... no."

Embarrassment colored her voice; I gathered her closer, hating to hear it. Her pain upset me, even if it came from the past. For a minute I didn't say anything as I thought about what I *could* say, without sounding either like an arrogant prick—or an asshole.

"We'll have to work on that."

"Save yourself the trouble. I don't think I'm built that way."

I refused to believe she wasn't responsive to sexual desire. I had felt her reaction to me when we were kissing. I had felt her heat when I thrust up into her. Her responses had been passionate, once she allowed herself to relax. She felt desire, of that I had no doubt. What she needed was the right person to help it burn.

I held her tight to me, teasing the sensitive skin behind her ear. I tugged the lobe between my lips, swirling my tongue on the sensitive skin. I smiled when I felt her involuntary shiver. I kept my mouth on her ear, murmuring, "I think I'm up for the challenge."

"Nathan . . ."

I nipped sharply at her lobe. "Hush."

"I might be a disappointment to you," she whispered into my neck.

"Not even possible."

I felt her entire body sag in defeat. I could feel her insecurities dwarfing her, and I hated it. "Together, Kourtney. We'll take each step together, at whatever pace you need to," I assured her encouragingly. "You trust me, right?"

"Yes, Nathan; I trust you."

"Then know *nothing* you do will ever disappoint me. And giving you pleasure will be the greatest reward I could possibly ask from you."

I lowered my voice. "I can't wait to see you come. It'll be the sexiest thing I've ever seen." I growled into her ear. "I know it." I groaned against her skin as she shuddered. "See, Chefgirl—feel that sensation—and imagine it magnified ten thousand times."

"You don't play fair," she breathed out.

"Nope." I smirked. "Not when I really want something. And make no mistake. I want you."

I was sure she whimpered. I pulled her down with me, drawing her face to mine, kissing her sweet mouth thoroughly. When I finally stopped, we were both panting. I dropped my head to her shoulder, struggling to calm myself. A grin broke out on my face and I snickered as I lay back down, pulling her to me.

"What?"

"Told you I wanted you panting in my ear."

A small giggle burst from her lips. I brushed a kiss on her cheek, and nestled her close to me. I could sleep now.

She was smiling.

THERE WAS FIRE EVERYWHERE AND I couldn't get out. No matter where I turned, I was trapped—something pinning me in place. I had to get out; I had to find a way . . .

I struggled, releasing the seatbelt that was holding me in place. I had to find the door handle and get out, but then I heard it. A voice calling my name. Pleading with me to save her.

Kourtney.

Kourtney was trapped with me, somewhere in the smoke. I had to find her. I had to save us both.

The smoke became thicker. I struggled to get enough air in to call for her, desperate to find her, to help her, but I was fading, the darkness overwhelming me. Pain shot through my leg and I screamed.

I sat up, gasping, struggling at the weight pinning me down, holding me back from getting to Kourtney, then I realized it had been a dream. The same dream I had all the time, except this time she was there—Kourtney. I felt the gentle touch on my face and I stared down, blinking and confused as a light snapped on. I looked into Kourtney's terrified expression.

"Nathan," she murmured anxiously. "It's okay, my love, I'm right here. You're safe." Her hands cupped my face and I felt the dampness on her palms. "I'm right here," she crooned.

Shuddering, I yanked her to me and her arms wrapped

around my neck. I dropped my head to her shoulder as she stroked my hair, whispering soft words of comfort into my ear. I felt my panic ease, my pulse returning to normal from Kourtney's calming presence.

She drew back and grabbed the bottom of my shirt. "Arms up," she commanded quietly.

"What?" My voice sounded weak, even to my own ears.

"You're soaked, Nathan. We need to take your shirt off."

"Oh." Like a child, I raised my arms and allowed Kourtney to pull the damp shirt off me. She stood up and started walking away, and instantly I felt the panic swell. "Chefgirl, don't go . . ."

She stopped. "I'm getting you a towel. Your pants are damp, too. Take them off."

I half-grinned, trying to lighten the moment. "I knew that would happen sooner rather than later."

She snorted as she came back from the bathroom. "One-track mind." She quipped. "Stand up."

Still unsteady, I did as she asked, feeling the towel pat the damp skin on my back, whisking away the moisture. "Turn around."

I complied, watching as she patted down my arms and chest.

"You have a tattoo," she commented; her soft breath wafting over my chest.

I nodded.

"What is it?"

I swallowed hard as she continued her ministrations. "In memory of my family. It's all I have left of them."

She traced the broken heart, her finger curling around the blood-filled teardrops at the bottom. "Did you have this done after you lost them?"

"Yes."

She reached up, and her lips ghosted a feather-light caress on my skin. She had kissed the symbol that meant so much to me. My heart filled with warmth at the sweet gesture.

"There was an accident . . . and fire," I began, closing my

eyes for a moment at the painful memory.

"I'm sorry."

"I have scars on my right leg."

She hesitated, her hand still on my chest.

"You can look. It doesn't bother me anymore," I offered, wanting to share this secret part of myself with her, somehow knowing she would keep it safe.

She stepped back, and gazed at the scarred skin that ran down my leg. She wrapped her arms around my waist and I was held to her warmth. "Is that how you lost your family? In a fire?" It was a hesitant question before she brushed small kisses on my chest.

I held myself close to her, accepting her tender sympathy. "I lost everything that night, Kourtney."

It was the closest to the truth I could share with her at the moment.

"The teardrops?"

"Each one represents a person I lost," I explained. "People I loved."

Her arms tightened. We stood in silence for a moment. Her grip loosened, her hand wrapping around mine as she led me to the chair. I watched, too weary to even offer helping. She efficiently stripped and changed the damp bedding, then lifted the light blanket for me, the same way I had done for her the other night. "I, ah, I don't have anything else dry to change into." I indicated my boxers. I didn't want her to be uncomfortable.

"I think, contrary to what your ego may believe, Nat, I can handle you in your underwear." She winked at me. "Your fine ass is, at least, covered."

I chuckled, easing back into bed, exhaling deeply when the light shut off, and she crawled in beside me. This time it was she who moved and wrapped around me, offering me the safety of her embrace as she stroked my hair. I closed my eyes in pure pleasure at her gentleness.

"I'm sorry I woke you," I breathed into the darkness.

"You were calling my name. You sounded so frightened."

"I was back in the fire and you were there." I swallowed the lump in my throat. "I couldn't get to you."

"I'm right here, Nathan. I'm right beside you."

A long, painful shudder escaped my throat. I hugged her tighter. "That's exactly where I need you to be, Kourtney. Right beside me. Don't let go."

I felt her hot tears on my bare chest as she gifted a warm kiss onto my skin.

"I won't."

Wrapped in her warmth, with her tender promise in my ears, I slept.

Chapter Twenty

I WOKE UP IN THE quiet morning, alone, in Kourtney's bed. I was buried into her pillow, clutching it tight, enjoying her soft, comforting scent. I still felt groggy, the effects of last night's nightmare lingering. Talking to Kourtney about her past had stirred up my emotions which always led to a restless night, and the dream I had was certainly a resulting factor.

Sitting up, I turned on the light, blinked and looked around, finally noticing the details of her room. Mossy green walls and dark furniture made it a welcoming space. There were more photographs on the wall, no doubt also taken by her. Her bed was huge—bigger than mine and way more comfortable.

Recalling our somewhat revealing conversation the night before, I was determined to learn more about her today. I had to figure out what was happening in her head so I could deprogram it. Whatever the negative influences had been in her life, needed to be removed—permanently—and I fully intended to do that.

But first, I had to find her.

I glanced at the clock, surprised to see it was early; only just after seven. The skies outside were as heavy and gloomy-looking as they had promised. I frowned, wondering if Kourtney had gone for a run without me. I wasn't going to be very happy if she had. Regardless of what she said of the asshole being a late riser, I didn't want to take any chances. I threw back the blanket and shivered in the cooler air. I was still in only my boxers. Getting up, I searched for my sweats and T-shirt, but couldn't locate them. After quickly making my way through my morning ritual, I followed the scent of coffee to the kitchen. I leaned on the doorframe, grateful to see Kourtney sitting at the table, her nose buried in a book. Smiling, I took in her black socks covered in little pink paw prints. I cleared my throat, grinning when she looked up, her cheeks turning a bright red as she noticed my appearance. Her gaze dropped as she mumbled a greeting. I pushed off the doorway and sauntered over, stopping in front of her.

"Chefgirl?"

"Yeah?"

"Cute socks. Did you wear them so they coordinated with my black boxers?"

She didn't look up. "I didn't know what color your boxers were when I put them on last night, Nathan."

"So you say. Speaking of which . . ."

"Yes?"

"Where are my clothes?"

"I washed them. They're in the dryer. The first load is done; the next one should be ready soon. I thought you'd still be sleeping and I'd have them dry for you . . ." She trailed off, sounding embarrassed and confused.

Chuckling, I lifted her chin. I gently tugged her glasses off and leaned down for a kiss. Her lips were warm and full under mine and I held her closer, deepening the kiss. Drawing back, I licked my lips. "Mmm, coffee," I murmured against her warm cheek. I dragged my mouth up to her ear, tracing my tongue along the soft shell of it. "You know, Kourtney, all you had to do was ask."

"Ask what?" she whispered, confused.

"Ask for me to parade around in my boxers so you could stare at my fine ass." I nipped at her lobe. "You didn't have to take away *all* my clothes. I would have happily obliged."

Her gasp was outraged. "I wanted no such thing, Nathan Fraser!"

I sniggered lowly at her use of my whole name. "Whatever you say, Chefgirl. As if you didn't try and lure me into the tub last night. I am so onto your tricks."

Her hand ineffectually pushed on my chest. "Get away from me." A buzzer sounded in the other room. "Your clothes are dry." She pointed in the direction of the laundry room. "Go put them on. Now."

"Okay, Kourtney." I turned and strutted across the room with a wicked grin on my face. "Enjoy the show." When I reached the door, I turned back and winked as I slapped one cheek for emphasis. "Next time you're gonna have to ask . . . and say *please*."

Her indignant yelp had me chuckling as I dragged on my sweats and T-shirt from the night before, grateful for the warmth. I folded the rest of my clothes, smiling when I saw how white the two pairs of socks were. I held up a pair of her socks and compared them to mine. Hers would easily fit into the heel of mine. For some reason it made me inanely happy to think about our laundry being done together. I was still smiling when I went back into the kitchen, catching Kourtney off guard as I grabbed her by the waist, spinning her around and kissing her hard.

She blinked up at me when I stepped back. "What was that for?"

I dropped another kiss onto her sweet lips. "For being you." I kissed her again. "For letting my socks touch yours in the laundry and be white again." Another kiss. I became serious. "For taking care of me last night." I kissed her—this time long and slow. "For putting up with me . . . and my teasing."

"I like your teasing," she admitted.

"Good. I like your reaction to it."

We stood, wrapped around each other. "Are you okay?"

I dragged in a deep breath. "I'm fine."

She pursed her lips. "Fine. I don't think I like that word."

I chuckled at her turning my words back on me. I stroked her cheek, keeping my touch light. "Okay. I'm as good as I ever am after one of those dreams. Better because you're here with me."

"Do you want to talk about it?"

"Not right now. I want to enjoy the *today* I have with you, not the past."

Her smile was soft. "Okay, then."

I smiled back. "Okay, then."

"Coffee?"

I rolled my eyes. "You really need to ask?"

"Do you want some breakfast?"

"You have cereal?"

"I have Cheerios."

"Cheerios?" I snorted derisively. "No Fruit Loops? Captain Crunch?"

"No."

I sighed. "I'm disappointed, Chefgirl."

She picked up the box and held it out. "They're honey nut."

"They're still Cheerios."

She giggled. "I'll make you a bagel?"

I shook my head, heading toward the patio door. "I'll go next door and get my own. I'll grab my tools while I'm at it. You can get my coffee ready while I'm gone."

She followed me, watching as I climbed the ladder. "Why don't you use the door?"

I grinned over my shoulder. "Because this is our thing—and besides, I know how you like to look at my ass as I go over the fence. I'd hate to deprive you of that guilty pleasure."

"It is a rather fine ass," she responded dryly, catching me off guard, causing me to pause my venture over the top. I gaped at her, then joined in her laughter before I swung myself over.

"I knew you'd see it my way," I called over to her. "Welcome to the dark side."

"Well, if you can't beat them, join them," she retorted.

I grabbed some clothes and stuffed them in a bag, and picked up my tool kit. I remembered the cereal and made my way back over the fence, dropping the bag down, swinging myself over. The door probably was easier, but this was simply *us*. I was glad our houses were separated from the others on the street. I could only imagine what the neighbors would think seeing me go over the fence all the time. Mrs. Webster would have a field day with it.

Kourtney was back at the table and I sat beside her, taking a deep drink of the hot coffee. I poured myself some cereal and munched away, watching her read as she sipped her coffee. The silence was surprisingly pleasant. It felt as if it was a regular, lazy Saturday morning being shared with someone special. After a few minutes I cleared my throat. "Kourtney?"

She looked up and for the first time I noticed her glasses. "Why are your lenses tinted?"

She shrugged. "I have them all tinted. You don't notice the weird eye color thing so much then."

I frowned. "Your eyes are *not* weird. They're beautiful."

"Most people don't see them the way you do, Nathan."

"It's wrong to cover up something so unique," I insisted.

Her face was a mixture of emotions. "I don't know how to respond when you say things like that," she murmured. "I'm not used to people saying nice things to me."

I felt the stirrings of anger as I absorbed her words. I leaned over and clasped her hand in mine. "Get used to it. I'm not going anywhere and I have lots of nice things to say to you."

Her gaze was shy as she glanced at me from under her lashes. Lifting her hand, I kissed the knuckles and squeezed it. I found my courage to bring up a subject I knew she was hoping to avoid. "Can I take you to the police station today to ask about a restraining order?"

Her face fell. "Do we have to? I'm sure he'll stay away."

"I don't want to take the chance." I tightened my grip on

her hand. "I can't risk you being hurt again. I want him kept as far away from you as possible." I frowned as I looked at her arm, knowing beneath the sleeve of her sweater there were dark bruises he had caused. "I don't want him to ever touch you again."

"You stopped him before he really hurt me."

I studied her defeated posture, my hand tense around my coffee cup. "Has he hurt you before?"

Her eyes shut and she nodded. "I was always his favorite punching bag when we were growing up; when he was upset he'd take his frustration and anger out on me—which happened often." She sighed softly. "Most of the time, he used words to hurt me, but sometimes he'd get carried away . . ."

I set down my cup; afraid I would squeeze it too tight and it would shatter in my grip. There were many things I wanted to say. So many things I wanted to do, which included going to find him and giving him a taste of his own medicine. I knew, however, it wouldn't solve anything or help her—it was her past. I crouched down in front of Kourtney and cupped her face, forcing her to look into my eyes. "He'll *never* touch you again. You'll never be subjected to his cruel words again. I swear it."

She leaned forward and brushed her lips on mine. "Thank you."

I held her face close. "You're safe now, Kourtney. I have you."

"I need to get used to that fact."

"Yeah, yeah you do," I agreed. "Because I promise you, it's not going to change. You're stuck with me, Chefgirl."

"I'm good with that."

"Good. Will you let me take you, to ask the questions and get the information?"

"Okay."

Relieved, I brought her mouth to mine, kissing her for a few long minutes, letting her feel everything I couldn't say—yet.

WHEN WE ARRIVED AT THE police station, Kourtney was beyond nervous. Her hands trembled, her entire body tense. I tucked her to my side and led her inside. The station was almost deserted, for which I was grateful. A female officer looked up, then came over, frowning. "Kourtney?"

Kourtney's eyes widened. "Joanne? What are you doing here?" She turned to me, speaking in hushed tones. "I went to school with Joanne. She was one of my few friends. We lost touch after I left for University."

"I transferred here after I got married. Why are you here?" She took in the way I was holding Kourtney. "Is something wrong?"

"Is there somewhere we could talk in private?" I asked. "Kourtney requires some advice."

"Certainly." She nodded, and focused her attention back on Kourtney. "Did you want to do this without . . . ?" Her eyes shifted to me.

"Nathan," I informed her. "Whatever Kourtney wants is fine."

"No," Kourtney insisted. "I want Nathan there."

"Okay. Follow me."

Twenty minutes later Joanne sat back, frowning, upset over the bruises Kourtney showed her. "Your brother was always an ass."

She then went on and explained the steps Kourtney would have to follow in order to get a restraining order. Kourtney became more anxious, and the grip she had on my hand tighter with every passing moment—especially when Joanne told her the police could decide to arrest him if they determined it was necessary, even without an order.

"I'm not saying it's going to happen. At the moment, this is only a private conversation," she assured Kourtney. "But, I agree with Nathan. You need to do something. We can discuss other options—but we need him to stay away from you."

"Can I think about it?"

Joanne met my gaze, as if sensing my frustration. "You

can, but don't wait too long. Don't give him the opportunity of coming back at you."

"He won't get the chance," I assured her.

Joanne smiled. "I'm glad she has you, Nathan. But you can't be with her twenty-four hours a day. Think about it, but think hard, Kourtney." She took out a business card and wrote on the back. "Here's my number here and at home. Call me. Anytime."

Kourtney accepted the card. "Thank you."

Joanne shook her head. "I never understood how someone as sweet and kind as you, could be related to your brother. He was such a jerk."

"Hasn't changed much," I informed Joanne. "He's lucky I only escorted him out of the door."

"Don't give him any reason to press charges and leave Kourtney vulnerable, Nathan."

That was a sobering thought. With my past, it was a good piece of advice.

"I'll be careful."

She rose to her feet. "I hope to hear from you soon."

KOURTNEY WAS QUIET IN THE car on the way home from the police station, the papers Joanne had given us clutched tight in her hand. I knew she was struggling with a decision, and I didn't want to push her, but I couldn't let her ignore it and give him a chance to hurt her again.

Looking over at her pale face, my chest ached with worry. I wasn't exactly sure how to help her, except to be there for her as long as she would let me. I had a feeling she had been doing everything alone for so long, she wasn't sure how to accept help.

I parked in front of my usual electronics store and squeezed her hand.

"I have to go get a few things to set up your TV and accessories. You want to come in with me?" I asked gently, searching her sad eyes. "If you don't, I can see you the whole time I'm in there."

"I'll stay here."

Leaning over, I kissed her forehead. "I'll be right back."

She nodded. I went in and grabbed what I needed, keeping one eye on the car. I knew the doors were locked and she was fine. Even if her brother appeared, I would get to her before he could even blink, but nonetheless, I was nervous. I had a feeling the events of the past couple days were about to break her open. I didn't want her alone when it happened. I sighed in quiet relief when I was back beside her in the car.

Once inside the house, I placed everything down and looked at Kourtney. She looked unsure and lost, glancing around her home, as if she didn't know what to do next. I embraced her, feeling a long shudder run through her. "You have questions," she whispered into my chest.

"I do. But we can talk about it when you're ready. Not before." I looked down at her pale face. "I know this is a lot to deal with, Kourtney. I know you have questions, too."

She looked at me, her voice unsure. "What are we?"

I smiled tenderly. "We're whatever you want us to be—I want you in my life. I want to be in yours."

"Why?"

I shrugged, unsure how to explain. "I wish you could see, that you could *feel*, what I do when I look at you. How you make me feel when you're close." I ran my knuckles down her soft cheek. "Then you wouldn't have to ask. You would *know*."

"I'm scared."

I frowned. "Of me?"

"Of how you make me feel," she admitted. "Of how very much I want you to feel the same way."

I held her close to my chest. "Stop being scared, Kourtney. You don't have to want it, because I already do. I care—very much."

Her words were muffled. "Nobody ever cared."

I tipped her face up. "As we've established already, I'm not nobody."

We gazed at each other, and I knew I had to help her get past this moment. We would sit and talk later, but I needed her to find her feet again and get her head out of all the churning, sad thoughts she had in it.

Leaning past her, I grabbed the box of elbow macaroni sitting on the counter. "Is this for me, Chefgirl?" I asked teasingly. "It seems to me, someone promised me homemade macaroni and cheese the other day."

She mock frowned. "I think someone asked, if I recall correctly."

"But it's for me, right?"

A smile broke out on her face. "Yes Nat, I'm going to make you mac and cheese."

I grinned in triumph. "Perfect. Get to it, woman. I had to make my own breakfast, after all."

She giggled as she grabbed the box from my hand. "Poor baby. I'll have to make up for that, won't I?"

"Damn right."

"I'll add a salad."

I groaned and rolled my eyes. "I hardly consider *that* making up for anything. Now cookies or brownies—that would be making up." I winked. "I bet you make fucking awesome brownies, don't you?"

She nodded.

This was perfect. She needed to be busy and I knew she loved to be in the kitchen.

"Will you make them for me?" I pleaded in her ear, kissing the soft spot behind it. "Now?"

Her shiver made me smile, as did her breathless *"yes."*

Grinning, I dropped a kiss on her head. "I'll go start working my magic and leave you to yours. I look forward to my rewards later."

"I hardly call mac and cheese and some brownies a reward, Nathan."

"That's not what I was referring to."

Her brow furrowed. "I don't understand."

I tilted her chin and kissed her, my tongue stroking hers languidly as I savored the feel of her mouth under mine. I dropped another soft kiss on her pink lips. "Those are treats, Kourtney. The reward is getting to spend the rest of the day with you, under the blanket on the sofa." I lowered my voice. "All afternoon. All alone." I nipped her bottom lip playfully. "Best fucking reward, ever."

She was smiling when I left the room.

Chapter Twenty One

"I MEAN IT, KOURTNEY; I'M never going back next door. I'm staying right here. I want you to make me mac and cheese every day." I groaned, contented, as I set down my bowl, and leaned back in my chair.

Kourtney snickered. "I think you might get sick of it—eventually." She lifted my bowl, inspecting it, then looked up with a grin on her face. "But are you sure you got enough, Nat? I'm sure there are a few noodles stuck in the pan. You could scrape them out if you wanted to."

"I only eat so much to make you happy. I don't want you to think I'm dissing your cooking or anything," I informed her haughtily.

"Ah, that explains your voracious appetite." She nodded with a smirk. "So kind of you. I take it you normally eat like a bird?"

I closed my eyes. "Yep. I nibble. All this effort is only for you."

I was surprised but pleased when I felt her warm lips touch mine. "I appreciate the effort."

My hand shot up, holding her face close to mine so I could

kiss her. We shared indulgent, caring caresses; our lips moved together smoothly, our tongues touched in soft passes. Neither of us deepened the kisses, but we shared a quiet moment of sweet intimacy. When we drew apart, I opened my eyes and smiled into her wondrous gaze.

"Hi, Chefgirl."

"Hi, Nat."

"I like this even better than the hand-holding." I waggled my eyebrows.

"Somehow I'm not surprised."

I grinned, running my hand through her thick hair, enjoying the feeling of the soft curls. "I like your hair."

Pink bloomed on her cheeks, like I knew it would. I stroked the warm skin. "I like this."

The color deepened, running down her neck.

"I *like* you."

Her teeth caught on her bottom lip and her eyes darted around looking everywhere but at me.

"Hey." I waited until her eyes met mine again.

"I really like being able to kiss you."

Her voice was quiet. "I like that, too."

I kissed the tip of her nose. "Good. Because I don't want to stop."

I released her and got to my feet. "Now, you ready to come see my magic?"

"It's all done?"

"Yep. I'll go put in a movie and you can bring the coffee . . . and brownies?" I asked hopefully.

"Deal."

"SO THERE'S ONLY ONE REMOTE now?" Kourtney asked in delight.

I nodded; my mouth so full of dark chocolate decadence I couldn't answer.

"Where did this come from?"

I swallowed and took a sip of coffee, trying to stifle a low moan of pleasure as the bitter of the coffee hit the sweet of the brownie and mixed on my taste buds. "I bought it this morning for you. It's the same one I have. It's much easier; you point it and hit the button for what you want to do. It turns on all the right components."

She frowned as she looked at it. "I'll probably fuck it up," she stated sadly, glancing up at me. "I always fuck up these things."

I threw my head back in laughter at her unusually colorful statement, leaned forward and kissed her warmly. "I think I'm rubbing off on you."

She wrinkled her nose. "Can you fix it if I do?"

"I can. Don't worry about it, Chefgirl. Between the mac and cheese and these brownies, I'm definitely not leaving. If you fuck it up, hand it over." I took the device out of her hand and tapped on the remote's face. She looked at the TV screen, confused.

"That looks like my front step."

"It is. Now when someone knocks, you can see who's there before you open the door. I programmed the blue key; touch it and it will do it all."

She looked at me, shaking her head. "How?"

I shrugged. "The wonder of wireless technology. There's a small camera over your front door now," I explained. "It's a safe thing to have, especially with all that's happened. When it's nicer out, I'll wire up an intercom, too." Then I pleaded. "Please accept it, Kourtney."

She pursed her lips in silent indecision. Finally, she sighed. "Thank you."

I clasped her hand in relief. I felt much better knowing this was installed. I handed her back the remote, explaining how to use it, then let her play with it for a few minutes as I sipped on my coffee.

I glanced with longing at the plate on the coffee table where the third brownie was still sitting. I knew she had brought me two and one for herself, but she had yet to touch hers since she had been too busy checking out her TV and equipment set up. She saw my look, and smiling, handed me the plate.

"That one is yours." I pointed out.

"There are more in the kitchen. I made them for you, anyway."

I set down my coffee and picked up the plate. "True, you did make them for me. I suppose, really, *I* am sharing with *you*. And *I* don't feel like sharing right now." I winked and grabbed the last brownie, grinning as I bit into it, enjoying her giggle. I offered her the rich treat "Bite?"

She leaned forward and took the corner in her mouth, pulling it off, and chewing; her eyes shut as she enjoyed the taste. I watched, fascinated, as her tongue flicked out to get the icing off the corner of her mouth and her throat moved as she swallowed.

In a move I hadn't planned, and she didn't expect, I tossed the brownie down and lunged over, pinning her to the back of the sofa, my body pressed hard into her softness, my tongue inside her mouth so fast, we both gasped. Her hands came up, gripping the back of my neck, as mine curved around her shoulders, holding her tight to me as I ravished her mouth. I couldn't get enough of her taste, which was only heightened by the sweetness of the lingering chocolate. Over and again I kissed her, my tongue delving and twisting with hers, exploring and seeking, until we were both breathless and panting for air. With regret, I stopped, seeking the tender skin of her neck instead.

"Should I apologize for that?" I breathed into her softness when I could speak again.

"No." Her reply was whisper-quiet.

"Good. Because it's going to happen—a lot."

"Was it the brownies? Do they, um, affect you?"

I smirked, looking down into her face, her lips swollen from mine, her cheeks pink from the exertion and her eyes reflecting the same passion I was feeling right back at me. "No, Kourtney.

It's you—*you* affect me."

"Wow," she mouthed.

"Wow is right." I held her to me, wanting her to feel how much she affected me. Her eyes grew round and her cheeks darkened as she stared at me, and I could feel her tensing up. I brought her back to my mouth. "This is all I want right now, Kourtney. Just you—just this. Relax," I begged against her full lips.

Her entire body shuddered, and I looked down at her, concerned by her change in demeanor. "Kourtney?"

"You make me want . . . more," she murmured, her fingers dancing along my face.

I turned my face into her hand, kissing the palm. "Good. More is good, but only when you're ready, Kourtney. No pressure. We'll get there. Together."

She sighed—the sound shaky. "Together."

I LOOKED DOWN AT KOURTNEY, who was asleep. After putting in a movie, I sat on the end of her sofa with the chaise lounge, put up my feet and convinced her to lie beside me with her head cradled by a pillow on my knee. A large blanket covered up both of us and I stroked her hair, pleased when I felt her relaxing into sleep. I continued to comb my fingers through her silky hair as I half watched the movie, but for the most part, watched her. I knew she was exhausted from the emotions of the last week and she had stayed awake long after I had fallen asleep, watching over me after my nightmare. Now I wanted to do the same for her.

The deep, protective feelings she brought out in me were astonishing. The desire she roused within me from a simple gesture or look almost brought me to my knees. She wasn't even aware of it. I had never experienced anything like it. I had cut myself off from emotions for so long, I found it all confusing. Losing my family had almost devastated me, and I never thought I'd allow myself to care about someone again.

But Kourtney—she entered my life so quietly, yet had such a profound impact on it, that she had become as necessary to me as breathing. Just the thought of going back to the solitary way I had been living made me shudder. I needed her—and I knew she needed me. There was no doubt we needed each other now, and I couldn't imagine my life without her.

Kourtney's nose wrinkled and she shifted her head, turning toward me. I waited until she had settled then resumed stroking her head, glancing around at the shadows from the late afternoon subdued light. I could hear the steady downfall of rain hitting the roof; its peaceful rhythm soothing to my ears. As my hand moved, my fingers ran over an impression on the side of Kourtney's head and paused. Curious, I pushed back her hair and looked down at the scar that ran under her hairline. It was jagged and twisted, about three inches long, and I frowned as I studied the nasty line marring her flesh. It would have taken some force to cut such a mark into her head. I felt the rapid fluttering of Kourtney's eyelashes on my wrist, and I lifted my hand back to see her gazing up at me. "Hey, sleepyhead."

Her voice was sad when she spoke. "You were looking at my scar."

I shrugged, feeling guilty. "I felt it as I was stroking your head. You've had it a while?"

"Since I was ten," she replied. "I have a few others."

"I have some good ones from my skateboarding years. I'll show you those later." I winked, but the sad look on her face didn't change.

Something about her expression bothered me. "How did you get the scars, Kourtney?"

"Andy."

I tensed at the name. She was ready to talk to me. I picked up her hand and held it tight.

"Tell me."

She took a deep, quiet breath, while gathering her thoughts—finally she spoke.

"I was a surprise. I was born four years after Andy."

"That's not a huge age gap."

"It might as well have been fourteen. My parents . . . they never wanted another child. I was unexpected." She glanced into my eyes. "And not very welcome."

I frowned. "How can any child not be welcomed?"

She shrugged. "They were happy—settled. They only planned or wanted one child and they had him much later in life than their friends did. Andy was everything they wanted in a child. Outgoing, popular, good at sports . . . and then I showed up. At first, Mom thought she was going into early menopause. But instead she got me."

I squeezed her hands. "Most people would consider that a gift. You told me it was your fault she died. How is that possible? She was in a car accident and you were a child. Just a child."

She stared at me, unblinking. "I wasn't like Andy, Nathan. He was wanted. My parents always referred to me as the problem child. I was chubby and shy. Sick a lot. Scared of my own shadow. Always falling and hurting myself." She shook her head. "According to my father, I was so needy, I drove her crazy."

She sighed. "One day, I was sick and needed medication. She went to get it, but never made it home. It was raining and the roads were slippery—she was in a car accident. Some man went through a red light and hit her head on. Things had never been . . . *great* . . . for me, but after Mom died things went downhill—fast."

She began to move, but I stopped her. "No, Kourtney. Stay close. Please, let me see you; I need to see you."

She settled back down on my knee, her eyes regarding me with worry.

"What happened?" I rested my hand on her cheek.

"Andy never liked me, even when I was a little kid. His favorite thing was to pick on me. He'd push me around, pinch me. He'd call me names and make fun of how fat I was or my freaky eyes. But after Mom was gone, it got worse. Mom at least tried to keep some sort of peace between us, but after she died . . ."

"Tell me, Kourtney. I'm right here, baby," I encouraged her gently, my thumb stroking her cheek.

"It was as if he hated me. The pushing turned to punching; the pinching became hitting, and the name calling . . ." Her voice was pained. "It was constant."

"Your dad didn't stop it? Or do anything?"

"I was never close with my dad. There was no doubt who was his favorite child. He always compared me to Andy. Why wasn't I stronger? Why wasn't I popular? Why was I always sick? And, after Mom was gone, it was as if he couldn't even be bothered to hide his distaste for me anymore. He drank all the time. He let Andy do whatever he wanted. In his eyes, Andy could do no wrong. If I tried to talk to him, he told me to buck up and quit whining." Her hurt-filled eyes looked at me. "I remember one day when he was drunk, he told me he wasn't even sure I was his. He said he couldn't believe he could father such a fat, ugly, useless waste of space. He told me if I was his, I was the biggest mistake he'd ever made, and he wished I'd died instead of my mother."

"*Kourtney!*" I tightened my hold on her, horrified at her words.

How could a father say that to his own child?

Her eyes shut. "Things only got worse as I got older. It never ended. One of them was always picking on me, criticizing me, berating me for something I wasn't doing right—which was almost everything. I did all I could to make them happy: I was quiet, I kept the house clean, I learned to cook, and I got good grades at school hoping Dad would be proud. But it was never enough. I was *never* enough. I became even more withdrawn and I never made many friends. I was picked on at school for how I looked, for being too studious, for being sick; it was always something, usually with Andy leading the charge. And if the big kids pick on you, especially your own brother, the younger ones think it's okay, so it never stopped. I never got any peace. When I got home it was the same thing, only worse.

He also loved pulling pranks on me." Her hand drifted up to her head where the scar was located.

I lifted her hand and kissed it, ghosting my fingers over the mark. "How did this happen?"

"I hated our basement. It was dark and musty and so"—Kourtney shivered—"awful. I despised going down there and I only did it when I absolutely had to. Andy had told me for years the boogeyman lived down there and would get me one day. He loved to turn off the lights when I was down there to scare me. One day, I came home from school and I went down to get something from the cold room, thinking I was alone in the house. I was partway up the stairs when the lights went off and the door slammed shut. I knew it was Andy and I begged him repeatedly to open the door. I could hear him laughing on the other side, but he wouldn't open it." Her eyes filled with tears as she relived her terror, and I could feel her shaking. My hand tightened on hers in silent support. "I heard something coming up the steps behind me, breathing heavily and whispering my name." She drew in a shaky breath. "I became hysterical, and I was screaming for Andy to open the door. The next thing I knew, I felt cold, wet fingers touch my neck, and I passed out."

That fucking little prick.

I wished he was standing in front of me so I could hit him. It took everything I had to keep myself calm. "That's not surprising. You were terrified."

"I was. When I woke up, I was lying on the basement floor, bleeding. I had fallen down the stairs, taking Andy's friend with me. He broke his arm; I hit my head on the wooden steps, causing this." She ran her fingers over the scar. "It didn't heal very well."

"Didn't they take you to the hospital?" I asked, horrified.

"When my father got home later that night, he took me—he had no choice. He wasn't happy about it, but he finally did because the bleeding wouldn't stop. He called me some of his favorite insulting names all the way to the hospital." She shrugged. "I was pretty banged up and they asked a lot of questions. Dad didn't like questions. I told them I fell down the stairs, and Dad and Andy weren't home. Eventually, they stopped hounding me, fixed me up, and sent me home."

"Was the fucker punished?"

"No."

"Why?" I spat out between gritted teeth.

"He told my father I had done it on purpose. I had pushed his friend going up the stairs, knocked him down, slipped and hit my head."

I snorted. "And he believed it, of course?"

"He was always happy to believe anything negative about me, Nathan."

"Did you try to tell him the truth?"

She shook her head.

"Why?"

She looked away, unable to meet my eyes. I hated the embarrassment I could see on her face.

I cupped her chin, forcing her to look at me. "Tell me."

"Andy told me if I said anything, he was going to tell everyone at school I tripped and fell on his friend and because I was so fat I broke his arm." She pushed away and stood up, looking at me, her eyes blazing. "Life was already hard enough without adding more humiliation to it, Nathan. I kept my mouth shut, and for a while, lived with the clever comments from Dad and Andy about not being able to see the steps because I was so fat. At least I didn't have to face it at school, too. When I didn't react to the remarks anymore, they eventually stopped."

My hands were clenched at my sides as I struggled not to show Kourtney how angry I was. "What else did he do?"

"After the basement thing, he switched more into intimidation. He still liked to push me around on occasion." She held out her hand and I could see another jagged scar across her palm. "He snuck up behind me one day while I was cutting buns for sandwiches and grabbed me. The knife slipped and I cut myself badly; right to the bone. I had to walk myself to the hospital that day for the stitches."

"Where was your father?"

"Drunk and passed out on the sofa." She shrugged, looking nervous. "I had no money to take a taxi."

I shut my eyes. That weak bastard.

Kourtney continued to talk, her tone almost robotic as she shared more of her painful past. "Andy threatened me all the time, called me names, pinched me so hard I would have bruises, whatever he could do to make me miserable. He would deliberately do things he knew would gross me out; put a snake in my bed or blow his nose on my pillow. One time he put dye in my shampoo and I had green hair for a week. That made school even more fun—freaky eyes, freaky hair—lots of insults to choose from for all of them."

"And your father turned a blind eye to all this?"

"Andy could do no wrong in my father's eye. According to him, it was simple sibling rivalry. Plus, he loved to poke fun at me. Call me Porky Pig or his favorite—Pinky the Pachyderm. He didn't care, Nathan."

She paced the room, her hands clenching and unclenching at her side. I let her pace, knowing she was gathering her thoughts.

"I figured out how little he cared when I was thirteen. I got sick. Really sick. After me begging for hours, because of the intense pain, my dad took me to the emergency room, but by then it was too late. My appendix had dislodged and ruptured. It was touch and go for a while, I was told. I have a huge scar from the surgery, since they couldn't find the appendix when they went in and had to keep cutting." She paused, lost in her own thoughts for a minute, before speaking again. "But the worst part was when I woke up alone. I was sick and confused, and there was nobody there." A tear ran down her cheek. "I wanted someone to be there, you know? To hug me and comfort me; tell me it was going to be okay."

She was quiet for a moment. I struggled to stay calm. I wanted to punch something and scream at the pain and loneliness she'd endured. However, I held in my feelings so she could share hers with me. I did reach out and capture one of her hands with mine, needing to feel that connection between us. Finally she spoke.

"I found out he told everyone at the hospital he had come home and found me ill, but the truth was he'd been there all day. He didn't want to be bothered." She looked at me with shame-filled eyes. "I was too embarrassed to tell anyone any different."

"Why were *you* embarrassed?"

"Because then everyone would know how I was unloved by my own family. How unworthy I was for my father to properly care for me. He didn't even care enough to come and see me the entire time I was in the hospital, except once to drop off a few personal things, and the day he picked me up to take me home." She exhaled. "And I covered the whole time. I'd tell people they had missed him, or he was working a double shift. I didn't want anyone to know how alone I was in the world."

"Kourtney," I whispered, outraged. Everyone in her life had failed to help keep her safe and happy. I was sad for the little girl who had been so alone and in need of proper care—and love.

"The saddest part was I hated going home. I was happier in the hospital despite the tubes and IV's. The nurses were nice and nobody bothered me. I could read and sleep and just . . . be." She played with the hem of her shirt. "But I did go home, and for the first time I realized things would never change—I would *never* be enough."

I shut my eyes at the prevalent pain in her voice. How did someone ever move past so much abuse and neglect?

"Things never got better? Even after they almost lost you?" I shuddered at the thought.

"No. They continued to ignore me and I stopped hoping they would ever love me." She paused. "They, ah, they bought me a welcome home gift, though."

"Oh?"

"They paid for a membership to Weight Watchers for me. They were convinced if I wasn't so fat my appendix would have been fine and I wouldn't have caused so much trouble. It was a great homecoming."

She wouldn't have caused so much trouble.

Because of their neglect she had almost died, and they made it her fault. At this exact moment, I wished I had Andy back under my fists. He wouldn't have left walking.

I sucked in a few deep breaths, trying to calm myself. My hands were clenched so tight I knew my knuckles were white, and I made the effort to relax them. "Your father is a heartless, spineless bastard. And your brother . . ." I dropped my voice. "I want to find him and beat the shit out of him." I stared at her, confused. "I don't understand why. You should have been thought of as a gift. Something precious." I thought of my sister and how I had always adored her. "You should have been loved, not hurt."

"Well, I wasn't. Andy told me once his life was great until I showed up. It was my fault our mom died—if I hadn't been sick again, she wouldn't have left the house. And my father told me more than once I was the greatest mistake he ever made. Both of them told me all the time I ruined their lives, and I owed them." She shrugged. "They still think I do. Hence Andy's last visit."

"You don't." I stepped forward, pulling her into my arms. "You never did, Kourtney. You were a child. Your mom was killed in an accident—it wasn't your fault. And your father, *fuck*, he was the adult. He should have protected you."

"They didn't love me. They still don't." Her lips began to tremble. "I was never enough, Nathan. I've never been enough for anyone. No matter what I did, they never tried to let me be enough."

"You're enough for me. You're everything I've ever wanted," I insisted, looking into her pain-filled eyes.

The tears that had been threatening began to run down her cheeks. "I'm not worthy of you, Nathan," she choked out. Her voice shook with the effort it took to speak.

"You are."

Her head shook from side to side. "I've never known what

it feels like to be . . . *that*. I've been alone my whole life."

"I'll teach you. You're not alone anymore; I'm not going anywhere."

A large gasping noise escaped her throat and she clapped a hand over her mouth, her eyes wild in panic. I tugged her hand away, my heart breaking at the sight of her trembling and vulnerable. "Let me in, Kourtney. Show me your pain." I cupped her cheek. "Let me look after you tonight."

I watched as she broke in front of me, painful sobs erupting from her chest. I tugged her to the sofa and brought her down beside me, cradling her in my arms as she wept. I hated hearing her sobs, but I knew she had to cry. She needed to let out the pain those bastards had inflicted on her for so many years.

Then I could prove to her she was worthy of being loved.

Chapter Twenty Two

WITH ONE LAST, SHUDDERING SIGH, Kourtney moved away.

I used my thumbs to remove some of the wetness on her cheeks, smiling in comfort when she opened her pain-clouded eyes. "Hey."

"I'm gonna go . . ." Her voice trailed off as she indicated the hall.

"I'll be here when you get back."

She stood up and walked to the door. Pausing, she turned back and looked at me; her expression dejected. "I wouldn't blame you if you weren't," she whispered and walked down the hall, shoulders bent.

I stared after her, worried, taking in her defeated stance. She was so sure I'd walk away, because she wasn't worth the effort to stay. There was only one thing that would prove her wrong, and that was time. I had plenty of that—a lifetime full of it— for her. I went into the kitchen, knowing she had coffee in the thermal jug, and poured us both a mug, adding cream. I moved back to the sofa, sipping at the warm beverage while I waited for her to return. I knew she needed a private moment to gather herself.

When she appeared, her eyes were dry, her hair brushed back into a ponytail, and she seemed calmer. I handed her the mug and we sat, listening to the rhythmic pattern of the rain outside.

"I'm sorry, Nathan."

I paused, the mug partway to my lips. "For what?"

"For crying . . . yet again. It seems that is all I have done since, well, since I came home. You must be quite tired of it."

"There's been a lot to deal with."

"I suppose. But I'm not usually that weak."

"You are not weak, Kourtney. My God, you can't see how amazing you are, can you?"

"I don't know what you mean."

I stood up, pacing to relieve some of my tension and collect my thoughts. I could feel Kourtney watching me, her gaze wary. I sat down beside her, gathering her hands in mine.

"Kourtney," I began, keeping my voice soft. "You don't see yourself the way I do. You're the strongest person I've ever met. Your childhood was horrendous, and I'm pretty sure I haven't heard the whole story yet. All you've known is pain and rejection. You could be the most bitter, angry person, but you're not." I tightened my grip on her hands. "You are such a giving, loving . . . *gentle* woman. You've overcome so much, baby."

She gazed at me in complete silence.

I met her gaze and continued. "You were abused, Kourtney. All your life."

"Not physically," she corrected in a whisper.

I shrugged. "Maybe not by your father, but I consider what your brother did to you physically abusive. He left marks on you. His pranks went way beyond sibling fun. But emotionally, they're both guilty. And your father . . ." I trailed off with a huff of anger. "His job as a parent was to protect and love you. He failed miserably at both. He failed *you*, Kourtney. Not the other way around." I cupped her cheek, hating the stark paleness of her skin. "You cry as much as you need to. It's time you let it out. It's not a sign of weakness. It's a sign you've tried to be strong, alone, for too long."

"I don't want to scare you away."

"You can't. Ever. I told you I'm not going anywhere. You're not alone anymore. If you let me, you'll never be alone again."

"I don't know how to do this, Nathan—I have no experience. I've never had someone care in the past," she spoke; nervousness evident. "I don't know how to be a partner. What if . . ."

"What if what?" I prompted.

"What if I'm so screwed up I can't be what you need?"

I leaned forward and kissed her. "You don't give yourself enough credit. I'm amazed how giving and loving you are; how selfless you are to those you don't even know. It's so instinctive with you. You're *exactly* what I need." I rubbed tender circles on her cheeks. "Kourtney, I wish your mind was like a computer and I could erase all the hateful things they said and did to you. That I could wipe away all the painful memories you carry." I shrugged in resignation. "But I can't. All I can do is try to overwrite them. Replace them with new ones. If you'll let me." I hesitated, holding my breath. "Will you let me?"

"I want to try."

"I know you're scared. This is new for me, as well. But I want this. I want you." I swallowed; my throat dry. "Do you feel the same way?"

I waited, the silent seconds dragging by.

Her quiet "yes," was the sweetest word I'd ever heard spoken.

I kissed her again. "Then we'll do it together."

Her beautiful eyes were filled with cautious wonder. "Together," she breathed, as if trying out the word.

I cradled her face in my hands, staring deep into her eyes. I wanted her to know I meant it. Every word. "Together," I promised.

"CHEFGIRL?"

Kourtney looked up from my knee. We had resumed our earlier positions on her sofa, content to listen to the rain as I stroked her hair and let her relax and calm herself.

"I don't want to upset you again, but can I ask you a few questions?"

She nodded, looking wary.

"Here's an easy one—how old are you?"

"Twenty-seven. You?"

"Thirty."

"Ah. An older man."

I leered at her. "Yep. Look out, little girl. I plan on having my wicked way with you."

She giggled. I ran my hand along her brow, my voice turning serious.

"You're pretty young to already be doing what you do, aren't you?"

She pursed her lips before answering me.

"Well, first off, my career choice doesn't take as long to accomplish as a practicing medical doctor—there's no residency to go through or as many years at school. As I told you earlier, I didn't have many friends or much of a life outside of school. But I loved learning, and I was pretty young when I decided what I wanted to do with my life. I always thought I wanted to be a doctor, so I volunteered in the summer at the hospital when I was a teenager. I thought it would be a great learning experience," she explained with a small grimace.

"Not for you?"

She shook her head. "I realized pretty fast the intensity of an active hospital, and dealing with the patients wasn't right for me. But I still wanted to do something medical—something that made a difference. One day I got sent to deliver a sample to the lab and I was instructed to wait for it. The technician was an older lady and nice. She saw I was interested and let me watch.

I was hooked. Afterward, I immediately went to the library and started researching things and knew what I wanted was to work behind the scenes. Help discover something to ease people's suffering."

She was quiet again. I let her gather her thoughts, stroking her hair. She looked up at me with hesitant eyes. When she spoke, her voice was quiet. "I like it when you do that."

"Yeah?"

"Yeah."

"Good. I like it, too. Your hair is so soft. I love how it feels under my fingers."

Shyly, she smiled at me. I couldn't resist bending down and kissing her; thrilled when she lifted her head to accept my caress. Her lips were warm and pliant as they moved with mine, sliding soft with each other. I kept it chaste and drew back, my thumb stroking her bottom lip.

"I like that best," I grinned down at her.

"Good." She wrinkled her nose adorably.

"Continue, please."

"As I got older I spent a lot of time at the library. Mrs. Braun was the head librarian and she was . . . Well, she was what made the difference in my life. She talked to me, helped me find the books I needed, encouraged me. She was the one person who seemed to *see* me, and the only adult who made me feel as if they cared. She always had time to talk to me, or listen, you know?"

"I'm glad you had her."

"I think she knew I didn't have a good home life and tried, in her own way, to make a difference."

"Kourtney . . ." I was unsure if I should even ask.

"What?"

"Why didn't anyone ever do anything to help you?"

She shrugged. "What were they going to do? I was fed, clothed; I went to school every day. My dad was the head of the local union and well thought of by almost everyone. My brother was outgoing and popular. If anyone suspected I had a less than happy home life, they never said anything." Her voice dropped to a mere whisper. "He didn't break the law, he ignored me. It wasn't as if they could make him love me, Nathan."

My heart clenched at her sad words and I shook my head. "He didn't only ignore you, Kourtney, he neglected you." I sighed. "But at school? Nobody there helped either?"

"The term *bullying* wasn't used the way it is today. I never complained, so who was going to come forward? I got good grades, I never showed any bruising or marks that weren't easy to explain by my own clumsiness, and Andy was smart enough he didn't mess with me in front of adults. I was a shadow. To them I was shy, not very sociable; another student who didn't fit in. Simple as that."

"They all failed you."

She was quiet for a moment. "Mrs. Braun was different, though. When I told her what I wanted to do, she encouraged me. As soon as I was able to, I worked every job I could: waiting tables, cleaning offices, tutoring other kids, anything to save money. And I studied a lot. Mrs. Braun even hired me at the library; although most of the time she made sure I studied." Kourtney smiled. "I trusted her, and I gave her all my money— she kept it safe for me, so Andy or Dad couldn't get to it. Not that they even noticed I wasn't home. I made sure they had their meals and the house was clean. They thought I was either at the library or tutoring—which I may have told them I did for free." Kourtney gave me a mischievous grin. "That was Mrs. Braun's idea. She didn't trust them at all."

I snorted. "The woman had good taste."

"She always made sure I had a little pocket money for things, but otherwise she put it all in the bank for me." She glanced up at me. "I think she added to it as well, but she never admitted to it."

"She sounds great. I'd like to thank her for what she did for you."

"She passed not long after I left for University."

"I'm sorry, baby."

"I still miss her." Her lip trembled a little, but she smiled. "She would have liked you."

"I think I would have liked her, as well."

Kourtney sighed. "I worked really hard, and I graduated high school a year early, with honors. I got a scholarship and went to University at seventeen. It was only a few hours down the road, but I was away from *them*. I lived in the dorms and ate Ramen noodles for months at a time, but I did it."

"I assume your father didn't help with the costs?"

Kourtney laughed. "No. When I told him I was leaving to go to University, he told me it was a waste of money since I would never amount to anything."

"That must have hurt."

"It did, but I was used to his insulting remarks. And for the first time in my life I ignored him and did it. I went and I worked; I studied and I paid for it myself, and I walked out of there with a PhD. in medical science."

I gazed down at her fondly. "I told you that you were brilliant."

"I wasn't brilliant enough."

"Why?"

"Just after I graduated, Andy called and told me Dad had fallen. I hadn't seen either of them since I left to go to school. I never went home for holidays or anything."

"I can't say I blame you."

"I didn't ever want to see them again, and with Mrs. Braun gone, there wasn't much reason to go back. But Andy kept calling and pressuring me, so I went to see him." She blew out a breath. "One thing led to another and before I knew it I was back there, looking after my father and brother."

I sighed in disappointment. "Kourtney."

"I know. I was stupid. I thought maybe this was the chance I had been waiting for. I was grown up, and they seemed to need me. I had been offered a job at a hospital in Mississauga and I thought I could look after Dad, work and maybe we would truly be a family," she admitted, sounding sad. "Maybe I would finally belong."

I stroked her cheek. "But it didn't happen, did it?"

"No. I didn't like the job and things at my father's hadn't changed. I was someone to look after them for free. My father was as distant and ungrateful as ever, and Andy—well, he was Andy. Nothing I did was ever right."

"Yeah. Charming."

Kourtney shifted and rolled toward me. I wrapped my arm around her, pulling her closer, sensing her need to be nearer to me. "What happened?"

"Dad wasn't getting better. In fact, he'd had some small strokes so he was becoming worse. He was getting to be more than I could handle and even his own doctor said he needed to be in a care home. He kept refusing, but I was running myself ragged between work and him. He wouldn't even accept home care to help me. I didn't know how I could keep going."

"What was Andy doing to help?"

Kourtney laughed. "Nothing. Absolutely nothing. He continued on with his life. Working at the garage, drinking with his buddies, making snide remarks about me."

"Fucker," I muttered.

"I got called out of the blue for a position at the Research Center here, which was where I had wanted to be after I graduated. When I was offered the job, I knew I couldn't do both—look after Dad and travel here every day." She shook her head. "I wanted this so much and for the first time ever, I put myself ahead of everyone else, and accepted the job. When I told them I was leaving and Dad would either have to pay for home care or go into the care facility . . . well, it was ugly. They said some awful things and Andy pushed me hard into the wall. I could barely move one shoulder for days." She looked up at me, her expression bereft. "I knew then, I would never be anything to them except a free maid. They didn't love me as a child, and they didn't love me as an adult."

I returned her sad gaze, tamping down my feelings of rage toward her asshole brother. He had better hope we never ran into each other in a dark alley. Or even a well-lit one. "What did you do?"

"I went upstairs, packed my few things and left after they went to bed. I started my new job, found a small apartment, and for the first time in my life, I lived on my own. I'd never had that kind of freedom before and I loved it."

"Did they bother you?"

"For a while. Andy would call and threaten me, telling me how much I owed them and how I had let them down, yet again. I had let Dad's doctor know I was leaving and he stepped in and got Dad into the care facility. He wasn't happy about it, but the calls stopped and I thought I was done with them. I hadn't heard or seen from Andy until he showed up the other day."

"Is your father still in the same care facility now?"

"Yes."

"And he wants to leave it?" I asked in a taut voice.

"Yes. He doesn't like it there."

I tightened my hands on hers. "I don't care. You're not going back there, Kourtney. You aren't free labor for them." I stared, my gaze intense. "I won't let them use or hurt you again."

"I know."

"You don't owe them anything. You know that, right? They have no control over you anymore."

"I'm trying, Nathan."

I cupped her face lovingly. "Good. I'll keep reminding you." I paused and changed my line of questioning; sensing she had answered enough questions about her family for now. "But I was wondering . . . What made you buy this place?"

"I had been saving for a while, thinking how much I would enjoy a place with a little yard. I didn't need anything big or fancy. My apartment was only about ten minutes from here. I used to come through the neighborhood all the time when I took pictures in the woods or went for a run. I saw the 'For Sale' sign go up and called the agent. I loved it right away and I put in an offer."

"I'm glad it was accepted."

She beamed. "Me, too."

"Yeah?"

"Yeah."

"Even if you ended up getting involved with someone who wants you to look after him, too?"

"We look after each other, Nathan. That's the big difference."

"There is another difference, Kourtney," I murmured.

"What?"

"This someone adores you."

Her eyes were huge in her sweet face. "You . . . adore me?"

I lifted my knees, pulling her up close. "So much, Chefgirl. So very much."

"I've never been adored before," she whispered brokenly. Her beautiful eyes swam with tears.

"Get used to it. It's not going to change." I covered her mouth with mine, showing her how much she was adored.

⌒〜

WE SPENT THE REST OF the evening quiet and together. Kourtney seemed to need to be close to me, and I was more than happy with that. I made her laugh with my magical microwave skills and heated up some leftovers for supper. Afterward, she curled into the corner of the sofa, reading, and I worked on my iPad; her legs draped over my lap. Outside, the rain continued to fall. Several times, I caught her gazing wistfully out the window. "What are you thinking?"

"I was wondering if the rain would stop, and I could go for a run in the morning."

"You run every day?"

"I try."

"I'm coming with you."

She rolled her eyes. "I had kinda figured that."

I squeezed her leg. "Good."

"You can't put your life on hold for me forever."

I looked at her worried expression and shook my head. "I'm right where I want to be. We look after each other, remember?" I took hold of her hand and reiterated in a quiet voice. "Together."

Her amazing eyes widened; the vivid colors brilliant as she gazed at me. "I like that," she whispered.

"Good."

I stood up and stretched. "It's been a long day." I held out my hand. "Bring your book and come to bed with me, Chefgirl."

She blushed, but accepted my hand. I tugged her off the sofa and into my arms, smiling as she accepted my embrace without tensing up for a change.

"I'm going to make sure everything is locked up, and I'll meet you there?" I kissed her forehead.

"Meet you there."

Chapter Twenty Three

A MOVEMENT CAUGHT MY EYE and I glanced over at Kourtney. She was propped up on her pillows, her dark hair spread around her, reading; or at least she was, until she had fallen asleep. Now her book was face down on her chest. Her reading glasses, with the tinted lenses I hated, had slid down her nose and her hand had fallen; it now rested palm up between us on the bed.

I pulled off my shirt, turned out the light, shut off my iPad and rolled over, propping myself up on my knees as I leaned over her. I closed her book and placed it on the nightstand, then tugged off her glasses and set them on top, frowning at them the whole time. I wondered if she would let me talk her into changing the lenses. Her unique eyes should be seen, not hidden from view. They were too beautiful to be concealed.

I sat back, staring down at her, drinking in her sweet face. It was still pale from the emotions of the day and her few freckles stood out against the pale of her skin; her beauty mark like a drop of ink spilled on paper. Her full lips were parted slightly, the tip of her tongue pressing on her bottom lip. I swallowed hard, battling the urge to lean forward and kiss her. She needed the rest. I couldn't, however, resist reaching up and tucking a thick strand of her rich hair away from her face. It fell into place with the other thick waves on the pillow. As my gaze fell back on Kourtney, I saw her eyes were now open and watching me.

"You fell asleep. I was moving your book."

"Didn't feel like my book you were moving."

"I can't resist your hair. It also needed to be moved."

The air around us grew thick with heat as Kourtney looked at me, a nervous longing filling her eyes. We stared at each other, the back of my neck prickling in intensity. "Your eyes are talking to me again, Chefgirl." My voice was husky with desire.

"What are they saying?" she breathed.

"That you want me to kiss you. Right now." I licked my bottom lip. "Hard."

"I hope you're listening."

I lunged forward, my hand curled around her head as my mouth found hers, and I did exactly that. The low whimper that escaped her throat only spurred me on. I gathered her to me as I ravished her sweet mouth. She wound her arms around me, pulling me close, and I groaned at the feeling of her soft body. Tonight, there was no hesitancy in her returning my passion. I reveled in the feelings she was sharing with me. Her hands were buried in my hair, tugging me closer. I began caressing her, stroking her passion, unsure how far she would let me take this, praying she wouldn't stop anytime soon. I ghosted my hands over her arms, down her torso and slipped under her T-shirt, finding her warm, supple skin that felt like satin under my fingers. Kourtney's hand flew down, covering mine and I felt her tense. I tore my lips away from her, dragging them up to her ear. "Don't, baby. Come back," I pleaded, nibbling on her lobe. "I want you so much."

Her shaking hand reached up and shut off her light, plunging the room into darkness. I sighed, prepared to pull back, surprised when Kourtney sat up. She pulled her T-shirt over her head, and lay back down, taking me with her.

A low moan tore from my throat at the feeling of her naked

warmth sliding along mine. My mouth found hers again, my tongue pressing, stroking, seeking hers in the sweetest of dances. We kissed until I was dizzy with desire. I ran my lips down her throat, laving, nipping, tasting her skin with my tongue, her quiet moans spurring me on. Her gasp was low when I found and cupped her heavy breasts in my hands, her nipples hardening as I stroked them gently with my thumbs, before feeling her tense up. I moved my mouth to her ear and whispered every sweet, loving thing I could think of to say. How lovely she was. How soft her skin felt under my fingers. How much I adored her, wanted her, and needed her. I felt her relax, and once again I reclaimed her mouth, kissing her deeply. Inch by inch, I allowed my touch to drift lower, caressing her, aching to feel all of her. I could feel her trembling and I cupped her cheek, panting. "Tell me to stop, Kourtney. I will."

"I don't want you to," she whispered. "I . . . I don't want to disappoint you."

"Never. You will never disappoint me," I assured her. "Let me love you, Kourtney. Let me make you mine."

"I want to be yours. All yours."

I cupped her face, bringing her mouth back to mine. "Let go for me, Kourtney. Let go," I encouraged. "Let me take care of you."

A shuddering sigh left her lips and her body quivered under my touch. I kept my caresses indulgent and light, until I felt her respond and her body begin to move under mine. I exhaled against her skin as I felt her desire winning over her nerves. "That's my girl," I praised her. "Feel . . . just feel right now." I lowered my head, capturing a nipple in my mouth. Kourtney cried out, arching up into me in pleasure. I moved to her other breast, loving how the full mounds felt under my tongue, their weight rich and heavy in my palms. I covered her mouth with mine; my hands slipped under her, settling on her rounded hips, pulling her up, wanting her to feel my desire. Her hands wrapped around my aching cock, and I groaned deep into her mouth, then slipped one hand between her thighs, finding her wet warmth. I swept my fingers over her, and began stroking, paying attention to her gasps and whimpers until she began undulating against my hand.

I worked off her underwear, needing to feel all of her. My own had disappeared at some point; I had no idea where they were, and I didn't care. Finally, we were molded together, skin to skin, hard meeting soft; our hands never ceasing their touches, our mouths seeking and finding purchase on sweat dampened skin, sweet lips and tender lobes. I trailed my fingers and lips over her, finding her dips and curves, loving each of them in turn, as her touches grew bolder and needier. Under my fingers, I could feel the beginnings of Kourtney's orgasm growing and I quickened my touch to push her over the edge. I wanted this moment. I wanted to feel her fall apart under my touch. To know it was my hand that brought her such pleasure.

"Let go, Kourtney." I groaned into her ear as she gripped my cock tighter. "Let me give you this, baby," I panted hard. "Come for me."

"Oh, *God* . . . Nathan . . . I've never . . . it's never felt . . . *oh God* . . ."

"*Kourtney* . . . baby . . . *let go.*"

"Please, Nathan," she begged. "I want you inside me, please. I want to feel you."

"Baby," I protested. This was for her.

"Please . . . please," she pleaded. "I need you."

I couldn't refuse her. I didn't want to refuse her. I wanted her too much. Slowly, I eased into her wetness, dropping my head onto her shoulder as I stilled, overwhelmed at the warmth and sensation surrounding me. I began to move, my hand finding and stroking her again, knowing neither of us was going to last much longer. I was lost in the pleasure of her tight, wet heat. She felt so good wrapped around me, but I refused to come before she did. I wanted this for her. I moved in and out of her with long, slow thrusts, drawing out her desire, drowning in my own. The deep need was overpowering and I struggled to hold back, needing to give her this pleasure. To show her how much she meant to me.

Her head fell back, her back arching as she shattered; her voice pleading as she cried my name loudly. She gripped me tight as if she never wanted to let go, her fingers digging into my skin, our eyes locked on each other. The moonlight bathed her face in a dim glow, the ecstasy of the moment making her even more beautiful. I stared at her in awe, thrilled to know I had given her this pleasure. I wanted to see her look this way every night. I wanted to be the one who made her this beautiful every time—to show her how much she was adored. I wanted her to feel nothing but pleasure from my touch and to know how worthy she was of such feelings.

My own orgasm tore through me, hard and fast. I roared her name into the dark, spilling deep into her as I shuddered; my body stilling, finally sated.

Unable to release her, I rolled over, tucking her up under my chin, holding her close. Small shudders racked her body and she sighed, one deep, lingering breath, before melting into me. The room was quiet except for the sounds of our breathing. We were both content, wrapped up in each other, as I nuzzled my lips into her thick hair and ghosted my hands up and down her back. I could feel her tracing my tattoo lazily and I sighed at the gentleness of her touch. I smiled as I thought about what had happened, the intense intimacy of being joined with her, unparalleled to anything I had ever experienced. Her sweet passion and warmth were even more ardent than I had hoped. The feeling of her warmth encasing me had been . . .

I sat up, startled, looking down at Kourtney in the dark. She shrank back at my sudden movement, gathering up the blanket up around her torso in defense. "What?" she whispered fearfully.

"Oh God . . . Kourtney . . . I hadn't planned . . . I didn't think . . . I was so caught up in you . . . in *us* . . ." I gripped my hair, angry at my own carelessness. "I didn't use any protection."

"I'm on birth control, Nathan. I have been since University," she assured me. "And it's been six years and I was tested, so I think you're safe."

I sighed in relief and lay down, pulling her back into my arms. "It's been a while for me, and I was covered." I brushed a kiss across her brow. "I wasn't only worried about me. We're both safe."

"I thought, ah, you had someone?"

"I haven't had a real relationship for a very long time. If you're referring to Sylvia, neither of us was looking for that sort of relationship. The last time I was with her was months ago." I exhaled deeply. "And you can't compare straight out sex to what happened between us."

"I don't understand."

I tilted her chin up so she could see how serious I was. "Sometimes sex is only a release, and for me, it has been. What we just did—what we *both* experienced, was way beyond that. We made love, Kourtney. I made you mine, and I belong to you. We connected on a level I didn't even know existed before now."

"Oh."

"You're the first woman I've felt like this about. The first person I've wanted more with." I kissed her, keeping my lips gentle. "Tell me you know that, baby. There's something strong between us. Tell me you feel it."

"I do."

"Does it still scare you?"

"A little. But . . . I like it."

"Good." I kissed her neck, smiling at her shiver. "Because like the attack on the sofa earlier? I plan on this happening—a lot."

She sounded hesitant. "So, it was okay for you?"

"*Kourtney*, it was more than okay. It was fucking amazing. *You* were amazing." I kissed her again. "You were everything I could have wanted . . . and more." I nuzzled her hair. "All the negative thoughts you had before? Forget them. You felt perfect wrapped around me. Perfect."

I felt her blush in the dark, her face and chest growing warm against my skin. "And we're only gonna get better, Chefgirl. You know, practice makes perfect. And I'm all for perfect."

"Oh. My."

I nipped her earlobe. "Brace yourself, baby. I'm only getting warmed up. Tonight was incredible, but I promise to show you more of my . . . *turbo*. I won't rev so fast next time."

Her shoulders shook as she giggled, snuggling close. "I look forward to it."

I grinned into her skin.

"Good."

I WOKE UP EARLY, BLINKING as I realized where I was and who was nestled on my chest. I looked down at Kourtney, smiling. I lifted a finger, drawing her wild hair away from her face. As I tucked the wayward curl behind her shoulder, I frowned at the T-shirt she was now wearing. When the hell had she gotten up and put it on? I had woken in the deep of the night spooned with her, desire filling me at the feel of her soft figure pressed into mine. Slowly, I had woken her with kisses and caresses, waiting until she was writhing and pleading before hitching her leg over mine and entering her from behind. I had kept my thrusts slow and deep, wanting to draw out her pleasure, loving her small whimpers and how she moaned my name as she came. My own orgasm had followed, hot and intense as I sighed out her name. When I fell asleep we had both been naked, molded together, and I had liked it. I much preferred her silky skin to the feel of the T-shirt. I hadn't felt her move after we had fallen asleep the second time.

With a start, I realized I had also slept through the night without having a nightmare. I knew, without a doubt, it was Kourtney's closeness that had brought me such peace. I kissed her forehead in silent gratitude for her unknown gift. Her eyes fluttered open, their sleep-filled gaze clearing as she blinked up at me, a sweet, shy smile appearing on her face.

"Hi," she whispered.

"Hi, yourself." I smirked. "All wrapped around me again, aren't you? You can't stay away."

She looked down, blushing, and began to pull away, but I held her tight. "Oh, no. You aren't going anywhere yet. You feel far too good to be moving."

She pushed half-heartedly on my chest. "You're just as wrapped around me."

I nodded. "True." I tugged on the sleeve of her T-shirt. "Would you like to explain how this magically reappeared back on you? Last time I checked it was on the floor somewhere. It looked better there; if you ask me," I reached down for the hem, pulling on it. "What are you—some sort of strange T-shirt ninja? You slip around at night putting T-shirts *back* on people? I suppose I'm lucky mine isn't in place!"

Her sweet giggles filled the air as she swatted my hands, trying to get away from me. "I couldn't find it!" She gasped between giggles. "Or I would have!" I continued my assault on her velvety skin. "Stop it!" she begged, rolling away and off the bed where she stood, clutching both the T-shirt and blanket to her chest. Her eyes widened as she took in the fact I was completely naked . . . and very happy to see her.

Grinning, I stretched out, not failing to see the desire in her eyes as she stared at me, her bottom lip now caught in her teeth. "Ah. Seducing me again, Chefgirl? I approve of how . . . *persistent* you are." I winked, reclining on one elbow. "See something you like, Kourtney?" I asked huskily, meeting her wide eyes, and waggling my eyebrows.

Her mouth opened, and her head shook wildly. "I . . ." She looked at me, rumpled, beautiful, and completely panicked. "I'm going for a run!" she blurted. She sprinted to the bathroom door, slamming it behind her. I was left rolling on the bed in laughter at her reaction, despite the fact I had a raging hard-on and the one thing I knew would appease it, had turned tail and run.

I sat up and sighed, spotting my boxers on the floor and grabbing them, trying to ignore my erection. She was still so shy, and yet I couldn't resist teasing her. I loved seeing her emotions play out in her expressive eyes and watching her react to my ludicrous behavior. I shook my head as I went to find my sweats and T-shirt I had left in the guestroom, pulling them on and finding a pair of socks in the laundry room. I needed to remember how new this was to her, despite her moments of bravado. When I came to the front door, Kourtney was lacing up her running shoes and I kneeled beside her to put mine on.

"You have little feet, Chefgirl," I commented, holding my foot along hers. "I noticed your socks were midget-sized yesterday."

She frowned up at me. "They're a normal size, Nathan. Not all of us have huge clown feet, you know."

"Well, you know what they say about big feet . . ." I teased and bent over to nip her ear. "And I think you saw proof of that statement last night—and this morning."

She scrambled to her feet, staring down at me, her cheeks ablaze in color. Then she giggled and grinned impishly. "That is true," she mused, as she grabbed her keys and opened the door. I followed her out and watched as she locked up.

Her face broke out into a mischievous smirk as she turned to me. "I can vouch for the fact, you know, and what they say is right." She paused and allowed her eyes to drift over me. I felt my cock twitch at her leering appraisal. "You do have a very large . . . *pair of socks*. I noticed when I did the laundry. Impressive, Nathan." With a lewd wink she took off running, leaving me behind her, laughing.

And completely horny.

Chapter Twenty Four

IT WASN'T A RUN. AS far as I was concerned, it was nothing but a long, torturous session of foreplay. Watching Kourtney in front of me, her hips sashaying back and forth while she ran didn't help with my erection. All I could think about was how her smooth flesh had felt under my hands as I held her tight while thrusting into her warmth last night. When she twisted her head to glance at me, all I wanted to do was pull her into the closest clump of trees, thread my fingers through her wild tresses and kiss her until she begged me to stop. Or let me fuck her. Either way I'd be a happy man. When she turned around, jogging backward, to ask me if I was okay when I stumbled, due to my mind being somewhere other than on my feet, I saw her full breasts ripple under her T-shirt, which only caused me to trip again as I grunted out a brief response. The sound of her panting, as she pushed us both harder, sent me back into the dark of the night when I had been buried deep inside her and her breathless moans were all I could hear.

I grabbed her arm long before the point I knew she used as her mid-marker for her runs and steered her back toward the house. Running with a hard-on was starting to be agonizing, and downright dangerous. If I didn't have her alone soon, the neighbors were going to get one hell of a show. She frowned in confusion, but something about the intense look on my face made her decide to stay quiet and she kept running, not slowing down until we approached the house. She proceeded to do some stretching, causing my cock not only to harden to the point of being painful, but solidify the fact she was, indeed, trying to kill me.

"I need a shower," she announced while digging in her pocket for the house keys.

I stared at the back of her head, my eyes narrowed. I forgot about taking it slow with her. I needed her—*now*. My hand closed over hers as she put the key in the lock. I yanked her back to me, my aching erection ground into her back as I lowered my mouth to her ear.

"I don't think so, Chefgirl." I growled. "After the little show you put on? I'm gonna give you ten seconds, and I'm coming after you. Wherever I find you, is where I'm gonna take you. You understand?"

"I didn't do anything," she squeaked in protest.

"You've been teasing me since you woke up." I nipped at her ear. "Talking about my large socks . . . eyeballing me." I grabbed her hips, holding her close as I rubbed up against her. "Making sure I got an eye-load of this sweet ass in front of me the whole time you were running. Never mind your little backward trick." I cupped her breasts, stroking their fullness over her shirt, the nipples hardening under my touch. "Did you think I wouldn't notice these?" I squeezed them, and her breath caught in her throat.

"I was only running," she objected feebly, but I felt her shiver.

I turned the handle and opened the door, then coaxed her forward.

"Ten seconds. You have ten seconds."

The door slammed behind her and I heard the lock turn. I snickered since the key was still in the lock so it wasn't going to stop me. I opened the door and stepped inside, the cool air welcome to my overheated skin from the run. But nothing was going to cool the desire I had burning inside of me until I was buried deep within Kourtney. I stood, listening, but could hear nothing. "Nice try," I called out. "You may have bought yourself another few seconds, but that's all! I'm still coming after you."

Only silence met my ears and I grinned. She was hiding, but she couldn't have gotten far. I sauntered into the kitchen and filled a glass of cold water, gulping it down as my eyes swept the room. I peered into the living room but realized there was nowhere there for her to hide from me. While I was filling the glass again, my eyes fell on the closed laundry room door, which I knew had been open earlier when I had grabbed my socks. I drank down the water, eyeing the door, then refilled the glass. Walking over, I eased the door open, scanning the seemingly empty room in the dimness. But, I could hear her—muffled little gasps were coming from behind the door where her small chest freezer was located, and I knew, without a doubt, she was huddled on the top. I stepped farther into the room, flicked on the light and hooked the door with my foot, slamming it shut. I turned to face Kourtney, who was pushed into the corner as far as she could get, her hands covering her mouth as she stared at me, her eyes wide.

I handed her the full glass of cold water. "You need to drink this."

She hesitated, then reached out with a shaking hand to take the glass. Her shoulders relaxed a little, thinking I had only been teasing her. I waited until she had begun to sip the water before leaning forward, dropping my voice again. "You need to be hydrated for what is gonna happen here." I tapped the top of the freezer. "Right . . . *here.*"

She froze with the glass partway to her lips. I reached over and tilted the glass to her lips. "Drink, Kourtney. Drink it all." I leaned closer. "You'll need it."

I watched the liquid disappear, my eyes never leaving her face. I licked my lips in anticipation, smirking when I saw her hand tremble again.

"I need a shower," she whispered, glancing down at her drenched T-shirt.

I moved closer. "No. I want you like this." I nuzzled her neck, my tongue swirling on her damp skin, tasting the salty flavor. "Hot, sweaty . . . *wet.*"

She whimpered.

"You done?" I asked, indicating the empty glass she had clutched in her hand.

"I'm still thirsty?"

I shook my head. "It'll have to wait now, Kourtney. I've been thirsty for much longer."

"For what?"

I leaned forward, wrapping my hands around her thighs, and pulling her forward to the edge of the freezer. "You."

She gasped.

I moved closer. "Do you want me to stop?" I asked. I didn't want her afraid. I never wanted to do anything to frighten her.

"No," she breathed.

"Good. Now . . . where was I?"

I grabbed her knees, spreading her legs wide and jerked her flush to me. Her gaze flew up to mine as she felt my cock; hard and ready. "I didn't do anything," she said.

"This is how you affect me." I cupped the back of her head, burying my fingers into her thick hair, covering her mouth with mine and kissing her, my tongue stroking and exploring her mouth. I wrapped an arm secure around her, lifting her a little, then yanked her shorts off and down her legs so fast, she had no time to protest. I grinned against her damp neck. "I'm another kind of ninja. Except I do it the right way; I *take off* the clothes." My hand stroked her hip, finding bare flesh and I stilled, pulling back. I arched an eyebrow at her knowingly. "Commando today, my lovely Chefgirl? How . . . *fortunate* . . . for me."

Her cheeks flushed. I reached down to grab her T-shirt. I wanted her naked. Her hand gripped mine, her head shaking wildly. "I want it on," she said timidly.

"I want it off."

"Turn the light off, please," she pleaded.

"I want to see you," I insisted.

Her face paled as pure panic flooded her features, her eyes filling with tears. "No, Nathan, please . . ." Her voice trembled.

I stilled at the fear I heard coming from her tone. I cupped her face gently, tilting it up to look at me. "Hey. Stay with me, Chefgirl. I'm not going to hurt you."

"I need my shirt . . . please."

I looked at her, confused.

"*Please.*"

"You can have your shirt, but I want the lights on," I compromised, remembering my promise to myself to allow for her shyness. I could work with that. "I want to watch you come," I added, my voice husky with desire.

"Okay," she breathed.

I captured her mouth again, needing her to just feel, to forget everything but my touch and what it did to her. I held her tight and was soon rewarded when her legs wrapped around my hips. Her hands restlessly gripped my shoulders and arms, then slid into my hair, holding me close. I kissed her until I felt her complete surrender to me—her body soft and trusting in my arms, her entire being lost in the moment. Using one hand, I yanked my sweats down, and my erection sprang free. I groaned when I felt Kourtney's hand wrap around me, stroking and pumping, and I bucked up into her touch. I covered her hand and dragged my cock through her heat, coating myself in her wetness. We both groaned at the sensation.

"I'm going to fuck you now, Chefgirl." I murmured against her ear.

Smiling at the strangled noise that came from her throat, I surged forward, burying myself in her wet heat. Her muscles tightened around me, and I hissed in pleasure at the intensity of her embrace. "Hold tight, baby."

I kept one arm wrapped around her waist, bracing the other on the wall behind her. I began thrusting in long, hard strokes; my raging desire staved off too long to even try and be gentle. Kourtney's head fell back, small pants escaping her lips as I took her. The need to fill her, to claim her as mine was prevalent. Nothing else mattered, nothing but this moment, these sensations and the woman causing them. I buried my head into her shoulder as I continued to drive into her powerfully, her moans a sweet noise all around me.

Nothing had ever felt this good. No one ever made me feel the way she did. I'd never wanted anyone as much as I wanted this woman. "Mine, Kourtney." I groaned into her ear. "Tomorrow . . . every time you move . . . every time you sit . . . you're going to remember who you belong to." I shuddered at the intensity of the feelings coursing through me. "*Say it . . . tell me you're mine.*"

"Yours." She whimpered.

I growled in agreement, bending her back and slipping into her even deeper, both of us moaning. The sounds of our sweat-soaked skin, echoed in the small room. Kourtney's voice, chanting my name like a prayer, was like wild music to my ears. Our bodies flowed and melded in perfect harmony, and I knew I would never have enough of her.

I could feel my orgasm beginning; my balls tightening, my spine tingling as I fought to hold it off, wanting her with me.

"So . . . fucking . . . good," I panted in her ear. "You feel so good, baby. Come for me, Kourtney. I want to hear you."

Her hands tightened in my hair, as she succumbed to her pleasure; the sexiest sound I had ever heard filling the air before she cried out my name. I watched her fall apart, her body arched and taut, her beautiful eyes wide in wonder, cheeks flushed and damp. The sight alone was enough to push me over the edge. I let go of the wall and gripped her as I came; all the air left my body and I gasped out the one word that mattered.

"*Kourtney.*"

I held her, my face buried in the nape of her neck, as I dragged in oxygen and the scent of her skin. Tremors shook my body, the aftermath of my orgasm, and I struggled not to collapse on top of her. I knew I should ease my grip or let her go, but I couldn't. I needed to hold her and feel her touch. Any space between us was too much right now. I shivered at the feeling of Kourtney's gentle hands stroking my neck and her sweet voice in my ear whispering loving endearments. Slowly, I felt sanity returning and I moved away, our eyes locking. I searched her face for any sign of unhappiness, sighing in relief when I found none.

I cupped her cheek, my hand trembling now. "You okay, Kourtney? Was it too much?"

She turned her face to kiss my palm, her shy expression saying everything.

My legs gave out and I crumbled to the floor, wrapping my arms around Kourtney's legs and resting my head in her lap, panting. "*Jesus*, baby. That was fucking . . . unbelievable. I swear you're gonna kill me."

Her hands stroked through my hair. "I didn't do anything," she protested again, confused.

My shoulders began to shake with laughter. I pushed myself up with my wobbly arms and kissed her hard. "You have no idea, do you?" I asked, astonished. "If this is how you affect me with *nothing*, I think I might be afraid of what you could do to me if you actually tried."

She shook her head. "Nuts," she whispered.

I kissed the end of her nose. "Just about you, Chefgirl. Just about you."

She giggled, and I gently brushed the hair over her shoulders. "Go have your shower, Kourtney. I'll clean up in here, and have one."

"Okay." She hesitated, accepting my hand to help her slip off the freezer.

I watched her leave, feeling sad. I wanted to go shower with her, but she didn't offer. I had to be patient until she was comfortable. I needed to find the right way to make her relax and fully trust me.

One day, we'd get there.

Chapter
Twenty Five

K OURTNEY GOT UP FROM THE table, her long hair still damp from her shower, and walked over to plug in the external backup device I had given her into the wall socket. She grabbed the coffee pot, sat down and filled our cups as she smiled at me, looking shy. I glanced back at the drive, smiling back at her.

"Chefgirl, what are you doing?"

She gave me a strange look. "It's Sunday, Nathan. You told me to plug it in every Sunday and backup my computer. I've done it every week, the way you told me to do."

"But your laptop is in front of you."

"Okay?" She frowned, confused.

"When I said plug it in, I meant plug it into your laptop. With the laptop turned on."

She sat, looking between the backup drive, sitting on the shelf, and her laptop on the table. "Oh. I guess that makes sense." She peered at me, looking sheepish, her cheeks beginning to flush. "I thought it was wireless or something."

"Ah, no."

"Told you I would fuck things up."

I burst out laughing, dragged her chair closer and enveloped her in my arms. I nuzzled the top of her head, amazed at how happy this woman made me. "It's okay—nothing is fucked. I should have explained better. I'll show you now." I pulled her teeth away from her bottom lip and kissed her. "Give me your laptop and bring the drive over here."

I was still chuckling as I showed her how to plug it all in. I got the backup running and frowned. "Kourtney? Your password; emptiness? Really? That's not the *you* I know."

She shrugged. "It's what my life felt like most of the time . . . before."

"Before?"

She smiled as she watched me type away. "Before us."

"*Us*. I like that. You want to change it?" I asked, dropping a kiss to her head

"Sure."

I brought up the directory, found her settings, then slid the laptop over to her. "Okay. Type in the new one."

She thought about it, and typed in something. "Hit return and you'll have to re-enter it," I explained.

She grinned as she did so, before sliding the computer back to me.

"You made it something you can remember without a problem?"

She nodded, her face beaming. "I'll never forget it."

"Good."

"Do you want to know what it is?" A mischievous grin lit up her face, making her eyes dance in glee.

I shrugged, even though I definitely wanted to know what was making her look that way. "If you want to tell me, sure, I'd love to know."

Her beautiful eyes glowed as she giggled. "Laundryroom1."

With a low groan, I crashed my lips to hers. I couldn't kiss her deep enough.

I wouldn't forget it either.

I LOOKED UP FROM THE paper and frowned. "You're squinting." I could see the crinkles at the corner of her eyes.

She sighed and looked up from her book. "I know. I have to see the eye doctor next week."

"Time for new glasses?"

She nodded.

I hesitated, but decided to ask. "Kourtney? Can I ask you to do something for me?"

"Anything."

"Don't tint your lenses. Please."

She removed her glasses and looked at them. "Why does it bother you so much?"

Sighing, I laced my fingers with hers. "I hate that it's been drummed into your head that something so beautiful should be hidden. Your eyes captivate me, Chefgirl. I like seeing them. I want to be able to see them every time I look at you."

She hesitated, staring down at her glasses. "I always have three pairs."

"Could you try one without tint? Just for home?" I drew in a deep breath. "For me?"

"Is this part of your overwriting, Nathan?"

"It is. I want to change all the negative stuff you think is true. I want to show you how wrong they were." I sighed. "About so many things."

She nodded. "Okay, then. For you."

Lifting her hand, I kissed the smooth skin on the inside of her wrist.

I'd let her do it for me. Until she was ready to do it for herself.

"ARE YOU MAKING LOTS OF meatballs?" I asked, watching Kourtney move around her kitchen.

She giggled. "I make lots of everything since I started feeding you, Tomcat."

I laughed and shrugged my shoulders. "Told you. I'm still a growing boy." I leaned back in my chair. "I assume you didn't cook this way before?"

She stopped adding whatever ingredient she had in her hand and pursed her lips. "When I was on my own I would cook one big meal, and heat up leftovers the rest of the week. The first night I fed you I had cooked extra for that reason, which is why I had lots to share." She smiled at the memory. "I had just gotten the barbeque and I was excited to use it. Of course, I had no idea the guy next door would be even more excited."

"Excited didn't cover it, Chefgirl. I was fucking ecstatic." I looked at her, curious. "Why did you keep feeding me?"

"You seemed . . . lonely. You were always so funny, but I sensed you were alone as I was—and it was fun to cook more often, as well as for someone." She grinned. "You were so complimentary and grateful. It was nice to have someone to care for who appreciated me doing so."

I stood up and went over, pulling her into my arms. "I was lonely. I didn't know how lonely until you came into my life. I did appreciate it then. I do now. I love how you take care of me."

"You take care of me, too. No one has ever done that."

I could hear the emotion welling up in her voice and I knew I needed to distract her. I kissed the tip of her nose and turned her back to the bowl in front of her. "Damn right I do. Now get to it, woman. Those meatballs aren't gonna make themselves and I want them."

I sat down as Kourtney's laptop chimed, indicating she had a message. I looked at the screen. "Um, *LabGoddess* is messaging you."

"It's Annie. Can you see what see wants?"

"You're sure? It may be private."

"Answer her for me, Nathan. My hands are covered in

meat."

> *WhyteElephant: Hi, Annie, it's Nathan. Kourtney is elbow deep in meatballs.*

> *LabGoddess: Hi Nathan. Never thought I'd hear Kourtney was elbow deep in any kind of balls. You must be a good influence. Keep it up.*

I laughed as I responded.

> *WhyteElephant: LOL. I'll do my best.*

> *LabGoddess: I wanted to tell Kourtney to keep Tuesday night open. It's time for a girls' night. Information needs to be shared. Tell her she can't say no this time.*

I chuckled as I read the message to Kourtney.

She groaned. "She's going to pump me for information about *you*."

I nodded. "No doubt. She was rather surprised to see me on Friday. She didn't seem to know I existed," I teased.

"I didn't know you existed like that, so I had nothing to tell her."

"Do you know now, Kourtney?"

She blushed. "I think so."

"I'll tell her it's a date?"

"Okay."

> *WhyteElephant: Kourtney is looking forward to it.*

> *LabGoddess: Great. You driving her to work again?*

> *WhyteElephant: Yes.*

> *LabGoddess: Okay, I'll drive her home after. Or Jason will if we have too much to drink. He is always on standby.*

> *WhyteElephant: Good plan.*

> *LabGoddess: Have a great day.*

> *WhyteElephant: Any day with Kourtney is a great day.*

LabGoddess: I think I'm going to like you.

There was nothing I could really say, so I left her with a smile.

WhyteElephant: :)

I read Kourtney the conversation, chuckling as she rolled her eyes and shook her head. "Sounds as if you're going to have some fun on Tuesday, Chefgirl."

"Annie is a great person. I like her a lot."

"Why did she tell me not to let you say no this time?"

Kourtney shrugged, looking sheepish. "She and I are friends at work, but we've never really expanded it outside that time. She is busy with Jason, the wedding and her family. But she's been trying to get me to go out with her for a while now, and we did have a good time in Vancouver."

I was baffled. "Why wouldn't you go out before now?"

Kourtney's cheeks turned pink and she kept her eyes downcast. "Annie is really pretty and outgoing. I always felt"— she hesitated—"like *less* . . . as if I wasn't good enough to be her friend."

I walked over and held her close. "You are good enough. You are more than good enough," I insisted, kissing her neck. "You need to know people don't look at you the way your family did, Kourtney. We all see what an amazing, lovely person you are, inside and out. You need to start believing that, too."

"I'm trying."

"So you'll go? Relax and have a good time?"

She looked over her shoulder. "Yes."

I kissed her soft cheek. "Good."

"What will you do?"

"Hopefully eat some spaghetti leftovers."

"Will you, ah, stay here?"

"Whatever you're comfortable with, Kourtney," I assured her.

"I'd like knowing you're here when I get home," she murmured.

"I'd like that, too. I like being here with you."

"Really?"

I grinned widely. "Yeah. Your food is way better than mine."

She chuckled. "Will I ever get to see your place?"

"Any time. I need to tidy up. You know, make sure the wife and kids are out of the way first. Otherwise it might get . . . awkward."

She turned sharply, and I winked. She shook her head, chuckling. "Nuts."

I turned her around so she was facing me. "Just about you, Chefgirl," I promised, kissing her until we were both breathless.

KOURTNEY LAUGHED AS I TICKLED her red, sock-covered feet that were draped over my knees. We were sitting on the sofa, she in her usual corner and me right beside her. I still couldn't stop touching her. I had orbited around her all day, needing to be close and I was constantly drawn to her lips. Every chance I got, I kissed her. Thankfully, she seemed to feel the same way, returning my caresses with her own. "How many more questions are you going to ask me?"

I chuckled, relaxing back into the sofa. "I'll keep asking until I know all there is to know about my girl. You've asked some yourself."

She had managed to get a few queries in, but I was far more interested in her. I wanted to know every little piece to the puzzle that made up Kourtney Whyte. I had been bombarding her since lunch. Favorite color. Book. Movie. Hobby. Ice Cream. Time of day. Music. Anything I could think to ask her that didn't include her family, or make her think I was trying to overwrite anything. I simply wanted to know more about *her*.

She sighed, looking content and relaxed. Silence fell between us, the quiet surprisingly welcome and comfortable. The smell of her spaghetti sauce was drifting into the room from the kitchen, soft music playing from the stereo and we were cuddled together in our little bubble, while outside the rain had started again. I couldn't remember the last time I had felt this relaxed . . . or this much as if I was where I finally belonged—as if I was home. It was all because of the remarkable woman sitting beside me; her eyes warm as she gazed at me. Absently, I picked up her hand, playing with her fingers, marveling how small her hands were in comparison to mine. When I closed my fingers around them, they disappeared. Grinning, I picked up one of her feet and studied it.

"What size feet do you have, Kourtney?"

"Six."

"Ah. I wear a thirteen."

She chuckled. "I know. Big feet."

I grinned back. "Midget socks. How tall are you anyway? Do you break the five foot mark?"

She sat up straighter. "I am five foot two and a quarter, for your information."

Smirking, I tweaked her nose. "Sorry, didn't mean to dis the two inches there."

"And a quarter," she insisted haughtily.

"I'm six three, Kourtney. I have twelve plus inches on you."

"Funny, I thought that's what you had in me earlier," she quipped back. Her hand flew up, covering her mouth, her face reddening, and her eyes widening as she realized what she had said.

I gaped at her, throwing back my head as I howled with laughter. She was so fucking brilliant.

She jumped off the sofa. "Come back here, I'll show you twelve plus inches," I laughed as she took off down the hall.

I struggled to my feet and followed her, stopping in the doorway of her room. She was sitting on her bed against the headboard, her cheeks flushed; still embarrassed and still fucking brilliant. I leaned on the doorframe, taking her all in. "You know, Chefgirl, you're not so good at this hiding game," I informed her, my voice husky to my own ears. "You run away, but I find you every time."

She bit her lip, unknowingly sexy in her shy embarrassment.

"Maybe I wasn't trying to hide."

I stepped forward, locking my gaze on her. "Are you trying to seduce me again, Kourtney?"

Her eyes glowed in the dim light of the late afternoon. "Seems to me I don't have to try too *hard*." She glanced at the growing bulge in my jeans. "Or at least so I've been told."

I tugged the shirt over my head and crawled up the bed toward her. Leaning forward, I stopped short of her tempting, full lips, feeling her warm breath mingle with mine.

"No, Chefgirl. You don't."

Then I kissed her. And this time I didn't stop.

I WOKE UP GRADUALLY; KOURTNEY nestled tight to my chest. Outside, the rain was coming down hard again, the wind wild in the trees, thunder rumbling in the distance. Kourtney began to stir in my arms. "Go back to sleep, Chefgirl. You're not going out in this weather," I murmured into her hair. She didn't even open her eyes as she burrowed deeper into me.

"Good. Don't want to," she mumbled and slipped back into sleep.

Listening to the rain, I was grateful I had gone next door and brought over a bunch of my things after dinner last night. I didn't want to have to get up and go over the fence this morning. We hadn't discussed how long I was staying, although I was perfectly content with the thought of never leaving. I was sure Kourtney had other ideas, though. I sighed, shut my eyes and allowed myself to drift for a few minutes; memories of yesterday flowed through my mind, bringing a contented sigh to my lips. Our passionate morning had eased into a warm, lazy, love-filled afternoon mostly spent in bed and had been followed by a wonderful evening. The day had closed with Kourtney tucked into my arms. I didn't want it to end, but I knew we now had to get back to reality.

I woke her up with slow kisses, making her giggle as I

begged for coffee and breakfast before we left; something I never got when I woke up next door alone.

The car ride was quiet, Kourtney's hand resting in mine the entire drive to her office. I parked by the front doors and started unbuckling my seat belt. "What are you doing?" she questioned with a frown.

"Taking you in."

She shook her head. "No, Nathan. He isn't here. I'm safe and I don't want to be walked in like a child."

"I wasn't doing that, Kourtney."

She stared at me, eyebrows raised, and I shrugged. "Okay, I didn't realize I was doing that." I kissed her, enjoying the feel of her full mouth against mine, pulling away regretfully. "Can I at least *watch* you walk in?"

She rolled her eyes, but didn't say no. She hesitated when she got to the door of the office, looking over her shoulder as she bit her lip. I climbed out of the car, and went over to her, not wanting her to get any damper in the rain. As I approached her, I held out my hand and she took it. I brought her close, cupping her cheek. "What's wrong?"

She shook her head. "Nothing. I . . . I wanted to say thank you, and have a good day."

She looked so unsure and vulnerable, and I wanted her to smile. I loved seeing her happy. Bending down, I kissed her cheek and put my lips close to her ear "Nobody's seen us yet, Chefgirl. You want to get back in the car, call in sick and stay in bed all day with me?" I waggled my eyebrows at her to make her laugh. "I'll let you play doctor. You can examine my stethoscope."

She giggled and swatted at my chest. "Stop it."

"I'm serious. I'm pretty sure I have a raging fever only you can cure," I teased, capturing her mouth with mine in a searing kiss. I forgot we were standing in front of her building. The only thought on my mind was making her smile again.

"Well, for the love of God, I think there is more information sharing needed than I thought," an amused voice spoke from beside me, startling both me and Kourtney.

We drifted apart to see Annie standing there, watching us with a wide, devilish smirk on her face. Kourtney's head dropped to my chest. I could feel the warmth of her cheek, but grinned back at Annie as I dropped another kiss to the top of Kourtney's head.

"Sending my girl off with a smile."

Her smirk widened. "Maybe I should send you out with Jason tomorrow night. You could give him some pointers on that, because it looks as if you did one hell of a fine job."

I winked. "Anytime."

I lifted Kourtney's chin and kissed her affectionately. "I'll pick you up tonight, okay?"

"Okay." Her vibrant, shy eyes blinked up at me, and I had to kiss her one last time, before Annie grabbed her arm, and dragged her away.

"God, the two of you, it's only a few hours. You'll survive."

I laughed watching her pull Kourtney through the doors. I lifted my hand to wave, as she looked over her shoulder one last time.

"Have a good day, dear. See you tonight," I called out.

"You too, Nathan," Annie called back sarcastically. "I'll make sure she makes it through without you."

I got back in the car, grateful there was someone who would watch out for Kourtney when I wasn't around. I knew she would be fine.

Nonetheless, for the first time in so long, the end of the workday couldn't come fast enough. I wanted to be able to go home. Because when I went home, it would be with Kourtney beside me.

And the thought of that made *me* smile.

Chapter Twenty Six

"**W**HAT'S THIS?" I ASKED AS Kourtney handed me a small bag Monday night, looking nervous and chewing her lip.

"It's, ah, it's, well, I thought maybe you would want it. Annie took me out at lunch to get it, but you don't have to keep it . . ." She trailed off, her eyes glancing everywhere but at me.

Opening the bag, I turned it upside down. My eyes widened when I saw the chef hat shaped key ring and the shiny silver key attached to it lying in my hand. I looked up at Kourtney, who was watching me with anxious eyes. I smiled as I kissed her. "Are you sure about this, Chefgirl? You'll never get rid of me if I have a key."

"I don't want to get rid of you." She looked up at me from under her long eyelashes.

I kissed her again. "Good." I leaned back, smiling widely as I held up the key. "I like going over the fence, but this will come in handy when it's raining."

"Your choice, Tomcat. You can use the fence or the door when you come over—whichever you want."

I frowned. "When I come over? Are you telling me you want me to leave, Kourtney? You've had enough of me?" My stomach clenched as I waited for her answer.

"No! I don't want that! I don't want you to go!"

I sighed in relief. I wasn't ready to go. The truth was, I didn't think I'd ever be ready to go.

She looked at me sadly. "I can't expect you to stay here indefinitely though, Nathan. I know you're worried about Andy, but eventually we have to go back to our normal routines. You can't put your life on hold because of my brother."

I regarded her in silence. Somehow, this felt more normal than how I had been living the past couple years.

"I'm not. I'm right where I want to be." I held up my hand to stop her from interrupting me. "I know I need to go back next door, but not yet. I need to make sure you're safe, then I'll go if that's what you want. But things have changed now. You're in my life. And I'm in yours. Regardless of where I sleep at night, it won't change, you understand me? As long as you want me around, then I'm yours."

She nodded.

"I plan on being right here, with you, as much as you'll let me."

"What about your place?" she asked quietly. "Don't you miss it?"

Rising to my feet, I held out my hand, knowing it was time to show her. I took her out the door, using my new key to lock it, and over to my place. I opened my front door, letting her walk ahead of me. Kourtney moved around, looking everywhere. I remained silent, knowing exactly what she was seeing. It was the exact same layout as hers, but like our yards, the difference was like night and day. Her place was warm, filled with comfortable furniture, muted colors and pieces of her everywhere. In the short time she'd been there, she had made it into a home. This house was stark; lifeless rooms with empty walls that screamed nothingness. It was a shell, somewhere I had been existing. Here, I was merely a shadow. Like the life I pretended to live before her.

"You're not happy here." She sounded sad, but knowing.

I shook my head.

She stared at me, her eyes filled with wonder. "You need me."

I sighed. "So much, Chefgirl."

"Maybe you should get a few more things while we're here."

"Maybe a few extra days' worth, yeah?" I paused. "For now?"

"Yeah." She nodded. "For now."

COMING BACK TO KOURTNEY'S ON Tuesday evening, alone, should have felt weird, but it didn't. Knowing she'd be home in a few hours made me smile and being in her space made me feel happy. As promised, she had left me spaghetti to eat for supper, so after filling up on delicious pasta, I decided to spend a productive evening while waiting for her to get home.

I made a trip to Home Depot and bought her two chairs for her table outside, as well as an umbrella. They matched pretty well and I felt better seeing them there. I thought she needed the umbrella to protect her pale complexion from the sun. I knew she would like the flowery design. After setting it up, I stood back, satisfied with my work, hoping she would approve. I also brought over my Blu-ray player and hooked it up to her TV. I knew how much she enjoyed watching movies and her DVD player wasn't working well. I held back on the sound system, at least for now. I carted over some beer to put in her fridge. Settling back on the sofa with a cold beer, I sighed in satisfaction. I liked it here. It felt right. Once Kourtney got home, it would be perfect. I leaned back, letting my eyes shut. It felt good having someone to wait for.

I woke up when Kourtney came home, tripping into the living room, all smiles, giggles, and hiccups as she observed me sitting on the sofa. "Hi, Tomcat."

I grinned at her flushed cheeks and bright eyes, indicating she was feeling no pain. "Were you and Annie drinking wine again, Kourtney?"

She nodded as she walked toward me, wobbling a little. "Jason had to come and drive us home."

I held out my hand, glad Annie hadn't attempted to drive. "Good."

She kneeled down at my feet, smiling up at me. "Did you have a good night?"

I stroked her cheek, the skin warm under my fingers. "I did, but I missed you."

She turned and kissed my hand, her lips lingering. "I missed you, too. Did you eat the dinner I left you?"

I chuckled at her need to look after me. "I did. Fucking awesome as usual, Chefgirl. I take it you had a good time? Lots of information sharing?"

She nodded enthusiastically and giggled, hiccupping again. "We did." She leaned forward. "I told her you were my boyfriend. And you gave me my first orgasm." She winked ludicrously at me. "And a few others since."

My eyebrows shot up. Information sharing indeed.

She regarded me with a frown. "Was that okay?"

"You tell her anything you want, Kourtney."

"She told me some stuff, too," she spoke low, attempting to waggle her eyebrows and failing badly.

I sniggered at how adorable she was in her tipsy state. "I'm sure she did."

"We talked about lots of good stuff."

"Good stuff?"

"You know—good sex stuff. She knows things."

I threw back my head in laughter. "She does, does she?"

Kourtney's eyes were dancing with mischievousness as she gazed up at me. "Yep." Her voice lowered. "Nathan?"

"Yeah, Chefgirl?"

"I want something."

I couldn't stop my grin. She could have anything she wanted. "Okay . . . what?"

Her hands ran up my legs, settling on my thighs as she leaned forward, her mouth seeking mine. I was only too happy to oblige. I cupped the back of her head, bringing her close and kissing her deep, tasting the wine she had been drinking. I tilted her head, deepening the kiss, groaning as our tongues slid together. The feeling of her warmth, and her quiet whimper, ignited the desire I felt whenever she was this close, filling me with need. I felt her hands tugging on the waistband of my lounge pants, and I raised my hips, allowing her to pull them off. She sat back on her heels; her hands stroking my thighs nervously while she gazed at me, and glanced down at my growing erection. "I want to . . . taste you."

My breath caught in my throat in anticipation when I realized what she was saying.

"I've never done this." Her cheeks were flushed, a nervous look replacing the impish one her eyes had held before.

"You don't have to," I assured her; even though the thought of her lips wrapped around me, caused my cock to twitch.

"I want to—if you want me to?" she asked shyly; sliding her hand up, to wrap around my now throbbing dick.

I groaned at the sensation. "Yes, baby," I hissed. "Believe me, I want you to."

My head hit the back of the sofa when I felt her tongue tentatively slide up the underside of my cock and around the head, swirling and gentle; the teasing feeling caused me to jerk in surprise.

"*Fuck.*"

She backed off, eyeing me warily, and I lifted my head. "No . . . don't stop, baby. That felt so fucking good," I encouraged.

She licked her lips, slowly engulfing me in the warmth of her mouth; sending flickers of heat along my spine. I couldn't stop watching her as she explored me; her hands and mouth moving in tandem, quickly working me into a frenzy of hot, blistering need. Her nervousness seemed to dissipate as she locked eyes with me, the desire blazing at me leaving me breathless. She rose up, her hair falling forward, its silkiness brushing my knees. The shift in position sucked me deeper into her mouth, and I wound my fingers into her hair, restlessly caressing her skin.

"Kourtney," I moaned, drowning in the sensations of her mouth's increasingly firm sucking, the way her tongue swirled and lapped, and her hand stroked and caressed. I hissed as the intensity amplified, my hips lifting off the sofa, bucking upward, wanting to go deeper into the source of pleasure. All of my senses were on overload and I knew I wasn't going to last. She was way too good at this and the pleasure was overwhelming. I could feel my orgasm burning through me, my body beginning to shake, my nerves tightening. I gasped her name loud, moving my hands from her hair and grasping onto the cushions tightly. "Kourtney . . . I can't . . . *baby* . . . you *need* to stop—"

Her rhythm never faltered, and I came. Hard, throbbing and intense, my eyes shut, as I spilled down her throat, feeling it flex as she swallowed. My grip tightened on the cushions, and I felt the fabric give away under the strain while I shouted out her name. I collapsed back onto the sofa, gazing down at her in awe. She moved back, a satisfied little smirk ghosting on her lips as she beamed up at me.

"You've . . . never . . . done that . . . before?" I gasped out between pants.

"No."

"*Jesus.*"

"Annie and I Googled it over dinner. And she gave me some pointers."

"You *Googled* it?"

She nodded, looking proud. "She has an iPhone, the same as yours. We used the ear buds so no one else heard."

I laughed at the thought of the two of them, drinking and Googling porn in a restaurant to help give Kourtney some tips on the subject of blow jobs.

I groaned. "You're a fast learner."

She frowned. "Annie said when I had more practice, you'd come quicker. I'll get better."

I gaped at her in shock. "*Get better? Come quicker?* Fuck, Kourtney, if you get any better at it, you're only going to have to *think* about giving me a blow job and I'll come in my pants. Game over. That was fucking *incredible.*"

Her smug, proud smile said everything. I hauled her close, kissing her deep, groaning as I tasted myself on her tongue.

"You, my girl, are far too clever for your own good." I paused, grinning. "But I like it.

"Anything else sexual you want to learn, I'm more than willing to be your guinea pig, okay? You can practice on me. Anything, anytime, Chefgirl—I'm your man." I glanced down at her ruined sofa cushion. "Although I can't guarantee the safety of your furniture. I owe you a new sofa."

She shrugged. "I think I can fix it. And if not, it was so worth a new sofa." She giggled, burying her red face into my chest. After briefly being the assertive one, my shy Kourtney was back, and I was okay with that. Chuckling, I tucked her beside me on the sofa and we sat quiet, while I stroked her head, both of us enjoying being back together.

When she yawned, long and wide, I cupped her cheek. "You ready to go to bed?"

She nodded up at me sleepily. "I don't drink much."

I laughed. "So you keep telling me . . . every time you're rather tipsy."

"It's Annie. She's a bad influence."

"I rather like her influence." I winked. "I encourage these information sharing dinners."

She yawned again, and I stood up. "Come to bed, Kourtney." I wrapped my arm around her as we walked down the hall. "You know, I know lots of good sex stuff, as well. And I'm always glad to share." Leaning down, I nipped her ear. "You won't even have to Google it. Only too happy to give you a hands-on demonstration—anytime."

She grinned. "I'll keep that in mind, Tomcat."

Another yawn escaped her mouth, and I brushed my lips over her forehead. "You go get ready. I'll meet you there. I'm gonna make sure everything is locked up."

Ten minutes later, I slipped in beside Kourtney, who was already half asleep, and I drew her into my arms. "Thank you," she said quietly, glancing up at me.

"For what?"

"For being here, for making me feel so happy, and safe."

"You are safe, Kourtney. I have you. And you make me just as happy."

She snuggled closer and the room was quiet. As sleep claimed me, I heard a pleading whisper in the dark, so low I wasn't sure it was real.

"I'll always want you with me. Stay. Please."

Chapter
Twenty Seven

WEDNESDAY NIGHT, WE WERE SITTING outside at the table, enjoying the evening, on the new chairs Kourtney loved. I was working on creating an account for her in Dropbox: my next planned learning experience for her with computers, when her message light lit up. Message after message came through, the beeps constant. Frowning at the name, I looked up.

"Kourtney?"

"Hmm?"

"Who is *Pistonman*?"

Her head snapped up; her face paled. "Andy." She stared at me. "Is that what all the beeps are?"

"Yes." My voice was strained. "Why does he have your IM address?"

"He set up the account for me when I was back at home."

"He built it?" I frowned, not liking the sound of that information. "Did he pick your user name?"

She hesitated, glancing over at me and looking nervous.

"Tell me."

"Yes. He always said I was the size of an Elephant and he thought it was funny."

"So this is another one of his insults that keeps following you around."

"I didn't know how to change it," she confessed.

I stared for a moment, then looked back to the screen. I hadn't yet opened the window. I kept my voice calm, although inside I was furious. "What do you want me to do?"

There was only silence.

I scowled. "He shouldn't be contacting you. Why didn't you tell me he was on your friends' list? I would have deleted him."

"I forgot. He never contacts me." She sounded upset. "Should I read them?"

"Are you interested in anything he has to tell you? Do you honestly think they're going to be pleasant?" I could hear the impatience building in my tone.

"It could be about my dad."

"Again, is that something you should care about?" I huffed, starting to feel the anger leaking out.

Kourtney's hand reached over, and I pushed the laptop her way. I stood up, not wanting to watch her do this to herself.

Angry, I went inside and grabbed a beer. I stayed in the kitchen drinking it, unsure what to do. Why did she continue to allow them the access to reach her? On some level, she had to know they were going to continue to hurt her any way they could. Why was she letting them do this to her?

I paced the kitchen for a minute and glanced outside. Kourtney was still in the same position I had left her in, the laptop sitting on the table. Her hand was on it but she hadn't turned it around. I could see her shoulders shaking and I knew she was already crying. My shoulders sagged in defeat. I couldn't leave her out there alone or ignore her pain. Sighing, I set down the beer and went back outside. I dragged my chair over beside her and sat down, pulling her into my arms.

"Tell me what to do." She sobbed into my chest. "Just tell me."

I shook my head, my anger dissipating in the face of her pain. "I can't, baby. You have to decide what you need to do.

You've had enough decisions taken away from you."

"You're right." She hiccupped. "I know you're right. They'll only be filled with hate. I don't want to read them and he shouldn't have sent them. Can you please delete them?"

I lifted her chin; my heart aching at the sight of her tear-stained face. "Kourtney, we should use them; show them to the police, and you need to get an order in place."

"It will make him even angrier."

I snorted. "He should have thought about that before he made such a stupid move. This is *completely* on him, not you." I drummed my fingers on the table. "Let me save them and delete the account. I'll make you a new one he has no access to, okay? One without another negative connotation attached to it."

"I didn't know how to change it," she repeated.

"I know, Chefgirl. But I do. Don't let him in. Don't give him this chance. You need to cut them both out of your life."

She hesitated, and I frowned. "What?"

She drew in a shuttering breath. "I don't want to talk to them or have anything to do with them."

"Good. Why am I sensing there's something you're not telling me?"

She met my gaze. "I know you think I shouldn't care—but I do. I help pay the costs of my dad's care facility. The government only pays for a ward bed. I cover the difference to a semi-private room."

I stared in amazement. Even after all they had done, all the pain they had caused her, Kourtney was helping to pay for her father's care. It shouldn't surprise me, given her generous nature. And she was right. I wanted to tell her she shouldn't care, but that was what Kourtney did. She cared. She always would care.

"Does Andy contribute?"

"No."

Of course not—that lazy prick.

"You want me to just ignore this, Kourtney? Is that what you're asking me to do?"

"I don't know," she confessed. "I don't know what to do."

"What if we were to speak with the officer who came and talked to you when we were there, at the police station? Maybe she could suggest the best plan of action. Would you listen to her?"

"Yes."

I sighed in resignation. I wiped away the tears on her cheeks and kissed her gently. "Can you get me the file so I have the email address, please?"

As she went inside, I opened up the message board and scanned the inbox, my eyes narrowing as I read his obviously drunken, vile messages. My anger built again at the nasty words and names he called her. I wanted to go find him and teach him a lesson he wouldn't forget. I knew if Kourtney had read this it would have devastated her. She had done nothing to deserve this sort of hateful treatment. I snorted at the last one: he informed her neither he nor his father ever wanted to see her again. Well, hallelujah. I noticed he never said a word about not wanting her continued financial support, though—the fucking selfish bastard. In my opinion it wasn't a loss for Kourtney at all. Good riddance. My fingers itched to start typing, to write back and tell him exactly what I thought of him, and his father, but I knew it would only incite him further and I didn't want to give him any reason to come around. Instead I copied it all, and opened an email to send to Joanne.

Kourtney came out and handed me the file, sitting in silence as she watched me send the email, then work to delete the username. I created a new account for her, stopping only to ask her what name she would like to use.

She smiled tremulously at me. "Chefgirl."

"Yeah?" I smiled back fondly, wanting her to know I wasn't angry with her. I was angry with the situation, *never her.*

"Yeah. I like it when you call me that."

After a few more key stokes, I pushed the laptop her way. "Password."

When she was done, I added both myself and Annie into

her contacts. "You can add anyone else later," I informed her; showing her how to do it.

She nodded. "They were mostly people at work anyway."

"Okay. Done."

"Did you read the messages?"

"I scanned them," I answered, wanting to be honest. "I think he was drunk . . . or he's a very bad speller, which I suppose shouldn't surprise me. It's obvious; you got the brains of the family."

"Were they awful?" she whispered.

I clasped her hands in mine. "Yeah, they were disgusting . . . and bullshit. The ramblings of a drunken asshole, who is so jealous and spiteful, he needs to lash out at someone to make himself and his miserable life seem worthwhile."

"*Jealous*? You think he is jealous of me?"

"Kourtney—think about it. Compare your lives."

"I don't understand."

I squeezed her hands. "Your brother still lives in his father's house. Alone. His business is owned not by himself, but your father." At her quizzical look, I shrugged. "I checked, okay? He owns nothing. His take-home-pay is based on the garage's earnings, which at times I'm sure isn't much, knowing how lazy he is. He contributes nothing to your father's care and has no real life of his own." I snorted derisively. "He drives a truck most seventeen year olds would be embarrassed to be seen in. He has no one significant in his life. He acts like an overgrown, middle-aged frat boy. He's going nowhere—fast."

I cupped her cheek. "Then there's you—his sister, who he claimed would never amount to anything. Ms. PhD: who owns her own home, has a successful career, is well-respected by her peers." I took in a deep breath. "And is in a committed relationship with someone"—I swallowed hard, stumbling over my words—"who adores her."

She stared at me.

"So, yeah. He is jealous, and spiteful. Because you did it all against the odds—you did it all on your own."

"I . . . I never thought of it that way."

"Because you don't see yourself clearly. You're so amazing, Chefgirl. And, someday, I'm going to get you to see that fact."

Grabbing her, I held tight. I shut my eyes as I thought about what made me pause while talking to her.

It had hit me like a Mack truck. I didn't only adore her. *I loved her.*

I was one hundred percent in love with her. I wanted to tell her. Yet, unlike her, I hadn't been open and told her about my past. Something she deserved to know.

I knew I had to talk to Grant, I needed his advice.

SATURDAY MORNING, I MADE THE drive and met Grant at our usual place—a long drive for me, a shorter one for him. It always gave me lots of time to think, and today I had been thinking hard.

Grant stared at me in dismay. "You haven't told her? Why Nathan? You've always been upfront about your past."

"I know."

"Why not this time?"

I searched for the right words. "I didn't expect to fall in love."

"It's not something that announces itself with a card." Grant pointed out dryly.

"I'm terrified that when she knows my past, she'll walk away. I don't think I could handle losing her," I admitted. "I never felt as if I had as much to lose as I do now."

"From the little you've told me, I don't think she's capable of such rejection."

I stared at him as his words sunk in. He was right. Kourtney had a huge capacity for forgiveness and love. Unlike my family, she didn't judge people harshly. She wouldn't turn her back on me.

Would she?

I thought of my life before I met her. Empty days, endless hours spent alone, too afraid to get close to someone, to open myself up to hurt again.

Until she moved next door. Without even trying, she broke down every defense I had with her quiet, caring ways. She brought out the man I should be. The one I wanted to be—for her.

"Tell me about her," Grant encouraged, startling me from my thoughts.

I sighed and started to talk. For an hour I spoke, telling him about Kourtney. About her childhood—the neglect and abuse, and how much it had scarred her. I told him about her cowardly, weak father and her asshole, bully of a brother. How vulnerable and broken she was, yet despite it all, so incredibly giving and sweet. He chuckled as I told him about our conversations over the fence; how she fed and teased me. I smiled as I told him how brave and strong she was and what she'd survived. And, finally, I told him how she made me realize I had to start living again, and in order to do so, I needed her with me.

We were quiet for a few minutes as he digested everything I had told him. Our waitress came and removed our cups, which had long grown cold and replaced them with fresh ones, which we both sipped, as he thought things through.

"Her father is a selfish bastard," he stated in an angry voice. "I wish he could be brought up on some sort of charges."

"He is, but short of trying to get Nurse Ratchet on his floor, there isn't much we can do about him." I chuckled without humor.

"Maybe I should ask a few friends to check out her brother a little closer, you know, make sure his taxes are filed, all his business licenses are in place?" he mused. "Send in an inspector to make sure things are on the up-and-up?"

"I'd like that," I admitted. "I'd love to mess up his life. Make him suffer. I want so bad to make him pay for what he did to her." I sighed and shook my head. "But Kourtney would *hate* it. She would say it was something they would think to do.

Make someone miserable only because you can—even though he continues to do it to her."

"What?"

I told him about the messages and my frustration with her first instinct to read them. Of finding out she contributed to her father's care, despite everything. I shrugged in confusion. "I don't understand it."

"From what you've told me about her, I'm not really surprised. She seems to have a huge capacity for forgiveness."

"She does. For everyone around her except herself."

"So this friend she knew from school—she's willing to help?"

"She's going to talk to him. Unofficially. But Kourtney agreed to move forward to the next step if she feels it's necessary."

Grant nodded. "He's a bully, and bullies tend to stop if someone scarier than them shows up. Maybe a visit from the police will do that. I hope she takes a partner."

I smirked. "She plans to drop by the garage during business hours in her uniform, with her partner, who she mentioned was a huge man. I hope it works. I want him out of her life."

"You need to be patient."

"I'm trying, Grant."

"Nathan," he began quietly. "Do you know that abused children, even adults, often protect the person abusing them?"

"I've heard that, yes."

"Do you know why?"

"No, no idea."

He smiled sadly. "It's all they know. They don't know love doesn't have to hurt."

I leaned forward. "But she has me now. I want to show her it shouldn't."

"And you will. But, Nathan, she's had you for a few weeks, less than that even. She's had *them* all her life. It's going to take time. It's all *she's* known."

I sat back as his words sunk in. He was right. She'd only

known pain and rejection for twenty-seven years and it was something she almost expected. I couldn't expect her to be healed instantly because I was in her life.

"I won't give up on her. Somehow I'll help her see she is more than the nothing they told her she was."

"Good. I'm glad you convinced her to talk to someone, and think about an order. Perhaps if this officer goes and talks to him, it might scare the shit out of him, and he'll leave her alone. If not, I might have to pay him a visit myself." He arched his eyebrow, and I grinned. This was the Grant I had gotten to know; protective and caring of the people he knew. I could only imagine Andy's face if Grant showed up to "visit" with him.

"You're right about one thing: he is a bully. If he knows he can't push her around anymore and he's being watched, he'll move on. He was probably drunk and made a stupid decision, but he won't appreciate the fact he was given a huge break from the one person who shouldn't give him anything." He shook his head as he looked at me. "Like you, I'd prefer to see him in trouble with the law, but it's her decision. Frankly, not reading the messages and letting you delete the account was a big step for her."

"I know."

"You think she is pretty amazing, don't you?"

I smiled. "She amazes me every day. She's the best person I've ever met. She didn't deserve what happened to her."

"And you love her."

I nodded. "More than anything." My hands flexed on the table. "I want a life with her."

He was quiet, for a minute.

"Can I ask a . . . personal question?"

"Sure."

"Is she . . . ?"

My eyes narrowed. "Is she what?"

"Heavy?"

I frowned. "Heavy? No." I thought about how to describe her. "She's . . . short."

"What the hell does that mean?"

"If she was Claire's height, Grant, she'd be a freaking supermodel. But she isn't. She's . . ." I exhaled as I searched for the right word. Somehow the words lush or voluptuous were too personal to say to him.

Grant whistled lowly. "Oh, fuck. She's a dish, isn't she?"

I frowned, confused. "A dish?"

He nodded and traced his hands in the air suggestively, as if he was stroking full curves. "All you need is a spoon and you're set. Short, curvy, sexy."

"Yeah, Grant. She's a dish. Although, a spoon wouldn't be what I would use." I winked at him.

He threw back his head laughing. "Didn't know you had that in you, Nathan."

I laughed with him. "She brings out a lot of things I didn't know were there."

"A smart, sexy, dishy woman. Those are rare qualities."

"I have the rarest. She is completely . . . I can't even begin . . . *She astonishes me.*" I leaned forward, my voice earnest. "I have to tell her. I have to be honest."

He turned serious again, staring at me. "Yes, you do. And you have to be prepared for her anger when you tell her. Give her whatever room she needs to come to terms with your story."

"Okay."

"I hope it works out for you. I want to meet this amazing girl of yours."

"Yeah?"

"Yeah, once you've told her and you're ready, I'd like to meet her. Bring her up to visit Claire and me." He paused. "If she wants to meet us."

"I think she would."

"Okay, Nathan. I wish you luck. Don't wait too much longer."

I held out my hand, grateful for his friendship. "I won't. I'll find the right time and tell her. Soon."

Chapter
Twenty Eight

THE HOUSE WAS EMPTY WHEN I got back from seeing Grant. Music was playing, so I knew Kourtney was there, and I walked toward the back to go and find her. I needed to see her.

The whole drive home, I wrestled with what he said. He was right—she had trusted me enough to tell me her story, and I had to do the same. I had to tell her the truth, answer her questions, hope she would forgive me for not telling her sooner, and she would still want me in her life. I sighed as I paused at the screen door, looking at her. I was also hoping she felt the same way I did—I wanted her to love me in return. I thought she had feelings for me, but how deep they were, I didn't know. That was the big question at the moment. Did she care enough to forgive me for holding back on her?

Her head was bent over some chore as she sat at the table. Her beautiful hair spilled over her shoulders and down her back, the sunlight catching the different colors in it as she worked away, and her bottom lip was caught between her teeth in concentration. There was a bag of some sort at her feet and the flash of knitting needles as her hands flew; a small pile of fuzzy items on the table beside her. I moved forward, the need to touch her too strong to hold back any longer. Her head turned at the sound of the screen door sliding open, and I was greeted with her warm smile as I strode toward her. I dropped to my knees when I reached her and cupped the back of her head, bringing her lips to mine, feeling instant happiness as I felt her mouth settle under my own. Languidly, I stroked her tongue, before I tilted her head, deepening the kiss as I held her tight. Her hands wound in my hair as she returned my passion. Drawing back, I leaned my forehead to hers. "Hey, Chefgirl."

"Hi," she whispered. "You okay? How was coffee with your friend?"

I dropped another kiss onto her sweet mouth, sitting down next to her. "Yeah, it's all good. I missed you, though." Bending down, I grabbed the knitting needles she had dropped and handed them to her. "What are you working on so furiously?"

She chuckled as she started her fast movements again. "Baby bonnets. I need some, fast."

My hand froze as I was reaching forward to pick up one of the small items on the table. My eyes flew to her, the sounds of the needles clicking growing louder by the second. She needed them . . . *fast*? There was a sudden, dull roar in my ears as I stared, with one large question looming in my brain.

"Kourtney?" I asked; my voice thick with distress.

Her head flew up at the sound of my unsteady speech, her eyes taking in my frozen posture. For a minute our eyes connected; hers confused, mine panic-filled.

"I thought . . ." I trailed off, unable to say anything else, unsure how to react. I swallowed and tried again. "I thought you said . . ."

A look of understanding crossed her face and she leaned forward.

"*No!*" she exclaimed, interrupting me. "No, Nat! I knit these for preemies at the hospital. They called earlier to say they were all out! I'm trying to get some done to take over later!"

I sat back, my shoulders sagging, feeling relief course

through me.

Kourtney looked at me for a moment, then started to giggle. "You should have seen the look on your face."

"You should feel my heart right now."

She looked at me. "I'm not pregnant. The bonnets are not for me." She paused, another giggle escaping her lips. "We've, ah, only been together a little while. And I'm on birth control." She shook her head. "And, if I was pregnant, do you really think my first reaction would be to start knitting bonnets?"

I shrugged my shoulders. "Maybe you were . . . nesting."

She burst into laughter. "Nesting?"

"It's a word."

"I know it's a word, but not one I thought you knew."

I sniffed haughtily; feeling relieved she wasn't upset over my reaction, but chose to see the humor in it. "I know lots of words, Kourtney."

She shook her head as she continued to knit. "So I'm learning. But not one you need to use right now." She looked up at me seriously. "If I had made a mistake like that, Nathan, I promise you I would find a better way to tell you."

Mistake?

I studied her, the sudden image of her pregnant with a child—with our child—entering my mind. I could see her, glowing and round, as she knitted something for them. I was surprised to find I liked the image.

I cupped her face, stroking the warm skin with my thumbs. "A child would never be a mistake with you, Kourtney—ever. I won't lie, it would be a bit of a shock right now, but not a mistake and it would be on both of us. Not just you." I met her gaze. "So, not right now, but someday . . . maybe?"

She stared at me, her eyes huge as she took in my expression and words.

"Maybe . . . someday."

I smiled. I think I had my answer.

WE DIDN'T VENTURE FAR FROM each other the rest of the day. Later that afternoon we were outside, enjoying the sun. Kourtney worked on some more bonnets while I checked things via email.

I looked up from my laptop. "Kourtney? Joanne paid a visit to Andy yesterday. She dropped by the garage with her partner."

Her head snapped up, her hands stopped their busy movements and her eyes round with panic. "Oh?"

I read the email again, frowning, as I edited somewhat. "Andy won't be contacting you again. He admits he was drunk and angry, and knows what will happen if he's that stupid again. She and her partner were, ah, rather blunt with him." I read a few more lines. "She thinks you're an amazing person."

She rolled her eyes at me. "Why would she think that?"

It was my turn to roll my eyes. "Because most people would have gone the other route—got an order done, or had him arrested for assault, and been done with it. They wouldn't care about the consequences. For him or your father."

She lowered her head and shrugged. "I couldn't do that."

Reaching over, I wrapped my hand around hers. "I know. Because, somehow, despite all the shit you've endured, you are the most generous, forgiving person I know." I kissed her hand. "You amaze me; everyday, Kourtney. *Every* day."

"So it's over? He'll leave me alone?"

I nodded. "I think he got the message. But Joanne agrees; he tries to contact you again, it's official. He only gets this one chance. Okay?"

She drew in a deep breath and exhaled. "Okay."

THE NEXT MORNING, I WOKE up alone. I sat up, confused, seeing the bathroom door open and no Kourtney. Glancing at the clock, I saw it was 5:30 a.m. Often by now we'd be out on our morning run. I looked at the closed bedroom door, and listened to the silence of the house and knew I was alone. Where was

Kourtney? I looked over at my running clothes and noticed hers weren't there beside them.

She wouldn't.

Frowning, I threw back the covers and grabbed my stuff, pulling it on. I had made it to the hall when the door opened and Kourtney came in, pulling out her earplugs.

"Oh, you're awake!"

"You went without me?" I snapped. "We hadn't discussed you running alone again."

She stepped forward and cupped my cheek. "Nathan, last night you slept through without a nightmare. You're finally sleeping well, and I couldn't bear to wake you. And it's time to move on. Andy isn't going to come after me while I run. No one is."

"I don't like you running alone."

"I've been doing it for two years. I have my cell phone," she stated. "I'm tired of letting him rule this part of my life. Or any part of it."

"I like running with you." I huffed, unable to let it go.

"Then you can come with me some days when you wake up. Other days I'll go alone." She tilted her head. "I like running alone, you know. It gives me time to think."

"Am I crowding you, Kourtney?" I was fearful of her answer.

"No. But I need some space at times. Just like you do, I'm sure."

"I'm upgrading your phone."

She kissed my cheek. "Not needed. But if it makes you feel better, fine."

"I'd also feel better if you'd stagger your run times."

She sighed. "If I did that, you'd relax a little?"

I held her hand to my cheek, nuzzling it. "Yes."

"Okay, then. I will." She paused. "Nathan?"

"Hmm?"

"I'm driving myself to work again."

Somehow this information didn't surprise me. "Okay,

Chefgirl." I swallowed a sudden lump in my throat. "Did you want me to, ah . . . ?" I swallowed again, the word "leave" too difficult to say.

I never got a chance to finish my thought.

Her eyes widened. "No! I don't want that."

I closed my eyes, hugging her.

"Good. I'm not ready yet," I mumbled into her hair.

I don't think I'll ever be, the voice in my head added.

WE HAD A NEW ROUTINE now. Some mornings I got up and ran with Kourtney, and a few I didn't. She was right; I was sleeping better with her beside me and often I was in such a deep sleep I didn't even feel her get up. Some days, I managed to persuade her to stay in bed with me and she went for a run later. We drove to work in our own cars, although on occasion, I convinced her to let me drop her off so we could grocery shop together after I picked up her up at night. I didn't tell her how much I missed those moments of quiet with her in the car every day, but I did.

For me, no day was complete now without her sweet kisses and tender caresses. The instant I was back in her company, I felt whole. I loved feeling her hands stroking my hair as we watched TV or her fingers working their way into a tight muscle when she gave me a massage to help me relax. Nothing pleased me more than hearing her laugh at one of my inane remarks or stories. The contentment that filled me when I saw her curled into her favorite corner of the sofa, knowing I could touch her anytime and be welcomed with her beautiful, warm gaze and smile, was as heartwarming as it was new.

Until this time with her, I hadn't realized how shut-off I had been from any emotional feeling since I had been on my own. The thought of returning to that state of almost suspension made me shudder. I knew I could have moved back next door, yet neither of us made any move to bring up the subject. I still went back and forth with my stuff, but it seemed more and more of my things were finding a home here with Kourtney's. I knew I'd found my home.

She was still somewhat of a mystery to me when it came to touching. She always held herself stiff when I would first embrace her, before eventually relaxing into my arms. It was as if she was waiting for something, but I wasn't sure what. Frustrating me the most was the fact her shyness still kept her covered in the light. I had hoped we would have moved past it by this point, but it wasn't happening. I did my best to remain patient, telling myself I had to give her time. I didn't know how much time, or how to make her see how lovely she was to me. I was determined to make her see the truth.

This past week had been especially good, with no drama surrounding us. Every day we learned a little more about each other. With every new discovery, I fell more in love with her.

I still hadn't told her about my past, and I knew I had to. I decided I would tell her this weekend. I wanted to tell her how much I loved her, and I needed her to know all about me.

As I sat at my desk, thinking of the best way to handle it, my message light lit up. I frowned when I saw it was Annie, right away thinking something was wrong, until I saw the first message.

LabGoddess: Hey Nathan—I stole your info from Kourtney when she gave me her new acct name. I've been holding back 'til now, but I need a favor. Chefgirl—suits her BTW.

Gnat: Yeah, it does. What's up?

LabGoddess: I need you to weave a little more of your voodoo magic on Kourtney for me.

Gnat: Voodoo magic?

LabGoddess: Nathan—she came to lunch with some of us today—the first time in the two years she's been working here. She went out with me—outside the office. I saw her locking lips with you—more than once. She smiles and laughs. She even makes the occasional joke. If that isn't voodoo magic, I don't know what is.

Gnat: She's shy, Annie, that's all.

LabGoddess: Thanks for the newsflash, bug boy. She's beyond shy and I know there's a story behind it. One day I hope she shares it—but 'til then I am thrilled to see her happy and coming out of her shell a little. Everyone is. She may be shy but people really like her. She just doesn't seem to realize it.

I shook my head. Annie was right about that. Kourtney was so used to rejection she anticipated it before it even happened. And she protected herself from it.

Gnat: What's not to like? I think she's pretty perfect myself. She doesn't see herself the way we do. But we'll get her there. She is too amazing not to.

LabGoddess: Knew I would like you. Now getting back to the subject at hand . . .

Gnat: Right—what do you need my magical skills for?

LabGoddess: There is a BBQ tomorrow night—a staff one. I don't suppose Kourtney has mentioned it?

Gnat: No.

LabGoddess: She never goes. Lunch today was the first social thing she's ever done. I thought maybe she might come if you were with her—I know you being there would make her feel better. Can you talk to her?

Gnat: I won't push her to do something that makes her uncomfortable, but yes, I'll ask her about it. Although how do I explain I know about her work BBQ?

LabGoddess: Oh, I will tell her I told you—I already told her I wanted her to come. But she got all nervous, so I thought I would ask you.

Gnat: Okay, I'll talk to her tonight.

LabGoddess: Perfect — thanks!

I stared at the screen, thinking. A work function. It would be like a date. I wanted to take Kourtney on a date. Although we had spent most of our time together since she came back, it was always at home. Aside from our morning runs and the occasional grocery store trip, we never went anywhere. She said she liked it at home, and while I loved having her all to myself, it was time to expand our world. And this might be the right step.

⟲

"NO."

"Why?"

"There'll be lots of people there, Nat."

I smiled indulgently, having expected this response. "That's what a party is, Kourtney. Lots of people."

Her hands began to twist the hem of her shirt as she tucked her knees up to her chest. I reached out and tugged her hands away, clasping them in mine. "Why does it make you so nervous?"

"I don't know most of them. I only know the people in my department, and not even all of them."

I frowned, hesitating, before speaking up. "Is it because they don't want to? Or you don't give them the chance?"

She gave me a startled look, her teeth working her bottom lip. "I don't know," she finally whispered.

"Annie tells me you are very well-liked at work—did you know that?"

"No."

I cupped her cheek, stroking the supple skin. "Maybe you need to try and let them in. Let them get to know you, and you know them. Not everyone is going to treat you like your family did, Chefgirl. And, you're not in school anymore. If someone says something that makes you uncomfortable, you can tell them to go fuck themselves."

Her eyes widened at my advice.

"I think—if you try—you might be pleasantly surprised. This might be a good place to start. Look what happened when you allowed Annie in to your life." I teased her. "Or me. That turned out pretty damn good, I think." I grinned, wanting to reassure her.

"It did."

"I'll be right there with you. We can do this together."

Her eyes were downcast as she struggled with her answer. I could *feel* the tension the conversation had caused her, and I knew she was holding back something.

"Tell me."

"Do you really want to go?"

"Yes, I'd love to take you, if you want to go."

"You'd be okay being seen with me?" Her voice was quiet, and she still wasn't meeting my eyes.

I sighed in frustration. "Hey. Look at me," I commanded.

Her troubled eyes lifted to mine and the worry I saw in them tugged at my heart.

"I would be proud to be seen with you, Kourtney. I want people to know you belong to me—like I belong to you." I cupped the back of her head, and kissed her until we were both panting. "Together, okay? You with me?" I leaned my forehead to hers. "I won't leave your side, Kourtney. Promise."

"Okay."

I beamed. "Okay. Hey—our first date."

She rolled her eyes at me, and I had to tease her some more. "I wonder if I can get to first base with you?"

She giggled, swatting my hands that were threatening to tickle her. I held her to my chest, grazing her ear with the tip of my tongue, enjoying the feel of her shiver. "Maybe I'll get even further, Chefgirl?" I nipped her lobe teasingly. "Something tells me I've got a pretty good chance. I am rather charming."

Her giggles turned into her low, sultry laughter. "Keep

laughing like that and we'll have a dress rehearsal right now." I growled playfully. "Or, even better, an undress rehearsal—" She pushed me away and stood up, smiling, but shaking her head.

"If we're going to the barbeque, I have to take something for the potluck," she informed me. "So I have to go make it."

"What are you making? I'll help."

She raised her eyebrow at me. "*You* want to help cook?"

I shook my head. "No, that would be a mistake. I can get what you need at the store. And, of course, I want to help taste test. Quality control. I'm all about that. Very important."

She laughed as she walked into the kitchen. "Such a hard job for you. Not sure I can ask you to make such a sacrifice."

I sighed heavily. "I only do it for you, Chefgirl. Only for you."

"OKAY, I'M READY TO GO." Kourtney sounded nervous and unsure.

I looked up, dropping the paper I'd been reading while I waited. "Chefgirl . . ." I breathed, taking in the sight before me.

Holy fuck.

Her eyes widened and she turned around. "I'll go change."

I shot out of the chair, realizing I had spoken out loud and she took my words as disapproval. "No!" I crossed over to her, taking her arm. "You look incredible."

She glanced down at her dress. "Annie made me buy it at lunch today."

I whistled. "Remind me to buy Annie a big thank you gift."

I loved seeing her in a dress and this one was spectacular. It was cut way lower than I was used to seeing on Kourtney, hugging her breasts, outlining their fullness, then flowing out to her knees. It was flowery and pretty; she looked like summer, all bright, airy and, very sexy. Her hair was drawn away from her face but hanging down her back in waves so I could thread my fingers through it, which I loved to do. I clasped her hand, that had been bunching up the fabric of her dress—one of her nervous habits. I brushed my lips along hers. "You are beautiful," I murmured against their softness, smiling as I felt her cheek warm up. "Don't change. Please?"

"Okay," she breathed.

I moved back, still smiling. "Should we really take all the stuff you made last night, Chefgirl? It's an awful lot of food."

She rolled her eyes at me. "It's two salads, Nat."

"Two huge ones. Maybe you should only take the coleslaw and leave the pasta one here. You know, for later."

"I made extra for you."

I grinned. "Yeah?"

"The way you were moaning over tasting it last night? I figured I had better."

I grabbed her, pulling her close, and kissed her hard. "I'll happily moan over something else later." I smirked and nipped her lips. "Thank you for saving me some."

She pressed her lips to mine. "You're welcome."

I watched as she picked up another container. My eyes narrowed. "What's that?"

"I also made brownies."

My eyebrows shot up. "When?"

She chuckled as she walked past me. "While you were snoring last night on the sofa, in a pasta-salad-taste-testing-induced coma."

"I don't snore."

Did I?

Kourtney looked over her shoulder. "Then your snoring twin is taking your place most nights in bed, Nat."

I locked the door behind me. "I'll have to speak to the bastard."

Frowning, I looked over at her in the car. "Do I keep you awake?"

"No. It's not a snore really . . . it's more a grunt-sigh-grumble thing." She made a strange sound in the back of her throat. "Like that. You only do it when you're really tired and it's rather adorable. I like it."

"You *like* it?"

She nodded, looking out the window, once again shy. "When I wake up and hear it, it reminds me I'm not alone anymore. I know you're there."

I picked up her hand and nuzzled it. "For as long as you want me, Kourtney." Then I chuckled. "But don't ever make that sound again. And hit me if I do."

She giggled and I squeezed her hand. I wanted her smiling. I always wanted her smiling.

"HOW ABOUT ANOTHER GLASS OF wine, Chefgirl?" I looked down at Kourtney, grinning. She was right; it didn't take much to get her tipsy. Two glasses of wine and she was pretty much on her way—and Annie loved encouraging it. It pleased me seeing her more relaxed and I was thrilled things were going well.

Everyone seemed happy to see her there, and as promised, unless it was to grab us a drink or fill up my munchies plate, I hadn't left her side. We had walked around, talked to people, and Annie and Jason remained close as well, so Kourtney seemed to be doing fine. She had relaxed enough to let go of the death grip she had on my hand when we had first arrived. Although she did stay close to my side, which I didn't object to at all.

It was her surprise at the level of warmth she was greeted with, that made me shake my head. She really had no idea how much people liked her.

"I need another drink," Annie announced, glaring at the bottom of her empty wine glass.

Jason grinned. "Kourtney and I will go. You want another Coke, Nathan?"

"Sure. Thanks." I wasn't drinking anything tonight. My passenger was far too valuable.

Kourtney glanced back over her shoulder with a nervous smile as she left with Jason. I winked and threw her a kiss, grinning at the instant color that stained her cheeks.

Annie snorted beside me. "You have it bad."

"I do."

"She's been a different person the last while."

"Funny, my co-workers say the same about me."

"You're good for each other. You give her the confidence she needed."

"We're good for each other." I agreed.

"Shit." Annie looked over my shoulder as she cursed.

"What?"

"I didn't think she'd come."

I glanced behind me, not seeing anyone I knew. "Who?"

"Colleen."

I turned and faced the direction where Annie was glaring. A tall, extremely thin woman was by the bar, her gaze taking in the group, looking far too formal for a staff barbeque. She was out of place in this casual setting; her clothes overdone, her posture stiff. How she even walked in the heels she was wearing was beyond me. Her cold eyes met mine, and a smug sneer curled the corners of her mouth as she appraised me openly. I turned to Annie, not at all interested in returning her unwelcome flirting.

"Who is she?"

"One of the administrators of the lab."

"You don't like her?"

"No one really does. She doesn't often come to these things. She, ah, she makes Kourtney very uncomfortable."

I stiffened. "Oh?"

"She makes . . . remarks."

"Remarks?"

"She referred to Kourtney once as 'a lump—round and doughy.'"

I frowned. "Kourtney heard her?"

"Yes."

"Has she said other things?"

"A few times—often about her eyes. I told her off once, but she ignored me." Annie sighed. "She's the reason Kourtney keeps to herself at the lab, I think. And it's not only Kourtney. She enjoys making others feel less."

My dislike for this woman grew exponentially. I especially loved Kourtney's eyes.

Her eyebrows shot up. "Look out, Nathan. Barracuda at ten o'clock."

"Hello."

I turned and faced Colleen. Up close she was even more out of place. Older than I originally thought, she was a woman on a mission. One I recognized—a hook up with no strings.

But that was before Kourtney. My sweet, insecure girl who was so easily crushed by words. Words this woman liked to use.

I studied her dispassionately, seeing things I would never have noticed before. Her clothing was out of place and too tight. Her hair was too vivid a shade of red to be natural and her make-up had been applied too liberally. She had an overbearing attitude and her stance screamed predator. Light blue, cold eyes gazed at me, so vacant of any emotion, I almost shivered.

Annie had the word correct; she was a barracuda.

I nodded politely. I wouldn't do anything that might reflect poorly on Kourtney. "Hello."

"I don't remember seeing you in the lab." She laid her hand on my arm, trying to sound seductive. "I'd have remembered you."

I shook off her touch and stepped back. "I don't work in the lab."

Annie spoke up. "Save it, Colleen. He's taken."

Her cold gaze flitted over to Annie, then returned to my face. "He's a big boy. He can speak for himself."

Before I could respond and tell her to back off, Kourtney's gentle voice spoke from beside me, a nervous edge making it shaky. "Nathan?"

I looked at her with relief, reaching out and winding my arm around her waist, tucking her into my side. "Hey, Chefgirl.

I missed you." Nuzzling her hair, I met Colleen's cold stare with a smirk. "I think you know my Kourtney."

Colleen's over-plucked eyebrows shot up. "*Your* Kourtney?" She blinked. "*Kourtney* is your girlfriend?"

"They live together," Annie announced with glee.

I didn't bother to correct her and tell her it was only temporary. Instead, I nodded. "Lucky bastard I am."

Colleen shook her head. "My, my what a dark horse you are, Kourtney. Who would have guessed you could attract a man like Nathan? You never mentioned the hottie you have held prisoner at home. You must never let him out of your two-toned sight."

Her choice of words was the wrong one to use, and I didn't appreciate the snide tone either.

"I'm the one holding *her* hostage, Colleen," I informed her, my voice cold. "You're lucky I let her come to work some days." I bent down, kissing the side of Kourtney's neck, while staring at Colleen. "Most days I don't want to let her out of my bed—especially when she looks at me with those beautiful, sexy eyes."

I felt Kourtney's blush and saw the flare of Colleen's anger. She didn't like rejection or being put in her place. Spinning on her heel, she marched away, disappearing into the crowd.

Annie and Jason both chuckled. "Nice job, Nathan."

I snickered. "What a bitch."

Kourtney sighed, turning to look up at me. "But she's so elegant."

I snorted. "She's overdone and cold. She makes my magic refrigerator look like a sauna."

"Really?"

I traced the heat of her blush along her cheekbone. "Really. She's desperate and trying too hard."

"She isn't, ah, your type?"

I yanked her into my arms. "No. My type is a short, pretty brunette with exotic eyes, who can cook like a dream." I kissed her. "And makes me happier than I've ever been."

"I like making you happy."

"Good. I like making you happy, too."

She looked past me. "I think maybe Colleen is lonely. That's why she's so desperate. Maybe if she found someone, she'd be nicer."

I leaned my forehead to hers, not pointing out the fact she'd been lonely and never chose to make other people feel less because of it. "You astound me. You always try and find some good in people."

Annie snorted and grabbed Kourtney's arm. "Okay, enough with the love-fest. You're making me ill. I have to pee and I hate going alone."

Jason leaned closer to Kourtney. "We need to talk strategy for the deliveries this week when you return, Kourtney."

Kourtney giggled before the girls walked away, and I turned to Jason. "Strategy?"

His eyes followed the girls for a minute, turning back to me. "I guess Kourtney hasn't told you about her little secret work project, has she?"

I shook my head. I was still learning so much about her.

"The floor she works on is divided into three different research areas. We all share a common lounge for breaks, casual meetings, that sort of thing. The bulletin board has a list of people's birthdays. Once a month, Annie would bring in a cake and everyone who had a birthday that month would share it with the rest of the staff. But then, people started finding a small gift on their desk on their birthday. Some small, thoughtful item. No card, nothing. Nothing to identify who was doing it." He smiled knowingly at me.

"Kourtney."

He nodded. "I didn't even know who was doing it at first. Problem was: there are a few locked offices on the floor she couldn't get into, like Annie's. Finally she had to come to me and ask for my help in unlocking the door to put the gift on their desks."

"And no one has figured it out?"

"Only Annie. It was hard to keep her in the dark. And she helps. Between the three of us we make sure it is delivered in secret and, I don't think anyone wants to figure it out. They know I have to be involved due to the locked doors. I think many people suspect it's Kourtney, since it started not long after she arrived, but everyone loves the mystery—you know you're getting something, but you never know when it's going to show up and what it's going to be. Someone started calling the mystery gift-giver the Birthday Elf and it stuck. Now, they all look forward to the Birthday Elf and their gift. Everyone's name is on the birthday list now." He chuckled. "The other floors are quite jealous of our little elf."

"What about on Kourtney's birthday?"

"Oh, your girl is smart. She put a box of chocolates on her own desk the first year, which, of course, she shared with everyone. Annie put something there this year." He paused, a sad look on his face. "I think it was the only gift she received."

I felt a tug on my heart. "I'm sure you're right. Annie is a good friend."

"Yeah, she's been trying. She likes Kourtney a lot. Has from the time Kourtney started."

"Is Annie in the same lab as Kourtney?"

"No, Annie oversees all the labs on the floor; she doesn't actually do research—didn't you know?"

"No, I didn't. I know she went with Kourtney to the last medical conference. I assumed she did research, as well."

Jason shook his head. "No, she runs them. More an office manager. Each floor has one. There is so much going on, it's needed. She also is in charge of overseeing when they go to conventions, etc. and she attends when needed. She went with Kourtney because of the last minute substitution. Kourtney rarely goes to them; because of her, ah—"

"Overwhelming shyness?" I interjected. "Her fear of speaking in front of people? Her deep-rooted fear of rejection?"

He nodded sadly.

"I'm aware of all those, Jason. Believe me. I'm hoping

between Annie and myself, we can help Kourtney overcome some of those issues."

"We feel very protective of her. She is—"

"Remarkable." I finished for him.

He nodded, and I glanced over to see Kourtney standing with Annie, who was talking to a group of people. I blew her another silent kiss, chuckling when her cheeks colored at my gesture. My heart warmed as I thought about what Jason had told me. Somehow, hearing what Kourtney did for her co-workers wasn't surprising. She made someone else happy, without drawing any attention to herself. A rush of tenderness flowed through me as I gazed at her, and I wanted her back by my side.

"You care for her a lot, don't you?"

I looked over at Jason who was watching me closely. "I do," I stated simply. "I'd do anything for her. She's changed my life."

"We see a change in her, as well. She has always been pleasant, kind and ready with a smile. But it never reached her eyes. Now when she smiles, it's real. And we know it's because of you."

"That may be the nicest thing anyone has ever said to me."

He laughed. "You do have it bad, don't you?"

I shrugged. "Yep. And I have no desire to hide it. She's too special."

"You're exactly what she needed."

"We're exactly what each other needed, Jason."

I COULDN'T WAIT ANYMORE. I glanced at Jason who knew what I was thinking and laughing, he clapped me on the shoulder. "Let's go."

I crossed the short distance to where Kourtney was standing, slightly off to one side of the small group. Reaching her side, I wrapped my arms around her, drawing her tight to me. Her head tilted back, but before she could say anything I lowered my mouth to hers, kissing her deeply, despite our audience. I drew back, but not before dropping a few more small kisses on her full lips. I smiled at her somewhat shocked expression.

"What was that for?"

"For being you, Little Elf," I whispered into her ear.

"Oh."

I kissed her again. "You astound me, Kourtney Whyte."

"I like seeing people happy."

I tucked her tighter into my side and nuzzled her fragrant hair. "I like to see *you* happy."

"You do that for me," she replied, looking up at me with her brilliant, beautiful eyes.

I groaned deep in my chest. "When can we leave and not have it be rude?"

"You only want to go home and devour those brownies."

I leaned down. "It's not the brownies I want to devour, Kourtney."

"Oh!" She breathed out.

My lips brushed her ear. "As pretty as your dress is on? It's going to look far prettier on the floor beside our bed."

A small whimper escaped her throat.

"Soon."

I nodded. Looking over, Annie winked at me.

I grinned.

Our first date was a definite success.

Chapter Twenty Nine

~KOURTNEY~

WOKE UP, WRAPPED UP in Nathan. His arms were locked around me, his head resting on my chest. I stayed silent, my hand drifting through his hair, the thick strands feeling like silk under my fingers. He had slept well the past few nights, no twitching or nightmares. I wished he would tell me what caused him to cry out sometimes at night, or cling to me so fiercely. I studied his face, peaceful in sleep, and still so handsome. His rugged features were softened in repose but very appealing. He was warm and loving, and completely perfect to me.

Too perfect for you, the negative voice in my head whispered.

Instantly, a deep feeling of inadequacy flooded my mind. I would never be able to satisfy and hold this man. Sooner, rather than later, he would grow tired of me and his wonderful, caring gestures would end. The thought of his warm gaze turning into the cold sneer I was used to from the men in my life, made me shudder.

As if sensing my thoughts, his arms tightened and his head lifted; his drowsy gaze meeting mine. "What's the matter,

Chefgirl?" His voice was a low whisper in the still of the room.

I forced a smile to my lips. "Nothing," I lied. "I have to, um, pee and someone is using me as a mattress."

He smiled back, all sexy and dopey, and kissed my chin. "Sweetest fucking mattress I've ever slept on," he murmured as he rolled over. "Hurry back."

Slipping out of bed, I went into the bathroom, shutting the door. I made my way through my morning routine and went back into the bedroom. As I suspected, he was sound asleep again, his head burrowed into one pillow, his bright-colored hair a shaggy mess around his head, while his arms were locked around mine. As with everything else in his life, when he did something, he did it wholeheartedly; whether it was digging into a meal I cooked him, working on my computer, or sleeping.

He was sleeping peacefully, and I knew it would wake him if I slid back into bed with him. He had kicked off the covers and I stood admiring the long sleek lines of his back, remembering how his skin felt under my fingers. How tightly his muscles rippled as he thrust into me, groaning my name. I shook my head sadly as I thought of how amazing he was. He was simply too good for me; I wasn't worthy of someone like him—and, soon he would realize it.

Even last night, he had sighed at my obvious discomfort after we got home from the barbeque. He had, indeed, peeled off the dress he liked so much, but I had pleaded for it to be in the dark and the disappointed look on his face before the light switched off was evident. Although his lovemaking had been warm and tender, I had sensed his frustration with me. I knew it was growing daily no matter how he tried to hide it. I was already becoming annoying to him. Fighting back tears, I grabbed my running clothes and changed in the guestroom, wanting him to stay sleeping. He didn't like me going out this early in the morning to run and I knew he would hate the reason I did so. He wouldn't like the fact I used the surrounding darkness to not be noticed.

If I woke him up, he would want to come with me, and at

the moment, I wanted to be alone. No one was going to bother me, especially Andy. But knowing he would want me to, I slipped the cell phone he had gotten me into my pocket before I left. Quietly, I made my way out the door and stretched, then turning on my iPod, I chose one of my angrier playlists and took off running.

An hour later, I let myself back in and went to my room after a long drink of cold water. I wasn't surprised to see Nathan gone. No doubt he had woken up and knew I had gone for a run, and left to go do some things on his own. He had mentioned having errands to run today. A small grin played on my lips as I wondered if he left via the front door or had used the ladder and gone over the fence. He seemed to prefer that method. He said it was because it was how we started. My smile faltered as the familiar, negative voice in my mind whispered it was because he didn't want people to see him leaving my house and know he was with me.

Last night he had shown me he wasn't ashamed to be seen with me. He had been open and affectionate all night, never leaving my side and introducing himself as my boyfriend. He had rebuffed Colleen's advances, firmly stating his place in my life. He even let her believe we were living together, on a permanent basis. Something I wanted, but had yet to find the courage to ask. I couldn't stop the voice in my head that told me it would change. Not to get my hopes up, because it would end and I'd be alone again.

Sighing, I stepped into the shower and welcomed the heat of the water as it poured over my aching muscles. I had really pushed it today, getting my frustrations out by running faster and harder than normal. When I felt clean and my muscles less sore, I got out of the shower, wrapped myself in a towel and padded into the bedroom.

Sitting on the edge of the bed, I reached over and picked up his pillow, burying my face in it as I breathed deep. Having the scent of someone other than my own in my bed was still very new, and the fact it was *his* scent was incredibly amazing.

He always smelled so good and holding his pillow made me feel . . . safe. It wasn't a feeling I was used to and I knew I would miss it when it was gone.

I lay back, allowing myself to relax. I had the whole day ahead of me to fill. As I rested there, I could feel myself drifting, the breeze from the window floating over my warm, damp skin. Maybe, a little nap would be okay before I got up and decided what to do for the rest of the day. I tried to ignore the part of me hoping, once he was done with his errands, it would be spent with Nathan. We were together so much now; I missed him when he wasn't around. I had never realized how lonely I was until he became part of my life. A part I wasn't sure I could live without anymore. I sighed sadly as I reclined on top of the bed feeling myself start to drift.

The mattress dipping, a large figure looming over me, and a husky voice woke me with a start. "Well. Isn't this a pretty picture to come home to?" Nathan whispered as his lips dragged up my neck. "Such a tempting offer, lying there, waiting for me."

"I thought you'd gone out," I gasped.

"I did. I went to get us some coffee and breakfast since you left me alone." He growled, narrowing his eyes. "Why didn't you tell me you were going for a run, Kourtney? You know I hate it when you're out so early alone."

My hand cupped his stern face, loving that even, if only for now, he was concerned for me. "It wasn't as early today," I placated him. "I had my cell phone. And, you were sleeping so soundly, I didn't want to wake you."

His face softened. "I sleep well when I'm here with you. I haven't had a nightmare all week. I woke up, thinking you were in the bathroom, but you were gone." He frowned. "I didn't like it. Don't do it again." Leaning down, he kissed me tenderly. "Wake me up. Tell me you're going—even if you want to go alone. I need to know, okay?" He kissed me again, this time a little harder. "I need to know where you are, that you're safe."

My breath caught at the intensity in his eyes. "Okay," I

breathed.

He nodded. "Okay. Now . . . back to this lovely offering before me." He grinned as his hand reached down and tugged on the towel I had wrapped around me. My hand flew up, halting his actions. He froze and looked down at me, his expression serious once again. He studied me for a moment. "Why, Kourtney?"

"Let me get a T-shirt," I whispered. "Please."

He shook his head. "No. This stops now. Today."

He sat up, dragging his hands through his hair. Standing, he began pacing. "Why? Tell me why. Why won't you let me love you the way I want to? Why do you keep hiding from me?"

I could feel the tears welling and I sat up, unable to meet his eyes. The room was silent, and I wondered if this was it. He would leave now, tired of my insecurities I couldn't share with him, and I would be alone again. However, he stopped his pacing and came over, kneeling down in front of me; his hands lifted my chin, forcing me to meet his intense gaze. "Kourtney, I need you to do something for me. I'm begging you right now. Please."

His eyes were so passionate, and I nodded. He tugged on my hand, bringing me to my feet. "I need you to trust me. Please trust me. I *won't* hurt you, I promise; can you remember that for the next few minutes?"

Confused, I nodded again and watched as he tore off his shirt and pants, and stood before me naked and breathtaking as the sun glinted off his defined muscles and skin. Unconsciously, my hand tightened on the towel I had wrapped around my body, a small layer of protection against the ugliness hidden beneath. Nathan took me over to the mirror in the corner of my room, placing me slightly to one side of him. Our eyes locked in the mirror, his intense and troubled, mine terrified and panicked.

What was he going to do?

His hand gently cupped my shoulder, bringing me to his side. "What do you see?" His voice was quiet but piercing in the room.

"You."

"What about me?"

"I see how incredible you are," I whispered the truth.

"Describe me. Describe how you see me," he insisted.

I hesitated.

"Tell me."

"Tall. Lean and muscular. Long legs. Broad shoulders."

"Keep going, Kourtney." His voice was tight.

My eyes drifted to his hand, which was still resting on my shoulder. "You have beautiful hands; a musician's hands. They're so strong, but they always touch me so gently."

"What else?"

I lifted my eyes to meet his gaze. "Your face—"

"Is?"

I frowned, trying to figure out the best way to describe him. "Handsome. No, more than handsome. Rugged, yet beautiful. Your eyes are like windows to your soul, they're always so expressive. The color reminds me of the blue of the ocean. I love how bright your hair is. It's like molten copper and it feels so good when I touch it. And your mouth . . ." I paused. "It's sexy—so full. The things you say make me laugh; the way you smile makes me smile with you. It lights up a room. You have so many different smiles, and I love seeing them. And when you kiss me . . ." I shrugged. "There are no words." I looked at him, marveling at his attractiveness.

"You're perfect, Nathan."

He snorted, shaking his head. "I'm not perfect."

"I see how other women look at you. They think so, as well."

He frowned. "Are you referring to that woman last night? Colleen? I'm not even remotely interested in her."

"Other women were looking at you, too."

"I don't care how other women look at me, Kourtney. You're the only woman whose opinion matters to me." Our eyes locked and his hands tightened on my shoulders. He inhaled a deep breath, letting it escape slow.

"I am tall, yes. Long legs—yep. I'm muscular with broad shoulders, because I work out like a freaking demon at the gym in the building every day. Otherwise, I'd look like a bag of bones. I've never been able to keep weight on. When I was a kid, I was this skinny geek who got picked on all the time for being a walking skeleton. Until a few weeks ago, the only thing keeping the weight on besides muscle mass was too much beer and horrid frozen dinners high in fat. Now, I feel better because I drink less, eat wonderful, healthy, home-cooked meals, made by my *girlfriend* and when given the chance, run with her."

I dropped my head, and his hand shot out and lifted my chin. "Look at me," he demanded, pulling me in front of him.

His chin rested on my shoulder. "My nose has been broken twice and it's crooked. It's got a little bump on it and sits a little to the left." He angled his face. "See?" He waited until I nodded before he continued.

"I like to keep stubble on my face to hide the scars left over from teenage acne, so I'm grateful it's acceptable these days. My eyebrows could have their own zip code and my teeth are kind of crooked." He stared at me, silently daring me to protest. "I think the color of my hair and the brightness of my eyes is a strange combination, but I'm glad they please you."

"They do," I breathed in admiration. How could he not see how handsome he was?

"My eyes do express what I'm feeling, except it seems, to the one person I want them to talk to the most." His gaze continued to captivate me, my eyes riveted to his. His lips dragged up my neck to my ear. "And my mouth is only perfect when it is making you laugh or covering yours to kiss you"— his lips nibbled on my ear, making me shiver—"or bringing you pleasure. Otherwise, like the rest of me, it is far from perfect and gets me into a lot of trouble."

I gave him a shaky smile. He did say the most outrageous things to make me laugh.

"What about my scars, Kourtney? Why didn't you comment on them?"

"They're part of you. I don't even see them. You're perfect to me," I insisted.

He nodded, understanding written all over his face. "I know that."

His arms dropped and wrapped around my waist. "Look again, Kourtney. Now tell me what you see when you look at you."

My eyes shut.

"Open your eyes, Kourtney. Now." His voice gentled. "Look at me, please."

I opened my eyes and stared into his. There was no judgment or anger looking at me. Only a warmth and a need for understanding.

"Tell me," he begged quietly.

I looked briefly at myself before dropping my gaze.

"I'm short."

"I like that," he whispered, encouragingly. "You fit perfectly under my arm."

I lifted my eyes to him. "I have brown hair. Strange, mismatched eyes. A plain face. Totally forgettable."

He frowned. "What else?"

I laughed—the sound bitter in the room. "You won't let this go, will you?"

"No."

I closed my eyes and let it all out. "My eyes are too round and big, and the color thing freaks people out. My nose is too big, and my mouth is too small. My hair is all over the place and has a mind of its own. My face is . . . round . . . chubby." I hesitated but knew I needed to say it—finally say it. "I'm fat, Nathan. Unattractive. Worthless. I know it's true because it's what I've been told all my life. It's what I see reflected in the mirror every day." The words started pouring out and I couldn't stop them. "I'm nothing. I'm not good enough for you. I'm too short, I weigh too much and compared to your tall, lean body, I am . . . short, lumpy and dumpy. I don't want you to see me in the light because you'll see all my stretch marks and how my body sags. It's hard enough imagining what you're thinking when you touch me, and I'm not sure I can stand to see the look on your face when you see how very unattractive I am in broad daylight, fully naked. I keep waiting for you to wake up and realize how much better you could do than me." I inhaled a painful breath. "I keep waiting for you to walk away."

The room was utterly silent, except for my harsh breathing and his shocked gasp when I finished. His arms tightened around me.

"*Kourtney.*"

The tears that had been threatening, dripped down my face, and I couldn't open my eyes. Nathan's arms loosened and he shifted so he was standing in front of me.

"Hey," he pleaded. "Look at me."

I forced my eyes open and looked at him, blinking to clear away the tears that kept filling them.

He used his fingers to gently wipe away the ones flowing down my cheeks and he frowned at me. "You are so wrong, Kourtney."

I shook my head.

He gripped me to him tight. "What have they done to you?" he murmured. He held me close for a few minutes, then stepped back, lifting my chin. "We're not finished here."

Wearily, I met his sad gaze. He was quiet for a moment, then spoke. "I saw you, you know. Before I came over the fence that day, I saw you."

My eyes widened in shock. "When?"

"The first time was a Sunday morning when I left early to go meet someone. Then I saw you again before I put it together the sexy little runner I was seeing, who I felt this incredible protective pull to, was indeed, you."

"Oh."

"And you know what I thought the very first time? And the next day? And every time after that?"

"No."

"How much I wanted to meet the person hidden under the

hood. The one who seemed to be hiding. I was drawn to you even then, Kourtney. I didn't think you were fat or unattractive. I thought you were lovely. And when I realized it was my Chefgirl I was catching glimpses of, I became even more determined to meet you, and get to know you."

He stepped back behind me, and before I could stop him, grabbed the top of the towel and yanked it away from my torso. I gasped in shock and tried to curl into myself, my shoulders hunching and my arms coming up to cover myself, but he would have none of that. He held me flush to him, pinning my arms at my side. "Stop hiding from me, Kourtney."

He waited until I stopped struggling, his hold never lessening. "Now, let's talk about what I see when I look at you."

Slowly, he loosened his hold, his hands running up my arms and across my collarbone. His head dropped to my shoulder, his lips at my ear. "Relax, Kourtney. Please, baby, relax. It's me. I'm not going to hurt you. I could never hurt you."

"You could, it'd be so easy," I whispered painfully.

His eyes met mine. "That's only because you keep waiting for me to do so, because it's what you know. But it's not going to happen. Not anymore," he insisted. "I need you to listen to me now, okay? Really listen." His hand continued to stroke my arms, his touch soothing, never rushed. "Are you with me, Kourtney?"

I nodded.

"Your skin is so soft," he murmured, warm and tender. "It's like satin under my fingers. I love touching you. And when I touch you, Kourtney? The only thing I'm thinking is how good you feel under my fingers. How much more I want to touch you . . . everywhere." His nose touched the base of my neck and he inhaled deeply. "You always smell so good. Warm, sweet, sexy. It's a scent that is all you. It calls to me. It calms me when I'm close to you."

He stared at me. "Your hair is incredibly gorgeous. It's not plain brown. You have red, gold, and all sorts of little colors in it—especially when you're in the sun. And I love running my

hands through it. It's one of my favorite things about you."
As if to show me he meant it, he gathered the tresses up and
tangled his fingers through them, then allowed the locks to
settle back down around my shoulders. He placed his hands
on my arms again, his fingers gently caressing the skin. He
was calm, but intense, when he spoke again. "You, Kourtney,
are *not* unattractive. You are lovely. And you could never be
forgettable. Ever. Your smile is contagious and your face glows
with warmth. I love it when you smile. I love being the one who
makes you smile. And your eyes . . . your eyes are breathtaking.
They aren't freaky or weird. They are exotic and stunning—
unique—like you. They draw me in and show your emotions so
vividly." He paused and searched my eyes in the mirror. "But
right now, I hate the emotions coming from them."

I started to look away. "No. Kourtney. Look at me." He
waited until I raised my eyes again.

"I understand why you think you're unattractive, but I'm
more than happy to spend the rest of my life showing you how
wrong you are. The assholes who drummed all the bullshit into
your head need to be taught a lesson in what is unattractive. I
think they can start by looking in the mirror themselves," he
stated with conviction. "You aren't a fake Hollywood beauty.
You aren't overdone like that woman last night. *You're real.* I
could look at you the rest of my life and never tire of your sweet
face. All the things you find imperfect, work for me. I love how
you look." He leaned over, kissing my nose. "Especially this.
There is *nothing* big about your little button here, by the way. It
fits perfectly on your face."

His hands reached for mine and he ran them over my
breasts. "You aren't scrawny like me. I know this. I like it. I
like your curves and how you feel to me. But you are *not* fat,
Kourtney." Our hands cupped my breasts, his larger ones
encompassing both. "I love how your breasts fill my hands.
How rich and full they are. They're incredible." He grinned at
me. "I want to touch them all the time. And I love sleeping on
them." He let his hands rest there for a minute, gently caressing

the skin as he ignored my breathing that had picked up. Our hands dropped and he caressed my torso, leaving one hand on my stomach while the other rested on my hip. His voice was low. "I love how your hips feel when I grab them. Soft, melting into my touch. How they look in your jeans or one of your pretty skirts. Round, shapely. Teasing me." He pushed forward, his erection hard on my back. "Can't you feel how you affect me, Kourtney? How fucking sexy I think you are?"

"I was heavier," I insisted. "I still wear a size sixteen, sometimes an eighteen. I have stretch marks. And so many scars."

His reply was patient. "They're like my acne scars, Kourtney. Or the burn marks I have. They're marks. They show me you survived something."

I looked at the silver marks running across my hips and stomach, and the huge twisted scar left by my surgery. "They're ugly."

His finger traced the deep, long scar that ran along my right side, his touch light, but he didn't comment on it. "Nothing about you is ugly, Kourtney. *Nothing.*" His lips trailed up to my ear. "The same way you don't see my scars, I don't see yours. I see *you*. Curvy. Beautiful. Voluptuous. Lush." He bit down gently on my ear. "Mine."

I shivered at his tone.

"You're as beautiful to me as I am to you, Kourtney. Nothing I see in front of me is ugly, or to be ashamed of. I see nothing but beauty and warmth." His eyes locked on mine. "I see nothing but you. And you, my Kourtney, are beautiful."

I stared at myself, not understanding what he was seeing. Beautiful? Me?

"You're healthy, Kourtney. You look after yourself. Does it matter if you're not a size zero? You're so much more than the weight you seem to think you carry."

"I've always been told . . ."

He interrupted me harshly. "They were wrong. And you admitted a moment ago you have changed."

"What?"

"You said it yourself. You were heavier. *Were*. You're beautiful, Kourtney. In my eyes you *are* perfect. Stop trying to please someone you can never please. Don't look at yourself the way they did. Stop listening to a voice that will only hurt you. Listen to a voice, to a person, who sees you for what you are—for who you are. How amazing I think you are."

I drew in a deep breath. "I want to."

Nathan turned me around so I was facing him. "Trust me, Kourtney. Stop fighting me. Stop hiding from me." He cupped my face tenderly, his voice low. "I *love* you, Kourtney. I want to show you how much. I want you to be free with me."

"You . . . you love me?"

He nodded. "I love you. Everything about you." His hands tightened on my face. "Do you think you could possibly let my opinion of you be the one to guide you rather than the opinion of someone who doesn't love you?"

I hesitated.

He loved me.

I had never heard those words spoken to me.

"Nobody has ever said that to me before. Ever," I whispered; my throat tight with emotion. "Nobody has *ever* loved me."

He gazed down, tears gathering in his eyes. "*I* love you, Kourtney. And I'll tell you . . . I'll show you every day, if you'll let me. Please let me."

"You don't want me to change?"

His tone was tender. "I do, actually. I want you to be happy. With yourself. With me."

"Nobody ever wanted that for me."

He frowned. "I'm not nobody, Kourtney. I'm yours, if you'll have me."

Mine.

This beautiful man wanted to be mine. He loved me. Just the way I was; scars, marks and curves included. And I loved him back. Fiercely.

Fresh tears poured down my face. "I love you so much." I

struggled to get the words out.

Instantly, his lips were on mine, his tongue pushing its way into my mouth, seeking and tasting. His kiss was possessive and powerful, overwhelming my senses. I could taste his emotional tears, mixed with mine as he held me closer, never breaking the kiss. His hands trailed up and down my back and sides, and for the first time I didn't cringe away from his touch. I could feel the love in his caresses. How gently he touched me. His hands weren't seeking what was wrong, but loving what he found right. And my curves didn't make him recoil; he liked them.

I wound one arm around his neck, bringing myself closer to his blistering kiss and reached between us, wrapping my hand around his erection. He groaned, pulling me with him as he walked backward toward the bed. He spun us around and lowered us both on to the mattress, never breaking contact with my lips. He leaned away a little, giving me more access to his erection as his hands cupped and stroked my breasts, teasing the nipples, which were hard and aching for his mouth. He pulled away, gasping, as I began stroking him harder; desire I had never experienced before shooting through me. He stared down at me, his chest heaving. "Can I love you now, Kourtney?" he rasped. "The way I want to? No holding back?"

I gasped at the look of pure lust in his eyes. No one had ever looked at me that way before. "Yes . . . *oh God*, please. I want you so much," I begged, my voice husky with desire.

He loomed over me, his lips trailing up my neck. "I want you." His hips thrust forward, his cock hard and leaking in my hand. "*Feel* how much I want you. How fucking sexy you are to me." He groaned as I started using both hands on him. "*Fuuuuck . . . Kourtney . . . Yes,*" he hissed, claiming my mouth again and I lost myself to the sensations he was evoking in me. Everything around me ceased to exist. It was only him and me. His mouth, his tongue, his body pressing into mine. He stroked me with his fingers and hands, his voice moaning and whispering sweet and dirty things into my ears, about everything he was going to do to me. Today, tomorrow, next week, the rest of his life. All the ways he was going to have me.

He moved his lips down, drawing my nipple into his mouth, his fingers continuing down, slipping into my folds. I gasped in pleasure at the sensation. He lifted his head, releasing my nipple with one final swipe of his tongue. "You're so wet, Kourtney. So wet for me, baby," he groaned. He kneeled on the floor, pulling me to the edge of the mattress. I stiffened but he refused to allow me to stop. "All of you, Kourtney. I want all of you," he declared, as his fingers continued to stroke my skin. "It's my turn to taste you."

I cried out with a startled, wanton gasp, as I felt his mouth on me. Pleasure I had never experienced coursed through me as he worked me with his mouth and fingers. Sounds I didn't recognize escaped my throat as I arched myself closer to his mouth, desperate for his touch. When he angled his head back, I whimpered in protest and lifted my head to meet his intense gaze.

"Kourtney"—he licked his lips as he stared at me—"you taste like sin. *Fucking, glorious sin.*"

I collapsed back onto mattress as his tongue returned to my aching, wanting center; my desire now at an all-time high. In a matter of seconds, I could feel my orgasm building, as his mouth licked and sucked, his tongue teasing, pressing, making me burn with a frantic, fierce need. My hips lifted, my body stretching itself taut and I came, my orgasm intense, as I screamed his name.

Nathan's lips gentled, and nuzzled me as I shuddered around him, drawing out my orgasm until I was a mass of shaking limbs. I felt the mattress dip as he crawled up my body, looking down at me with a wicked gleam in his eye. Bending down, he kissed me deeply, and I moaned when I tasted myself on his tongue. "I'm not done with you yet, Kourtney," he murmured against my lips as he dragged us both farther up on the mattress. "I want inside you, pretty girl. Now." He moaned my name as he pushed my legs back to my chest. "Tell me you want me. Like this. Right now," he demanded quietly. "I need to know you want this."

"I do." I gasped, arching my hips for him. "I want you."

"This isn't going to be gentle," he warned. "Or take very long. I want you too much."

"*Please.*"

His hands tightened on my legs as he thrust forward, entering me with a deep groan. In another move I wasn't expecting, he grabbed my legs and flung them over his shoulders as he began thrusting powerfully. In this new position, I could feel every inch of him as he moved deep within me, hitting a place inside me I never dreamed existed. I moaned in pleasure as he moved strongly above me. His eyes were locked on mine as he smirked and arched his eyebrow at me. "You like that, my girl? You gonna come for me again?" He growled, lifting my hips off the bed, continuing to pump into me hard.

I groaned his name as I felt the coil twisting inside me again; tightening quick, ready to burst at any given second.

He lowered his head as his orgasm approached. I could feel him swelling and felt his body tensing around me. "Come for me, Kourtney. I want to feel you coming with me," he begged before he threw his head back, groaning, clutching my hips as he thrust deeper, frantically calling my name. Watching him fall apart, I shuddered around him, losing myself, feeling his intense orgasm almost as if it was my own, before falling with him once again.

He collapsed on my chest and the only sound in the room was our ragged breathing. I lifted my hand and caressed his hair as he lay on top of me, his weight warm and solid. After a few minutes he pulled out of me, rolled to the side and dragged me to his chest, his arms holding me snug as he nuzzled his lips in my hair.

"I love you, Kourtney."

I snuggled even closer, his quiet declaration making me feel complete. "I love you," I said, trying to stifle the yawn that escaped as I spoke.

"Sleep, my sweet girl." His voice was tender and amused.

"I'll be here when you wake up." His arms tightened around me. "Promise me you'll be here when I do."

"I will. I'm not going anywhere."

He sighed. "Good. I need you with me."

I smiled as I drifted into sleep.

He loved me.

He needed me.

Me.

This perfect man.

Perfect for me.

And the other voice . . . was finally silent.

Chapter Thirty

K OURTNEY WAS SLEEPING, HER BODY curled into mine. My fingers stroked her thick hair spread out on the pillow as I gazed down at her. Her self-image was distorted, she couldn't see it, but she was beautiful—and so vulnerable and broken. I smiled sadly, thinking of the fact I had just experienced the most meaningful sex of my life; with a woman who was completely convinced she wasn't good enough to be loved by anyone, yet deserved to be loved more than any person I had ever met. I hadn't meant to tell her I loved her today. I didn't want to do that until she knew who I was and what I was hiding from her. But seeing her pain earlier, her panic at allowing me to see her fully, I had to let her know how I felt about her.

I had thought she was really shy, but there was so much more to her fears than I had realized. Hearing the fact she cringed away from my touch, fearing a negative reaction, had caused my heart to ache. My fingers cupped the back of her head, as I remembered the pain in her eyes when she looked at me, expecting rejection and coldness, while she at last revealed her fears to me. She would never get either from me. I had fallen in love with her spirit, her giving, thoughtful ways and her physical appearance was only enhanced by what I knew lay underneath. To me she was perfect. And I would do whatever it took to help her see herself the way I saw her, not the image she had been forced into seeing all these years.

I knew from the things she had told me, she had spent most of her life knowing only criticism and the feeling of never being enough. I frowned as I thought about her loneliness and isolation, of the constant denial and neglect she had experienced. How the effects of the treatment she'd experienced had lingered, causing her to shy away from people since she now expected rejection.

My rage was huge toward the people who caused her to feel she wasn't enough. I thought of the times I had been told I was loved: by my parents, by Sophie and Trevor, even the occasional friend threw it out there. The fact she had been denied those words *all* of her life made me furious. How could they not see the wonderful, *stunning*, giving woman in front of them? How could they have ridiculed and berated a young girl to the point she stopped believing she could ever be enough for anyone? That she was worth less than them?

I could feel my wrath building as I thought of my sister Sophie. All my life I had protected my younger sister and I couldn't understand how Kourtney's brother had been the one causing her pain, joining her tormentors at school and in public, then continued his callous behavior behind the closed doors of their house. Or her own father, who not only allowed him to hurt her, but joined in on a regular basis. I couldn't fathom how they lived with themselves and what they'd done to Kourtney.

I wrapped my arms back around my sleeping girl and brought her closer. Would I ever be able to make her fully see how infinitely precious she was to me? She would never be denied warmth, caresses or loving words. She would never again be subjected to treatment like that. And I would protect her against anyone who tried. Silently, I promised to safeguard her. To be everything she had never had growing up.

To love her unconditionally.

Closing my eyes, I drifted off, wrapped up in the warmth and scent of *her*. My Kourtney.

KOURTNEY'S GENTLE HAND WAS RUNNING over my chest and shoulder, tracing my tattoo over and again. I opened my eyes to watch her touch my skin; her bottom lip caught up in her teeth as she studied the movements of her hand. I had to smile at the look of concentration on her face, and as if sensing I was now awake, her gorgeous eyes flew to mine and she withdrew her hand.

I shook my head and released one arm still wrapped around her. I placed her hand back on my chest. "Don't stop. Touch me, Kourtney. I love how it feels when you touch me."

She smiled nervously, but went back to her loving caresses. "I like touching you," she whispered.

I hummed. "That's a good thing." I ghosted my hand up and down her side, relishing the feeling of her warm, supple skin stretched over her curves. "I love touching you. " I murmured. "Your skin feels like silk."

I felt her stiffen, but she didn't pull away. I continued stroking her, silently willing her to relax. To accept my touch as it was meant—a way of showing my adoration. "I love your curves, Kourtney. I love how you feel under my fingers." I grinned and shifted, pinning her underneath me, chuckling at her quiet gasp. "I love how *you* feel under me." I nuzzled my face into her neck, kissing and nipping my way up to her ear. "I love how I feel inside you, how you feel wrapped around me. Nothing compares to the sensation of being buried inside your warmth," I groaned.

I saw the look of nervous want on her face. She still couldn't believe someone could find her desirable or I could find her sexy. I stifled a sigh, knowing I had to be patient and show her until she *knew* without a doubt how amazing she was; as a friend, a lover and a person.

I drew her mouth to mine, kissing her deep, drinking in her taste. I didn't stop until I felt her relax under me, until I knew she was as lost with my kisses as I was with hers. I swept my hand over her, my mouth never leaving hers as I touched and caressed her entire body. I slid my fingers along the warmth of her skin, as I slowly stoked the growing fire between us. I ground my aching cock into her, needing her to feel my want. The want I had for her. Only for her.

Her touch was hesitant at first, but became bolder as we lost ourselves to each other. Light, tender caresses became firmer and more confident; her hands began pulling me down to her, molding my body to hers as she began rocking up against me. Nestling between her legs, I felt her heat and wetness, desire coursing through me once again.

Her head fell back with a sexy, passion filled moan. "Take me, Nathan. Make me yours again," she pleaded.

Growling low in my throat, I eased my aching cock into her warmth, stilling at the feeling. She arched up, taking all of me and groaning at the connection. I wrapped her up, and without breaking contact, rolled us so she was on top of me. Her eyes flew open as she sat up and stared down at me in shock; her hands crossing over her chest as she stilled. "What are you doing?" she whispered, panic evident in her voice.

I sat up, pulling her mouth down to mine, kissing her hard. "*You*, Kourtney, take *me*. Make *me* yours," I commanded softly as I lay back down, watching her with hooded eyes. "Show me you want me as much as I want you. Take control—" I urged.

Her wide eyes met mine. I loosened her arms she had folded across her chest. "Don't hide from me, Kourtney. Don't cover yourself up from my eyes." I held her hips tight as I thrust upwards, watching her eyes widen again at the sensation. "Trust me. Be with me . . . give me this. Please." The last word was a low groan as I felt her clench her muscles around me with her desire.

My thumbs traced small circles on the flesh on her hips. "I love how soft you are here. How you fit in my hands." I leaned up, wrapping her in my arms. "How your breasts sway as you move . . . it's so fucking sexy to me, Kourtney. How you flow into me . . . it drives me wild," I murmured huskily into her ear, loving how she shuddered at my words before I laid back down, watching her as she struggled to let go of her fears.

"I want you, Kourtney. All of you. Have me now . . . make me yours," I pleaded with her, arching back up into her again. "Ride me, Kourtney," I groaned, pleasure spiking through my body.

Her face changed, her uncertainty lifting as pure desire lit her face.

"Yesss . . ." I hissed as she began moving over me, filled with need at the vision before me. Slowly she built a rhythm, and I followed her actions, letting her control both of us. Watching her as she writhed above me, I moaned in satisfaction. Her hair floated past her shoulders in a dark cloud, her breasts jutting out as her head arched back and she started riding me in deep, languid movements, her hips rolling smoothly as she pushed and pulled, building the heat and pushing my need for her to the limit.

Sitting up, I yanked her close, lowering my head and using my lips and teeth on her full breasts, cupping them as I kissed and teased her hard nipples. Her panting breaths in my ear as she clung to me turned into a low gasp as her body went taut, and she shuddered as she found her release. My name fell from her lips as she convulsed around me, causing my own orgasm to tear through me as I crushed her to me. I thrust up into her one last time, riding out the spasms before I stilled, holding her tight. I couldn't stop myself from trailing kisses over her rich hair or my fingers from running up and down her back as we clung to each other in the moment.

Gently, I held her with me as I lay back down, keeping her close when she tried to move off. "Don't even think about it, Chefgirl," I warned softly. "And stop thinking what you're thinking. You're perfect where you are," I mumbled into her hair, refusing to let her move, loving the feeling of being wrapped up in her. She allowed herself to relax and we both sighed in peace.

"I love you," I breathed as I grazed my lips across her crown yet again, unable to stop kissing her.

Her arms tightened on my shoulders. "I love you, Nathan."

"That was the sexiest thing I've ever seen, Kourtney."

She lifted her head from my chest and I propped mine up to look back at her. Her voice was shy when she spoke. "Really?"

I nodded, lifting her hand to my mouth to caress it. "The woman I love, trusting me—that itself is a turn on . . ." I stared, watching the color creep onto her cheeks as my voice dropped. "But watching you ride me, Kourtney? Fucking hot. And something I want to see again and again. You're so sexy; you have no idea."

She chuckled and boldly pressed her hips down where we were still joined, causing a small groan to escape. "I think I may have a pretty good idea how turned on you were," she whispered as she waggled her eyebrows at me, making me chuckle along with her. Her hand reached up and gently traced my lips. "You make me feel . . . sexy, Nathan." Her cheeks deepened again as she shook her head in wonder. "I've never felt like that before," she added.

"You are sexy, Kourtney. I thought it the first time I saw you and I think it now. It isn't going to change."

"Be patient with me, please," she whispered. "This is all new to me."

I rolled us over, and gathered her into my arms. "I will be, Kourtney. Please trust me. I love you. *You.* Not your dress size, not the imperfections you see when you look at yourself. Just you. Understand?"

She nodded against my chest.

"I'll try."

I held her closer.

"That's all I ask."

Chapter Thirty One

THE NEXT FEW DAYS, I strove to show Kourtney how I felt about her. Our evenings were spent together, always touching. Now that I knew all of Kourtney's fears, her insecurities and the level of neglect she had experienced, I realized what had been missing all her life and I was determined to rectify it. For so long she had been denied the simplest of all things: touch and acceptance. She had been taught she wasn't worthy of hugs and kind words. All her life she had been made to feel ashamed of her own body so she had learned to hold herself back.

At every opportunity, I held her, caressed, and kissed her, trying to convey with my touch how much I cared for her. We started going for walks at night, holding hands as we explored the neighborhood together. We often stopped and chatted with Mrs. Webster, and I smirked at her side-long, knowing looks.

There were long kisses goodbye in the morning and even longer, deeper ones when we reunited at night. Every chance I found, I praised her, enjoying the fact my words could cause her smile to blossom. The words "I love you" left my lips several times a day, my own smile breaking through when I heard them returned from her mouth. Every night I made love to her, groaning deep with the intense sensations brought forth from being joined with her intimately. Each day, we grew closer and each day the thought of ever leaving her grew more abhorrent to me. When I was with her, I felt complete.

I was grateful to see the end of Thursday. It had been a long, hard day, with problems all over the building. I was late coming home, bringing a laptop with me to work on. Kourtney was across from me, folding laundry, her low laughter making me look up from the keyboard. "What?"

"Four of your five pair of socks have holes in them. You need new ones."

"I have a new package in my drawer next door. I'll get them after I get this started."

"I'll go."

"I have to get the box of discs from the drawer in the desk."

"I can get them for you."

I held out my keys. "Okay. Look in the right top drawer of the dresser for the socks. Left drawer, blue box of discs from the desk in the main room."

"Got it."

I went back to work, realizing after a little while, she hadn't come back. About to go and look for her, I heard the front door open and I glanced up, ready to tease her about finding my hidden porn and being shocked when I saw the look on her face.

Her pale, upset face.

"Kourtney?"

She stared at me, holding up a thick envelope. "I searched the wrong drawer."

Fear, like icy water, ran down my spine, making me shudder. She held the large envelope containing all my letters to my mother and sister, and my legal documents.

I'd waited too long to tell her, and now she found out about my past the wrong way.

"You . . . you were in prison, Nathan?"

"Yes."

"You lied to me—all this time?" Her voice quivered with repressed emotion. "Did you lie to me about everything? Has this all been a . . . diversion?"

I stood up, reaching for her, already feeling her rejection when she stepped back from my touch. "No, Kourtney! The way I feel about you is honest and real—I love you. You mean everything to me!"

"Still, you lied."

"I did," I admitted. "I was afraid."

"Why?"

"I was too scared to tell you the truth—I was terrified you'd walk away from me."

"Why were you in prison?"

"Will you listen? Will you hear my story?"

She hesitated, looking distraught, and making my heart ache.

"Please let me tell you." I swallowed the lump forming in my throat. "If you want me to leave after, I will."

It felt like an eternity before she nodded. "Okay, Nathan. I'll listen."

After she sat down, I sat beside her; not touching, but close. "I went to prison for manslaughter."

Her gaze widened; her expression wary. "You killed someone?"

Slowly, my hands tightened into fists. "Yes."

She stared at me, her eyes filled with fear. "On purpose?"

"No! Don't look at me like that, baby, please. Don't look at me as if you're now afraid of me. It was an accident—I swear."

"Tell me," she demanded, whisper-soft.

"I was in prison for involuntary manslaughter and reckless driving. I went in when I was eighteen and got out on early parole just after my twenty-second birthday." I inhaled a deep rush of air for courage. "I was driving my car and lost control, killing one passenger and injuring another."

"Nathan," she breathed.

"I killed my little brother." I had to stop for a moment. "And my sister Sophie was injured, but she survived."

She gasped, her hand covering her mouth. I took the chance and inched closer, wanting to feel her closeness.

"If it was an accident, why did you go to jail?"

"I need to tell you the whole story so you can understand."

"All right." She drew in a deep breath. "I'm listening, Nathan."

I captured her hand, kissing the tender palm, then releasing it. "Thank you."

I stood up and walked around the room, a place that wasn't mine, yet felt so much like home because of the woman who lived there. The one I desperately prayed I hadn't lost because of my cowardice. Every nerve in my body felt as if it was on the outside of my skin—burning and snapping—not allowing me to remain in one spot.

"I grew up on the East Coast in Nova Scotia. My dad died when I was ten. My mom remarried not long afterward, and the man she married, Ryan, had a young son—Trevor. He was six years younger than me, three years younger than Sophie."

"Did you get along with him? Ryan, I mean?"

I shrugged. "Mostly—at first anyway—things went downhill pretty fast. My mom doted on Trevor—we all kind of did—he was at that age, you know? He was a cute little bugger—easy to love. People thought I resented him, but I didn't. I didn't show it the way my mom and sister did, but he was my little buddy, and I never thought of him as Ryan's son, but my little brother."

"What happened?"

"I became a teenager. Ryan and I butted heads a lot. He was on my case all the time and I rebelled. I rebelled often." I laughed dryly. "I was grounded a great deal of the time."

"What about your mom?"

"She sided with Ryan most of the time. I'm not saying she was wrong, but sometimes I felt as if she could have stuck up for me a little more. I know I gave her a hard time, though."

"And Sophie?"

I smiled a genuine smile. "My little sister was a hippie from a bygone era. She believed in love and peace. She wore these flowy dresses, her hair was this wild mass of blonde curls, and she was one of the sweetest souls I'd ever known. I called her 'Gypsy-girl' because she reminded me of a free spirit. She always stuck up for me." I met Kourtney's unique, cautious gaze. "Until I met you I didn't think anyone like that existed anymore."

"Don't." She looked away, and I cleared my throat of the emotion I felt building. I needed to stick to telling my story and save my apologies for afterward. If she'd let me apologize.

Trying to loosen some of the tension, I rolled my shoulders, and continued. "When I was sixteen, my mom gave me my dad's old Mustang. She'd kept it all those years for me. I don't think Ryan was too happy about it, but by that point, I didn't really care."

I looked down at my feet, gathering my thoughts. My fingers flexed and relaxed in a constant rhythm—a nervous habit I'd picked up in prison when I needed some sort of physical release. "The car needed a lot of work. I got a part-time job to pay for the parts, my friends helped with labor, but it still took almost eighteen months to get it done. I was so fucking proud of that car. I heard Ryan telling my mom I'd get bored with it and abandon the project—but he had no idea what it meant to me. It belonged to my dad—my real dad—and I could remember driving around in it with him. I knew how much he loved it. It was like having a piece of him."

"What happened?"

I stared out the window, silent. "I was young and stupid, Kourtney. Not long after my eighteenth birthday, I was home with Trevor and Sophie—I was grounded again, I think. Mom and Ryan were out. I was restless—I'd had another argument with Ryan earlier, and I was stewing in my room, thinking it was time for me to move out and be done with him. Trevor and Sophie came to my room, wanting to go for ice cream. And in a moment of weakness, or rebellion maybe, I said okay."

"Why a moment of weakness?"

"Ryan wouldn't allow them in my car."

"Oh."

"It was perfect—my own way to get back at Ryan with him never knowing. They promised not to tell, so I drove us to the local ice cream shop and we had cones. On the way home, they both begged for a longer ride and I was stupid enough to agree—after all, what could go wrong?"

"But something did?"

I sucked in a deep breath. "It had rained earlier in the day and the back road I went down was muddy. We were having such a good time—we were laughing, the windows were down, the music blaring and we were just driving. Trevor begged to go faster and I did." A long shudder ran down my spine. "I misjudged my speed and how fast I could take the bend in the road."

Emotion overwhelmed me and I leaned on the window sill, gripping the wood hard. "I lost control. The car rolled and we ended up ramming into a tree."

From behind me I could hear Kourtney's murmured words of sympathy. My words came out faster—now I had started telling her, I wanted the whole story out.

"The car caught fire. I woke up; the car was filled with smoke and I was upside down. I was disoriented, panicked, and I had a terrible searing pain in my leg. My seat belt was still in place and it took me a bit to get it undone and get out of the car. I pulled Sophie out of the back—she was unconscious and bleeding, but she was alive. I raced to the other side of the car to get Trevor out." I shut my eyes as the memory of his limp, blood-spattered body sliding from the upside down car into my arms washed over me. "He was dead."

"Oh, Nathan. How awful."

I didn't want to talk about the accident anymore. If I did, I was going to lose it—big time. I could feel the emotions bearing down on me, making me tremble with their intensity. I plunged my clenched fists into my pockets to hide the shaking.

"I was brought up on manslaughter and reckless driving charges. I didn't fight it—I pled guilty and I went to prison here in Ontario."

"Why didn't you fight it? Why didn't your parents try and stop you?"

A bitter laugh escaped my throat and I turned to meet her gaze. "My parents, especially Ryan, blamed me for the accident and Trevor's death, and they were right. I wasn't supposed to take them in the car. I shouldn't have been driving so fast. It was my fault—I killed him and I hurt Sophie. I walked away with some contusions, broken ribs, and a few scars on my leg. But I was alive. Why would I put them through a trial and try to duck the blame?" I shook my head. "I was considered an adult and it was my decision. The only thing I argued about was the reason. Ryan told everyone I always disliked Trevor—I was jealous of the attention he got and he thought I did it on purpose, but I didn't. I was irresponsible and stupid—yes. But I didn't do it on purpose." My voice broke. "I—I loved that kid."

"You went to jail."

"Yes."

"And your family—they didn't come see you?"

"My stepfather came to see me the first week I was in prison. He told me they wanted nothing to do with me anymore. I didn't believe him. I started writing to my mother, begging her to listen, to know I didn't do it on purpose—I would never hurt Trevor or Sophie intentionally. I never got a response. I tried to call her, but the number was changed and unlisted. The number the prison had for emergencies was Ryan's private cell phone. Eventually some of the letters came back marked undeliverable. I found out later they had moved."

"You kept all the letters?"

"I did." I shrugged, unsure how to explain it. "It was all I had."

Her hands clutched her knees so hard, the knuckles were white. She regarded me sadly. "So you were all alone?"

"Yes. All my friends were back east so I had no visitors. I

was too ashamed of what I'd done to try and stay in contact with anyone. I convinced myself it was better for everyone that way. Grant tried to tell me differently . . . but I didn't listen."

"Grant? The friend you had coffee with?"

I nodded. "He was the mandated counselor I was assigned when I was in prison. I wasn't exactly a model patient at first, but gradually I started to trust him. He became a friend—he left the prison not long before I was released. It was his testimony at the parole hearing that got me out early. He and his wife, Claire, took me in for a while until I got on my feet. They co-signed my loan so I could buy my car and again for my house. They live up north and I go see him every month or so." I sighed. "If it hadn't been for their kindness when I got out, I'm not sure what would have happened to me."

"Why?"

"Ryan was waiting for me when I walked out of prison. He gave me the first of the letters I had written, and said none of them wanted anything to do with me. He told me to leave them alone—to forget they existed because they had already forgotten me. He was there to make sure I got the message."

"Are you sure he was telling the truth?"

"The letters are marked *return to sender* in my mother's writing. There was also a note saying to leave them alone. I got the message. I had to beg him to tell me if Sophie was okay—if she had recovered. He said she had, but she didn't want to see me."

"Have you . . ." Her voice trailed off.

"I looked when I first got out of prison. I know they moved away from the East Coast, but I've never searched for them past that—I couldn't handle more rejection. I thought I found Sophie once on Facebook, but it wasn't her. Grant offered to help find them, but I didn't see the point. Ryan and my mother made themselves very clear. I wasn't welcome. They had their life, and I had to go and find mine."

"But, you're her son. And your sister—"

I shrugged. "Sometimes, you can't forgive, Kourtney. They

couldn't."

"Why did you keep this a secret from me?"

I scrubbed my face with my hand, feeling weary. "Grant asked me the same thing. I didn't want to see the way you looked at me change." I frowned. "I didn't want to see you look at me the way you are now. Like I'm a complete stranger."

Kourtney didn't say anything—she simply stared at me. Remembering Grant's advice, I decided I needed to leave her alone and process what I'd told her.

I pushed off the wall where I'd been leaning, picking up my keys from the table. "I made a huge error in judgment that night and I killed my little brother, and lost my family. It's something I have to live with every day, for the rest of my life. It seems I made another huge error not being honest with you. I'm sorry about that—more than I can say. I hope you can forgive me. I hope you'll think it over and let me try to make it up to you. That maybe, you could trust me again."

I waved at the laptop and messenger bag still lying on the table, too tired to care about them at the moment. "I'll get those later. I'll go back next door and wait to hear from you. If I don't, I'll understand. I'll hate it, but I'll understand and I'll forever be grateful to have had you in my life while I did. You showed me there are good people left in the world." I hesitated and looked directly into her eyes. "But I pray you can forgive me. I already lost so much—I'm not sure I can survive losing you, too."

Turning around, I had only made it a few steps when Kourtney spoke up. "Why do you say it that way?"

I frowned in confusion. "Say what?'

"You always call your place next door, or over there, never home, or even my house. Why?"

"That's not my home, Kourtney. It's only the place I was living while I was waiting for you to find me. You're home to me."

Her eyes filled with tears, her lips trembling. "I don't want you to leave."

I froze, my entire body beginning to shake. Did she mean

what I thought she meant?

She held out her hand. "I want to know everything. I want you to stay."

I crossed the room in seconds, dragging her into my arms. She held me tight as I buried my head into her neck, breathing her in, letting the tears I held inside for so long, soak into her skin as I gasped out my apologies.

She led me to the sofa and I fell onto it, taking her with me, unable to bear the thought of losing the connection with her.

Her softness surrounded me, her tender voice in my ear, as she comforted me, allowing the relief of her forgiveness to wash over me.

I drew back. "Kourtney, I know you have questions, and I will answer them all, but right now, I need you. I need to be close to you."

She stood up, tugging on my hand.

Relief flooded through me as I followed her. She knew the truth and she was still with me.

She was still mine.

WE DIDN'T MAKE IT HALFWAY down the hall, when I had her pushed up against the wall, my desperate need to feel her overwhelming everything else. I captured her face in my hands, kissing her deeply, groaning at the sensations she stirred. My body held her captive as my tongue delved and swirled, caressing her possessively, my desire overtaking all my other senses. I clung to her hard; lost and still frantic at the thought of losing her. It was the realization of how tense she was and the fact her hands were ineffectually pushing at my chest that alerted me I was holding her too tight, kissing her too rough. I pulled backed, dropping my head to her shoulder, ashamed at how I was acting. "Kourtney, I'm sorry," I pleaded, holding myself stiffly away from her.

Her arms reached out, wrapping around me, drawing me back to her body. "I've got you, my love," she murmured in my ear. "I'm not going anywhere. Relax and let me take care of you this time."

Nodding, I allowed her to lead me into the bathroom, watching in silence as she filled the tub. She kneeled in front of me, cupping my cheek, her thumb drawing gentle circles on my skin as she gazed up at me. I rested my hand over hers, and turning my head, I kissed the palm of her hand in contrition.

"You want me to have a bath, Kourtney?" I stared into her beautiful, forgiving eyes.

She shook her head. "No, I want *us* to have a bath. You need to calm down and I think you need me to hold you right now."

I tightened my hold on her hand. "I need you to hold me forever."

She sighed and stood up. "I'm right here, Nathan."

"Good. I need—"

"Tell me what you need," she encouraged.

"You. I need you."

"You have me."

"Let me see you, Kourtney. Please."

She bit her lip, still nervous and shy when it came to me seeing her naked. Slowly, she disrobed and stood in front of me, her full body as exposed and vulnerable as her wide-eyed gaze. Reaching out, I pulled her to me, burying my face into the gentle swell of her stomach. I kissed her scars with feather light pecks, trailing my lips over her marks and imperfections that bothered her so much and yet to me were nothing. Just as mine were nothing to her, except scars from a past we had both survived. I looked up at her as she gazed down on me.

"I love you. All of you. Be with me, right now." I pleaded. "I *need* you, Chefgirl."

She blinked, and a tear trickled down her cheek, then she nodded and moved to the tub. I stood up and discarded my clothes, following her into the warm water. I sank down, my back pressed to her softness, my head nestled under her chin, as her arms held me tight. The warm water, the gentle glow of the candles she had burning and her calming touch relaxed me—and I slipped deeper into her embrace. She nuzzled gentle kisses on my temple, murmuring soothing words of comfort and love. When my body shook violently with sobs, her arms tightened and she offered me the safety of her body to finally grieve aloud for the family and the life I had lost.

When the emotion had passed, we climbed out of the tub, Kourtney insisting on helping me dry off. We nestled under the covers, our bodies melded together, skin to skin. My lips found her sweet mouth and our tongues fluttered with soft touches. I worshipped her curves lovingly, her tender ministrations having eased my earlier desperation. She returned my caresses and kisses with a quiet passion of her own, pulling me into her heat with a breathy moan, rocking with me as I thrust in long, slow strokes. Our eyes locked as I felt her orgasm ripple through her and she stilled, shuddering around me, breathing my name.

"Nathan."

I buried my face in her neck as I spilled into her, unable to speak, only to feel, as the waves crashed over me, leaving me heavy and spent.

I rolled over, keeping her close, still needing to feel her unspoken solace.

"Stay with me," I pleaded into her skin.

Her arms tightened. "I have you, my love."

Surrounded by her love, I slept.

AS USUAL WHEN UPSET, NIGHTMARES plagued me all night. Every time I woke up, shaking and crying out, Kourtney was there. It was her tender voice, whispering words of love and comfort in my ear, and her gentle caresses that would lull me back in to sleep. When I finally opened my eyes to the muted light, peeking through the curtains, it was her concerned, sincere gaze that met my weary eyes. As I blinked, tightening my already firm grasp on her torso, relief seeped through me that she was still there with me.

"Hey," she whispered as she stroked my cheek.

"Kourtney." I leaned up, and captured her lips with mine, pulling her down to me as I kissed her, putting all the emotions and words I couldn't express into the warmth of her mouth. Languidly, I stroked her tongue, as I held her close, unable to let her go. I released her mouth, and burrowed my head into her neck, breathing her in. "I'm sorry."

Her arms tightened. "I know."

"I should have told you sooner."

Her low sigh ruffled my hair as she exhaled. "I know that. But I understand why you didn't."

"There is so much we need to talk about. So much more I have to tell you."

"We have all day, all weekend, more, if you need it. I'll listen."

I looked at her, searching her face. "You've forgiven me?" My voice was barely a whisper and my throat tight, worried she might have changed her mind during the night.

"Yes."

The one small word exploded in my head, my entire body relaxing. She drew me back down to her chest and I melted into her embrace, drifting quietly as she held me in her arms.

I glanced over at the clock, pulling myself up as I saw the time. "*Shit*. I'm late."

Kourtney shook her head. "I texted Shannon and told her you were ill and not coming in today."

"You texted Shannon?"

She waved my iPhone in front of me. "I figured it out all by myself. Shannon says she hopes you feel better. I assured her I would look after you." Then she frowned. "Annie, on the other hand, said something about you working voodoo magic on me since I've never taken a sick day before. I'm not sure what she meant."

I kissed her lovingly, returning to her warmth. "Look how far you've come. Tackling an iPhone all by yourself." I chuckled. "As for your friend—Annie, she makes me laugh."

"She's a good friend."

I nodded. "She is."

I let the quietness of the room calm me before I spoke again. "We should get up and talk."

"Okay." She rolled out of bed and held out her hand "Let's talk."

"WILL YOU EVER TRY AND find them again?"

I shook my head sadly. "I've thought about it, but no."

Kourtney's eyes were unhappy as she regarded me. We had gotten up and spent the late morning talking; she asked many questions about my family and my time in prison. I found it to be an emotional release to be able to talk about them—to share memories of happier times; although I was more guarded in my replies about my time in prison. There were too many things I wasn't ready to share about that dark time—painful memories and twisted emotions I wasn't sure how to explain it to her—yet. She was interested to find out how I'd finished my high school degree, then took computer courses while in jail. I told her about living with Grant and Claire; about going back to school to study computer science; and how Grant had helped me land the job I still worked at today.

Kourtney had gently directed the conversation, encouraging my ramblings and stories. She laughed with me over some of the antics I told her about getting into with Sophie and Trevor. She'd clasped my hands when the memories would get too vivid and held me when the emotions got too strong for me to contain.

"Have you accepted that?"

I wasn't sure how to respond. "I don't know. I've been . . . drifting, Kourtney. I go to work, I have a couple of people over occasionally to watch a game, I work on some projects for a few clients, but I haven't been living. I just—"

"Existed."

"Yes. And I didn't even realize it until you came into my

life." I turned to her, clasping her hands tight in mine. "You've made all the difference to me, Kourtney. I can't do this without you." I implored. "I'm not sure I want to do this without you."

"You don't have to."

I studied her open, loving expression and cupped her face. "I love you, Kourtney. You mean everything to me."

Her beautiful eyes widened, tears welling in the corner and slipping down her cheeks.

"I love you, Nathan," she responded.

"It's not easy being involved with someone with a criminal record. Things are more challenging at times."

"I don't care. I would follow you to the ends of the Earth, Nathan. You've existed on your own for the last few years without anyone to love, so you understand how painful that is." Her eyes filled with more tears. "I've never been loved before . . . by anyone. I'm not giving you up because things might be difficult. Life is difficult. But if we're together, that's all that matters." Her lip trembled. "I'm not letting you go. Ever."

I could feel my own eyes tearing up as I listened to her declaration. "You'll stay with me? No matter what?

"No matter what."

I crushed her to my chest, finally able to take in a deep breath.

I had her.

She was mine.

Forever.

WE SPENT MOST OF THE day curled together on the sofa, Kourtney asking questions as she thought about them. Her fingers picked at a stray thread on my T-shirt and I could sense she wanted to ask something, and she was unsure how to proceed.

"What?" I asked, dropping a kiss on her head. "You're thinking far too hard."

"Can you travel?"

"I haven't applied for a passport yet, but I will, although getting a passport and being allowed into another country are two different things."

"Do you want to travel?"

"If I can. I'd like to travel with you."

"Can you, ah, get married?"

"Are you asking me?"

Color stained her cheeks. "No, I was only inquiring as to the rules."

I snickered at her haughty tone. "Yes, I can legally get married." I dropped another warm kiss on her head. "So yes, Chefgirl. I can marry you."

"I didn't ask that, Nat."

I sat back, grinning. "But, if I asked *you* and it was a sunny day, you'd maybe say yes?"

"Meh. If I was in a good mood, or slightly tipsy, perhaps. And totally depending on the size of the rock you put on my finger," she deadpanned.

I burst out laughing. "I'll keep that in mind. I'll tell you jokes, and get you drunk before I pop the question." I smirked. "And hide your glasses so you can't see the size of the ring."

I could see the grin playing on her lips as she stared at her lap. "Good plan."

I watched her quietly for a few minutes.

"Kourtney?"

She tilted up her head in question.

"Like the baby bonnets? Someday, for sure . . . someday." I inhaled deeply. "Someday soon. Okay?"

"Okay," she breathed, her eyes misty as she ducked her head back down.

But I saw her smile.

And it was stunning.

Right then, I knew we'd make it through.

As long as we were together, we'd both be all right.

Chapter Thirty Two

"**N**ATHAN, TELL ME."

I looked up from my plate. I had been pushing the food around and trying to figure out how to tell her what I had found out today. I wasn't sure how she would react.

It had been two weeks since I told her about my past. Two weeks of simply us—no drama or worry. Our conversations were open and frank. We had nothing left to hide from each other. I knew her greatest fear was my rejection and she knew I feared her leaving me.

Neither fear would ever be completely gone, but they would diminish over time and soften.

We only needed that time.

I ran a weary hand over my face. I hated knowing I was about to put an end to the tentative happiness we'd been feeling.

Her worry-filled gaze was filled with questions, but her tone warm when she spoke. "You're not eating, so don't tell me nothing is wrong. Did something happen to Grant or Claire?"

I dropped my fork and sat back. "No. Nothing like that, Kourtney."

"I'm listening."

I sighed, feeling my frustration escaping. "The building I work in has been sold to a private company, which is taking over the entire place. The company I work for will be losing the contract to service it and a lot of the tenants will be leaving. The IT crew will no longer be necessary, which means I'm out of a job in a month."

She clasped my hand. "Oh, Nathan. I'm sorry."

"They offered me another building that they service, but it's north of Toronto. I'd either have to move or commute." I shook my head. "It would be a long commute."

She looked at me, worried. "What did you tell them?"

I held her hand firmly. "I said no. I'm not moving away from you, and the commute would be hell. I'd never see you and that's not acceptable."

"But . . ."

I shook my head. "I'm sure I'll find another job. I don't know how long it will take. But I'm not leaving you, Kourtney."

She let out a shaky sigh. "I don't want you to, either."

"Good. It's settled. I have some vacation time and they offered me a severance package, which I accepted. I'll start looking right away."

Kourtney was quiet, then pulled her chair closer. "What if you did something different?"

"Different?"

She drew in a deep breath. "You told me how much you miss writing code and developing programs for clients. Maybe you should open your own business, offering those services, as well as IT. All the businesses that were in your building are still going to need help when they relocate, won't they?"

I thought about it for a minute. "Some will."

"And you know them. They know you. I bet if you spoke with them, you'd have some clients right away. I know Annie hires outside independent contractors all the time for computer stuff. I could speak with her." She pursed her lips, looking thoughtful. "You said you worked with some talented people.

They'll be looking for jobs as well, yes?"

I nodded.

"You could hire them."

I smiled at her enthusiasm. "All that would cost—cost a lot, Kourtney. I don't have that sort of capital. And I'm not sure I could get a loan considering everything, or if I'd even be able to apply for that sort of thing with my record. I had trouble with the house and car."

"I have some money. I had several of my articles published and I was well-paid. I've never touched the money."

I held up my hand. "I'm not taking your money, Kourtney."

She stood up and took our untouched plates to the counter and left the kitchen. I sighed, looking around the room in the place I now thought of as home, because it was where Kourtney lived. I still hadn't gone back next door and she hadn't asked me to. I hated even thinking about being without her.

When she came back, she was carrying a file folder. Without a word, she handed me the file, her teeth worrying the plump flesh of her bottom lip.

Reaching over, I tugged her lip free. "What's this?"

"I've been doing some research."

I winked. "That *is* your line of expertise, Kourtney."

I was rewarded with one of her sweet smiles. "On the internet."

I grabbed my chest in mock shock. "Listen to you, Chefgirl! Using the internet! Found some new recipes to try out on me?"

She rolled her eyes but I could see how nervous she seemed to be.

"What were you researching?" I asked, curious as to her seeming worry.

"The housing market here."

"You want to move?"

She shook her head. "No." She hesitated. "I want you to."

"Me?" I was confused. I told her I didn't want to leave.

"Yes, I want you to move."

A wide grin split my face, my heart beat picking up.

"Chefgirl, are you telling me you want me to sell my place and move in *here*, with you, permanently?"

"If *you* want to, yes."

I cupped her head, dragging her mouth to mine as I kissed her deeply. "There's nothing I want more."

"Really?"

I rested my forehead to hers. "I don't want to ever be away from you, Kourtney. I've been waiting for you to tell me you've had enough of me and it was time for me to leave." I hated the mere thought of leaving her. "I didn't want to go back there and live alone anymore."

"You don't have to. I don't want to be away from you either."

I kissed her again. "Then it's settled."

She nodded. "You can sell your place, move in here and use the money to help set up your business."

"There are lots of things to consider, Kourtney. It might not work. The only nest egg I have would be gone. I don't know if I'm willing to gamble on that high a risk."

She shook her head. "It won't fail. You're too smart for that to happen. I know you can do this. And I know you'll be successful. I have every confidence in you, Nat."

"I don't want to be dependent on you."

She pursed her lips. "What if the roles were reversed?"

She knew exactly what would happen; I would want her to reach for her dream. She wanted the same for me—her faith in me was incredible. I huffed in resignation. "I need to think about it. Write it all down." I paused, thinking. "Talk to Grant."

"I know. You should do that."

"Regardless of whether I do this or simply find another job, I'm staying here, though." I grinned. "Most of my stuff is here anyway."

"What about your furniture?"

"There isn't much. I have some more clothes and a few things, plus the TV and other electronics. I'll have it cleaned and maybe painted fresh and sell it as is, or give the stuff away."

A shadow crossed her face.

"Hey." I shook my head. "Don't be sad. That part of my life is over and I'm happier than I ever thought possible. I have you now."

"We have each other."

I pulled her back into my arms. "Each other."

KOURTNEY FIDGETED BESIDE ME, CLENCHING and unclenching her hands. Reaching over, I covered them with mine. "Relax. It's going to be fine."

"What if he doesn't like me?"

I tucked her into my side and nuzzled my lips into her soft hair. "Impossible."

"But . . ." Her voice trailed off, as her fearful gaze met mine.

I cupped her pale cheek. "He'll adore you, Kourtney. I know he will."

As if on cue, Grant slid into the booth across from us. "Break it up you two."

Chuckling, I turned to him. He smirked across the table at us, his eyes going wide as he took in Kourtney sitting beside me. I felt her tense as he stared at her and I held her closer.

He whistled low in his throat. "Holy shit, Nathan. You weren't kidding." He held out his hand across the table. "Nice to meet you, Kourtney." He grinned widely. "Nathan said you were stunning, but he didn't do you justice. Not even close."

Kourtney hesitated before offering her hand in return; her cheeks pink from embarrassment with his remarks. I was about to tell him to shut up when he spoke again. "You have the most gorgeous eyes I've ever seen, young lady." He winked. "Don't tell my wife I said that. She'd have my balls on a platter."

Both Kourtney and I snickered at his comment. I felt her relax a little. Kourtney shook his hand, smiling. "Nathan's told me a lot about you as well, but he was pretty accurate, I'd say. He said you were a charmer."

Grant laughed. "Oh, beautiful and funny. Great combination, Nathan; you lucky bastard, you."

I grinned as I leaned down and nuzzled her head again. "That I am, Grant. That I am."

GRANT CLOSED THE FILE HE'D been reviewing. He was quiet for a minute. "You've given this a lot of thought, Nathan." He rapped the top of the file folder.

I nodded. "We have."

"It's risky, especially these days, opening your own business."

"I agree. That's why I'm starting small. I've spoken with some of my current clients and they've agreed to hire me. I'm going to work from home for the next few months until I've built up a big enough client base. I'm only hiring one other person right now, but once I'm confident things are working I'll lease office space and hire more staff."

Grant looked at Kourtney. "You support him on this?"

"One hundred percent."

He leaned back, taking a long sip of his coffee. "And you're sure you want to sell?"

"Yeah. Absolutely. Kourtney is my home now, Grant. Where she is, I am."

He smiled. "Look at the two of you."

"What do you think? Nathan trusts you. Your opinion means a lot to him," Kourtney asked.

"It's a good, solid plan."

"You think I should do this?"

"I think you should. Kourtney's right—it's the right time to try."

I felt better knowing Grant felt the same. "It's not what I had planned, but things have changed."

Grant regarded us seriously. "I'd say your life is heading exactly where it should be, Nathan. You have a new career to look forward to and an amazing woman at your side." He paused, drumming his fingers on the file. "Claire and I want to help you if you need it. We'll co-sign a loan, or loan you the money ourselves if the bank says no. It's very difficult to get a loan right now, even without your past."

He held up his hand before I could protest. "Nathan. We think of you as a son. Let us be a part of your new life. Your future. We want that." His voice softened as he looked at Kourtney. "All we ask is you work hard and keep making us proud."

I flushed at his words.

"Claire wants a visit—soon. She wants to meet the amazing lady who means so much to you."

"I'd like to meet her, as well," Kourtney responded with a shy smile.

Grant returned her smile. "It will be nice not having to worry about you anymore, Nathan. You've moved ahead and started living. Really living."

I picked up Kourtney's hand and kissed it, knowing he was right. "Amazing isn't a big enough word, Grant."

He laughed. "Amen to that, Nathan."

Kourtney cleared her throat. "There was something else I wanted to ask, Grant."

I looked over, surprised. I thought we had covered everything.

Grant tilted his head. "Sure, Kourtney. What is it?"

Her fingers fiddled with the edge of the paper napkin in front of her, shredding it into tiny fragments. She didn't look at me, but kept her gaze on Grant.

"Nathan told me you offered to help him find his sister. Is that offer still open?"

I gaped at her, caught off guard by her question.

Grant looked over at me. "Is that something you want, Nathan?"

"I don't know. It wasn't something I'd been thinking about."

Kourtney turned to me, with cautious eyes. "I think you

need to put the past behind you, once and for all, in order to really move forward, Nathan. You miss Sophie. Whether you'll admit it or not, you miss your mom. You need to find out if that door is truly closed or not."

"Kourtney," I whispered, my voice tight. "What if it is?"

"Then we deal with it—together." She picked up my hand, holding it tight. "But what if it's not? What if you can forge a relationship with one or both of them? I know what it's like not to have any family who care, Nathan. Don't throw away a chance."

Grant spoke up. "I agree with Kourtney, Nathan. So much time has passed. You're starting a whole new journey. Reach out this one last time. If you fail, then you know you tried." He gazed at me, encouragement in his eyes. "You give me the word and I'll ask my contacts to help."

My mind raced. My initial reaction was to say no. The thought of their rejection made my heart ache. But Kourtney's words rang in my head. Since falling in love with her, I found myself more open to feelings—ones I had cut off long ago. And the thought of reconnecting with my sister, and perhaps my mother, was a desire I kept hidden for far too long.

Kourtney's eyes pleaded with me: both to accept and to understand why she had asked Grant. I brushed my lips across her cheek, letting her know I wasn't angry or upset. If anything, I was grateful—my girl loved me enough to suggest something she knew I longed for, deep in my heart, but was too afraid to express.

"I'll think about it, Grant."

"Okay, I'll be waiting."

Chapter Thirty Three

I DRUMMED MY FINGERS RESTLESSLY on my desk, my stomach in knots. I looked down at the slip of paper in front of me for the hundredth time since Grant had handed it to me. I didn't have to look at the numbers anymore. I had worn the edges of the paper so thin they curled up, the corners fraying from my fingers worrying them, and the numbers were embedded in my memory.

Ten digits. Ten innocent digits that could possibly change my life—or, as Grant pointed out stoically, confirm my fears and I could shut the door on my past once and for all, knowing I'd done everything I could.

My gaze drifted to the picture on my desk of Kourtney and me, taken last week. We were both smiling; her with a shy glance at the camera while I beamed down at her, my feelings clearly written on my face.

When she had surprised me by asking Grant to try and find my sister, I didn't know what to think or feel. Grant admitted he felt the same way—that I needed to reach out one last time. After examining my feelings, I knew they were right and finally I agreed to let Grant help me. Thanks to his contacts, it didn't take long to find Sophie.

It turned out she lived in Ontario, a mere hour away from me.

And now, I held her number in my hand.

Kourtney's gentle voice startled me. "You don't have to do this, Nathan."

I looked up, shaking my head, grateful for her presence. I had almost not told her what I was planning, thinking I would somehow spare her my pain if Sophie rejected my olive branch.

Thank God I listened to Grant, who reminded me of the last time I tried to hide something from Kourtney. Needless to say, he was right, and now she was beside me; her support given without hesitation.

She'd been at my side every minute of the nerve-racking opening of my company. She held my hand when my loan was rejected, then handed me a money order the next day, telling me another one was on its way from Grant and Claire. All three of them celebrated with me when the business took off.

They were all my family now, but she knew how much I missed Sophie. She had encouraged me, making me listen the way no one else could. She reminded me of the love I still carried for my sister; that in all of this she was the one I missed the most and in all likelihood, had been the one caught in the middle of the entire situation. "She was fifteen when this happened, Nathan. What power did she have about seeing you? She lost both you and Trevor that day."

As usual, she made a good point. But I was still nervous—because of me Sophie had been hurt as well. Had she forgiven me for that? A lot of time—years—had passed and I had no idea how either of us were going to feel about me making contact.

"I want to," I responded. "I'm—"

"Nervous," she finished for me.

"Yes."

"You were nervous when you told me you loved me, and look how that turned out."

Smiling, I stood up, leaning over the desk to kiss her. She

was right. I took a chance then, and I had to take another one now.

I picked up the phone and dialed the number.

"Hello?" A woman's voice answered, although somewhat different, still achingly familiar.

I opened my mouth, but nothing came out. Only a rush of air which I exhaled into the phone.

"Hello?" she repeated; impatience evident in her tone.

I swallowed, trying to clear the dryness in my throat. "I—ah—"

"Listen, asshole, I have call display and I'm in no mood for some creep to call and breathe heavy on the end of the phone. I'm calling the cops, shithead."

For a second, I gaped at the phone. Sophie never swore. At least the Sophie from my memories didn't. Finally, I found my voice.

"Sophie? Sophie Fraser?"

"Who wants to know?" she demanded.

"Um, I . . . I'm looking for Sophie Fraser."

"Sophie Johnson," she corrected tersely.

"But you were Sophie Fraser?"

"Who is this?" Her speech was slow and cautious.

I cleared my throat and reached out for Kourtney's outstretched hand, holding it like a lifeline.

"Sophie, it's Nathan . . . your brother."

I PACED THE ROOM, MY nerves taut, my anxiety at an all-time high.

Kourtney watched me with concerned eyes, not speaking, but allowing me the space I needed.

After telling Sophie it was me, all I heard was a gasp, followed by sobbing and the sound of the phone hitting the floor. When a man's voice picked up the receiver, demanding to know who it was, I explained the best I could, given my nervousness. Silence greeted me, then he informed me he was Sophie's husband and asked for my information to call me back. I hung up, dazed and looked at Kourtney, unsure what to say.

"You shocked her. I doubt she expected a call like that out of the blue," she soothed me. *"I'm sure she'll call back."*

I didn't know what to think or say until the phone rang again and Sophie's husband, Ian, asked me if they could come and see me in person. I gave him the information and now we were waiting for them to appear. We stayed at the office, thinking it would be good neutral ground. I had no idea what to think, or how I should be feeling.

Was it a good thing Sophie was coming to see me?

Would she recognize me?

Would I recognize her?

The door to the office opened and in an instant, all my questions were answered.

My baby sister stood in front of me—I'd know her anywhere.

The long blonde curls were replaced with a shorter, darker version of waves and her face had matured, but her eyes, the same ones that stared back at me in the mirror every day, hadn't changed. Nor had her sweet smile, which was genuine and wide, even as tears ran down her face. She was dressed like my memories of her; in a gypsy skirt with a ruffled blouse—an older, not-too-different version of my little sister. One second she was hesitating by the door and the next she was in my arms, both of us crying. We shared mumbled incoherent words, neither of us caring what they were, happy to hear each other's voice.

Finally, I drew back, staring down at my sister. "Sophie," I whispered through my tears.

"I tried to find you, Nathan . . . I tried so hard," she whispered back, her voice thick with her own emotion.

That was all I had to know. "We'll figure it out, Gypsy-girl." Her smile grew as I called her by her old nickname. I kissed her forehead and wrapped my arm around her. "I have someone I want you to meet. Sophie, this is my Kourtney." I drew in some much needed oxygen. "Kourtney, this is Sophie"—my voice caught as I gazed at my girl—"my sister."

Kourtney smiled shyly at Sophie. "I'm happy to meet you, Sophie."

Sophie grinned; the dimple I remembered on her left cheek as prominent as ever. She held out her hand. "Good to meet you, too."

I met Kourtney's gaze, the emotion in her eyes warming my chest. She always expressed her love so intensely through her eyes. The emotion soaked into my soul, easing whatever troubled me, calming my frazzled nerves. She let me know she was beside me, no matter what. She was the nucleus of my world, and everything else revolved around her.

She looked around at our strange, apprehensive group. "Why don't we sit down? I have coffee."

Sophie's husband, Ian, spoke up. "Are those cookies?"

Our laughter broke the ice, and I grinned. "Kourtney makes the best cookies in the world. Let's sit down and talk."

I GRIPPED KOURTNEY'S HAND HARD, and blew out a deep breath, after Sophie told me my mother had passed away. "When?"

"About five years ago," Sophie murmured. "She had cancer, which she was diagnosed with a couple years after you went to prison. She fought it long and hard, but it finally beat her. I'm sorry, Nathan."

"And Ryan?"

She glanced at Ian, who gave her a subtle nod of encouragement.

"I don't know where Ryan is—no idea. I wasn't very close to them after I turned eighteen—especially Ryan. Once Mom passed, I had no reason to stay in contact with him. The last I heard he was still in Florida."

I was shocked to hear that piece of news. All this time I had assumed she was still close with them. "Why, Sophie? What happened?"

She sighed, threading her fingers through mine. When she spoke her voice was quiet and resigned. "After you went to prison, Ryan told Mom and me that you didn't want us to see you there. You wanted no contact with us. I was forbidden to write you or attempt to find out which prison you went to—he wouldn't tell me."

"I never said that—I thought you wanted no contact with me."

She shook her head. "It wasn't until well after I turned eighteen I found out you were out of jail, Nathan. By that time, I was fed up with Ryan and his rules. We'd moved three times and my life was in constant flux. His rules were strict—even stricter than when you were with us. Mom and I fought all the time it seemed."

"About him?"

She shrugged. "Him. You. The restrictions I lived under." She lifted her gaze to mine. "She told me once she'd already lost too much: Dad, Trevor, you—she couldn't lose another person. They kept me under such close scrutiny, it drove me crazy. They pushed me away instead of keeping me closer. When she got sick, things got better, but it was never the same."

I clutched her hand. "I tried to reach out—I wrote you both. All the letters were returned. When I got out of jail, Ryan was there. He told me none of you wanted anything to do with me." My voice shook with the emotions I was fighting. "He gave me back all the letters I had sent at first—before you moved. Then he told me to leave you alone. He reiterated you still wanted nothing to do with me and that you hadn't forgiven me for hurting you or killing Trevor. I was so alone, Sophie."

"We never got your letters. Everywhere we lived we had a postal box and Ryan picked up the mail. Anything you sent, he kept hidden. I never knew until after Mom died."

"How did you find out?"

"He got drunk one night after the funeral, and without meaning to, he said a few things—enough for me to realize he'd been lying the whole time. The next day we had a blow up and I walked out. By then, we were living in the States and I hated it. I came back to Canada and moved to B.C." She smiled at her husband. "I went to University and made a life for myself. It's where I met Ian. He had a job offer in Toronto last year, and we moved here, to Mississauga."

She turned to me, frowning. "I looked for you, Nathan. I tried on Facebook, I checked records, I even contacted the prison, but they wouldn't give me any information. Short of hiring a private investigator—which I didn't have the money for—I didn't know how to find you. I thought you really didn't want to see me, so I left it. Did you . . . did you look for us?"

"At first, a little. But when I got out and Ryan told me to stay away, I was in such a free fall, I shut down, Sophie. Grant and Claire took me in and helped me get on my feet." I paused, shutting my eyes with the pain building in my chest, reaching blindly for Kourtney's hand. "I pretty much kept myself closed off until I met Kourtney. I was too afraid to care that much again; too afraid to lose someone else. I thought . . . I thought you hated me for what happened to you and Trevor."

"It was an accident, Nathan. I knew that. I was there, remember? My body healed, but my heart . . . it never did. I missed Trevor, I missed you. I didn't understand why you cut us off." She swallowed and wiped a few tears that had fallen. "I lost you both that day."

"I was ashamed, but I wanted to see you."

"Ryan kept us apart."

"I guess he was the one who hated me." I was silent for a moment. "Did Mom . . . did she . . . ?" I couldn't even bring myself to say the words.

"Mom regretted not pushing more," Sophie confessed. "She wished she had been able to tell you she was sorry."

A tear leaked from my eye, running down the edge of my cheek. "Why was she sorry? I'm the one who killed Trevor and ripped our family apart."

"Once Mom got over the shock and the grief, she knew it was an accident, and she regretted her actions. She never hated you the way Ryan led you to believe. But it was too late—thanks to him, she thought you were lost to her. She was sick and weak for a long time—she never had the strength to fight it. But she did love you." Her voice broke on her next words. "I never hated you at all. I missed my big brother so much. I thought you were lost to me as well."

I lifted her hand to my mouth and kissed her knuckles. "I'm right here, Gypsy-girl. We can start again—get to know each other, if you want?"

She smiled through the tears rolling down her face. "Try and get rid of me now, big brother. I'm sticking like glue!"

Kourtney spoke up. "We'd love to have you come for dinner. You can spend some more time together."

"We'd love to!"

I beamed at the two women I was sitting between. Despite the sadness I felt about hearing of my mother's passing, I also felt a weight lifted from my shoulders. She hadn't hated me. Ryan and his anger had infected every part of our lives—taking away the years we could have spent together—as a family. But I had Sophie back, and now we could rebuild our relationship and move forward. We had many years to catch up on, so much to learn about each other.

Thanks to Kourtney and her love, to her ability of allowing my heart to reopen, I had a chance to know my sister again— to hear about my mother and her memories, to learn about Sophie's life—the good and the bad.

THE WARM WATER AROUND ME felt good. Kourtney's arms holding me close felt even better. She knew exactly what I needed after Sophie left. She let me hold her until the first wave of emotion passed. When we got home, she poured us a bath and slipped in behind me, surrounding me with her presence. She stayed quiet, allowing me time to process what Sophie had told me.

"I wish I'd looked harder. I wish I had the chance to say goodbye."

"I know, my love."

"Ryan really hated me."

"I think his grief twisted his judgment."

"She wasn't a bad mother. Did I make you think she was?"

"No, Nathan. I know what a bad parent is. Your mom wasn't one, she was . . . human. She made mistakes, but it sounds as if she wanted a chance to fix them." Her arms tightened. "I'm sorry she never got the chance—that you never got the chance to reconnect. But you know now she forgave you, and she loved you."

Twisting my head, I looked up at her. "Because of you, I got a chance to get to have my sister back. I get to reconnect with her—to have her in my life."

"You did the hard part. You took the chance."

I ran my fingers down her cheek, smiling at the trail of bubbles I left behind. "I was able to because of you. All the good things in my life have happened since I met you, Chefgirl."

"The same goes for you."

"Then I guess we're perfect for each other."

Her smile could have lit the whole room.

"Yes, we are."

Chapter Thirty Four

"IS THIS THE LAST OF it?" Kourtney smiled, as I lifted a small box over the fence and handed it to her.

"Almost."

"Have you enjoyed your little trip down memory lane, Nat? Using the fence?" she asked as she placed the box on the table before coming back to her ladder and climbing up a couple of rungs.

I chuckled. "It felt right."

"Just think, you'll have to retire the ladder now, unless of course, you want to leave it for the new people moving in. Maybe I'll have to feed them as well?"

I shook my head. "They are a nice, retired couple, Chefgirl. I'm sure they can fend fine for themselves. I might let you bake them some cookies to say welcome, but the rest of what you cook? It's mine."

"Always so protective of your food."

I stood on the top of the ladder, looking over the fence at Kourtney, who gazed back at me, amused. "I am. Not as protective though, as I am of the person who makes it. She's my reason for everything."

Kourtney blushed as she reached up, and I wrapped my hand around hers. "This is where it all started."

She grinned and shrugged. "Who knew when I heard a voice groaning how fucking awesome my dinner smelled that this is where we would end up."

I laughed thinking about that first dinner. "You literally had me that night, Kourtney. I was already a goner."

"Well, it actually took us a while."

"I wouldn't trade a minute of it." I rapped the top of the fence. "As much as this was a barrier between us, it gave us the time to really get to know each other. Time we both needed, I think. I loved our conversations and hearing your laughter when I said something inane." I paused. "I remember how right it felt to hold your hand the first time. How much I came to rely on hearing your voice. How fast I started needing you."

"Me, too."

"This fence kind of symbolizes a lot of us, Kourtney. It's a part of our history. Do you realize we haven't been apart one night since the first time I came over the fence?"

Her hand clutched mine. "I know. I can't imagine being without you anymore."

I felt my nerves take over and I swallowed the lump in my throat. "I don't ever want to be without you. Ever."

She beamed up at me, her eyes dancing. "Then come over the fence one last time and stay."

"I have one more box, Kourtney."

"Okay, give it to me and I'll go open the garage and you can put the ladder in it, then we're finished."

I held her hand tighter. "Kourtney?"

She looked at me, confused, and gingerly climbed another rung of the ladder, so she could grip my hand better. "Nat? What's the matter?"

"I'm not quite done." I placed our entwined hands on top of the fence. "This was the beginning of our story. Me climbing over it was the next chapter. Falling in love with you and having you love me back was the heart of the whole tale."

Her voice was filled with warmth. "You moving in is the next one, right?"

"It is." I paused, and cleared my throat. "But I want to expand on that chapter."

"I'm not sure I'm following you."

I swallowed nervously and placed one final box on the top of the fence. A small leather box.

Kourtney's eyes widened as she stared at the small item.

"That's your last box?" she asked, barely above a whisper.

I nodded, clearing my throat. "This one is special."

"Nathan?" Her uncertainty was evident in that one quiet word.

"We started right here. I want to close this part of our life right here, right now. I don't want to come over this fence to live with you. I want to marry you."

Tears filled her eyes.

"It's someday, Kourtney. Be mine. Please. Tell me I can keep you forever. Marry me?"

She stared at me, her lips trembling. I took her left hand and grinned down at her. "It's sunny, Chefgirl. I made sure you had a glass of wine with lunch, I've made you laugh, and your glasses are nowhere to be found. I think I got it all right. So all that has to happen now, is for you to say yes." I drew in a deep breath. "Please, say yes."

Her smile was brilliant. "Yes."

Grinning, I picked up the box and pressed it into her hand. I swung myself over the fence one final time, landing in front of her, helping her down off the ladder. I grabbed her tight in my arms, rejoicing when I realized how she allowed me to do so with no reticence; thrilled at how far we had come since the first time I held her.

I gazed down into her breathtaking, beautiful eyes that gazed back at me filled with more love than I had ever seen. Love that was for me and only me. The promise of the future beckoned in her intense stare.

A future I had given up thinking ever existed, until I heard her voice, over the fence.

My mouth founds hers; emotion driving me as I swept her tongue with mine, tasting her sweetness. I held her close, loving the feeling of her in my arms. How right it was. How right we were.

I drew back. "You haven't looked at your ring."

"I'll love it."

"Open it, Kourtney."

I loosened my grip on her, watching her expressive face as she slowly opened the box, with shaky hands. Her eyes flew to mine after she stared at the small token of my love nestled in its satin lining.

"I wanted something you could wear all the time," I explained. "Your beautiful eyes are my most favorite thing about you and I wanted them represented." Reaching over, I plucked the ring from its mooring and lifting her left hand, slid the thick ring in place. The brilliant sapphires and emeralds caught the light, and the small diamonds threw rainbows onto the glass behind her.

"It's beautiful," Kourtney breathed out as she held her hand up, twisting it to see the colors dance more as she did.

"Our fence is represented, as well." I grinned and pointed out the straight lines of the sapphires. I turned her hand a little to the right. "If you look at it this way it looks like the ladder. I couldn't find one with a barbeque on it though. But I thought two out of three was pretty good."

Her rich laughter made me smile.

"You like it, Kourtney?"

"I love it. I'll never take it off." She hesitated. "Do you, um, want to wear a ring?"

I dragged her back into my arms and nuzzled her neck. "Yes, Chefgirl. Buy me a ring. Mark me as taken. As yours. It's what I want to be." I kissed her soft skin. "And I want to do it soon, okay?"

"How soon?"

I shrugged sheepishly. "I already downloaded the wedding license off the net. We can fill it out. Send it in and have it back in a couple weeks? Make our plans?"

"You really want to marry me?" Her beautiful eyes misted over and her voice trembled with suppressed emotion.

I gathered her hands in mine and kissed her ring. "More than anything. Yes."

She sighed. "I love you, Nathan. I can't wait to be your wife—to belong to you."

"You do belong to me, every second of every day. You're mine, Kourtney—you have been from the day you were sweet enough to care about the hungry person on the other side of the fence and brave enough to climb a ladder and let me into your life." I placed our hands over my heart. "And, in the process, give me back mine."

Her smile could have lit up the entire world. "Yours," she breathed.

"So that's a definite yes?" I teased.

"Yes."

I wrapped my arms around her, knowing I'd never let her go.

My world was now complete.

Epilogue

I call this: Glimpses. Chefgirl and Nat's life through one of their favorite mediums; texting.
Nat's texts are bold.

I'm going to be late again, Chefgirl.

That new client?

Yeah, pain in the ass. Meeting again in an hour. I'll be home as soon as possible.

I understand, Nat. This is huge for you. I'll be waiting. I love you.

Huge for us. Love you so much.

xx

Claire called.

How is my favorite older woman?

She wants us to come back soon for another visit.

Can you blame the woman? I am rather charming.

LOL. Not to mention modest.

Actually, I didn't mention it—you did. But thanks for noticing. Is she OK? Grant?

They're both fine. She wanted me to tell you thanks for bringing me to see them and to do so again soon.

If she'd make another meatloaf like the one she made this weekend we could go tomorrow. I'll clear my schedule.

You're so easily swayed with food.

Kourtney—that was the best meatloaf I've ever eaten. I'd forgotten how much I loved it. And the pie? God help me.

She gave me the recipe.

For both?

Yes.

Forget her, then. We don't need her anymore. Besides, you have something she doesn't.

What is that?

The cutest socks . . . always with the cute socks. Nothing compares.

LOL—I love you.

I love you, Chefgirl. And whenever you want to go back, just tell me. Or they can come here before the wedding.

She says we're perfect together.

We are.

See you at home.

Kourtney?

Yes?

You're making the meatloaf tonight, right?

Love you, Nat.

Is that a yes? . . . Kourtney?

How's your day, Nat?

I miss you. Thank you for marrying me last week. Did I mention how beautiful you were?

About a hundred times.

Hmm. Not enough. You were beautiful.

I love you, Nat.

I want you.

Um . . . at work. So are you.

I could slip out. I am the boss. How's that headache of yours?

Pounding.

Meet me at home. Now. I'll show you pounding.

Leaving now.

I love you, Chefgirl.

Stop typing and get your fine ass home, Nat. I want it bare and buried between my legs.

Fuck.

That's the idea.

In the car. On my way.

Thank you for the flowers—they're beautiful.

You were remarkable last night, Kourtney. Articulate, beautiful and perfect. So proud of my wife. Sophie thinks you're amazing, too.

I hate talking in front of a crowd. But knowing you were there, supporting me, helped me so much. Having Sophie there was a bonus.

I'll always be there, Kourtney.

I know.

In my heart I'm always beside you.

I love you, Nat.

I love you, Chefgirl. See you at home.

I'm leaving a little early, Nat.

Yeah?

Did I mention I'm wearing new socks today?

I didn't see those this morning. Color?

Pink and white. Hearts.

Hmm . . . need to see those. Guess I'm leaving early, too.

OK—me and my socks will be waiting. Meet you in our room?

Meet you there. I need something to tide me over. Give it up.

xx

That's my girl. On my way.

Did I mention last night how sexy it is to see my name on your body?

You might have shown me, Nat. A few times.

I love the tattoo. I love you. Thank you. Best surprise Wednesday gift ever.

Really? It beat out the red polka dot lingerie from last month?

Hmm, hard call there, come to think of it. I have an idea.

This I can't wait to hear.

Why don't you model the lingerie tonight and I'll see which I like better—tattoo with the lingerie on . . . or tattoo with the lingerie off?

This sounds like a set up.

Never, Chefgirl. Only trying to make sure I give it a fair assessment.

You do remember the tattoo is on my arm, right? Not sure I need to model it with the lingerie off.

Oh there's a need. A hard, pressing need. I promise you.

Nat?

?

I love you. Even though you have a one-track mind and you're a complete nut, I love you. And I will take care of your hard pressing need tonight.

I'll bring home dinner . . . save you some time and energy. We're gonna need lots of both Chefgirl. The need is growing.

How embarrassing for you.

God, I love you. See you at home. Come early.

Without you?

NO. Don't even joke. Come HOME early. You come with ME.

I will. Suddenly I'm also feeling needy.

Perfect. I like you needy for me.

xx

Thank you again, my wonderful husband—yesterday was so . . . beyond anything I could have ever dreamed of. It was perfect.

You're the perfect one, Kourtney. I'm glad your birthday was a good day for a change.

GOOD day? Nat—it was amazing. I still can't get over the presents and the dinner . . . and everything else you did. You spoiled me.

Your birthday will be a day I want to celebrate every

year. I missed too many of them already. I had to catch up. One gift for each birthday I missed, and a few for this one. And the dinner? Our friends were thrilled to celebrate with us. They love you too, you know.

I loved every one of them. Thank you for bringing Claire and Grant down.

Anytime. I'm glad they're staying for a few days . . . and I'm equally glad they're staying at a hotel. You were very enthusiastic with your thanks last night, Chefgirl.

Complaining? Did I tire you out?

Nope. I'll show you tonight how un-tired I am. Especially if you wear that pretty pink thing I saw Annie gave you.

You peeked in the bag!

Hey—I saw something lacy. It screamed at me. You can model it for me when you show your thanks again.

I'll do that.

Good—when you get home take them for a nice long walk . . . tire them out so they leave early. I myself might have a huge headache and have to retire early.

One-track mind.

For you—Yep. Love you, Chefgirl.

Love you, Nat.

Nat—The realtor's office called. They found us a house you might like.

Big kitchen for you?

Yes.

Big basement for me?

Yes.

Bedrooms?

Yes.

Smartass. How many?

4. 5ᵗʰ could be downstairs.

Okay. That works. Fence?

LOL. Yes. There's even a den on the main floor.

Make an appointment.

You sure you want to move?

We're going to have babies someday—lots of them— Chefgirl. Need the room.

Someday, Nat. Not today. I just came off birth control.

Better be prepared. And you never know. I bet my boys are strong. Ninja-like sperm.

OMG—I give up—I'll make the appointment.

Chefgirl?

?

I love you.

xx

⟳

Nat—I need you.

What's wrong, Kourtney?

I got a call—my father died. I know I shouldn't care . . . but please, I need you.

Of course you care. I'm on my way. Don't drive.

I love you, Nat.

So much, my girl. I'll be right there—I've got you, Kourtney.

How are you feeling, Chefgirl?

I still can't believe it.

Told you my swimmers were strong.

Yes, you did.

I'm going to be a daddy.

Yes, you are.

You are my life. I love you.

I love you, Nat. You're going to be the best daddy.

I need to kiss you right now.

xx

NO. Not good enough. I'll be there in 10 minutes. Be out front.

Nuts. You are nuts, Nat.

Just about you, Chefgirl. And our baby.

Okay, now I need to kiss YOU.

Pucker up, Mommy. On my way.

Showing off my ultrasound picture.

Again?

Hey . . . I want people to see how good-looking my son is.

Yes, Nat, our son looks JUST like you.

I am sensing sarcasm.

Never. The shadowy image is your spitting image.

Shadowy but detailed. MY BOY.

I love you.

Chefgirl?

?

Do you need anything? Can I go buy ice cream or something?

No, I'm good. I only need you.

You have me. I love you.

xx

Did I mention how much I love the nursery?

You did, Chefgirl, but quite happy if you want to show me . . . again. Especially if you're on top . . . again. That drives me wild. And I bet you're blushing now. I like

that, too!

I will not answer you since that only encourages your cheek.

You already did, Chefgirl. LOL.

You never told me last night. How on earth did you get one of our fence boards from the old house?

I used my appealing charm.

Okay. Right. No, really, how did you do it?

I'm insulted my wife doesn't find me charming. I, ah . . . okay fine . . . check the freezer. There may be a cake missing. I knew Deb had a sweet tooth and if I told her the fence story, while she was all sugar shocked, and how I wanted a board to go in the nursery so we could use it to track the baby's height as he grew, she would let me have it. I replaced it for them. And it looks great in the nursery with the farm thing you picked out. I have even impressed myself with my handyman skills.

Motif, Nat. Farm motif. And you did an amazing job. Your son will love it.

My son. Our son. I love you. xxxxxxxxxxxxxxxxx

Oh my—such excess.

Never enough xx's for you, Chefgirl. To infinity.

And beyond. Love you back, Nat. Um, you didn't take the caramel cake did you? I was craving that.

Ah . . . gotta go, Chefgirl. Someone is calling. I'm sure that was my name.

You are in such trouble, Nat! You know I'll get you at home. You can run but you can't hide.

I'll distract you at home.

Really.

Yep. Me. My charm, my fine ass and my hot loving.

That hot loving better include caramel cake.

I'll make sure to stop at the store.

Good decision, Daddy.

Would you make me your sweet and sour chicken tonight, Chefgirl?

We had that two nights ago, Nat.

What can I say? I have a craving. I NEED IT.

Um, I'm the pregnant one. Shouldn't I be having the cravings?

Sympathy cravings. Besides your cravings are constant.

?

For me, Chefgirl. Seems to me I barely get in the front door these days and you're all over me. I'm lucky I can walk in the morning.

And you're complaining?

NOT A BIT. Just saying.

Now that you mention it, Nat I think I suddenly have a craving . . . an intense one. And I need it eased . . . right now!

Chefgirl, I'm blushing. And we're rather far apart.

You're the boss. You can leave.

And you? How will you get out?

Morning sickness is just a myth. It can strike at any time of the day.

Excellent. Let me get this straight—I'm gonna sneak out of here and you're gonna go make some horrid retching noises, get some sympathy, meet me at home and have your wicked way with me?

Yep, that's about it.

I'm surprisingly good with that. On my way to the car now.

I'll meet you at home. Be ready. Naked for me. I need to feel you.

WOW. CHEFGIRL. Suddenly my craving kicked into a pulsating need. YOU get home to me, woman. I am ALREADY ready.

I like you pulsating. In me. On my way.

Fuck—I had no idea pregnancy would turn you into this . . . wanton wench. I like it.

Wanton wench? I'll show you wanton . . . Get home.

Um . . . Chefgirl?

Yeah?

I still get the chicken . . . after the wanton-ness . . . right?

Nat—I think your son might be anxious to meet you?

Uh-oh. Is he moving around a lot today?

No.

What makes you say that then?

My water just broke.

Fuck! Running to car!

Stay calm, Nat. Annie is here with me at my desk.

At your desk?? Why aren't you lying down?

I am fine. Please come.

I'm on my way. Don't go anywhere. Wait for me.

Where the hell would I go, Nat?

In the car. Coming. I love you.

Love you too, Daddy.

Kourtney, is everything okay?

Relax, Nat, we're fine. You've only been at work a couple hours.

I would rather be home with you and Liam. I miss you both.

We miss you. We'll be waiting when you get home.

I'll come home early. In fact, I may work from home a couple days a week for a bit. Perks of being the boss.

Why does this news not surprise me? I like these perks.

Good. I like you.

That is a good thing.

You are a good thing. You are, in fact, the best thing that

ever happened to me.

I think you should come home now.

On my way.

I see I missed 4 texts. Sorry—the appointment took longer than I thought.

Are you okay? Going mad with worry here. What did the doctor say?

You need to come home.

Kourtney. Tell me now. What did the doctor say? I wish you had let me take you. The meeting could have waited.

It's not the flu.

Where are you?

In the parking lot of the doctor's office.

Liam?

Asleep in the back.

Tell me.

Your ninja-sperm have done it again.

Kourtney!!!

I think I need to lie down.

I think that's what got us into trouble in the first place . . . or should I say . . . second place.

No, it was you and your strange fixation with my cute socks, which led to your investigating up my legs and using the kitchen counter for purposes it was never intended for . . .

Well, they were rather sexy—all red and fuzzy and calling to me.

My socks call to you? You're deranged. Totally deranged.

Right now I'm rather giddy, I admit.

Where are you, Nat? I think I need you.

In my car already, my girl. Coming home to my family so I can kiss my wife and welcome our new blip properly. You have a picture for me? Are you okay to drive?

Yes, I have a pic and yes, I'm fine to drive. You're okay with this? Liam isn't even a year old. We hadn't planned on more babies yet.

Chefgirl, I'm ecstatic. I'll show you how ecstatic as soon as I see you. Drive safely.

I love you.

So much, my girl. SO MUCH. Stop texting and come home to me.

A girl. We're gonna have a girl. A baby Chefgirl. A Chefette?

LOL.

I love you. I love our daughter. Our son. Our family. Our life.

I love you, Nat. Are you showing off your new picture?

Yes. What a beauty she is.

She is half yours.

And half yours. I hope she looks just like you. A little mini Chefgirl running around. My little dumpling.

Nuts.

Only about you.

That never gets old for you, does it?

Nope. You tired?

Yes. Exhausted actually.

I'll look after dinner—Liam and I will have a boys' night and you can relax. Deal?

Deal.

I'll be home early.

This news does not come as a shock.

Sass. Love you, Chefgirl.

I love you, Nat.

Nat?

You're supposed to be resting.

How's Liam?

He misses his mommy but his nana and pops are spoiling him. Sophie and Ian are on their way, too. How is my daughter?

Emaline is fine. She is all snuggled up here on my chest. I think maybe her eyes are going to be like mine. The irises look slightly different.

I already saw that. Perfect.

Nat . . .

Kourtney—she is going to be surrounded by love and I will tell her every single day how utterly perfect she is— like her mother. She will never ever doubt herself. She'll never suffer like you did. I will make sure of that. I also plan on teaching her how to throw a good right hook, just in case.

I love you.

I love you, Kourtney.

Can you come back?

Already on my way, my girl. Liam is asleep and I have to be there with you—Claire laughed at me and threw me out. I'll be there in about 10 minutes. And I have your frozen yogurt. I'm about to leave the store.

You remembered.

I remember everything about you, Kourtney. And I especially remember your desperate need for this after Liam was born. I figured better safe than sorry. And once I get there I'm not leaving you again until I bring you and my daughter home. Liam is anxious to meet his baby sister tomorrow. Nana is very excited, as well.

You take such good care of us. I'll . . . we'll be waiting.

You're everything, Kourtney. See you in 10.

Everything okay, Nat?

We're all fine, Kourtney. We're having lunch. Auntie Sophie is here, too. How's the meeting going?

It's okay. They want me to stay on in some capacity, so we're trying to hammer it out.

Told you they wouldn't want to lose you. Are you sure about this?

Yes. I want to be home with our children. Especially now that #3 is on the way. If we can work it out that I can work a little and write some articles at home, then it works.

As long as you're happy.

I am, Nat. Always.

I am attaching a photo. Remember how to look at it?

Yes. Got it. Um, what am I looking at?

LOL. Our fencepost in the nursery, Chefgirl. I measured the kids for the first time. See the blue and pink lines?

Oh.

Chefgirl? You okay?

I'm good.

I don't believe you. What's wrong?

They're growing too fast, Nat.

Don't cry, Kourtney. Please.

How did you know?

I know you.

It's the pregnancy hormones.

No. It's you. It's your beautiful heart. I love you, Chefgirl.

I love you. I'm coming home. I'll finish this tomorrow.

We'll be waiting. Drive safely.

Nat—where are you?

I'm on my way back. Nana and Pops have everything under control. Waiting in line for your yogurt. Do you need anything else?

Only you. Did you kiss them for me?

Three times. And I took pictures for you.

Caitlin is sleeping.

My little cupcake.

You and Liam are outnumbered again.

We're good. #4 will even it up again.

Um, Nat. I gave birth 5 hours ago. I am not ready to talk about #4.

Fair enough. We'll discuss it tomorrow.

Good luck with that.

Next week, then. I have no objection to continuing this process until we have a nice even number—maybe a dozen.

Nat?

?

Now you have shared this information with me, you and your ninja-sperm filled penis are never coming anywhere near me again.

People are looking at me, Chefgirl.

Why?

Because I'm standing by our car, laughing so hard over your use of the words 'ninja-sperm filled penis' via text. I'm so proud.

Nuts. You are still nuts.

About you—yes, I still am. Always will be. I love you, Chefgirl.

I'm so lucky.

In the car now. Thank you for my daughter. You were magnificent today. Again. Thank you—for you, our family, our life.

Stop. Now you're making me cry.

Then I'll come and kiss away the tears. On my way.

xx—I love you Nathan.

I love you, Kourtney—always.

ACKNOWLEDGEMENTS

So many people to thank.

Ayden, Ashton, Caroline, Heather, Meredith, Pamela, and Suzanne—Thank you for your support, your eyes, your encouragement, and most of all, your friendship.

Carrie—your unending friendship and support helped me through so many rough days. Your patience and help are more appreciated than you know.

Trina—Thank you for the love and laughter you bring to my life.

Meire and Flavia—Thank you for your belief and support.

Carol—Thank you for your support and all the effort to help. I am blessed to have you in my corner.

Melissa—Your lovely cover and sweet enthusiasm for this project made it a joy.

Deb—Your red pen and notes made this so much better. Your friendship makes my life better.

Matthew—I can never say thank you enough. Your love, gentleness and patience are gifts I will always be in awe of. You are the greatest man I know, and I am honored to be your wife.

For all the bloggers and reviewers who give so generously of their time and spread their love of books, you are a gift to all of us who write.

For all my readers—you are a blessing in my life. Thank you.

To my street team—Melanie's Minions—you ladies rock my world. Love you!

ABOUT THE AUTHOR

Melanie Moreland lives a happy and content life in a quiet area of Ontario with her beloved husband of twenty-six-plus years. Nothing means more to her than her friends and family, and she cherishes every moment spent with them.

Known as the quiet one with the big laugh, Melanie works at a local university and for its football team. Her job, while demanding, is rewarding as she cheers on her team to victory.

While seriously addicted to coffee, and highly challenged with all things computer-related and technical, she relishes baking, cooking, and trying new recipes for people to sample. She loves to throw dinner parties, and also enjoys travelling, here and abroad, but finds coming home is always the best part of any trip.

Melanie delights in a good romance story with some bumps along the way, but is a true believer in happily ever after. When her head isn't buried in a book, it is bent over a keyboard, furiously typing away as her characters dictate their creative storylines to her, often with a large glass of wine keeping her company.

OTHER TITLES BY MELANIE MORELAND

Made in the USA
San Bernardino, CA
08 August 2015